Theodore Weesner
THE TRUE

DETECTIVE

SUMMIT BOOKS
New York

This is a work of imagination. Places are named, but only to suggest reality. None of the persons who appear in these pages is intended to represent anyone, living or dead.

Manufactured in the United States of America
1 2 3 4 5 6 7 8 9 10

Library of Congress Cataloging in Publication Data

Weesner, Theodore.
The true detective.

I. Title.
PS3573.E36T7 1986   813'.54   86-14468

ISBN: 0-671-40024-X

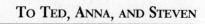

TO TED, ANNA, AND STEVEN

Who haunt every night the hallways of my mind

PROLOGUE

PORTSMOUTH, NEW HAMPSHIRE, 1981

MURDER STOPPING AT A SMALL TOWN may have the effect of a nail dropped into the mechanism of town life. In large cities, by contrast, any number of murders may be processed and left behind daily, and only a glut creates a stir. A town or small city, even as it has no choice but to continue on its way, is likely to pause. It will look within, may gaze even harder and longer if the crime seems to have stepped down from a bus coming in from Boston or New York, L.A. or Atlanta. Questions will be asked. Why here? Did we do something? Is this the start of something new?

A new bridge bypassing Portsmouth offers a view that could be from a plane. Below, where the river opens to the Atlantic, are the town's older bridges, the Route 1 Bypass and the Memorial Bridge. There, too, are its white and blue and cream-colored pleasure boats in stalls, its Naval Shipyard worksheds painted battleship gray, and the immediate merging of sky, river mouth, and ocean. Close upon the shore are the town's brick buildings and narrow streets, pressed by rows of wooden houses and old tree tops, held throughout by salt water washing into the town's coves and harbors, creeks and bays. Directly under the bridge a depth of water pours one way or another in its tidal slide, and as always a lobster boat is sputtering by, leaving a thin white wake in the swollen green surface, drawing along a gull or two like toys on a string.

The antique seaport of thirty-odd thousand is on the northern border of New Hampshire's momentary coastline, and the wide river coming and going is the Piscataqua. The new bridge turning through the sky is spliced into Interstate 95, three lanes going each way, leaving the ground like a long line drive, curving east in its trajectory north, cresting above the water at 165 feet—a dozen feet more at high tide—and returning to earth in another state. Southbound (*Live Free or Die / Bienvenue Au/ New Hampshire*) and northbound (*Welcome to Maine / Vacation Land*), the green superstructure is intended to carry civilization into New England's high corner well into the coming century.

Sea sounds and smells are here in all seasons. Over land and water gulls and sea ducks complain and argue, buoys and ships' bells clang and hammer, and the clam flats and rock formations with their catch basins and green beards—unlike the blond beaches on the nearby ocean proper—perk and hiss and send off their foul breath at low tide. There are old docks and piers and seawalls around town, too, covered with generations of minuscule barnacles and crustaceans, which at a distance are not dissimilar from other colonies up on shore. There is life underwater, too, where seaweed-black lobsters the size of baseball gloves thumbstrut throughout the dark mystery as if they have seen it all, as if there is nothing new under the sun.

On land, where the town is in the process of becoming a small city, wood-framed houses along the narrow old streets are being salvaged and painted yet again, and the occasional red brick mill or shoe factory is being converted to offices, apartments, boutiques, cafés. It is a town being rediscovered and repopulated, and along its old waterfront streets and in its wooden-floored mom-and-pop grocery stores, the term *mixed blessing* has found new currency. But so, elsewhere in town, have the terms *paradise,* and *pride,* and not so rarely, *San Francisco of the East.*

When the local lieutenant of detectives dresses up it is in a necktie and possibly a V-neck sweater under a wool shirt jacket from Kittery Trading Post; not dressing up, he dispenses with the necktie. An early riser, he often takes a walk in his town on Saturday morning, while his wife Beatrice sleeps in. He walks in town, or about the waterfront, or through a neighborhood. He may walk through one of the old downtown cemeteries and try to perceive something of life in a reading of markers. Or he may drive to one of the nearby beaches, to stroll and see what has washed up overnight. He will pick up broken glass if he sees it, if its edges have not been washed smooth, and deposit it in a trash barrel as he returns to his car. And he may stand for a time near the seawall at Wallis Sands and watch gulls and squads of sandpipers work the beach within its roar and mist, as waves roll in and break and leave behind a glistening effervescence of table scraps.

What he enjoys above all is to watch the far-off smudges of boats to see if they are advancing, like time, on the horizon. A child's pastime, he often thinks. And he often thinks, too, that it is one of the pastimes to which he would introduce children, if he had children, even as this thought has reminded him lately of an account by a lawyer acquaintance whose path he is forever crossing at the courthouse or in the police station. More than once, in elevator and marble lobby, the man has told him of walking with his son and daughter on the beach at Ogunquit, passing through the grassy dunes and happening upon two naked men lying together—well, more than lying together, the man has said, one man, it seemed, but then two—just as the sun was coming up and he was walking with his son and daughter.

Gilbert Dulac is fifty-two years old and twenty-six years a policeman, an overweight, oversized immigrant of French Canadian birth—he carries 260 pounds on a frame six feet four inches tall—and he has regarded the town as his for a dozen years or more. The feeling is a consequence, he knows, of being a policeman, of being a detective and the lieutenant of detectives, and of the town being small enough to understand, but also of being an immigrant, even if it was only to shift down, some thirty years ago, from Quebec, more as a neighbor marrying in than as a foreigner putting down roots. Like other immigrants, as immigrants know if others do not—as they believe their seriousness to be the country's secret weapon—he is more aware of the ideals of his adopted land and life than are the natives, and it is this added charge which gives him satisfaction in his self-appointed role, one he exercises quietly, as town father in an American town.

Everyone should be so lucky, he reminds himself ever more often as time slips along and his horizons seem to diminish at a quicker rate. Children would have been the greater good luck, he has always thought; that he has none is his life's only deep-seated regret. Children, just one or two, would have provided all that he and Beatrice might ever need or want to move on into the shadows ahead, and into the darkness. He'd have them out this morning, in fact; he'd have chased them out of bed whatever their ages and taken them for a stroll on the beach, just as he always went with his own father on Saturdays when he was a boy and his father was free from work, when they'd take their sea green Hudson Hornet down to the garage and hang out with the other men and boys and speak of cars and motors, of geese and Atlantic salmon, of Rocket Richard, of Lindsay and Howe.

It was in 1981 then that an incident happened to startle the town in its headlong rush into restoration, new brick walkways, and new taxes. On a

Saturday evening in February, a twelve-year-old boy walking home close to downtown disappeared, leaving only traces of circumstantial evidence. Like a creature lifting out of the water, the incident sent a chill through the area, stole a beat in the town's preoccupied preening upon its new wardrobe; all the world paused, if it knew it or not.

PART ONE
Magazine Photographs
SATURDAY, FEBRUARY 14, 1981

HERE IS ERIC WELLS, on Valentine's Day, lying on the living room floor, giving love a chance. Chin in hand, he keeps catching himself looking all the way through the TV screen where otherwise, on buzz saw feet, the Roadrunner is zipping everywhere. The old screen's black-and-white images don't quite matter now. Red colors keep coming up there. Blushes of valentine red. He is twelve years old and the colors are raising a warmth in him.

The card was in his desk at school yesterday. At the time he could only sneak a glance, but as he carried it home after school, trying to ignore that it was in his pants pocket, bending with his leg, its red colors kept stirring in him. Taking it into his bedroom, he closed the door. He looked at it and looked at it. If valentines were such mush, he wondered, why did it feel so good?

He gives the Roadrunner another try, until the feeling is in him again. He thinks, yuck. Then he thinks, this could be love, and catches himself tittering all the more as he tries and tries not to guess who could have put the dumb thing in his desk.

From the kitchen, close by, his mother says, "Eric, at least come have some toast."

Toying with a Matchbox car, he doesn't say anything. Always before he would have answered. The sensation is in him and he doesn't answer in the first moment and then not at all. Nor does he feel anything like hunger. Their apartment is small, and his mother is hardly a dozen feet away. How could a Navy Seal, he wonders—he's been dreaming for months of someday joining the U.S. Navy Seals—feel like this about a valentine?

Matthew, lying in bed with his eyes closed, is not asleep. There are two roll-away beds in the partitioned end of the apartment he shares with his little brother, but the winter sun seems this morning to heat only his own. Matthew is fifteen. His mood is terrible. The smell of chili cooking out there angers him and vaguely he wishes he were anywhere but where he is.

He gives a thought to a girl in school, a black girl of all things, who spoke to him yesterday, who seemed often lately to flirt with him. To another girl, over something in algebra, she said, "Let's ask Matt Wells. He always has his work done."

She was teasing; he never had his work done anymore. But there was her smile and there, too, were several tiny gold rings on the fingers of one hand and a gold earring in her ear. The combination suddenly struck him: gold and chocolate.

But lying in bed now within the aroma of chili, his mood is so awful he is close to tears. When he knows his mother has opened the door, he keeps his eyes closed and lets his anger thrive on her presence.

"Matt, don't you think it's time you got up?"

He holds.

"Matt," she says.

Still he holds.

"Matt!" she says.

"*What?*" he says.

"I know you heard what I said."

He doesn't respond. He stops himself from shouting, or from collapsing within.

"Matt, you've got to stop being so hard on everybody," his mother says. "We can't live like this."

Guiding one of his paint-worn Matchbox cars, Eric gives an uncertain ride to a pair of plastic soldiers. Dumping the pair on the other side of a gorge, he drives back to pick up two more. He changes his mind, though, and glances over where the Roadrunner is still zipping around. That bird is so dumb, he thinks. Turning onto his back, he places his hands under his head and looks into the universe where there used to be but a ceiling.

"Eric, you don't have a fever, do you?" his mother says.

"Nope."

"Are you sure?"

He doesn't respond.

"I wish you'd eat something," she says, although on a pause her wish disappears with her back into the kitchen.

Returning from his journey, Eric looks once more at the television screen. He and the nineteen-inch, black-and-white set are the same age, and too often in her nostalgic moments his mother has told him that when she brought him home from the hospital they spent hours together watching everything that appeared on the tube. Except when he was nursing, she always adds, which was practically all the time. Maybe a year ago, when he was old enough to tell her how icky it made him feel when she talked like that, she told him that someday he'd enjoy recalling such things as how he put on his first pounds.

Well, here it is, he thinks. This is it. Sitting up, but not by choice, and in the grip of something serene, he touches his chin to a bridge between his knees. His insides continue on their spinning ride into the heavens. He'd have to admit—these things don't feel bad, these valentines and thoughts. They feel good right there at the tip of his spine, in the center of all that he never tells.

As the freedom of Saturday morning is pleasantly under way, Claire is cooking a pot of chili, on consignment from the Legion Hall where she works weekends as a waitress. The weather outside is unusually warm—a February thaw—and she cannot resist humming a little as she guides a wooden spoon through the deep mix. She enjoys cooking. All her life she has enjoyed Saturday mornings. They are her favorite hours of the week, the only time she hums.

Otherwise she is a packer at Boothbay Fisheries. Growing up in rural Maine, leaving school in the ninth grade, Claire has worked at the fishery eight years now, since her husband left—his whereabouts are unknown—and since she moved here with her two sons. If Claire is worrying over anything this unusually pleasant morning, it is her oldest son, Matt. He seems so unhappy anymore, seems to be going backward instead of forward. If only she could tell him something helpful. If only she could get him to stop being so mean to his little brother. And to himself, she thinks. She wonders if it's too late to dish out a good spanking. Would it do any good? Would it make things worse?

Who would believe it, Eric thinks, as he finds himself gazing yet again into the mystery overhead. He's never gone cuckoo like this before. His dreams have always been to build things. He'd use his vehicles to bulldoze roadways and airstrips; he'd throw pontoons over steams or bridge them with Popsicle sticks, and use rope and winch to save whatever trucks and troops he happened to allow to slip in their passage from one side to the other. *Combat Naval Engineers* was one of the neatest names he'd ever heard. So was *Airborne Rangers. Frogmen. Special Forces.* The names made his scalp sing, made his loins tingle, called up in him an urge to go out and build a fort or climb a tree. Who would believe something like this might so easily get in the way? Girls? Valentines?

Who would believe that on a Saturday morning, of all things, he wants to be in school? Wow, he thinks. He has to be going crazy.

Vanessa Dineen is the black girl's name. Thinking of her, Matt is taken with a desire to gaze at women in his hidden magazines. He is attracted at once to the escape the color photographs offer, the intersecting pink valentines—the glistening cuts of veal and pork—at the same time that he has no wish to take on the guilt he always feels afterwards.

He knows he's going to do it, though. It's always like this. He's too much in its grip already to turn back, unless someone walks in.

Someone does—just as his motor is revving up.

Lying on his side, the sheet tented by his shoulder, he has explored little more than a page or two when Eric blasts into the room. *"What're you doing?"* Matt snaps at him, letting the sheet collapse.

"Nothing—getting something—what do you care?"

Leaving, quickly, Eric leaves the door standing open. Matt could scream at him but doesn't. He could tear after him and smash him in the face, but he doesn't. Again, he could cry, but he doesn't do that either. Putting the magazine back under his mattress, he lies there. He stares at something just an inch before his eyes. His strength has left him; the feeling to cry nearly has him again, and his eyes blur as a spinning-away urge to exist no more passes through his mind.

In the distance a gull shrieks and calls up in Claire a feeling of spring. Soon again she is purring music of no known origin, guiding the wooden spoon. Not her mother, but her father used to hum like this. In their farmhouse near Lewiston, sitting around in cold weather, doing whatever repairing and tying and polishing there was to do, he often hummed. He winked. As the youngest, she received most of the winks. He was old— her parents were old enough to be grandparents when she was born—and their interest in her always seemed as fresh as day-old bread. Both were gone now, and here she was, living like this, a divorced mother, living in an apartment.

She nips a taste of chili. It should be satisfying, she thinks, to just be home like this on a Saturday morning, preparing food. It is—almost. Except for what seems to be wrong. She'll have to come up with something, she thinks.

What would a father do? Would a father rail at Matthew? Deny him privileges? What privileges does he have in the first place?

When he closes his eyes—Eric has just learned—the outer space, valentine sensation will come up in him. Awesome, he thinks, eyes closed to the ceiling, a door going up on his heart, all his organs playing him this serenade they have never played before.

Merely to respend the pleasure, he looks back at how it started. There is the white envelope with his name. Inside is the red card. And there, as the card is opened, is the message, flying on its arrow directly into his chest: *I have my eye on you! Won't you be my Valentine?*

In a felt-tip pen it is signed *Guess Who.*

He has guessed a little. He has guessed almost everyone, and no one. Mainly, in the flush of things, he has settled on no one. Nor does the problem of loyalty go away as he lies staring at the ceiling. There are his comrades in battle, under mortar attack. Someone has to throw a bridge over a ravine and save lives. And there is his sweetheart back home, and she nearly has a name by now. How weird, he thinks, that this new call is so much stronger than the other.

Matthew's eyes remain closed; the cooking smell continues to upset him. His other escape, after those under the bedsheet, is to think of his father. He likes to invent secret futures in which his father returns or in which he goes away to find him. Runs away. He can come up with dreams, almost any time, in which life appears new and possible again. He and his old man on the road. Tooling along in a car. Working construction. Running cable, like they do on TV.

He'd give anything, he thinks all at once, to be eighteen, to be on his own.

Maybe he'll take off. A couple years ago they heard that his father was working construction in New Orleans, and in his school's reference room he looked up the city in the atlas. He studied a patch of yellow on the map, which indicated the city's size; he envisioned his father there, deep within the map's color, working about the skeleton of a new building. What if he wrote to New Orleans? What if he took off and hitchhiked south?

Getting out of bed at last, Matthew stands in his underwear beside the chilled windowpane, looking down over the tops of parked cars. In recent days a new thought of his father has been in his mind. Standing with other boys in and around school, it has struck him how they are all making moves in their lives, and not for the day alone or for the semester, but for bigger things. Jobs. Cars. Money. They were getting driver's licenses, working part-time in the offices and shops where their fathers work. Girls. They were walking boldly with girls. They spoke of dates, of stopping at girl's houses.

His father was a journeyman electrician, Matt has thought, and would be one still. If he were here, he thinks; if his father were here, working construction like he did before, then he could say things in school himself. He could speak up in the company of boys, and of girls too, and in the company of teachers, for journeyman electricians, as everyone knew, made what was more important than anything else; they made good money.

TWO

A DOZEN MILES INLAND, along the river and across the Great Bay, a young man, Vernon Fischer, is waiting for a telephone call. Twenty-one, a senior at the University of New Hampshire, Vernon is sitting at a picnic table in a pondside cabin two miles west of Durham, where the university is located. He is sitting over an empty coffee mug, over pencils, school papers, books, glancing over the surface, but really over his life, and letting time slide by.

He knows his friend isn't going to call. At the same time he has an ear perked for the telephone's ring. His thought is to take up the receiver before it rings a second time and awakens his housemates. He wants to at least have privacy, in case the words he has to hear, or speak, are difficult.

They will be difficult all right, he knows, just as he knows the telephone is not going to ring. Would he be able to speak at all? In these past days his capacity to talk has been getting even worse. All his life he has had difficulty facing such problems, and lately he has not been able to face them at all. His friend, he knows, is not going to call.

This is so hard to believe, he tells himself. This isn't him. He isn't sitting here like this, confused over such a thing. A friendship with a teenager at that, he thinks. It isn't anything really, and it is based on practically nothing—except, of course, that it was the first time he had ever let himself go in such a way.

Taking up a wooden pencil, he rolls it in his fingers. He glances at a textbook, a pad of paper. He could at least get some reading done while he waits, he thinks. At the same time, he knows he has no capacity to take in the demanding words and meaning in the book before him, called *Molecular Biology as Art and Science.* Each thin, silken page, he knows, presents a maze of complexity. A devoted student—if nothing else, he reminds himself—he has devoured many such books. In the best of times, though, he had to shut out the surrounding world, had to take on each phrase, each diagram, illustration, and concept, had to fix it, look at it from another side, all the time urging himself to *see* and *think,* to *put things together,* to *succeed,* to *show them,* to *show every person he had ever known who had had no belief in him, who had avoided him . . .*

Stop it, he says to himself, as he thinks again of the fool he made of himself last night. He sees himself waiting at the door to Anthony's dormitory, acting as if he were not waiting to catch him with someone else. What an impossible scene. How could anyone act so badly?

Getting to his feet, Vernon walks over to look through the window above the kitchen sink. He knows the telephone, on the counter to his right, is within reach of his arm. He decides yet again, however, that it isn't going to ring. He knows the worst thing to do is to listen for it to ring. Please ring, he says to himself. Let me have one more chance. Please let me have one more chance.

He looks through the window. He wonders for the moment who he is, and how he has come to be where he is today. The hurt he feels is so strange, he thinks. How could it be this way? Was it because he had been bottled up all his life?

He looks again through the glass, although the position of his head has not changed. From this angle the pond spreading out below has the shape of a dollar sign. Ice covers the pond. A single curving piece, he sees. It fits perfectly. There have been so many secrets in his life, he thinks. Secret games and stories. They lasted all day, sometimes all summer or all year. Some lasted still. In fact, anything that had ever been important to him had been a secret. Secret hopes. Wishes. A wish that someone might speak to him in school, take a seat next to him. Appear on the sidewalk if he turned a certain corner. Telephone on Saturday afternoon. Now he has this secret wish in him that the telephone will ring and that it will be his friend, even as he knows this wish will go the way of all his previous secret wishes.

The air near the window feels different. The gray surface of the pond looks soft under the sun, like lukewarm water, and tells of a thaw coming in. So many years in New Hampshire, he thinks. Ten winters. Would he have been different in a different location? Would he have talked more, become more of a person somewhere else? He might have his red cheeks and look younger than he is, but who knows what he might have been like if they had gone somewhere else? What if they had gone to a large city, with a giant-sized high school, instead of a small town. Would there have been a place for him? Would he have come out of himself?

You're okay, he tells himself. You're going to be fine. This will pass. It will go on its way. Other friends will come along. It would be a mistake to make too much of a small thing like this at a certain time in your life.

He hears something. Leaning over the sink to the window, he directs an ear, to listen. He hears nothing then. He listens to nothing. He hears only the country sounds. They are far off. Still waters run deep, people have said to him. The idea has made him almost sick with rage. But he has never said so. Like everything else, he has turned the idea back into himself.

Is it a truck on the highway? The oil trucks sing like that. Maybe it's an airplane. The cabin is two or three hundred yards from Route 125, a two-lane highway, and nearly a mile, by winding dirt road, from a paved secondary road. It's a quiet pocket. Too quiet, Vernon thinks. Maybe it's part of the problem. Next year, if all goes well, he should be in Boston. He'll find himself there, he thinks. Even if he is lost here, he will find himself next year in Boston. That has to be his beacon.

Then, at once, the thought of being anywhere else is irreconcilable. It isn't possible to be anywhere else.

The airplanes up there fly between Boston and Montreal. It's what was said in Laconia. He wasn't sure if anyone knew where the planes were really going. They were so high their vapor trails, reflecting sunlight beyond the horizon, were more visible on the ground than the planes themselves. Unless they reflected the sun. Anthony will be in those planes, and he will see him from the ground in his small town, he thinks. He will be a prisoner in his small town all the rest of his life and will feel this way every time he looks at the sky.

Again, he thinks he hears something. He returns to the picnic table. There is movement in one of the rooms. Maybe it's just someone turning over in bed. God, if they knew what he'd been doing lately.

He does hear movement now; it is clear. He directs his hearing toward the closed doors. Then, again, he hears nothing. He listens still, but hears nothing. Maybe he was listening too closely, he thinks, hearing something when nothing was there?

The stringy-haired, slumped-shoulder kid *was* there, he thinks. Could he be blamed for that? Dear God, to think that he attempted to be polite, to introduce himself, even to shake hands. What a fool he made of himself. He sees the boy again. His shoulder-length blond hair. His raincoat about a foot too short. Hunched there in the dark. A beak nose. He wonders if Anthony joked about him to the other boy.

Again he hears something. Someone is up, moving around. A dresser drawer opens and closes. This is so impossible, he thinks, looking down at the table again as he hears a bedroom door open. What if Anthony does call? He hopes it's Duncan, the student from New Jersey who is the oldest of the four and who, like Vernon, took the room through a posting on the campus housing bulletin board. The other two, high school friends from Manchester who share the third bedroom, are never so friendly. Leon especially, a high school hockey player, is usually sullen, almost mean, and always quick—Vernon believes he does it on purpose—to pull a tab on a can of beer and turn on blaring radio music, which always sends Vernon out to his car, on his way into town to the university library.

Vernon turns his face to his school papers, avoids looking as he hears the person walk to the bathroom. He hears water running; the toilet flushes.

Vernon takes up a pencil, to appear to be working. Nor does he look up when he hears the person pad into the kitchen. "Quiet Man, you're up?" a voice says.

Relief. It's Duncan; as always, there is something friendly in his manner. "Morning," Vernon says.

"You hung over?" Duncan asks.

"No," Vernon says. It is more of Duncan being friendly; he knows Vernon would not be hung over.

"I'm still half in the bag," Duncan says.

Vernon smiles some. He is thinking how he has always been able to tell, when people teased him, if they liked him or not. It was another of his secrets. Duncan likes him. Calling him Quiet Man, as he often does, there is something in his voice. When Leon uses the name, it comes out differently. The same is true of Leon's roommate, Wayne, although Wayne usually lets Leon do the talking.

Duncan is fixing instant coffee. "I thought I heard you come in late," he says. "I mean even later than me."

"I was out," Vernon says. He would say more; he would explain something, but as usual he cannot.

"I bet it wasn't drinking that kept you out," Duncan says slyly.

"No," Vernon says, pleased that Duncan is teasing him. "Not drinking."

"Vernon, you got some little sweetie out there, don't you?"

Again, Vernon smiles. "No," he says, like a child.

"Me neither," Duncan says. "You want to go steady?"

They laugh; Vernon laughs as if for the first time in his life. His eyes fill.

Duncan sips coffee. "Vernon, listen," he says. "I've been meaning to ask you to help me with my calculus. I don't know why I need it for economics, but I do. I mean sometime when you have a chance. But soon."

"Sure," Vernon says.

"You'll help me?"

"Sure."

"Tomorrow?"

"Okay."

Sipping again, looking at him over his cup, Duncan says, "Man, are you okay?"

"Sure," Vernon manages to say.

Duncan keeps looking at him. "I mean you're always sort of weird," he says. "But lately, you really do seem weird."

"I'm fine," Vernon says.

Watching him still, Duncan nods. Carrying his cup then, he starts back in the direction of the bathroom. "Okay," he says. "Calculus tomorrow."

Vernon sits at the table. He'd like to have said more, as usual, but didn't. It could be so pleasant, he thinks. He could so enjoy someone being friendly with him. Taking the lead, though, because it was something he'd never been able to do. Did any of them have any idea how much he suffered by his reticence?

Getting up, believing he has heard a voice—it would have to be Leon or Wayne in the other bedroom—Vernon slips back to his own bedroom, to close himself in. He couldn't face those two right now, he thinks. Not today.

Sitting at his desk, next to the door, he hears them moving around in the kitchen and bathroom. At times like these Leon always wore a pair of gray sweatpants that revealed the droop of his genitals, which embarrassed and angered Vernon. Something about Leon always seemed to say, look, see what I have here—so Vernon sensed—which made him avoid looking at all costs.

This is awful, he says to himself, sitting in his room. What is so strange, he thinks, is that the one person who could lift him out of his depression on nothing more than a couple words is the one person who isn't about to.

He sits at his desk. In a moment, on a thought, he digs into the bottom of a drawer to remove an erotic magazine—in a manila folder—he has had in his possession since childhood. Called *Summertime Friends*, the magazine is something he had yet to show to his friend, and he is wondering now if it would have any effect on him, if it would excite him— two prepubescent boys engaged in page after page, scene after scene, of sex play? Would it help now?

He glances through the magazine, scans its pages. It's been a long time, months, since he has last looked at his two young friends, but he knows the pages well and feels some comfort now in their presence. There were times in his life when the two boys seemed to be—they were—his only companions, and glancing over the pages, it seems less the two of them he is seeing now than himself, himself alone, perhaps studying the photographs, kissing them, tracing them, daring all sorts of things with them in the kind of escapes they allowed him to experience. Childhood.

The telephone in the kitchen rings. Vernon's heart stops; he doesn't move as he hears someone walk past his door.

The telephone rings a second time. Vernon holds.

He hears Duncan speaking. Hearing Duncan laugh, he knows the call isn't for him. It means he'll have to go ahead with the meeting. *If I don't call . . .*

Duncan would be getting a call from his father in New Jersey. This seemed to happen every weekend, when they caught up on how all the sports teams in the East had fared since they had talked last. Was that how fathers and sons talked? Was it a secret code?

Vernon closes the magazine cover and the manila folder. Checking his watch, coming around, exhaling, he decides he might as well go on his way, go ahead and get it over with.

On his feet, he checks his pants pocket to be sure he has his keys. He leaves the secret magazine where it is on his desk. Does he hope it will be found? he wonders. Turning out his desk lamp, he leaves his bedroom, pulling the door nearly shut.

Crossing the kitchen—his coat is on a hook in the doorway—he raises a hand to say so long to Duncan, as does Duncan in turn, capping the phone and saying, "Later, Quiet Man. Calculus tomorrow."

In an odd leap, as if through a blank space, Vernon is outside. Perhaps the momentary time lapse had to do with the weather, he thinks, for the air outside is immediately sunny and warm. The air is almost hopeful. He walks around the cabin to a row of cars in the sun, to unlock the door of the third and last in line, a faded, silver gray 1975 Pontiac Sunbird.

THREE

KATHLEEN MOREAU! Eric thinks. Yes—yes, Kathleen Moreau! She is so small and shy. She sits on the edge of class and never in the middle. Just like someone else he knows, he thinks. And she has looked at him. Leaving the building, on sidewalk and stairway, across their busy room and in turns at the board, glances have slipped from her small dark eyes like folded notes. Gee, he thinks. They could end up getting married. Talk about going off the deep end.

A girl, he thinks. It's so strange that on the slightest attention from a girl he'd find himself sidetracked like this. A Navy Seal turning to mush, all at the hands of one of those puzzles with brains and long hair.

Her small ankles, though, and the shanks of her legs. There is her profile, too—around the side of which her glances seem to *click*—and the small bones of her shoulders like seashells within her blouses and sweaters.

Out of control. Kathleen Moreau.

He rolls over. Well, it could be somebody else, he is telling himself when, suddenly, the bottom of his foot is kicked, hard, and hurts at once. *"Hey!"* he cries out.

Matthew, standing over him, slaps his head as he tries to pull away, as Eric cries, "What're you *doing?*"

"See you got a valentine from Frieda," Matthew says.

It's an old line of teasing. Not the previous summer, but the summer before that, at an outdoor camp, girls from a neighboring camp visited one afternoon for field events and a marshmallow roast, and a young girl named Frieda was said to "like" Eric because he was "nice." The girl lost a bracelet, and Eric, taking on a search—any search challenged something in him—found the bracelet and returned it to her. When the boys in turn visited the girls a day later, the girl invited Eric, within his brother's hearing, to play shuffleboard, and the teasing, launched by Matthew's raised brow at the time, had never quite ceased.

"Mom," Matthew is calling out. "See the valentine Rockport got from Frieda."

Making a face at his brother, Eric tries a new tack. "Neat, ain't it," he says.

All at once, but harder, Matthew backhand slaps Eric's head. Stung, tears starting, Eric whips his foot around in a kick at his brother's shin and misses.

The fight—and Eric's tears—are under way. Matthew kicks a foot, smashing Eric's ribs under his arm as he tries to twist to the side. The fight is real, but there is their mother, shouting at them, *"Stop it! Both of you! Stop it right now!"*

"What a jerk he is," Matthew says.

"No more!" Claire says. "Eric, my gosh, will you get these cars out of the way!"

Stung again—what did his cars have to do with anything?—Eric picks up one car and then another, and tosses them into the shoe box. He would cry out that he hasn't done anything, but it doesn't seem to matter this morning.

"I won't have any more teasing from you," his mother is saying to his brother. "Certainly not because a girl sent your brother a valentine."

"Oh, Mom, nobody sent me anything," Eric cries.

"Well who did what then? What's this all about?"

"He's such a dope," Matthew says. "Stupid card's from his teacher. Why'd you even bring it home, you dumb jerk?"

"Up yours!" Eric wails. "You think you're God or something?"

"Enough!" Claire says. "Not another word from either of you."

Shoving his shoe box of cars and soldiers under the TV table, Eric feels his heart is sinking away. His *teacher?* What an idiot he is, he says to himself. His *teacher!* Mrs. Ackman?

Going along the short hallway, he locks himself in the bathroom and stands with his back to the doorknob. How could anybody be so *dumb?* he thinks.

He sits on the stool cover in a slump, too disappointed with himself to cry. He hopes his brother will try the locked door, in which case he will say he isn't through yet, which answer he will give for two hours at least, hoping Matthew will be unable to avoid disaster.

It isn't Matthew, though, who taps on the door. "Eric?" his mother whispers.

"Who is it?" he says, about to cry again.

"Eric, please open the door," she says.

"I didn't *do* anything," he says.

"Just open the door. I don't care who did what. Open the door now before I get mad."

He doesn't move, not yet.

"Eric!" she says.

"Okay," he says, going over and turning the handle.

"What is going on with you?" she says, letting herself in.

"Nothing."

She stands there. Who knows about childhood hurt, she wonders. He's had his share, at the hands of his brother mostly, she thinks. Years ago, accidentally Matthew said, he hit Eric across the nose with a baseball bat, an injury that blackened both his eyes. But it was less the injury after all that hurt Eric than a realization later that his nose might all his life bear a somewhat flattened bridge. She recalls finding him closed in this un-lighted bathroom, late on a summer afternoon, caught up in unmanage-able heartache. What in the world was wrong? His nose, he cried to her at last. Matthew and the other kids—they said his nose would *always* be like that.

Holding him now, Claire says, "I just don't understand why you two can't get along."

In a breathless whisper, Eric says, "Why is he so *mean* to me? I don't do anything to him."

Claire pauses, looking down at him. Well, she says to herself, that's it. It's gone on long enough. That's it.

"We're going to have a talk," she says to Eric. "Just don't be upset now. We're going to have a talk."

Leaving the bathroom, headed for the living room, she is wondering again how a father, a man, anyone, would handle this. Uncertain what she is going to say, afraid already the two might turn and laugh at her, she strides into the living room, her heart turning one way and another.

Matthew is on the floor, watching the flickering screen. Above him, Claire says, "We're going to have a powwow. Right now. Just turn off the TV."

"I'm *watching* this," Matthew says.

"I said turn off that TV!" Stepping over him, she snaps off the set. "Get in the kitchen—now! Don't make me say it again." For a moment Claire is filled with a desire to fight.

The two slink along before her.

"Matthew," she says. "One thing. One thing. Your brother's name happens to be Eric. It is *not* Rockport—whatever that is supposed to mean. I don't *ever* want to hear you call him that again. Do you under-stand?"

"Yeah."

"And don't say 'yeah.' Don't you sneer at me. This is a family emer-gency. And it's going to be straightened out—now. Or nobody's leaving here—all day long."

They sit there. She wonders if she has gained some ground.

"Okay," she says. "It's just high time you both understand that we are a family and what that means. We're a different family, because we don't happen to have a father here. But we're still a family, and we sure don't have any business hurting each other for no reason at all."

"Oh, Mom," Matthew says.

"You—just clear the cobwebs out of your ears. It's you I'm talking to! You act like a juvenile delinquent around here. Maybe I should have laid down the law a long time ago. I don't know." She takes a breath, feels she is getting off track. "Now," she says. "The little boy sitting next to you is your brother. He will turn out to be the best friend you will ever have. I bet you didn't know that, did you? He's going to grow up to be a strong young man, and *you* are going to be *proud* of him. I guarantee you of that right now. You'll be as proud as can be that he's your own brother. Do you understand?"

"Yes," Matthew says.

"Eric. I don't think hardly any of this is your fault. Now don't say a word, Matthew, because it isn't his fault. Not as much, even, as it's my fault. I know you're going to say I favor him, and maybe I do, sometimes, because he is the youngest, but it doesn't mean I don't love both of you just the same. Matthew, do you hear what I'm saying?"

"I guess so," he says.

"Okay. Now, there's something I want both of you to do. And you are not going to get up from here until you do it, either. I want you to promise me that you'll try, really hard, from now on, to get along with each other."

Looking at their faces, she adds, "That doesn't mean there won't be times you'll feel mad. That's only natural. But you are brothers. And we are a family, even if we don't have a lot of money. Do you hear what I'm saying? Matthew?"

"Yes."

"Eric?"

"Yup."

"Good. Okay. Now what I'm going to do, I'm going to ask you, both of you, to say, right now, the time you were most proud of each other."

"Oh, *Mom*," Matthew says.

"I know that sounds corny. But this is an emergency. Nobody leaves. Nobody does anything until you do as I say. That's all there is to it. That's the way it is going to be."

The boys exchange a glance of the faintest amusement, and Claire says, "Eric, you go first."

"What should I say?" Eric says.

"You know what I said to say! Now you do it! When were you most proud of your brother?"

"I don't know."

"Yes, you do! Now you say it!"

"I don't know," Eric says. "The time, I guess, he took me to the football game at the high school and took me around the field and stands and explained stuff. I guess."

Eric is looking away from his brother, but Clarie is relieved. "Hear that, Matt?" she says. "There's a time Eric looked up to you. Aren't you glad of that?"

"I guess."

"Good. Now it's your turn."

Quickly Matthew says, "The time he stomped on the mustard."

As the two boys laugh, Claire, unable not to join them, says, "What?"

"Nothing," Matthew says, even as he and Eric keep giggling.

"Well, *tell* me," Claire says.

"Well . . . we were down by Mister Donut, and this bossy woman told us to clean up the sidewalk. We were just standing there, and this woman who I guess thought she was the principal of the world said, 'You two—' And Rockport just took a look at her—"

All three are laughing hard.

"He just took a look at her," Matthew cries, "and lifted his foot—and stomped! And the mustard went *bloop* . . ."

"Okay," Claire is saying. "That woman shouldn't have been so bossy, but that wasn't a very nice thing—"

"Oh, Mom," Matthew says.

"Okay," Claire says. "But tell me when you were really proud—"

"*Then!*" Matthew says, and a new explosion of laughter breaks from the two boys.

"Well, tell me something else, too," Claire says.

"Well, I guess the time he spotted this big pheasant down by Damart. It was in a field there—this humongous bird—it scared me when I saw it. Old Rockport though—I mean Eric—went right after it like some big-game hunter. I thought, gee, he's a pretty tough little kid."

Eric, thrilled and embarrassed, cannot help laughing, and listening.

"You caught a pheasant?" Claire says.

"No, we just chased it," Matthew says.

Claire glances from one to the other. "Eric, see? Matt likes you. As his brother. Don't you, Matt?"

"Yes-yes-yes," Matthew says.

"And you like Matt, too, don't you?"

"I guess I do," Eric says.

"Pride . . . is a kind of love," Claire says. "You know?"

There is no response. "Okay, that's all I wanted to hear," she says. Getting up from the table she adds, before the moment is lost, "Have some chili now, if you like."

Moving to the stove, raising her eyes to the ceiling in amazement—with them and with herself—she dips the wooden spoon into the pot. She is going to take a taste but doesn't. She glances back at the two boys, on a thought—to tell them to hold fast to each other as long as they live—but it is nothing she knows how to say.

FOUR

PARKING IN THE Shop 'n Save parking lot, Vernon crosses the street to walk through the campus, to kill a few more minutes. The front of the library, his destination, is a couple hundred yards away.

Lines and puddles of melted snow are forming; they look black but sparkle and flash the white-orange of the unusual sun. A Molson empty is stuck in a crust of snow beside a walkway. The bottle is green, the snow is layered with dirt. He passes other bottles. Green, clear, brown. One appears filled with piss. College life. It has never quite worked for him, he thinks. Almost every day here, from the very first, he hasn't been happy. Or not alone. Until half a dozen weeks ago.

The dirt path he is on leads behind the Union Building, through a ravine, and meets other paths in the center of the campus. There are more bottles along the path. There are fir trees overhead and needles on the ground and mixed in the old snow. Some bottles pick up sunlight as it glances through the trees and reflects in flashes. Over a brook, the path leads to a tarmac walkway which leads to a series of flights of cement steps which, climbed, lead to the front of the libary. The time is at hand.

Once, going to a dentist as a child, he felt like he does now. He tries to smile over the thought but has no luck.

It wasn't sex exactly that he wanted, he thinks, and that may have been his downfall. What he wanted was what came after. He thinks.

Sex is sorcery, he thinks. Black magic. In parks, public bathrooms, he had reached and made gestures a few times, shown it as instructed and assumed one position or another under the sorcerer's spell, and longed afterwards, sick at heart, to have himself back again. He wanted it, but when it was over, he was left confused, cut in half.

Should he warn Anthony of the danger? As if he didn't know.

Up the stairs, he returns to the sunlight. There is the library with its million volumes about everything, and there, posing in the sunlight on a low wall before the entrance, is his friend, Anthony. He sits in his neck scarf, facing the sun, resembling some character from *Masterpiece Theatre*, although one cast too young for his part. Vernon cannot help smiling faintly, however nervously, in the same old way. "God, you look, so decadent," he manages to say, however uneven his breath.

There is the boy, who is sixteen, who has power over him, to whom he would have difficulty denying a request that he step from the top of a building. Shifting, holding one knee in both hands, Anthony looks, smiles faintly, mischievously. He doesn't speak—not yet—continues posing, Vernon observes. The silence grows. It might as well be autumn in England somewhere, Vernon is thinking, glimpsing a stunted, leftover leaf stuck to the pavement and the private loss it conveys.

Not to him, but to the space before him, the boy says, "I'm enjoying this—in a way. I'm sorry your feelings are being hurt and I don't enjoy the pain that might cause. At the same time, I feel I have command of something. Like the air. Or the sky. I feel good, because I'm being honest. Does that make sense?"

"I guess it does. I don't know."

"I know this is a new experience for you," the boy says. "I'm sorry for that because I know rejection can be painful. It's hurt—that isn't yours to control. But I know you'll be okay."

Vernon more or less nods.

"Everyone you see walking around—if they haven't gone through this, they will soon enough."

"It's this other person?" Vernon manages to say.

"And other things, too."

"What things?"

The boy hesitates. "It's not worth it," he says.

Vernon says nothing; the boy keeps looking at him. It's just, Vernon is thinking to say, that he will be alone again. Like he was before. He doesn't say this. He says, "You're sure?"

"Yes," Anthony says.

Vernon feels his throat thickening. In a part of his mind he is considering making some plea, asking if he might not have another chance, calling up the intellectual excitement he has discovered and experienced through the person before him, the companionship . . . and the small town silence and aloneness to which he sees himself forced to return. He doesn't make a plea. Rather he says, "I won't be there anymore. If it doesn't work. I won't come back." Surprised at himself, he holds the other's gaze, feeling his hands begin to tremble. The boy nods.

"I'd like to just speak, if we should pass," Vernon says then.

"Of course."

"You won't just look away?"

"Not at all."

"Well—" Vernon begins, his breath getting in his way.

"I'll go," the boy says.

"No, please. I want to."

The boy looks; looking back at him, Vernon sees a tremor in his face he feels in his own. "I—" Vernon begins, but lifts his shoulders, unable to finish whatever he was going to say.

On a turn he is walking. He becomes aware of himself walking—time has skipped a beat again—aware of a feeling of self-consciousness about his shoulders and ears as he makes his feet walk away.

On another turn, going down steps, he knows he is out of view. At a sidewalk intersection then he turns in the wrong direction, going on to cross a pedestrian bridge over a runoff. Nothing seems to change. *You can't let yourself go to pieces over something as slight as a brief friendship*, he is telling himself. *There are more important things in life to worry about*, he is telling himself. Still, nothing in the air about him seems to change.

FIVE

CLAIRE STANDS LOOKING AT THE POT of chili, at the problem of moving it to its destination. It's something she's known all week and has kept putting off. How—without a car—is she going to get all this chili over to the Legion Hall on Islington Street? Her agreement with Smitty was simply to show up with the goods; he'd give her fifteen dollars over her receipts, he'd said, if he didn't have to have anything else to do with it. Not too smart, Claire thinks. Here she is holding the short end of the stick, because of her dumb need to please. The story of her life.

Studying the volume of chili, Claire is trying to gauge if she can make it fit into her assortment of plastic containers. Even so, she thinks, how will they get them there? Walk back and forth? She and Eric? Even if she could get Matthew to help—who knew where he was by now?—not even the three of them could manage this great big tub. What in the world had she gotten herself into?

Crossing to the doorway she looks in on Eric where he is lying once more before the television set. Watching him, she wonders what is going on inside that head of his. All that war stuff he likes to read about and watch on television. It would be a lot better for him, she thinks, if she could shoo him outside to play. He could look for animals or build a tree house, do something other than have his head filled with laser beams and destruction.

"Eric, how are we going to get this chili to where it has to go?" she says.

"I don't know," he says, keeping his eyes on the screen.

She watches him another moment before returning to the kitchen, asking herself, what in the world has gotten into him now?

At least they're okay, she tells herself. At least she doesn't have that to worry about. Of course she worries about it anyway, if only in four-fifths of her mind. That has to be why she likes to cook, she thinks. Because when all three of them are sitting down to eat, they're a family and her mind and heart can be at ease, can bask even, in a pleasure of family love. It may not be so passionate, she thinks, but it's what she has, and it's the most important really—isn't it?

Betty. Betty is her only possibility; she has to face up to it. Not Betty, of course, but her husband John. He'd be glad to move the chili in his station wagon. They could spread it out among several pots so it wouldn't spill, and refill the main pot at the hall.

Claire's thought isn't on John, though, but on Betty. It's an old, vague problem and one she has handled a number of times once she had learned it was a problem. Betty was the one she'd have to ask. Betty was her friend, Betty and John were her friends, still she knew enough not to ask the wrong one of them first. As a single woman she'd been shut out by wives more than once where their husbands were concerned, even if she was, she was sure, the last person in the world they had to worry about. It seemed almost silly to think of such a thing, but she knew it wasn't silly at all. She'd never forget the time at the Legion Hall when, on his invitation, she walked over to join Bill and Maggie Zimmerman in a booth for, of all things, a cup of coffee. On a Sunday morning.

"You know," she calls to Eric, looking away from the unpleasant memory. "Betty and John have their station wagon. Think I should ask them?"

"We could pull it in my old wagon," Eric says.

"The whole pot?"

"Sure. Or buy a car."

"What would you like, a Cadillac or a Buick?"

"Ask John," he calls back to her.

At the telephone, pausing, it occurs to Claire how funny it is that she is thinking to ask for Betty should John answer. Not funny, of course, but too bad.

The phone rings almost under her hand, however, and startles her. The sound of Matthew's voice is reassuring; wherever he is out there, it means he is safe. "Cormac stay overnight?" he says.

She cannot refuse, although she knows the time isn't right. "I don't want you two giving Eric a hard time," she says.

"No problem," Matthew says.

A moment later, Betty is saying the same thing. "It's no problem at all," she says. "I'll pick you up whenever you say. Then you won't have to worry about it, Claire. That kind of thing can just drive you crazy."

Before the stove once more, she takes up her stirring. She imagines the two boys, at the table, eating. She imagines their friends with them. Cormac. Maybe the other Eric from down the street. She imagines a plate of saltine crackers in the center of the table, glasses of cold milk, and their milk mustaches and horseplay. Is she supposed to want something more than that? she wonders. Something different? If so, it is clear she's forgotten what it was. She has learned to do without, to appreciate what she has. "Eric," she calls suddenly.

"What is it?" he says.

"Nothing," she says. "I just wanted to hear you say something so I'd know you were there."

"Mom, you're weird," he says.

SIX

VERNON IS DRIVING AGAIN. His car, left in the sun, had grown warm inside, but he feels chilled. It *is* February, he tells himself. There is warm sunlight out there, but frost in the shadows. He is only trying to settle down. On the radio, "Torn between two lovers/Feeling like a fool" is playing, and within him everything is churning.

He doesn't know what he wants or where he is going. Things aren't so bad, he tells himself. He only needs to settle down. Along a two-lane road north of the university, he considers driving to Portsmouth. Hah. There is gay life there and along the beaches to the north. So he has heard. It's something he hasn't tried before and the thought of it frightens him as he thinks of it now. Still, the thought keeps coming up in him.

Getting picked up. Was that a way to get a hold of himself? Go out and touch bottom? Or would it only make things worse? He has heard several times of a place near Ogunquit called The Magnificent Obsession. Was that a way to go? Be indiscriminate? Degraded? Take in something—*suck and fuck, call anytime*—to dispose this awful hurt? Hurt Anthony somehow, if he could?

North of Portsmouth, over the state line, he pulls in and parks on gravel just beyond a portable red-and-yellow electric sign that reads Sex Barn. There is a red barn with a cinderblock extension. In the mid-afternoon shadows, the yellow sign box is lighted; perhaps a dozen cars are in the parking lot.

Once before Vernon has passed time in a porn store, and he pauses here before entering. It is exactly the depression from the other time, in Manchester, that persuades him now to enter. He wants his spirit degraded, he thinks, so he won't think of other things.

Passing through a doorway, causing a bell to tinkle, he finds himself within an offering of walls of hardcore magazines, glass cases of films, black and pink rubber goods, customers—they seem all to be men—stepping along and looking. He moves along, too, keeps his face largely on what is before him. There is flesh everywhere, in sexual positions and arrangements, and it makes his ears ring with embarrassment and confusion. This part of life is so strange, he thinks. It's the main force, the need to connect, which is his need, too, but means and end still confuse him. Men confuse him, really, he thinks, because it is himself he wants accepted, not just parts of himself.

He keeps his face on what is before him and shifts along, not unaware of side-glances being sent his way. His urges remain thin. Anthony would ridicule him for this; frightened of something all at once, Vernon begins to tremble.

Around a corner of magazines he looks on two doorways with white-lighted signs overhead. One, to the left says Peep Shows 25 cents. To the right is a more elaborate sign, black letters over milky glass:

Children in Bondage
Triple XXX
$5 NonStop Movie $5

The idea of the film does something to him, in his nervous state, as if it may be a chapter in himself he has not seen before. Still, it isn't possible for him to walk over and enter. Everyone would stop and look, he thinks, like the commercial on television. Nor can he afford five dollars, he tells himself.

He shifts along before the walls of color photographs, as do the others. There are sections given to "Leather, S & M, Gay Men, and Lesbians. He notices two women with short blond hair at the glass countertop near the door examining rubber penises, long double-ended devices, strap-on devices; they appear so casual they could just as well be in a department store looking over Rubbermaid kitchen goods.

Vernon looks on magazine covers of women with dogs and horses. Long drooping penises, penises cherry red, carrot-shaped. He moves along. What is he doing? he wonders. Would the movie help him escape? Would it disrupt his hurt? What is all this?

He stares at a glossy magazine before him entitled *Young Cocks/Tight Cunts*. Even though it is cellophane-wrapped like the others and cannot be opened, he takes it up, boldly, to look at its back cover. The couple there, the same as on the front, look to be in their late teens. Replacing the magazine, he moves along.

In another Gay Men section, a cover shows two boys who appear to be fifteen or sixteen, but they do not look happy. They look lost. They look like he feels, Vernon thinks, and he realizes what he is doing. He is look-ing for a way to make a decision on the five-dollar movie.

He browses the glass case then where a man is stationed at a cash regis-ter. He looks through glass at Swedish VCR films in red and orange boxes. On the counter is an unsealed magazine called *The New England Connection*, which he takes up and opens. He turns some pages. There are ads, appeals, dim photographs in black and white. He reads:

Mother and daughter desire discrete feminine games. Mature females only. Only inquiries with photo an-swered. RL-403.

He is propositioned. Not three feet from the clerk, a man at his side says softly, "Look good?" Vernon glances and the man adds, "Want to meet outside? Motel's just down the road."

Vernon turns, steps a step away; in a moment he senses the man moving off.

Of a sudden urge, taking the last step and leaning to the clerk, he says in a near-whisper, "Any younger materials?"

"Nope," the man says, not raising his eyes.

"Stuff isn't available?" Vernon whispers.

"I said no!" the man says.

"I'll pay," Vernon whispers.

The man looks at him then. "Want me to call the fucking cops?" he says.

Vernon retreats. Stepping past another wall of magazines, he removes his wallet, removes a five-dollar bill as he walks. What does anything in his life matter? he is thinking. What does anyone care what he does or who he is? No one cares. Could it be any more clear than it is here that no one cares?

SEVEN

WALKING IN TOWN, Matt is saying, "I'd pay the price. I really would. Wouldn't it be something? Wouldn't it be great, if *any* band in the world was here right now? And we had tickets. This afternoon. Wouldn't that be great?"

"Well, nobody is," Cormac says. "Portland's the closest place and as far as I know—"

"I know that," Matt says. "Jesus, don't you think I know that?"

"I don't see what's so bad about *here*," Cormac says.

"Forget it," Matt says.

"We can go to my house and watch the tube."

"Screw it," Matt says. "I want to *be* a video, not watch them on TV."

"You're in a great mood," Cormac says.

Matt doesn't reply. Moments later, in Variety Mart, at a twenty-foot wall of magazines, he looks up, though, and there is Vanessa, the black girl from school. As if on the lifting of a magician's handkerchief, he is smiling at her, as she is smiling at him.

"Hi," she says. A black girl beside her looks up.

"Hi," Matt says. His agitation has flown.

Not light-skinned, Vanessa is chocolate and smooth. Her long arms and legs, her long neck with its scant topping of glossy hair convey to him now a black swan. Looking back to his magazine, seeing nothing, he hears laughter ripple from the two girls.

"Who dat?" Cormac whispers.

"Screw you," Matt says.

"She's cute," Cormac says.

"Up yours," Matt says. "She's nice," he adds, a thrill passing through him. Hearing more laughter from the girls, he says, surprised by his own daring, "Interested in the friend?"

"What?"

"You heard me."

"You're not serious," Cormac says.

"Why not?"

"They're black."

"So what? Let's."

"Let's what?"

"Talk to them. Do something."

"Not me."

"*Come on.*"

"Jesus, I'm not that hard up."

"Don't be such a drag. This town is driving me nuts."

"Not me. No way."

"Thanks," Matt says. Seeing that the magazine in his hand is *Electronic Music* and realizing there is no likelihood of his ever owning anything from its pages, he returns it to the rack. Jerk, he thinks. You have no idea what a jerk I think you are.

Seeing that the girls are moving away, he says, "They're taking off."

"Look at this," Cormac says, his face back in his magazine.

"Who cares?" Matt says.

Cormac looks up. "What's your problem?" he says.

When they have left the store, however, and are walking along the sidewalk, there are the two girls, returning toward them, and Matt sees at once that he and Cormac are being given another chance in a continuing game. "Look, here they are," he says. Cormac doesn't respond.

Laughter is coming from the two girls as they approach. Matt laughs, too, and at a dozen feet, in someone else's voice, he says, "You came back."

There is some giggling and tittering, and as Matt pulls up to circle, so do the girls. But Cormac keeps walking, and Matt mutters, "C'mere, Cormac, you idiot."

"My friend, Barbara," Vanessa is saying, although both glance at Cormac.

"Hi," Barbara says.

Matt, too confused to know what to say, says, "Cormac, what're you doing? C'mere!"

"Nah," Cormac says.

"Oops," Vanessa says.

Matt glances from one to the other; there is a flash about Vanessa's fingers of her gold rings.

"Let's go," the other girl says.

The girls are walking away, just like that. Laughter breaks between them all at once, and the way their shoulders move makes Matt wince. He turns away, too disappointed to speak.

"Look, I'm not about to hang out with jungle bunnies right in the middle of town," Cormac says.

Matt cannot speak. He walks along. What a jerk, he thinks. He will end this friendship, he is telling himself.

"I mean it," Cormac says.

Matt is still unable to speak.

"Well, do you really—" Cormac starts to say.

"*Forget it!*" Matt says, as next to each other they continue along the sidewalk.

EIGHT

THE ACTION ON THE SCREEN has taken time to mean anything. A young boy and girl dressed in Victorian-looking clothes have peeked for a time through a partially opened door into a lighted room. Vernon has felt like he is coming out of himself, although he hasn't shifted physically from his withdrawn posture in a seat he has taken near the wall. The boy and girl in the dark hallway are young; however the film may have made its way here, they look to be little more than twelve or thirteen.

His interest has begun to grow. Within the lighted room—it appears to be on an upper floor of a mysterious Victorian mansion—a young woman, naked and heavy-breasted, is tied with leather thongs, arms outstretched, to a wall. Of the two men standing by, one is holding a cat-o'-nine-tails, the other a switch. The two men wear Victorian dandy clothes. The two children, to be sure, Vernon realizes, will shortly be discovered, bound, and similarly punished.

So it follows. First, though, as they spy through the door, the boy and girl become aroused. They rub into each other and utter how warm they feel. The girl asks what the bulge is pressing against her thigh and the boy tells her she will know soon enough. From behind her then, as she kneels on the floor to gaze into the room, the boy lifts her several ruffled skirts onto her back and gets down in a crouch to kiss and caress her openings. Making no move to resist, only to accommodate, the girl asks what he is doing and why it feels so hot down there.

It is after he has lowered his knee-length pants and entered her from behind and they become lost in their passion that their sighs give them away and they are discovered. "Well, what have we here?" one of the men says. Dragged and pushed into the room, the two children are ordered at once to undress to be punished for their transgression.

Vernon watches from his corner of the small cinder-block theater. The boy is tied first, with leather thongs, his wrists tied both together and between ankles, causing him to kneel in an exaggerated anal presentation. The two men all along offer comments and touches. One of the two men undresses from the waist down, removing velvet knee pants and white knee stockings, "to allow freedom of movement," he says. His own nearly erect penis visible between his shirt ends, he takes up the switch to lay on the first swat.

Vernon stares, aware from breathing and movement that someone not far from him in the darkness of the theater is masturbating. His own desire is to rescue the boy on the screen. He would care for him and make him happy. He knows what it is to be happy. He would give him attention and toys, food and clothes. He would walk with him and listen to him. He would be his friend. Sensing someone is moving to the seat directly beside him, angered at the interruption, Vernon gets up and pushes his way to the aisle—"Well, sorry," a man's voice whispers—and a moment later, Vernon is outside in his car, rolling once more along the highway.

Was he actually in there? he wonders. Was it another time lapse? Was it himself he had run away from? Why was the interruption of his fantasy so maddening?

NINE

CLAIRE AND ERIC ARE WALKING, soft-ice-cream cones in hand. The chili is delivered and Claire has time to kill before going back to the Legion Hall to pull her shift. Thanking Betty several times, she told her she had to stay and set things up, but it was only an excuse not to impose too much. Besides, she had promised Eric an ice-cream cone for helping her.

They walk along working on the cones. Claire has remarked on what a nice day it is. Otherwise they have hardly spoken. It has occured to her, though, how much she enjoys having time like this with Eric. He's her sidekick. They can talk or not talk. She needs to be careful, she thinks, not to smother him, not to love him too much. A boy without a father. If Betty was driving them home, she'd be with Betty. This ways she's with Eric. She likes Betty, but being with her twelve-year-old son, as Eric would say, is prime.

Meteorologists along the coast often use the term *land air*, as they have today. Compared to air coming in over the water, land air is usually warm and dry. Here she is, approaching middle age, Claire thinks. But she feels young today in the warm and dry air. "It's almost balmy, isn't it?" she says.

Eric sort of acknowledges that she has spoken.

They go along. Noting a ghetto fence over a storefront across the street, Claire says, "Things are sure changing around here. Maybe we'll get mugged."

Eric says, about as she expected, "Don't worry. You're with me, you're safe."

She laughs. "It's how I feel," she says. "I do feel safe with you."

"Somebody tried to rob us, I'd just bash in their brains."

Claire smiles but doesn't say anything. They continue, working on their cones. She hears Eric say, "I'll learn karate and all that stuff when I go in the Navy."

It's something of an issue, but she lets it pass. Her mind has shifted to Warren, to summer nights, as if in a dream of the past. She sees them out strolling in tiny South Berwick. Warren's appetite always amazed her and was the source of not a few skirmishes between them. He couldn't abide her comments about his eating; she couldn't resist making them. He bought the largest possible ice-cream cone—chocolate, always—and would put one away, it seemed, in three or four bites. His mouth, when he irritated her, resembled a Mason jar.

"I wonder you don't chill your tongue the way you eat," she would say.

He might, perhaps to spite her, do another round to the dairy bar and follow with an entire quart of expensive hand-packed ice cream, sitting on the front porch in the dark. His appetite came from his work, certainly in the summer when he might work ten hours, or twelve, out in the air and come home ready to eat a horse, and maybe she shouldn't have criticized him. Why did she do it? Was it because food was scarce in her childhood? Or was it because she did not take the time to understand?

Or, she reminds herself, he wouldn't come home from work at all. He'd stop along the road and fill his body, like a sponge, with liquor. In exchange for his money.

What a shame alcohol is, she thinks. Probably nothing in the world has caused more hurt and heartbreak than alcohol. Not even war.

Of course when he was drunk, she recalls, he'd get on her about getting on him about his eating. "You don't know one goddamn thing in the world about what it's like to be a working man," he'd say.

At last, as she can see this warm afternoon, at this distance, he was right. She should have just fixed him heaps of food, heaps of potatoes and gravy. For food was part of his life. She had been a fool not to understand, for of course she had loved him at the time. Arguing over food was something she had no business doing.

"*Kah!*" Eric says suddenly, slicing the air with the side of his arm and hand, at the same time tossing his ice-cream napkin into a trash receptacle standing next to a post. "Just like that! Karate chop! *Ha!*"

Getting rid of her own soggy cone tip and napkin, Claire says, "Just don't get too anxious to go off and leave your mother."

It is his turn now not to respond, and as they go along, her thoughts slip back to alcohol. What in fact gets poured away, she thinks, is love. And life. Life of all kinds. That's where *he* was in the wrong. He drank up their life.

To think, she thinks in the old rush of pain, they once had a house of their own—a porch, a garden, flowers, the boys asleep in rooms of their own, asleep in peace while they sat on the porch steps and Warren smoked one of his cigarettes. Money enough coming in. Plenty of money, really. Warren sure couldn't handle it, but he wasn't bad at making it. To think that both of them took so much for granted, paid such a price.

Now, for goodness sakes, karate against robbers. A boy wishing his life away to join the Navy. Her son, she remarks to herself as they turn onto the street where they live, where she cannot help thinking that streets of apartments are streets of broken dreams.

Enough of that, she tells herself. The thing to do is to keep plugging along. That's what she needs to do. Keep plugging along, and get these two guys grown up. Then she would be someone, to them and to their children. The times of the day, the days of the week that made life whole, would fall back into place. She would have done her job.

TEN

THEY SIT NEXT TO EACH OTHER in the side-street movie theater, their faces highlighted by the screen. Little from the movie is occurring within Matt, however, and when Cormac laughs, in a moment, Matt glances at him and experiences dislike of a kind that brings him close to lashing out at his friend with words, even with his fists.

He thinks of the black girl and feels some relief. Does he sort of have a crush on her? Is that what it is, even if it was only yesterday that she spoke to him for the first time? Is he hard up, like Cormac said? There beside him is Cormac's face. It seems connected to the screen by lines of light; it smiles, its smile holds. It looks ignorant.

Shifting suddenly, Matt says, "I gotta get some air. I'll see you later."

"What?" Cormac says.

Matt is getting up; nothing is going to stop him. "See you," he says.

"You're going?"

"See you in school."

On his way up the deep-red aisle, Matt doesn't look around. Screw you forever, he says to himself.

Passing through the theater doors, he takes in the brisk air. Half a block along, he angles across the street. In a sudden urge, he starts to run. His sneakers push off the pavement as he dashes around and between people along the sidewalk; he turns at the next corner, taking a direction in the city it seems he has never taken before.

He sprints along the full block of the street, into the gutter to circle pedestrians, and turns still another corner, to be certain of his escape. At last he slows to a walk, to recover his breath.

He knows—believes—Vanessa lives in the direction of the Mall, although he doesn't know how he knows that. Going in that direction might somehow get him intercepted by Cormac, though, and he doesn't turn back. He continues—Bow Street, around the harbor, is his destination—on a path to leave Cormac absolutely behind.

Would she be home by now? Well, sure, why wouldn't she? It's dinnertime, and she and her friend—Barbara, he reminds himself—would not hang out downtown into the evening. Still, it is the likelihood that she won't be home that makes up his mind. At the first telephone, he will call her. He will do it. The decision comes in on a new thrill, a new version of himself.

She is not in the telephone book, though, and the name that the operator offers scares him. "I have a Paul T. Dineen, Lieutenant Colonel," she says. "Woodlawn Circle."

A pilot? Matt wonders. He imagines Darth Vader dressing him down for his presumption at calling his daughter. Still he says to himself, do it. Don't be like Cormac, do it, and he redeposits his dime.

Clearing his throat as the telephone rings, he stares at the circle of numbers and letters before him. A deep male voice takes its time. "Hullo."

"Vanessa there?"

Silence follows; Matt's heart starts dropping away. "May I ask who is calling?" the black lieutenant colonel says.

"Matt Wells?" Matt asks.

He knows I'm white, Matt is thinking. Jesus. Now he's going to let me have it.

But the voice says, "Just a moment, please."

When the receiver is picked up, a fluid voice says, "Matt, hi."

"Hi."

"You still in town?"

"I took off from Cormac. He's such a jerk."

"Color line bother you like it does your dopey friend?"

"No. No, it doesn't."

"This ain't just a guilt call?"

"No. You're—ticked off I guess, aren't you?"

"Well, yeah," she says. "Barbara's mad at me, too. I get us put down like that. Yeah, my feelings were hurt. They still are."

"I'm sorry."

"I thought you were cool, in school, you know. Then me and Barbara get served up a plateful of humiliation."

"I never knew he was such a jerk."

"That why you called?"

"Not just that. I . . . wanted to talk to you. I don't know. I wanted to say something to you."

"Like what?"

"I don't know. I forgot."

"Come on, you didn't forget."

"I wanted to say hello."

"That's all?"

"Well . . . I like your rings."

"My rings?"

"All that gold. You might get stolen."

"That really why you called—say you like my rings?"

"Yeah."

"Man, what about me?"

"What do you mean?"

"You don't like me? That ain't got nothing to do with why you called?"

"Sure, but I like your rings, too."

"Between my teeth and my fingers I'm a walking gold mine. You think the rest of me is worthless?"

"Sort of."

"Funny, Matt."

"I think you and me . . . got a lot in common, you know."

"Baby, it's 'you and I.' "

"What?" he says.

"Nothing. The grammar. I shouldn't do that."

"Well—you called me baby."

"It's just an expression. Don't get carried away."

"I am, though," he says, his heart lifting suddenly.

Pausing, she says, "This ain't a social call then, an apology?"

"What do you mean?"

"You called to be friends?"

"Yes."

"You call back then sometime?"

"Sure. Tomorrow."

"Okay, I have to set the table now. Slaves ain't all been freed yet."

"I'll call," he says.

Hanging up, Matt holds still a moment, as if to get his breathing straight. God, she's neat, he says to himself.

ELEVEN

HIS HOUSEMATES ARE DRINKING. Perhaps they are drunk; he isn't sure. He has almost never been around the cottage at this time and wonders if it wasn't a mistake to return here now. In a moment he knows it was. The taunt comes from Leon, who seems always to be after him. "Vernon," he says, "are you gay?"

Leon's roommate/friend, Wayne, sipping a can of beer, snorts suds and laughter. Duncan, though, says to Leon, "Hey, take it easy."

Did they see his magazine? Vernon wonders. Were they talking about him?

"We were wondering," Leon says. "All year you've never had one fucking phone call. Until lately. And they ain't been from no girl."

"Someone called?" Vernon says.

"See!" Leon says.

"No one called," Duncan says. "Leon, those are low blows. Vernon's phone calls, or anything—they're none of your business."

"Low blow, high blow, any blow will do," Wayne says.

"Shut up," Duncan says.

"Is he some kind of closet queen or not?" Leon says.

"I'm not," Vernon manages to say.

"Man, you are overdoing it," Duncan is saying to Leon.

"Where does he go, what does he do?" Leon says. "Nobody could spend that much time in the fucking library." On this he throws back his head, pours away some beer.

"I can't believe this," Duncan is saying. "It's none of your goddamn business, none of it."

"I wish I'd known if he is," Wayne says. "Could be our house faggot, save me beating my meat so much."

"Hey, *come on!*" Duncan says. "There's no reason to be cruel. What's with you two?"

"Don't like faggots, man," Leon says. "Sure as fuck don't like living with one."

"My God, I can't believe this," Duncan says.

"So don't believe it," Leon says. "That mean you're one yourself?"

"Man, you are getting me pissed off now. I don't care how drunk you are."

"It's simple," Leon says, crushing a beer can and tossing it into a standing grocery bag. "Either he is. Or isn't. I have a fucking right, you see, to know, see, who the fuck I live with. Vernon, you a faggot or not?"

"You're an asshole!" Duncan says then. "You hear me! You fucking ignorant asshole!"

"Let him answer," Leon says. He turns back from the refrigerator with a can of beer, pops the tab.

"He doesn't have to answer anything," Duncan says. "Even if he's gay, that's his business. Who are you, with all your fucking *Hustler* magazines? What's the difference between you reading *Hustler*, jacking off in the fucking john all the time, and Vernon spending his time at the library. If that makes him a bookworm, it makes you a fucking outhouse."

"Okay. I read *Hustler*. I jerk off in the bathroom. It's true. Only that's normal. The fucking library, as I'm sure you know, is used for more than reading books."

"You're disgusting," Duncan says. "What the fuck you doing in college?"

"The point is," Leon says, "the point is, you may not like me, and you may not approve of what I read, but I have the right, I do have the right, to know who the fuck I live with!"

Pausing, Duncan says, "You don't read anything, you look."

"Beside the point," Leon says. Turning, he says to Vernon, "Well?"

"You—" Vernon says, trembling. "Talk about right. You have no right. To ask me anything."

"I do," Leon says. "I have the right to live with people of my choice." Leon forces a smile. As always, when he smiles, the end of his nose tips, and Vernon hates him all at once for the ugliness and cruelty he sees in the tipping of his nose.

"I don't believe this," Duncan is saying. "You don't have rights like that. You do not have the right to insist that anyone—anywhere, any time—make that kind of disclosure. It doesn't even matter that you advertised these rooms. Sex, religion, politics, fucking taste in clothes or music. You can live where you like, you can like what you like. But you cannot—under no circumstances, legal or human—batter someone, if only verbally, to answer your stupid, fucking, self-indulgent questions. I tell you I'm ready to take a stand on this. You want to go outside, take it on, I'm ready. I won't stand for your bullying. That's it."

"I don't like faggots," Leon says

"Talk to me," Duncan says. "You're a hick, that's what you are. What're you doing in a university? You're a drunken hick who sits around reading skin magazines. You shouldn't be here. You should be somewhere cleaning pig pens."

"Now *you* take it easy now," Leon says.

"Why—" Wayne starts to say.

"*Shut up!*" Duncan snaps. "I'll tell you this," he says, raising a finger.

"You want to get down to fucking cases, I'll tell you this. As for being truly gay—my guess is a serious case could be made for you two! All you do is read jack-off magazines. Is that why you came to college? Read about throbbing ten-inch cocks and jack off? Salivate, I imagine—one of you going at it in the bathroom, the other in the bedroom. What you'd probably really like to do—you two *buddies*—would be to reach over and take hold of each other's dongs. Down in there somewhere, *that* is fag city—you fucking hicky high school homoerotic *buddies* from fucking nowhere New Hampshire! Maybe that's what you didn't want to live with. *You ever think of that?*"

"I think you better not say any more," Leon says. "Any second now I'm going to get violent."

"You go right ahead—you motherfucker. Don't think you can intimidate me. You asshole! Don't ever think that. You fucking hick. You fascist! I'll fight you to the fucking *death*, you cocksucker, you!"

When Leon has no response to this, Duncan, swigging beer himself, adds, "You can dish it out, but you can't take it, can you? Truth gets to you, doesn't it? I'm a little surprised. Since I moved in here, I see you collecting all those shit magazines, I thought it was kind of funny. Strange-funny, you know. I thought: I call him on it, he's straight, he'll laugh. He gets defensive? Ooh, something funny in there, man. You and Spot here, your faithful companion."

"That is funny. Ha ha."

"Too late, Leon."

"Fuck you. I happen to know I'm normal. And fucking looking at *Playboy* and jacking off are normal, too. Okay?"

"You are so pathetic," Duncan says.

Leon is drinking his beer. "No," he says, indicating Vernon, who hasn't moved in this time. "That is pathetic."

"As soon as I can, I'll move," Vernon says.

"Please do," Leon says.

"You're not moving anywhere," Duncan says "You move, I'll move. Know something?" he adds, turning back to Leon. "I was warned about coming here to school. Go to a small private school, people told me. Know something else? This is the first—serious—question we've taken on since we've been here. The *community college* I transferred from—we sat around a fucking dirty cafeteria *every* night and had good arguments, good discussions. And we all thought—dumb-ass bozos that we were— we all thought that *real* student life existed elsewhere. We were wrong. All you do here is play. Me, too. It makes me want to cry. My God, to respect *Playboy*—which is nothing but a jack-off magazine that you are rube enough to buy. Know something else? It makes you a joke. It makes me want to walk in front of a fucking truck. There was a time, man, *I was hungry to learn things,* and you have the fucking gall, you do, you have the fucking gall to make fun of New Jersey."

"You're drunk," Leon says.

"You're fucking right I'm drunk," Duncan says. "That doesn't mean I'm wrong. It means I'm telling the truth—you fucking turd."

Vernon thinks to leave, to go to his room, but he stands there, as do the others, as if caught.

Leon, a catch in his voice, seems about to cry. "I'll tell *you* something," he says. "I love this school. Say what you like. I love it."

There is a pause. Duncan, face down, looks to actually be weeping, too, although tears of another kind. Vernon walks between them and across the kitchen to his room. The pause continues. Closing his door, standing inside in the late afternoon shadow, he senses the three of them on the other side.

There on his desk is his magazine in the manila folder, looking untouched. He returns the folder to his desk drawer.

Do I have to move? he wonders. Do I? Is that what happened?

Sitting on the side of his bed, he sees no answer to his question; nor does he have any idea what to do or what to think. What is it? he wonders. What is happening to him?

An outburst of laughter comes from the kitchen and startles him. All three, it seems, laughed at once.

There on the metal bar of his cot are socks he washed by hand and hung to dry a day or so ago. He takes them down, mates and rolls them into pairs. He has underwear in the bathroom on a small drying rack he bought—and is taunted over, as he is for the regular hand-laundering he does in the bathroom sink—but he has no intention of retrieving anything now. Only in his weeks with Anthony did his sink-laundering fall out of rhythm.

Socks rolled, he remains sitting on the edge of his bed. He has realized he is crying, but he doesn't know if it is one thing or another. He seems to know only of the aloneness around him.

Moments later there is a light tapping on his door. He looks over but doesn't say anything.

"Duncan," a voice says. "I come in?"

The door opens several inches.

"You okay?" Duncan says.

Vernon nods; he would say yes, but the kindness is confusing and the word doesn't come out.

"You know," Duncan says. "You're the one might think of going to a different school. I say that as a friend. There are schools that are more—well, I don't know—that aren't so base, you know."

Vernon only looks back at him; the suggestion would be generous except, as Duncan should know, it is Vernon's last semester.

"The animals are going out," Duncan says. "So am I. You wanna go?"

Nor can Vernon say no, as he moves his head back and forth.

"I understand. See you later, man."

Closing the door softly, Duncan is gone. Vernon sits there, wishing he had said yes. He seems to listen to the house, or to the sky. He doesn't know if what he hears is within his head or without.

They all leave. He hears the cabin door out there open and close; a car starts up, backs around, and drives away. Vernon feels some relief to have them gone. Then, at once, the familiar aloneness is within him again.

To avoid the feeling, he goes ahead and carries his scant laundry bag of socks and underwear to the bathroom. Lights are on in the kitchen, to his left, and a stillness there takes him back to childhood, when his mother left him alone so many times in the evening.

He wishes not to think, but he thinks that washing his clothes like this is a strong thing to do. Shaking detergent on the sinking socks, pressing them into the water, his mind keeps looking to the question of how he is going to get through the night. His odd life. He won't be able to sleep. Will he live?

Looking into the mirror, it occurs to him that he will go out. He should go out, this early evening, and do something. Maybe he should go somewhere and let himself be picked up. Is that how it's done? Go somewhere, degrade himself if he can. He will bathe, and dress in clean clothes, he thinks. He'll sprinkle talcum powder over his stupid heart, and soul, and go out and give himself away to anyone who will take him. In degradation, maybe his aloneness will fade.

TWELVE

"THAT CARD WASN'T FROM FRIEDA, was it?" Claire says, as they approach the Legion Hall.

"Heck no. *Gosh*."

"It's okay if it was," she says in a moment. "And it's okay now or any time, if you have a girlfriend. Or a friend who is a girl. You don't want to let your brother's teasing get in the way of that."

Maybe he nods, as they continue walking. In her glance at him, she wonders what is in his mind, what he knows. Is she doing all right by him? she wonders. Is it guilt that has her acting so affectionate? Having him walk her to work? Well, the main thing, going to work on Saturday night and leaving him alone? Was that it?

At the same time, the twenty or twenty-five or thirty dollars she earns long ago became a necessity. And when she returns home and Eric, counting her tips at the kitchen table, announces the verdict, they both seem to know a kind of satisfaction. It always seems right then, when the week's lunch money for all three of them is in hand.

Besides, she'd have to admit, she enjoys the few hours she puts in each weekend waiting on tables. It's the only chance she has to act like a hostess, a wife almost, serving food and drinks to people who are in a good mood, who are having a good time and know her by name.

THIRTEEN

LEANING AGAINST A BRICK WALL, Matt overlooks Bow Street and Ceres Street, the sheltered lee in the harbor around which are taverns and glassed-in terrace cafés, tugboats and yachts. And out-of-towners. The sunless air on the horizon is dusty orange, and for the first time he feels an allure here. The feeling of Vanessa keeps coming up in him. It fills, like a balloon. A moment later it fills again.

From where he stands, the Interstate 95 bridge is in view. He gazes for some time in that direction. Perhaps he has never looked to the horizon before, or within himself. The bridge arcs through the sky like something more modern than the city, and in reverse focus he imagines the view of Portsmouth below, its buildings and houses, the wide river, its lobster boats, and at last—would he be visible?—himself standing here. No, he thinks. But what an idea. Does it mean he is in love with a black girl? Boy, are you losing it, he says to himself.

He strolls some. Sleek cars slide by here, close to the restaurants around the harbor and the Theatre-by-the-Sea. He watches a chauffeur-driven Rolls-Royce drift by. Women passing are different, too, and he strolls, eye-searching both for European cars and for the appealing droop of free-flowing breasts. In his mind this early evening, breasts uncontained look to be presenting themselves, ready in their faint sag to be lifted and held like kittens in his hand, to have their noses touched by his thumb.

What if he called her again. No, he thinks. Too uncool. He said he'd call tomorrow. Or sometime. That's what he had to do. Be cool. That was the way to make out with a girl. He could see why, too. Calling her now would be the uncoolest possible thing anyone could ever do. Talk about being a twit.

"Goodness, twice in one evening," Vanessa says. "Is this getting serious or what?"

"You still eating?" Matt says.

"All done," she says.

"Could I meet you somewhere? Can you come out?"

"Tonight?"

"Right now."

"Gee, I don't know. I know I can't be out past nine. Is something wrong?"

"No."

"Where are you?"

"I'm still in town. I just been hanging out."

"I can meet you, I guess. But I have to be back by nine. I'm sort of on probation."

"Where could we meet?"

"The Mall? I could have my father drive me there. He thinks the Mall's cool."

"Where in the Mall?"

"By the plants, in the center?"

"Okay. I'll be there in twenty minutes."

Leaving the translucent telephone shell, Matt is all at once surprised. What are you doing? he asks himself. What is all this?

FOURTEEN

PARKING HIS CAR ON THE SIDE, walking around to the door on the high-way, entering into a noisy crowd, a true crowd, he is trembling with apprehension. He pauses a moment. Disco music is playing. It sounds like *Saturday Night Fever,* and so it is. So many people are lined up, packed along the bar, he has to reach and step sideways between customers to achieve a view of the other side. Then, when a bartender, a young man with smooth hair and a black bow tie, pistol-points an impatient finger at him, Vernon isn't ready with something to say.

The finger shifts. In the crush, not giving up his place, Vernon pulls two dollar bills from his wallet. Within the near roar of talk and music, he overhears a voice call out, "Chablis on the rocks, *mon cher.*"

Ready, he holds out his money. "Chablis," he says when his turn comes. "On the rocks."

Two-fifty. Drink in hand, held shoulder high, his two dollars gone, he has to work with his free hand as the bartender waits. He retrieves another dollar, working one-handed, extends it between shoulders. Two-fifty for a glass of wine! Is that what these places cost?

Quarters in hand, the drink in his uncertain left hand, he slips—"pardon me"—away from the bar to a less-crowded opening. Pocketing his change, shifting the heavy glass, he sips and glances above the glass edge around him.

It occurs to him that he fears rather than anticipates someone approaching him. He is wondering, as he had when he drove into the parking lot, if the police collected numbers in such places, kept tabs, filed reports. Should he use a name other than his own?

Five minutes at least have passed and nothing has happened. How does it happen? he wonders. This all seems so ordinary, even happy. Will someone wink at him?

Sex. It has to be the compelling force, but he feels nothing of its call himself. Not now. He wonders, not at all for the first time: Is he really what he seems to be? Does he know what he is?

He sips, widens his gaze. No one bothers him or seems to notice that he is standing there alone, sipping modest swallows of white wine from a large glass. Do they know that he is here to offer himself?

Feeling he is standing on air, a thought runs through his mind of driving home to see his mother. It's a thought he seldom has anymore. Might they reconcile at last? Might he drop out of school and go back home and do everything over again? Start over again? Be a child again and make himself over?

All around there is smoke, movement, laughter, and music. And talk. Red, orange, and blue strobe lights flash from the doorway, exclaiming, it seems to Vernon: *You! You are here! This is life! This! There is no turning back!* Sipping, he remembers a remark he read somewhere, attributed to a woman: "Going to a gay bar informed me for the first time that I was not alone."

He shifts a couple steps, glances. There is an occasional woman in the crowd, and there are signs of intimacy, a hand on a shoulder or on a forearm, a person standing within the invisible shadow-embrace of another. Do we lose fear in pairing up? he wonders. He recalls a boy in grade school whose father, every time he saw him, had his hand around the boy's shoulder or on his neck. Did the absence of that affection then, he wonders, have anything to do with its presence now? Close to his ear, almost into his thoughts, a voice says, "Some crowd."

Turning, Vernon sees a man in a suit, tie, and vest, looking nothing other than conversational. "Yes," Vernon says. "It is."

It could be an exchange in a bank line. The man wears glasses, has thinning hair, looks to be in his thirties. His face looks lightly tanned.

Through the noise, the man says, "First time here?"

"Yes," Vernon says and nods.

The man smiles some. There is something friendly and genuine about him, and Vernon wonders if *he* knows what kind of bar he has wondered into. Then the man leans closer, to be heard, and calls, "You look like a frightened rabbit, you know that?"

He smiles; Vernon smiles in turn this time. "That's how I feel," Vernon calls back. What he feels in fact is an amount of relief.

"Haven't been to a place like this in a few years," the man calls. "It's a meat market."

"Is it?" Vernon says.

Nodding, the man says, "It must be the weather. I just felt like talking to someone new, someone I didn't know. I enjoy that at times."

Vernon nods; it's a fair reason, he thinks.

"Are you in trouble?" the man calls.

"What did you say?" Vernon says.

The smile continues on the man's face. "You heard me," he says, in his pleasant manner.

Vernon cannot resist smiling again, almost laughing. It seems the closest laughter has come to his face all day.

"Well?" the man says.

53

"Yes," Vernon says. "Yes."

"Personal problems?" the man says.

"Yes."

His head turned to listen, the man nods almost professionally. "What's your name?" he calls.

"What?"

The man almost glances. "I said, 'what's your name'?"

"Tony," Vernon calls back, believing the man sees through this lie as readily as he saw through his evasion.

"Wes," the man says, offering his hand.

"I beg your pardon," Vernon says.

"Wes."

Vernon nods, without eye contact. The man sips his drink, and Vernon follows suit, glancing at the man now as he does so. He is not good-looking, at least as Vernon has ever calculated good looks. He is friendly, though, Vernon thinks, and he seems quite intelligent. If he looked at him now, Vernon would smile, he knows, cooperatively.

The man doesn't look at him, though; as if to the floor, shifting his head near Vernon's face, he calls, "There's another room there. Let's sit in there where we don't have to shout."

Vernon nods.

They shift along, Vernon following. Stopping near the door, the man says, "What are you drinking, Tony? I'll get us a couple to take in."

"I'll—" Vernon begins, as if to reach for his wallet.

"No, no, on me," the man says easily, handling his glass to Vernon. "What are you drinking?"

As Vernon tells him he nods, seeming to know already. Pointing, the man says, "Meet you right at the door in exactly two minutes."

Vernon steps over, holding the two drinks. Well, he feels better already, he says to himself. Maybe he should have come here, come out long ago. Maybe he'd get over what had happened to him. Maybe he wouldn't have been so insecure with Anthony in the first place. Maybe he would have had the psychological advantage with the teenage wonder.

Glancing into the room, into an infrared darkness highlighted by the revolving strobe lights, he sees faint orange lamps here and there, then a cigarette lighter flaring; to the left is a partial view of a translucent floor over which are sliding and walking the silhouettes of couples dancing. It doesn't fit with the man, he thinks. Dancing in a roadside bar as the sun goes down. Or is it himself, as always, who doesn't fit? What would his mother say, he wonders, if she saw him now? Oh, God. Anthony would berate him for being a fool, for giving in to trashy impulses.

The man, appearing, smiles politely, winks somehow, and says, "Better follow me."

Vernon follows. He thinks again how much less alone, less at sea, he feels already, no matter what Anthony might say. Across the room, placing the drinks on a table and sliding into the vinyl seats on either side, he says, "Why is it so dark?"

"Tacky, isn't it?" the man says. "It's so people can make out. It's intended to be sexy."

There is the subject, the reason he is here, Vernon thinks. He lifts his drink, realizing all at once how anxious he feels, and sips.

"Here's looking at you, sort of," the man says.

Vernon sips again, to join in the toast. "What do you do?"

"You shouldn't really ask that," the man says. "But I'm a lawyer, in a nearby town. I keep my personal life quite apart from my professional life."

"Well, I'm sorry," Vernon says.

"No problem. What do you do?"

They both laugh. "Nothing, really," Vernon says.

"You're not a student?"

"I have been," Vernon says. "Not anymore. Yes and no."

They drink. You don't have to lie, Vernon is saying to himself, not here in the dark.

"Well, what is your story?" the man is saying. "Why are you unhappy? Why in trouble?"

"Oh," Vernon says, "it's okay. I mean, I'm okay."

"I would say," the man says, "either it's a coming out or it's a loss, a death maybe, or a broken heart."

"It's a couple of those," Vernon says.

"Which couple?"

"Well, I've never done this," Vernon says. "And I'm not sure I should. I guess I'm doing it because I got rejected by my friend. I didn't know what else to do."

The man drinks, slowly. "Some things I guess you just have to go through," he says. "If you could afford therapy, that would certainly help. I think it was smart of you, your instincts were right, to get out, you know."

"I'm glad I met you," Vernon manages to say.

"Well, how can I help? We could go to my place and talk. Relax. Take a long, hot shower. Talk things out. Have a couple of drinks. No pressure, I mean. You understand? Who is this ex-friend of yours? What does he do? Do you want to talk about him? Is he older than you?"

"Well, the person I've been close to, he's not a man like that. He's a boy. He's younger than me. Quite a bit younger."

"Really."

"Yes."

"You're just a boy yourself."

"I'm twenty-one. Twenty-two. I don't even know how old I am."

"You could pass for seventeen or eighteen. You look, to tell you the truth, like a high school student. You look like a high school athlete who wandered into the wrong place altogether."

"I did wrestle in high school," Vernon is pleased to say. "It was because I was way overweight at the time. I've never regained the weight, though." He smiles; it occurs to him how he has warmed to this man, how easy it is to say things to him here in the dark.

"I think you won the struggle," the man says.

"Thank you," Vernon hears himself say. "I didn't mean to say . . . that I didn't want to go with you. I don't mind that. You're the first person who's been nice to me in a long time."

"Now, I hope that's not true," the man says.

I'd say ever, all my life, but I know you wouldn't believe it, Vernon thinks. "It's true," he says. His eyes seem about to fill. Is it the wine? he wonders.

The man only stares back, perhaps in embarrassment. It's true, Vernon is thinking. It is true. "I came out," Vernon says then, "I came out here to debase myself. Because I couldn't stand who I am. It's not working like that."

"I know what you're saying," the man says in a moment. "I wish I didn't. But I'm afraid I do."

FIFTEEN

CLAIRE HAS TWO PLATES in each hand, on her way to a booth of four, and there is Eric at her side, saying something, nearly getting in her way. *"Not now!"* she says. *"My gosh, I'll talk to you in a second!"*

She feels upset for being so short with him, and anger with him for being so inconsiderate. Returning from the booth, circling around tables, taking up dirty dishes on the way, Eric is at her side again.

She knows what he said the first time—he is asking for money—and it is money she is responding to when she says now, "My gosh, Eric, can't you see I'm working?"

He tags after her to where she places the dirty dishes in a plastic tub.

"All I want is a dollar to stop at Smiley's."

"I heard what you want. The answer is no, Eric. I'm sorry! You know darn well we don't have money to waste every time we turn around. You just had an ice-cream cone."

"I'm hungry."

"Have a peanut-butter sandwich when you get home."

"I don't want a peanut-butter sandwich."

"Eric, I have to work. That's what I'm getting paid for."

He says nothing.

"What time is your program on?" she asks.

"Eight o'clock."

"Well, you go watch it then. And have yourself a sandwich. And a glass of milk."

"It's not on yet."

"Eric, come on now, stop being such a grump."

She returns to work, walks away from him. Moments later, through the wide doorway into the adjacent pool table room, she looks over the faces to see if he is still there.

She spots him. She feels relief. A pool game is taking place, and he is standing at the wall in a line of others. Nothing on his face says that he is watching though, and she wishes Matt were with him. In another moment, carrying a refill bowl of chili to a large bearded man sitting at a table with his wife, her mind shifts to other things. It's fine that they like the chili, she thinks. But if they keep ordering it like this, there won't be a drop left for her to take back home.

SIXTEEN

THE MAN IS BAREFOOT, although Vernon has not seen him remove his shoes. "You have to try to relax," the man says, as music reaches down around them from above.

Vernon tries. Being in a stranger's house with its particular odors and objects has him tense, however, until, as instructed, he closes his eyes. This seems to help, even as he squints and peeks some at first. The music is classical piano, well recorded, carefully amplified.

He allows himself to be undressed. Looking down, eyes closed most of the time, like a shy, complacent child, he lifts a foot, raises an arm when told to, maintains his balance. Standing in this darkness, in his underpants, he hears water spittle and spit its spray in the shower stall behind him.

"Warm water will help you loosen up," the man is saying close by.

Vernon is peeking and squinting less, enjoying the darkness, and he cooperates as the man slips his underpants down and off over his feet. Standing, keeping his eyes closed then, he experiences nakedness in a way he has not known before.

"I guess I'd forgotten just how needy you were feeling," the man says, guiding him by his elbow into the stall.

Vernon peeks some here, as he settles in under the water. The shower stall is contemporary, off-white and double-sized, with chrome nozzles and flexible hoses between the handles and the main shower nozzle, which is as large as the head of a sunflower. A contoured bench seat is on one side, and the curtain is transparent. On a glimpse of the man, naked, approaching—Vernon did not know what was going to happen next—he turns more or less into the spray and closes his eyes once more. His feet on skid tread on the floor, his eyes closed, he feels for a moment as if he is in childhood again.

"Feel better?" the man says, stepping into the shower stall behind him.

Vernon keeps his eyes closed and doesn't say. He wants to ask what is going on. He wants to say that he doesn't feel sexual, that he only feels lonely, that this isn't what he wanted. He imagines Anthony shaking his head and laughing at what a fool he was to go out like this.

"Keep those eyes closed," the man says.

Vernon does, as he knows the man is lathering soap over himself close by. Vernon tries, too, to feel as a child again, but it isn't working now. He feels himself sliding back into despair. "I'm just going to wash your back now," the man says, his voice and face feeling too close.

Vernon stands there, eyes closed, as the man lathers over his shoulders and back. "Come on, Anthony, relax," the man says. "Loosen up."

"I don't feel . . . sexual right now," Vernon manages to say.

"No need to," the man says. "I'm just trying to help you relax. But you have to try, too, my friend."

Vernon tries once more to relax. The man washes down over his legs, to areas of his ankles he had never known were alive to touch of the kind. Feeling more childlike then, his anxiety does seem to be washing away, even as the man is washing and lathering up over his cheeks and in between. "That's better," he hears the man say.

Is this a child's feeling of security? Vernon wonders, as he works to relax, as he thinks of attention of the kind given to him by his mother. Was she ever so fond or affectionate in her attention? he wonders. No, she really wasn't, he thinks. She wasn't rough, but neither was she gentle. Mainly, of course, she wasn't anything, because she usually left him to do things for himself. Almost forever, he thinks, she left him on his own.

Oh, his poor mother, he thinks. She was young and it wasn't that she wanted to be like that. It was more like she didn't know. Nor did she want to dislike him, he thinks. It was more that she just didn't know what to do with him. Nonetheless, he thinks, she didn't have to leave him alone and neglect him as much as she did.

He returns to the present. Time seems to have slipped away again while his mother was on his mind. And he seems to have dozed, as the man lathers him, as it occurs to him how extremely tired and in need of sleep he is, here upon all the sleepless hours he has known over the past days.

"Only then what happened," the man is saying, "is they pushed me ahead of them along this alley. Then they turned into what was a kind of abandoned repair garage for cars, made of cinder block. It had a lot of small, translucent windows, and the floor was cement. God, I remember that. Old oil stains everywhere. Beer cans. Rubbers. Cigarette butts. An odd light through the windows, like the color of Coke bottles. And that, thereafter, even that color took on erotic significance. Became part of my repertoire."

Continuing to lather or massage Vernon's back, the man's hands work up to and around the sides of his neck, sending pleasant shivers through him. The man keeps a distance; except for his hands, he avoids contact and Vernon is only occasionally aware that the space between them is not empty. "Of course," the man is saying, "because I did know the one boy from the high school, I probably wasn't as frightened as I should have been. I'm not sure I had a reasonable idea of what it was they had in mind. Although I suppose I did. It certainly was the time when *I* was debasing *myself*, because in a way I was going along. Looking to die in shame, to live again at last. What you say you haven't gone through—which is remarkable for someone your age. What I mean is, they were calling me faggot names and so on as they pushed me along, and they said other things that were rather clear, and in some deep, deep way it was something I know I desired.

"There I was. I was thirteen. What was most important to me was that I was in the company of this boy from the high school who I happened to believe was a sort of god, you know, as you do at that age. He certainly was, to me, just about the most incredibly *striking* person in existence, even as he was pushing me in the back with the others. He was an absolute hood and terrible in school—I suppose he dropped out before long—but he had to be the most fearless, most *daring* person in the world. Fairly tall, fairly thin, an Italian stallion with long blond hair, of all things, hanging down to his black leather jacket. From behind he looked like a woman's ad for Clairol. Artie DelGreco was his name.

"Once, when I was in the high school, on a stairway, and saw him coming down the stairs, I froze. I stood there and stared at him, starstruck, although I didn't know at the time that it was anything more than boyish hero worship. He was so famous. I remember seeing some friend, saying at once, 'Hey, guess who I just saw . . .'

"They began to get a little rough. Saying things, saying they knew what I liked to do, things like that. I didn't mind at first, but they started to hurt me. One of them—it wasn't my hero, thank God—slapped my face backhanded, so my nose started to bleed. 'You *wanna* suck us off, dontcha?' he kept saying. 'You wanna suck our cocks, dontcha?' I cried and said no no no, and swallowed blood and wiped blood from my mouth and so on.

"The same boy just blasted me in the stomach then. I buckled and went down, and when I tried to get up, which I can tell you wasn't easy, he shoved me, by my shoulders, as hard as he could, and I went sprawling. He was saying they were going to kill me if I didn't do it, and so on, and then Artie DelGreco said, 'Take it easy; let's just ask him in a nice way.'

"Well—what I did, there on that oil-stained cement floor—I turned or twisted in a way that I was looking up at this boy over whom I had had this remote but serious thing. And I said, 'Just don't beat me up. Don't beat me up.'

"This little smile came over his face. He was looking right into my eyes. As he did this, as he looked, he rubbed his hand over his crotch several times. He said something like 'This is what you want, isn't it?'

"I didn't say anything. I just looked up at him, at his eyes, while he felt himself. But I was taken.

"Just like I am now, just thinking about it," the man adds in an even softer whisper, as his face comes forward and Vernon realized he has just touched his lips to the side of his neck.

"He unzipped his jeans," he says. "Let his tool sort of unfold out. There it was sticking straight out. Only I was hard, too, and very excited. 'Don't let them hurt me,' I said to him, for all kinds of obvious reasons. He said 'here' or something, and reached himself out, and so I did it. I just let him put it in my mouth, and right into my heart, you know, and I was born. He just rode it in and out, and . . . the truth was, I was so taken with it, and with him, and with who he was to me at that time in my life and how deeply connected we were as human beings—which I bet he knows, too, today, no matter where he is or what he is doing—that I just closed my eyes and let it all be. Nothing in my life or in the world mattered, not anything, for at least those few minutes. Maybe forever after.

"See?" the man adds, sliding up over Vernon from behind. "Every time I recall that day it gives me the most genuine feelings. See? I know, I know I promised not to press you, and I won't, but . . . it might relax you, too, you know." There are the man's lips again, on his neck. He presses closer; where Anthony was as smooth and hairless as a pear, this man feels like he is covered with steel wool, with hundreds of small wires lying flat.

Vernon doesn't reply; he isn't sure where the man is and is confused and doesn't know what to say or do. As he shifts away, the man maintains contact, reaches around him on both sides to soap his chest and belly, teasing about his center without touching. "Feel how high I am," he whispers. "We can do anything you like. Your ass feels wonderful. I can make it awfully nice in there, if that's what you'd like."

Vernon keeps what distance he can. A spark—a shock—shoots across his temples as he feels trapped or claustrophobic and required to pay. He feels he is degenerating, as the man continues around him and he has nowhere to go. *This is a nervous breakdown,* Vernon is saying to himself as the man slips his hand down over him and stops. And holds. Vernon urges response in spite of his tension. He closes his eyes. No response is forthcoming, though, and the man drops him. "Shit," the man says.

Vernon dies a little, standing there.

"Goddamit," the man says.

Vernon is becoming naked now and doesn't know what to do.

"I guess I thought we'd get right through things and have a good time," the man says. "I'm sorry."

"Well, it's my fault," Vernon says.

"Doesn't matter," the man says.

"I just—I don't know," Vernon says.

"I think you'd better go. It's just going to get worse."

"Go?" Vernon says.

"I think so."

"You want me to go?"

"If you don't mind. The party's over."

"Oh."

"Get on with your life and so on. I don't mean to be rude."

"Oh," Vernon says again.

The man moves past him, leaves the shower, and Vernon hears him say, "You better rinse off."

Naked now, Vernon doesn't know what to do next, cannot get himself to move. His skull feels as thin-shelled as an egg, feels close to cracking from pressure within and spilling. He sees the drain on the floor; he would slide away into the drain if he could, into the city's waste, into the oblivion of the ocean nearby.

He has to step out; he has to have the man see his face, on the slightest glance. He cannot die and escape so easily; he still has to pay. The several steps, a slight eye exchange are what he must do, what he must put up with, he is thinking. So he does put up with them; they are a part of dying, he thinks as he steps, washed, past the translucent plastic shower curtain and reaches for his underpants on a wooden chair painted banana yellow; his eyes are filled with tears as he steps into and lifts the underpants up over his damp legs.

SEVENTEEN

TAKING UP PLASTIC-COVERED MENUS, Claire follows a man and woman making their way to the last booth. Her legs have started to fill with sand. It's how she thinks of waiting on tables. Her legs are hourglasses, empty at first, when the work is most pleasant, but with sand sliding in on every step she takes carrying menus, napkins and silverware, cheeseburgers, fries, bowls of chili, smiling, talking, wiping tables, carrying dirty dishes back to the plastic tub.

Every week it seems the sand flows in just a little more quickly.

Chili. More orders for chili. "How's the chili?" a man asks.

"I guess it's fine,"she says.

Thinking of Eric, on her way to the kitchen, she glances past the pool table to where he had been standing. She runs her eyes over the men and boys leaning against the wall, and seeing that he isn't there, seeing the slightest space of blank wall where he had been standing, and missing him, she goes to the window opening to place the order.

EIGHTEEN

TOO NERVOUS TO SIT, Matt stands in the heart of the Mall, watching the flow of people entering. There are benches before him, among red bricks and indoor plants, but he feels he would *really* look like a wimp if he was sitting down when she walked in. Guarded by the plants, he watches, and there she is, coming his way, moments ahead of time, for which promptness he all once adores her. To his surprise, though, she moves a little less boldly than he would have expected, even as a foolish smile is breaking out on his own face. She is black, he sees and remembers; yes, she is black.

He heads around the centerpiece to meet her; she is scanning shoppers sitting there. He sees her eyes discover him. "Hey," he says in a laugh and, reaching—he had no idea he would do such a thing—takes her hand for an instant in both of his.

They turn to walk along the Mall's avenue, past jewelry and cookie displays. He hears her say, "You seem really different."

"I do?"

"Like you've changed," she says.

Glancing at her face he sees that yes, it is the girl Vanessa, with her black skin, her flash of red lips and white teeth. And they are together, which gives him this complicated and sensational feeling.

"I hope nothing's wrong," she says.

"No," he says.

"Not having second thoughts about being with a black chick?"

"Oh, no. No. Not at all. Are you?"

"Me? Heck, yes, man. Well, not second thoughts."

"Say that again?"

"I'm *aware* I'm here," she says. "It's a little cool, but a little scary, too."

"We just look like friends, don't we?"

"Which is what we are—friends."

"Want to get a Coke or something?"

"I guess it's a little more than friends. That's why it feels scary."

"I like the way you say things," he says.

"Meaning what?"

"You don't fool around. I just like to talk to you."

"Yeah? How about Papa Gino's then, white boy, for a Coke?"

Turning, they go through an awkward reversal of direction and an amount of smiling. He touches her arm above the elbow, and it is nearly daring. What they are doing is no longer imaginary, he thinks. They are together.

At the counter, while she sits at a table covered with red-checkered oil-cloth, he orders and pays for two medium Cokes. Standing among the pizza buyers, he smiles at the menu on the wall and smiles still as he carries the two paper cups to the table. He has never felt more self-conscious. To complicate things, she suddenly says, "Now what are you thinking about?"

He looks at her.

"Tell me," she says. "I can tell you're thinking about something."

He lies. "I was thinking about what a good idea it was to call you up," he says.

She seems not to buy it. *"Really?"*

"No, that's not true," he says. "What I was thinking was, looking at your hands—was that I'd like to touch your hands."

"Well?" she says.

He looks at her.

"Why don't you?" she says. "I could go for that."

He laughs and still doesn't dare. It's all too much, he says to himself. As if seriously, he looks into her eyes; she looks into his in the same way.

"Want to go someplace we can mess around?" she says.

He keeps looking at her and doesn't move, as blood determines on its own to occupy his face. "Where?" he gets out.

She takes a moment. "Our garage," she says. "My mother's Buick. She never uses it."

"Far from here?" he manages to say.

She only continues to look at him as if to say, what a silly thing to ask.

His face is flushed and he cannot hold her gaze any longer; he glances down. He strains at once to look up at her, but his neck is so stricken it doesn't want to cooperate.

"God, I have messed up again," she says.

"No. Oh no," he says.

"Oh, I have," she says. "I'm sorry."

"It's not anything," he says. "I'm out of it, that's all."

"I shouldn't come on like that," she says.

"No, it isn't you, really," he is saying. "It isn't."

"Let's just back up and start over," she says.

"It's okay," he says.

"Tell me something *else* you're thinking," she says.

"Just what you said," he says.

"Listen, all I meant by that was—well, I didn't mean what you're probably thinking I meant."

He looks at her.

"I just said that, you know, for shock value."

"Well, that's okay."

"Except you look like you found a rattlesnake in your lunch bag."

He laughs, shrugs as if to say it's true.

"So," she says. "Tell me what you're thinking *now*."

"Same thing," he says.

She pauses. "Okay, let's go then. But it ain't to do what you think."

She smiles, looking at him over the red-checked oilcloth; he suddenly leans toward her and, surprising himself as much as he might surprise her, says, "I'm just dumb about stuff."

He resumes his position, and now she is the one who appears confused. "Which means what?" she says.

"Just what it says."

"You've never even kissed no girl before, have you?"

Well, that's what he meant, he is thinking, and as he looks at her her larger meaning turns in his mind. "I gotta go to the bathroom," he hears himself say.

He is in the center of the Mall, walking among people he doesn't see, when he asks himself, as if realizing he has committed some kind of social error, do you say to a girl you have to go to the bathroom?

He walks through a wide opening into a department store and finds and then enters the men's room, with its beige tile and brushed stainless steel, and seeing himself in the mirror, he cannot deny that something about what he sees is different. As an afterthought, he tries a breath in his hand.

Heading back, he feels no less light-headed. As if, he thinks, all his life he has been housed, held—in a membrane—and here at last he is breaking through. It was a little like this when he first realized he could swim.

Around him are women's nightclothes, colors so lightly blue, so faintly pink and beige, so laced and silken that they seem to tend toward creating some puzzle of a creature within the trees. In the looks of a saleswoman whose lips glisten red, whose eyes and eyelashes look like miniature birds in small cages, whose cheeks are dusted perversely pale—in the midst of her perfume he seems to receive another glimpse.

"Ready to go?" he says, approaching the table, not sitting down.

Reaching to take his hand, to steer him into sitting again on his side of the table, she whispers, "One thing I want you to know. Don't you go thinking I meant what I didn't mean. I think it's cute you never done nothing with no girl, if that's what you meant. But don't you think I meant what I didn't mean, because that's not what I meant at all."

There are her eyes, her red mouth, her glossy hair like icing on a cake. There are her gold earrings. "I know you didn't mean that," he says.

"Let's go do it then," she says—and adds, "Just kidding."

NINETEEN

He HAS DRIVEN PAST SOMETHING that has alerted his mind and shifted his eyes to his rearview mirror. As if in a movie, in its odd reflection, there is a young boy walking on the sidewalk through the early evening air. Already there is a new beating in his heart, as he returns his eyes to the street before him and lets his car roll along.

Approaching an intersection, slowing to a near stop, he has no idea where he is going or what he might do. He turns right and rolls slowly along the side street. Where there is space along the curb, he pulls over and stops.

The boy may not come this way, Vernon thinks. He may have already passed back there on the larger street. He doesn't look back; he decides not to let himself do so, so he turns off the motor. Life is chance, he thinks. Nor does he let himself use either of the car's mirrors. Reaching under the dash, he pulls the car's hood latch, sees the hood jump up an inch or two.

Opening the door, he steps into the evening air. He still doesn't let himself look back down the street.

He lifts and props the hood. He leans into the motor's warmth, as if to see something, and his thoughts are running over a notion of recurring distribution of lives within bodies, a notion that if a boy does appear, they will have known each other in the past or the boy will have been with him in the past.

Reaching a hand near the motor's hoses, from which heat is generating, he touches two fingers to a rubber hose coated with oiled dust; he is rubbing his soiled fingers over his thumb and standing upright, and the boy is there—he is there—coming along the middle of the street.

Taking a step from the fender, brushing his hands, Vernon says to him, "You know anything about cars? Can you give me a hand?"

The boy steps over. He looks into the car's opened mouth. Stealing a glance at his hair, Vernon looks under the hood as well, and he says, "It won't start. I don't know what happened."

"What did it do?" the boy says, gazing into the dark mystery of metal and rubber.

"It just cut out," Vernon says. "It could be the fuel line," he adds. "I was thinking, if you got behind the wheel and tried to start it, I could check the fuel pump." He glances at the boy. He is eleven or twelve years old. "You know how to start a car?" he says.

"I think so," the boy says.

"Let me show you," Vernon says, leading him to the driver's side.

As he says, "Jump in" and the boy does so, Vernon is careful not to touch him. "That's the key, the ignition," he says. "The right pedal on the floor is the gas. All you do is turn the key and step on that pedal. When I say so. Step on the pedal lightly. You've never driven a car?" he adds, straightening away from him.

An excitement is in him he has not known before, a boundary he has never crossed. He hears the boy say, "Not really," as if at a distance.

"It's a good thing to learn how to drive," Vernon hears himself say, allowing himself now to glance upon the boy's profile.

"When I say start it, turn the key," he says.

Stepping around the door, Vernon returns to the fender beside the raised hood. He really hasn't done anything, he is telling himself; who could say his car had not stopped for some reason? Is anyone watching?

Looking to the windshield, he says, "Give it a try."

He pretends, as the engine fires and trembles before him, to conclude some handiwork. Okay, he thinks, lowering the hood, letting it drop into place.

"Good!" he says, opening the door where the boy, just able to reach the pedals and glimpse over the steering wheel, sits smiling. "Slide over, I'll give you a lift," he says, slipping into the car, closing the door, sensing success of a kind as the boy obeys.

Vernon looks to his side only, and to the rearview mirror. "Once you start a car," he says, "it's easy to learn how to drive."

"That sure wasn't hard," the boy says.

Vernon pulls away from the curb. He is trying to think of what to do next, what to say, and his mind skips over his old fantasies of adoption, of meals and games, of the friendship of a brother, and of schools and bicycles, baths in a tub, watching television . . .

"You know there's another car," he says. "I have this other car to worry about, which belongs to my friend. It would be great if you could help me get that car started, too. It's just a few minutes from here. Maybe ten is all."

"What's wrong with it?" the boy says.

"It's something, I think, to do with the starter. I think the two of us could get it started, though. Just like we did this car. I could pay you five dollars for helping me to get it started."

The boy says nothing to this, and Vernon makes a move at once. Turning into a driveway, backing around, expecting the boy to say, simply, *no*, he accelerates in the other direction. "It won't take long," he says. "Just a short drive."

"Where is it?" the boy says, and Vernon believes there is no suspicion in his voice.

"It's back this way," he says. "It's right by this pond."

The boy says nothing.

Vernon drives along. For the first time in the car, at an intersection, making his turn, he glances upon the small person in the adjacent seat. There is his slight frame, his sandy hair, his nose; Vernon realizes in a rush of affection how trusting the boy is. He would reach and touch his shoulder, and smile at him, but he restrains himself. "You have any brother or sisters?" he says.

"Just a brother," the boy says.

"How old is he; what's his name?"

"Matt. He's fifteen."

"And you, are you fourteen?"

"No," the boy says.

"How old are you?" Vernon says.

"Twelve."

"Tell me your name."

"Eric."

"I'm Vernon," Vernon says, feeling an unexpected rush.

He glances again. "This is an easy way to earn five dollars," he says.

Hands on the steering wheel, watching ahead, he blinks to clear his eyes of the curious emotion stirring there. What is crossing his mind is how much he likes this boy already, how his innocence makes him so likeable. Does he look like someone he has seen before? It seems he does.

On Route 4, driving west, he thinks how he would simply like to drive on into the world with this young boy, this new young friend who trusts him so naturally. "I like your nose," he says.

"My nose?" the boy says, and laughs.

"That little flattening makes you look strong, you know. Girls will be after you in no time."

"Got blasted with a baseball bat," the boy says, although it is clear this reading of his nose is something new.

"Well, I guess you paid a price," Vernon says. "It looks special, though. You could grow up to be a movie star."

The boy laughs. "It sure hurt when it happened. I had two black eyes."

"Really?"

"And—" he begins, but stops.

"And what?"

"I got teased a lot."

"That must've hurt, huh?"

"Yeah."

"Your brother teased you, I bet."

"Yeah. Other kids, too. It was my brother who blasted me. But it was an accident."

"It's too bad people are mean like that," Vernon says. "The teasing, I mean."

The boy makes no reply; Vernon has to take in a breath all at once, to conceal his emotional feeling. This is so wonderful, he thinks. Driving like this. This fullness of life in his car at day's end where always before there had been emptiness. "Do you have many friends?" he says.

"Sure, a few," the boy says.

"Not many?"

"I don't know. I guess so."

"Some people have just one friend," Vernon says. "And some people have a lot of friends. I didn't have many friends when I was your age. Well, that's not true. I didn't have *any* friends, really. I met people sometimes that I wanted for friends. I think just having one good friend is what I would have liked. You wouldn't be lonely then, you know, maybe like having a brother."

The boy says nothing; skylight is visible now only on the horizon. Cars have headlights on. "Your brother isn't your friend?" Vernon says. "Or your parents?"

"I only live with my mother," the boy says. "My father's gone somewhere."

"I always dreamed," Vernon says, "of having a brother. Who was my *friend.*" When the boy says nothing to this, he says, "I guess it doesn't always work that way though, does it?"

"Hm," the boy remarks, as if not knowing how else to respond.

"My father," Vernon says. "I never really had a father either. I mean I never *knew* him. He died in Vietnam. I'm not even certain my mother was married like that, although she says she was."

As he keeps the car on its line, it occurs to Vernon how childlike he is sounding, and he reminds himself to be careful. "You don't have a stepfather?" he says.

"No."

"Maybe that's better," Vernon says. "I mean, if your mother's your friend. Well, my mother hasn't ever been my friend, but I think she wanted to be. What about girlfriends? You have girlfriends?"

The boy laughs. "No," he says.

"Sit over here closer where I can hear you," Vernon says, patting the seat. To his amazement, the boy shifts some, and he experiences a new wave of affection over the boy's innocence. He blinks as if in the presence of something he has not known before. "You know," he says cautiously, "I could be your friend."

The boy seems to hunch his shoulders. He doesn't say anything.

Vernon looks ahead, continues driving.

"How far is this place?" the boy says.

"Not far."

"It better be pretty soon or I have to go home," the boy says. "I didn't know it was this far."

"We'll be there in just a few minutes," Vernon says.

They continue rolling along under the darkening sky.

Against sudden nervousness, aware the boy is growing frightened, Vernon starts talking again. "I've always had this dream," he says. "I could spend a whole summer with my friend. Just to have a friend like that. We could be together. We could spend the whole summer at a lake, you know. Do anything we wanted."

"Well, what does that mean?" the boy says.

"It doesn't mean anything," Vernon says. "Just what I said." And he adds, "Another dream I've had, just recently, though—well, it would be to adopt someone, you know, a boy who would be a friend like a little brother, someone who was like myself. Who didn't have a father to grow up with, you know, or very many friends, either. I'd take real good care of this friend—buy him a bicycle, and toys, things like that. Take him to the movies."

The boy doesn't say anything for a moment. Then he says, "That sure isn't me."

"Well, I didn't say it was," Vernon says. "I just said it was a dream. What's wrong with that?"

The boy doesn't answer.

"I didn't mean to say that it was you, necessarily," Vernon says.

The boy remains silent; Vernon looks to the road ahead.

"I think I have to go home now," the boy says.

"I'm going to *take* you home," Vernon says. "Just as soon as we get this car started. I sure wouldn't bring you all this way for five dollars for nothing."

"I don't want to do that anymore," the boy says.

"Oh, now," Vernon says, "why are you being like that? Just because I offered to be friends?"

The boy is silent.

"We'll be there in just one minute," Vernon says. "Then I'll take you back home, just like I said I would."

Again, in silence, they roll along. But Vernon cannot put aside his growing tension, and he says, "I was only trying to tell you some things that would help you for the rest of your life. No one ever told me anything like that, when I was your age."

Nor is there any response to this; the boy holds in place.

"If you were my friend," Vernon says. "If you were my friend now, you'd know there wasn't anything to be afraid of. I could help you in all kinds of ways. By showing you things. Telling you things. I was your age, too, you know."

Still the boy doesn't say anything, and Vernon doesn't know if he should feel anger with him or cry out in disappointment and frustration. Turning from the highway at last, headlights showing the way under the cover of trees and branches, they follow a two-lane pavement. The turn-off to the back road to the cottage—a narrow gravel road—isn't far now, and Vernon slows down. For the first time, he is visited by fear over what he is doing. This is illegal, he thinks. What if someone sees him? At the same time an urge is in him to hold the boy, to touch his face to his hair.

"I want to go home," the boy says; there is trembling in his slight voice for the first time.

"I'll take you home," Vernon says. "In just a few minutes."

Engaging the car's turn signal well ahead of time, Vernon hopes that the green light flashing from the dashboard will reassure the boy. Turning onto the gravel road, close then within tree branches, he maintains some speed, thinking the boy might try to jump from the car and get away. As they bounce along at perhaps thirty, he says, "We'll be there in a minute. It's right up here."

There is no response, and glancing, Vernon perceives the boy's face, the forehead wisp of his hair, in the dashboard's glow of light.

Through the darkness around them, between trees, occasional orange and yellow lights of other cottages around the pond pass in and out of view. If someone is at the cottage, Vernon is thinking, if lights are on, he will drive out the other way and take the boy back to Portsmouth and drop him off.

No one will be there. He knows this, even as knowing it makes him nervous. Gone on a drinking outing of some kind, he has never seen his housemates return before the middle of the night. They don't stay around the cottage on Saturday's lonely hours. Only he has done that. Here and elsewhere. Everywhere.

He rolls along. "I just want to be with you," he says, on a rush through him of pins and needles.

The boys gives no response.

At the Y-intersection he follows the winding dirt road down toward the pond's surface. Under and between tree branches he glimpses a silver reflection of sky on the thawing ice, and he sees, through fir trees—where lights would appear in the cabin—that only darkness comes from the windows. All things come to this, he is thinking. All work. All ambition, imagination. This feeling. His urge is to embrace the boy, to adore him with passion. "I just want to be with you," he cries to him. "It's all I want."

"What does that mean?" the boy says.

Letting up on the gas, turning away from the pond to approach the cabin, Vernon realizes he is sinking into surprising, unexplainable sadness. "Everything," he says. "It means everything."

Parking, switching off ignition and lights as always, he doesn't touch the boy. Nor does the boy move or speak. "Just driving like that," Vernon utters. "Being with someone. It's new to me; it's everything. That's what I meant when I said it was all I wanted. I didn't mean to scare you."

Vernon can see little. There is the boy in silhouette, but Vernon doesn't know if his head is facing to the front or to the side. His urge is to touch his hair with his fingers, to lift it over his forehead as gently as a mother. His urge is to thrill him as he believes he may thrill him.

He has the boy's wrist in his hand, reaching and taking it, and there is pressure in the boy's small arm to pull away, as he cries, *"Leave me alone! Stop it!"*

Vernon's eyes have filmed; he holds the boy's wrist more tightly. He reaches his other arm and hand to the boy's shoulders, to pull him closer. *"I want to hold you,"* he cries to him. *"It's all I want."*

The boy resists. He tries to pull free, cries *"Stop it!"* and *"Don't!"* and *"Stop it!"* and *"Don't!"*—

Vernon holds him. Through his own tears and gasps he is trying to kiss the boy's hair and neck, his ear and face. As the boy struggles, as he jerks with surprising strength, Vernon holds, contains him, cries to him, cries upon his neck in desperation, *"I'm not going to hurt you. I love you. Don't you understand? This is love. This is love."*

TWENTY

THEY ARE NOT IN THE BACK seat but in the front seat of the darkened Buick. They are in a darkened garage, under the darkening sky, and one knee and then another has banged the dashboard. The floor gearshift has been in the way, too, but it is too late to consider moving, to tumble into the back seat like children. It is too late for everything.

Matt holds her. He hears her breathing and hears his own, feels her warmth against him as another minute falls away. He doesn't know what to do now and seems to be trying to think, to understand. Something like forever has been in his mind, and he is troubled with odd disillusionment, with a wish to go back and be what he had been before.

Lifting his head from her neck, he opens his eyes. He says to her, "I just opened my eyes, but I can't see anything."

She doesn't move. Nor does she speak. A faint breath in her throat tells him that she heard what he said, that she knows what he means.

PART TWO

Anyone with Information
Is Asked to Call

SUNDAY, FEBRUARY 15, 1981

ONE

At a few minutes after seven, as the morning sun is just lifting out of the ocean, Dulac is in Lyle's Lunch to pick up the Sunday *Globe*. Four or five people are ahead of him in line. At this hour, he remarks to himself. Everyone keeps telling them to be courteous to the newcomers, however, and he determines to take it in stride. Lyle's Lunch. It's a nondescript coffee shop, two blocks uphill from the water, and he has been stopping here forever, since he was a newcomer himself, come down from Quebec.

How, he asks himself yet again, could a run-down dive like this become popular?

Lyle's wooden floorboards meander now as they always have, and Dulac wonders again—does he do this every Sunday?—if proximity to the salt water has raised the waves in the boards. At the same time, a row of new booths has been hammered into place down the center of the place—where there used to be Wonder Bread on shelves and packaged pies only schoolchildren seemed to buy—and the booths seem not to lean or sag. Newcomers sit there now, over blueberry pancakes and fat copies of *The New York Times*. Their imported cars are lined up along the side streets, where for the first time ever parking space has become a problem.

It's okay for these people to come with all their money, but when parking space . . .

Okay, the overweight detective says to himself at last, as some unknown customer ahead is asking Jenny questions. Let's move it along now, how about it?

A young woman in a purple jogging suit appears in line behind him.

He notices that the check in her hand is the same mint color such checks have always been, and he notices her. He manages a passing glance. He doesn't stare, for that would be both rude and unprofessional; shifting along with the line, he looks ahead. In his private method of recall, however—another of his pastimes—he files the woman in his mind. His method, one he has yet to take to court, is to call up someone the person resembles. It could be Jackie Gleason or Jane Fonda, a neighbor or a friend. Bert at the Amoco station. Anwar Sadat. Shirley Moss at work. Only the nose was such and such, the hair was this darker color, and he or she came up to here on his shoudler. Add your own details, he has said to young officers. Eh? Lock it in your mind as a variation of your Uncle Phil.

Jill Clayburgh. Yes, Your Honor, Jill Clayburgh. Pale cheeks, soft lips. Eyes circled with a little color. Eyes a little tired. Light brown hair. Ruffled some near her shoulders, and a smell of sleep about her neck. No, I'd not seen her before, and I assumed she was a newcomer to the area or a visitor.

The line moves along. On his turn at the counter, aware that it is a foolish thing to do, he orders the *Times*. As lumpy as a rhino and unshaven this morning, he says, "*The New York Times*, Jenny," approximately in the angled presence of the woman in the purple jogging suit.

Paying the fare, a dollar fifty, he carries the paper out onto the sidewalk, where he is not unaware of the engaging springlike air coming in again today. He goes along slowly. Holding the *Times* in both hands, he pretends to be reading the front page, to give Miss Clayburgh a chance to catch up, to fall in place beside him with her copy of the *Times*.

Behind him, Lyle's door opens and swings shut. He listens for her footsteps. In these seconds, too, however overweight and solidly married he happens to be, he imagines the women writing to her best friend in New York: *I met him in this quaint little mom-and-pop store . . . you know the kind . . . we just fell into conversation . . . he's a policeman but I knew he was someone special when I saw him buy the Sunday* New York Times.

Nothing happens. Five second pass, perhaps five more. When he glances over his shoulder, he sees Jill Clayburgh going the other way. Turning the corner on a pivot, she is starting uphill, and she carries no newspaper. As if on tiptoe, not rapidly, she begins to lope.

Hoisting, shifting his bulk into his unmarked four-door Chevrolet, tossing the heavy paper to the passenger seat, Dulac heads into town. He lights a cigarette. That little number, he thinks. Seabrook is probably the closest she's ever been to New York City. She's probably down from Skowhegan or Province du Québec; she picked up the jogging suit at a yard sale in Kittery, and she works as a frontline waitress at Valle's on Route 1.

And he has that paper to read which will not include a single score from anything more recent than Friday. Yes, Your Honor, I turned fifty-two last July and I know what you're going to say.

Half a mile away, at the Portsmouth PD, nosing his car up to his marker—*Lt. Gilbert Dulac*—he begins the reverse process of lifting himself out of his car. He can unload quickly if need be, he always tells himself, but of course it is Sunday and he is both off-duty and the ranking man present. The chief's and the captain's parking spaces, the only spaces to the left of his own, stand empty, as they generally do on Sundays.

On his feet, Dulac shakes out his wool shirt jacket. He leaves the paper where it is. The station house is his unofficial Sunday morning club, where he often stops to talk, to have coffee and cigarettes and read the paper while Beatrice sleeps in until nine or so, and although he can tell from the scant number of cars in the lot—most, he knows, will belong to officers out on patrol—he is not of a mind this springlike morning to settle in with the paper. Not quite yet. Not without anything on the Celtics or Bruins from at least yesterday. You'd think Portsmouth was closer to Halifax than Boston, the way the news traveled.

The station house resembles a small-town stone church or library, and walking around to the side entrance he is taken with the urge, and very nearly turns back, to go ahead and drive to one of the nearby beaches. To take a stroll in this remarkably warm air. Raising a hand to the cadet on duty at the main desk, who buzzes him through a waist-high gate, Dulac moves back through to the squad room, to the coffee station, to see if anyone is around. If so, maybe he'd tell them about Jill Clayburgh in her purple jogging suit and the foolish tub of lard who bought *The New York Times* to impress her. It wasn't anything, he thinks, he'd be likely to pass on to Beatrice.

Styrofoam cup in hand—no one is around—he wanders back out to the main desk, to read over the entries in the log. Checking entries, from the bottom up, is a daily habit as well as one of his responsibilities as Lieutenant of Detectives. It's a curiosity, too, for nothing crucial would have gone down or he would have heard of it long before reading it in the log.

He doesn't quite pause on the report of an armed robbery of a gas station near the air base, or over an entry concerning a twelve-year-old male runaway, but he does note them. He continues, skims various alcohol- and traffic-related calls and complaints entered since he last checked the log at about four yesterday afternoon, before leaving for home. Domestic disturbance, shoplifting, burglary from a garage, domestic disturbance, unlawful driving away of an automobile, domestic disturbance, simple assault. An entry which *is* unusual is the arrest, and release to custody, of three Portsmouth High students, two male, one female, apprehended while drinking beer in the home ec lab of the high school at 0240 hours.

"This armed robbery, you notified Sergeant Mizener?" he says to the cadet.

"Well, no, I didn't, but I think he was notified."

"You came on at midnight?"

"Yessir."

"How about this runaway? Anything else on him?"

"No sir, I don't think so."

"You didn't take any calls, since you came on?"

"No sir."

"You didn't call his house?"

"No sir. Was I supposed to?"

"You could, I guess. He should be home by now, wouldn't you think?"

"Yessir, I'd think so."

"Maybe they haven't called back—his family—but who knows. It doesn't say here if he's run away before. Did you check that out?"

"I didn't know I was supposed to do that either, sir."

"Well, it wouldn't hurt, would it? Then you'd know."

"Yessir."

"Why don't you do it now. See if we got anything on anyone at that address or by that name."

Straightening to sip his coffee, Dulac watches as the cadet shifts his chair and begins to tap on the computer keyboard. He watches the screen as the name, entered, produces no file, as the same thing happens with the mother's name at the address. "Nothing," the Cadet says, looking back. "That's all we have."

"Kid would be hungry by now, wouldn't you think?"

"Well, yessir. I guess he would."

Taking up the telephone, Dulac says, "He's probably sitting at a counter somewhere scared shitless of what his old man is gonna do to him when he gets home."

"Yessir," the cadet says, smiling.

"There's nothing wrong with calling," the lieutenant adds. "If it would help."

"Yessir," the cadet adds.

"Mrs. Wells?" the lieutenant says. "Lieutenant Dulac, Portsmouth Police. We haven't heard any more about your son, Eric. We're just wondering if you've heard anything?"

Listening, looking more or less above the cadet, the lieutenant says. "You haven't."

Then he says, "You did."

Then, "You don't think he fell asleep somewhere?"

And then, "Has he ever run away like this before?"

And, "Well, it was entered here as a runaway."

In another moment he says, "What about relatives? Did you call them?"

In another moment, "Was he upset or angry about anything?"

Then, "You think he might have been mad because you wouldn't give him money to stop at the party store?"

And then, "Fifty cents? Would he run away over fifty cents? What else did he take with him? How much money did he have?"

And, "Mrs. Wells, please, try not to be upset. He's probably fallen asleep somewhere. Even in a car. This happens. He could be at a friend's house."

Listening again, the lieutenant says, "Where is Mr. Wells?"

And, "You mean he's deceased?"

And, "You have no idea of his whereabouts? Is he delinquent in support payments?"

And, "I see."

And, "Mrs. Wells, listen, call his teacher and see if he's been having any unusual problems at school. Ask his brother the same thing."

Then, "Mrs. Wells, I'll tell you what. I'm going to stop by and talk to you and your older son. In about twenty minutes to half an hour. Listen, before I get there, there's something I want you to do. Look through your son's possessions. Eric's possessions. Look carefully. See what's missing he might have taken with him. It could be a watch or a coin, or anything. A favorite jacket. Some personal treasure. A photograph."

Listening another moment, he says, "This valentine is still there? It's the same one?"

And finally, "Check your own things as well. See if anything is missing. Valuables. Money. And try not to worry. This isn't that unusual. Boys who are twelve begin to have a lot of adventurous ideas."

Replacing the phone then, Dulac stands a moment thinking or puzzling. "That's odd," he says.

Then to the cadet he says, "The mother is quite worried. She doesn't think he's run away, although they did have a little argument over fifty cents the last time she saw him. Last night."

The cadet doesn't respond, merely sits watching and waiting.

"Odd," the lieutenant says to himself.

"Does any mother ever think her son's run away?" the cadet says.

Dulac returns from his pondering and looks to the cadet. "Oh, I guess not," he says.

81

"I mean—" the cadet starts to say, but the lieutenant has raised a hand to hush him.

"Listen," Dulac says. "Several things I want you to do. I want you to run a check on Warren Wells. The father. Check with South Berwick, and with the State of Maine."

"Yessir."

"Wait a minute. Some other things. Repeat the description of this missing boy to all patrol units. Looks like it only went out last night at 2310. Anyway, repeat it. Get it out, too, to the Maine State Police, New Hampshire State Police, Massachusetts State Police. Say it comes from me. Gil Dulac, Portsmouth PD. Notify the MPs at Pease Air Base, too."

"Yessir, that's a lot of calls," the cadet says.

Dulac glances to the cadet, sees him making notes, decides he is merely being conversational. "That's okay," he says. "They're just sitting on their asses drinking coffee. Tell them this. Say there's an extremely worried mother here in Portsmouth who is waiting for her twelve-year-old son to get home."

"Full description plus that message?" the cadet says.

"Yes. Also, if my wife calls, tell her something came up and I'll get back to her. This is probably a simple runaway, but it does have this funny feel to it, so I'm just going to stop and have a look."

"Sir, I'm supposed to go off duty at eight."

"What does that mean?"

"It's just that I don't know if I'll get all these calls made by the time I'm supposed to get off and—"

"Pass it on to whoever comes on. Regular dispatcher's in there, isn't he?"

"Yessir. I didn't mean to—"

"I'll call back in a few minutes, see if you have anything on the father. Warren Wells. Formerly of South Berwick. Okay?"

"Yessir. I just meant to say that it is Sunday morning and I—"

"You check Warren Wells yourself," Dulac says. "Do that right away." Dulac smiles some, as if to say one thing or another.

Returning his smile, the cadet says, "It's the lieutenant's day off, too, sir."

"Dedication," Dulac says, as if to share a joke, however surprised he is at the cadet's remark.

Writing the address in his pocket memo book, he adds, on his way out, "I'll call back in ten or fifteen minutes."

Crossing the parking lot, however, he finds himself increasingly bothered over the exchange that has just taken place. It's as if, even with this young cadet, he has presented himself in some dishonest way. The story of his life, he thinks. The old ethnic fear of looking dumb. A fat man's fear.

He goes through the chore of loading his bulk into his car but doesn't start the motor. The unsettled feeling remains with him.

All at once, he finds himself unloading from the car. On the pavement he says, evenly, "Goddamit," as he slams the door, as he starts back around to the side entrance.

He passes through the door and there is the cadet, standing, just lighting a cigarette, which he begins at once to snuff out.

"No no, I don't care about your cigarette," Dulac says.

"Sir?"

"Did someone tell you—have you been taught not to do a good job around here?"

"Sir, I don't understand."

"You're how old?" Dulac says.

"Nineteen, sir."

Dulac is nodding. "I'm going to tell you something," he says. "It's okay to make an extra telephone call. You understand? It's okay to do a good job."

"Yessir."

"It's taken me most of my life to know that."

"Sir."

"State Troopers. Maine State Troopers. It's okay to disturb them. They really don't mind. That's what they signed on for. Me, too. Long time ago. I mean the money, the security, that's all fine. But there're other reasons, too, why we're here. Women and children first. Am I making sense?"

"Yessir."

"Good. Then you make every call I told you to make. It doesn't matter if it takes you all day and all of another day and you miss everything you ever wanted to do in your life, every girl you ever wanted to love, and you don't earn an extra penny. Do you get what I'm saying?"

"Yessir."

"Good. I'll call you in ten or fifteen minutes."

TWO

THE ROADBED HERE IS GRAVEL; ice water in the potholes looks black. Not long ago, a dented Subaru drove by. Before, as first light was hardly in the sky, a pickup truck passed slowly, and the lone driver looked hard at them but did not stop. In the rearview mirror, the pickup moved away slowly, like someone walking on bedsprings

Vernon watched it go, thinking the man was trying to see something. Everybody is trying to see something, he thought. Then he returned his face to his hands on the steering wheel, to a jumpy feeling which keeps passing through him and which he has been unable, for even a moment, to escape. Everybody is trying to see something, he thinks. Trying to see other people's secrets. No matter what they say.

He sits here, chilled. The only thought he seems able to form is that he has never, no one has ever, been as sick at heart as he is now. The wine. His head, his temples into his eyebrows offer gradual waves of pain. The fear in his heart is constant. It is the day after.

Now there is sunlight glancing at angles through the trees, and he guesses the gray Sunbird is not very noticeable in the dappled light. As if it matters, he thinks. As if anything matters.

Has he done this? he wonders. Has he done what he knows he has done, or is something, someone, playing some cruel game with him?

The boy isn't talking. Even though Vernon untied his hands from behind and retied them in front, to have him stop crying so much. Nor can he be cold, with the flannel Boy Scout sleeping bag up to his chest—but he only looks away, looks to the side window at nothing, or at his reflection, with that expression on his face. Anger. Maybe it's anger. It's all he does is look that way. He hasn't looked at Vernon now in twenty minutes, at least.

Vernon *is* sorry. He admits this to himself. Given a chance he would say so to the boy. He is so sorry, so regretful, he becomes all but sick in the waves of fear and confusion which keep sweeping through him. If only the boy would tell him it's okay. If only the boy would say it did not matter that much, then Vernon could cry to him how deeply sorry he is and take him back home. Give him the money he had promised to give him. More than he had promised. And return to his mere problem of losing his friend.

The boy stays at his distance, though. He only shows anger, or hurt. The scowl on his face—if he had any idea how unattractive it made him look this morning.

Nor is there anyone Vernon can call. If anyone cared for him, he thinks, he could call and explain how he'd gotten into a situation—in the dark of night, he might say, in a grip of passion, because of the rejection he was suffering, the wine, he would mention the wine—and maybe the person would help him or tell him what to do. He keeps thinking that Anthony would know—money, or words, something—but the thought of Anthony is as far as he can carry the idea. Calling him seems impossible. So does it seem impossible to turn to his mother. She'd hear so much. She'd be concerned in her way. She might even try to help, or say she'd try to help. But she'd turn on him then. *How could he do such a thing? Was he insane? Why, why, why was he always trying to ruin her life?* she'd cry at him.

What could he say to her? How could he tell her what he did not know himself? He could only cry back to her that it happened. His entire life had been that way. It happened. It was all he knew. *It happened. He did it.*

The boy sits there. Turning his face from the steering wheel, Vernon looks at him through his own dilated eyes and reaches to turn his chin, on the thought of begging forgiveness, but the boy jerks his head away. Neither of them has had more than moments of sleep. The boy's eyes are puffy, Vernon sees, and he cannot help thinking yet again that he just isn't cute this morning like he was last night.

"Are you hungry?" Vernon says.

The boy gives no response.

"You want to get something to eat?" Vernon says.

"*I just want you to let me go!*" the boy says to him. "*That's what I want. I want you to let me go.*" He bawls a gasp.

Vernon, watching, tries to check himself from being affected by the boy's hurt. "I'm sorry," Vernon says then and almost starts crying again himself. "I'm sorry you feel bad."

Vernon sits looking, but the boy maintains his gaze away. Vernon tries yet again. "Eric," he says. "We've done what friends do. That's all we've done. It's all I wanted—was to be your friend. If I was your friend, if I knew we were friends, I could let you go. I'd just take you home. I'd give you the money, like I said. I'd buy you some breakfast."

"*I said I won't tell!*" the boy cries. "*I said I won't tell!*"

"You don't mean it, though," Vernon says, in a moment. "I can tell you don't mean it. How can I let you go if I know you don't mean it?"

"*I said I won't tell!*"

"You will, though," Vernon says. "I can tell you will. As soon as I let you go, you'll tell somebody. Then I'd be in trouble because they wouldn't understand. What kind of friend is that?"

The boy sits there, whimpering at a distance.

"I can tell if someone is my friend," Vernon says. "I can *tell*. I can tell you're *not*. You wouldn't be mad at me if you were. I know you wouldn't. *So how can I let you go?*"

"I'm not mad," the boy cries. "I said I'm not mad."

They are quiet again. Another car approaches, a newer car, and Vernon is thinking the morning hours will bring more cars along even this scraped and rutted dirt road.

The car passes.

Vernon rests his face on his hands once more on the steering wheel. He is wondering, if the boy did tell, could he be traced? If the boy told the police? Would the police bother? What if he just told them the boy befriended him, asked to go for a ride, or was hitchhiking, and said he didn't want to go home because he wasn't happy and everyone was mean to him? Could they prove anything? What if he said the boy got fresh with him and so they fooled around a little? The boy put his hand on him and said he liked to play dirty. Wouldn't it be his word against the boy's? After all, he didn't have a record. He really isn't hurt, is he? Vernon thinks. In any way that will show?

Another car is coming. It turns out as it passes, though, to be another pickup truck, eyes looking down hard again to see the front seat of the parked car, and Vernon thinks again how everyone wants to see, how others could just as easily be sitting here.

"Eric," he says. "Listen. I would be willing. I would be willing to say to you that I'm sorry. That you feel hurt. Not just because I like you and want to be your friend. But because I can tell you *do* feel hurt a little. If I said that, that I was sorry, and I really meant it—and you wouldn't be mad at me and you swore you wouldn't tell on me—then I could take you back. And untie you. Do you understand?"

The boy is looking alert to this; his eyes are moving.

"Do you?" Vernon says.

"You'll say you're sorry?" the boy says.

"Yes. Yes, I will," Vernon says.

"You have to say it," the boy says.

"I'm sorry," Vernon says. "I'm sorry you feel hurt if that's how you feel. All I wanted was to be your friend."

"Okay," the boy says. "Okay. I promise I won't tell. I promise. So untie me."

"Some people might not understand," Vernon says. "So you can't tell anyone."

"Just untie me. I said I won't tell."

"People would make trouble. For me. For you, too, you know. If you told anyone, kids would tease you and make fun of you. Just because you had someone who was your friend and wanted to tell you things and show things to you. Adults do things like we did all the time. All the time. So do a lot of kids, kids you know, too, only they wouldn't ever tell you or anybody else. Because it can be a lot of fun and can make you feel really good, only adults usually don't want you to learn anything about it, because they just want you to be quiet and do what they want you to do. Do you know what I mean?"

"Yes," the boy says. "Just please untie me. I said I won't tell."

"Eric . . . if I let you go . . . will you still be my friend? Will you promise you won't ever tell anyone? If I could believe that, I'd take you back right now. I'll give you the money and everything. It's up to you."

"Yes," the boys says, although he seems to be starting to cry again, losing his breath. "I said I will. Just untie me. You said you would."

"You'll be my friend?"

"Yes," the boy cries.

"You will? Will you meet me, and we'll go to the movies next Friday night? Will you meet me in Portsmouth? Will you do that?"

The boy is crying, but he manages to utter. *"Yes, I will, I will, I'll try to."*

Vernon sits still as a moment passes.

"I said I will," the boy cries.

"No, you won't," Vernons says calmly then. "I know you don't mean it."

"I mean it," the boy cries. *"I mean it!"*

"That's not even the question at all," Vernon says. "I asked—to see if you would really be my friend—if you would meet me to go to the movies on Friday night. You didn't say you would."

"I said I would!" the boy cries. *"I said I would!"*

"You didn't. You didn't say you would when I asked you."

"I will," the boy cries. *"I will. I promise I will, I'll do whatever you want me to."*

A moment passes. The boy continues crying.

"I said I would," the boy cries then. "I wouldn't promise if I wouldn't do it. Please untie me. It hurts. Please."

Vernon turns to him. "You swear, on your honor?" he says. "You swear you won't tell anyone? And you'll be my friend, too?"

"I swear," he boys cries. "I swear I'll do it. I'll be your friend."

"You know the kids at school will make fun of you, they'll tease you all the time if you ever tell anyone. It's because they're too young to understand."

"I know," the boy cries. "I won't tell anyone. I promise I won't."

Vernon looks at him. Tears are coming once more into his own eyes. Reaching, pulling the sleeping bag away, he stuffs it over the back of the seat. "Okay," he says. "I'm going to do it. I am. It's up to you."

Untying the boy's ankles first, he says. "You can't ever forget what it is to make a promise. You can't ever go back on a promise."

Eyes filled, tears on his cheeks, his nose running, he is untying the boy's wrists by feel. "I'm letting you go because I'm your friend . . . because all I wanted was to be with you as your friend. That was all I wanted."

The boy lifts his hands. Vernon, sniffling still, sits back as the boy starts working to unlock the door. "No, no," Vernon says to him. "It's too far to walk. I'm going to drive you back."

"I'll walk," the boy is saying, pushing open the door. "I'll walk. It doesn't matter if it's far." He slides from the car, saying yet again. "I'll walk. I don't care."

Vernon lets him go. He presses his forehead to his hands once more on the steering wheel as he hears the boy slip and fall, it seems, in the accumulated crust of snow on the shoulder, as he feels cold air enter the car. He hears nothing then, nor does he see anything as he looks to the front of the car.

The boy comes up beside the fender. It looks like he is losing his footing, trying to get around to the road. His hands free of the car, he is moving then, but it is clear at once, as he struggles to walk, that he is having difficulty moving his legs.

Vernon closes his eyes, lowers his face to his hands. He is hurt. It's so clear that he's hurt. And he's going the wrong way. He's walking the wrong way. Everything is wrong. He doesn't know where he is. Everything is wrong. "Oh, God," Vernon cries into his hands.

The boy is trying to hurry, Vernon sees, as he looks up once more and watches him. He's hurt and he's trying to hurry away.

Through his tears, Vernon sees the boy moving along the dirt road. He doesn't know where he's going. Neither of them know where they are going. He sees the boy reach a hand to his seat in pain. He sees the boy hold himself like a child struggling to make his way to a bathroom. He goes on, though, stiff-legged, and it is so clear that he is hurt.

Vernon stares down at the dials of his car for a moment. Then he turns the key.

As the motor starts, he sees the boy glance over his shoulder. He sees the boy try to quicken his step, but there is no way for him to escape.

Vernon presses the accelerator. The car's wheels spit back some ice and gravel as they depart the shoulder, as they shift to the rutted roadbed.

THREE

CLAIRE IS SEARCHING. She understands the implication of Eric's things not being there. Let things *not* be here, she is thinking. She is in their bedroom, on a chair at the closet door, when she hears the knock from below. Have ten minutes passed? Twenty? Where is Matt; why isn't he going down? "Matt," she calls. When there is no reply, she gets down from the chair and steps to the bedroom door. "That's the policeman. Can't you go let him in?" A spot in her mind is that she hasn't found anything missing; but then she hasn't had a chance to really look.

The knock sounds again, the loose-hanging screen door slamming on each rap. *"Where are you, Matt?"* she calls, going into the hall, knowing from the closed bathroom door that he is there, hearing everything.

Down the steep narrow stairway to the landing, she opens the door to an enormous man—he fills the doorway, in height and width—who is holding in view a police badge on a piece of leather. She says something, as does he, and then she is leading the way back upstairs, thinking how unwashed she looks, how worn and weary is their attic apartment, afraid all at once that the police won't really help them because they are poor.

Then they are in the living room. The man is glancing around; she watches him. He seems to fill the room, more like an elephant than a horse brought up the stairs, yet in his large wool shirt he looks ordinary. "I haven't been able to find anything missing," she is saying, trembling with odd fear.

"Nothing, really?" he says, still looking around, taking things in. "Where's your older son?" he adds, glancing down at her.

"He's in the bathroom; he'll be right here."

The man nods. He seems so casual, as he keeps looking at things, which is bothering her by now. "You think he's wearing what he had on when you last saw him?" he says.

"Yes," Claire says. "I would think so."

"No sign he stopped here, put on another jacket or something?"

"No," she says. "I haven't found anything missing—not yet."

"Different shoes, something like that?"

"I don't think so."

"You called his friends?"

"I've called everyone I could think of."

"What did his teacher have to say?"

"She hasn't seen him. Not since he was in school on Friday."

"Did you look in your own car, see if he was asleep there?"

"Well, we don't have a car."

"Okay. You say his feelings were hurt over some money?"

"It was fifty cents."

"His feelings were hurt badly?"

"I don't think so."

"How much money could he have had with him?"

"Maybe twenty cents. We don't have money."

"Would he have a bank, a piggy bank, any money he'd keep at home?"

"Gosh, I don't think so. Not that I know of."

"His brother might know, but you don't think so?"

"No, I really don't think he could have any money."

"You keep money around, cookie jars, change, things like that?"

"No."

"None at all?"

"Well, no. We just don't have money."

"Money for the paper boy?"

"No."

"Okay. Well, I'll need to ask your older son some questions, Mrs. Wells."

"Let me call him," Claire says. Walking out and along the hallway, she whispers to the door, "*Matt, will you come out of there! This man needs to talk to you!*"

As she returns to the living room, the oversized policeman says, "Tell me what happened last night, Mrs. Wells. Start with when you last saw Eric, up to when you called the police."

Claire describes looking over to see Eric standing at the wall by the pool game, and looking over again to see the empty space. They fix the time as six forty-five to seven P.M. She tries, too, to recall anyone else Eric knew, men or boys, being or not being there when she looked.

She can recall no one offhand.

"There's a bar there? Most of the people there are adults?"

"Well, there's not a bar in the pool table area, but it's right through an open door there."

"Did you see Eric talking to anyone?"

"Well, no, I didn't."

"Anyone, male or female, young or old? *Anyone?*"

"No, no one at all."

"He had maybe twenty cents?" the large man says.

"About that much."

"You called home then because you were worried, or because you usually call home?"

"Well, the first time because I usually call when I'm working like that.

Or Eric calls me. But that's one of those things he's sort of growing out of."

"So you called home? What time was that?"

"That would be about quarter to eight."

"What happened?"

"Well, there was no answer."

"So you went back to work?"

"And began to worry, yes. Eric wanted to see this movie on TV and it just wasn't like him not to come home. But, then, he is getting older and I thought he'd gotten sidetracked. Or that he was still mad about the fifty cents and wasn't going to answer the phone. He was kind of tired, and he wasn't in a real good mood."

"What happened then? When did you call again?"

"Well, I was working. I kept thinking—what I do, at work like that when I want time to pass, I don't look at the clock. It's always like that when I'm not with my kids. I don't mean at work during the day, but on weekends."

"When did you next call home?"

"Half an hour later, I guess."

"Still no answer?"

"No."

"How many times did you call and when did you get an answer?"

"I guess three more times."

"The third time you got an answer?"

"Yes."

"It was your older son?"

"Yes."

"Matt?"

"Yes."

"What time was that?"

"That was about nine thirty. Or twenty-five to ten. I was really watching the clock by then."

"Okay. And the call previous to that? What time did you make that call?"

"I guess nine twenty. About nine twenty."

"Matt was here then at nine thirty. What was he doing? What did you say to him?"

"I'm not sure what he was doing. He'd just come in, and he hadn't seen Eric. I had him check Eric's bed while I held the phone. But Eric wasn't here."

"Well, what did Matt say? Had he seen him? Did he have any idea where he might be?"

"No, he hadn't seen him and he wasn't too worried. I said to him I was really getting worried, and he said, oh, he probably ran into some friends. And when I told Matt to call up friends of Eric's who lived along the way—there were just two of them—he got kind of annoyed because, he said, he wanted to fix something to eat and watch TV. Anyway, I insisted and told him to do what I said and to call me back right away, and he did that."

"What did the friends say?"

"Well, they hadn't seen him since Friday in school."

"So Matt called you back and told you that, and then what happened?"

"I just told Smitty I had to go. I really left them holding the bag down there, but I just said something was wrong at home and I was sorry and I had to go."

"What time was this?"

"About ten."

"How'd you get home then?"

"I walked. Like I always do."

"How long a walk is it?"

"Ten minutes."

"What was Matt doing when you got here?"

"Well, he was in front of the TV. He was having a peanut-butter sandwich and a glass of milk."

"What did you do?"

"We shut off the TV, and I had him help me call people. Eric's friends. We called everybody we could think of."

"No one had seen him?"

"No, not since Friday in school."

"Then you called the police?"

"Well, first I went down and looked around the garage out there and the basement, although neither one of them belongs to us. I even looked under the beds. Just in case he was hiding there and playing some kind of joke. I just couldn't believe he wasn't here. I still can't."

"Then you called the police?"

"Yes."

"They told you about the twenty-four-hour policy?"

"Yes, they did, but these two officers did stop by here. At about eleven thirty."

"Well, the reason for that policy is that most kids who run away show up again within twenty-four hours."

"I just don't think Eric would run away. That's what scares me."

"Okay. Still, most often it is the case, and most often the parents don't think their boy or girl would do it. What it means is that there is a good chance Eric will come strolling back home any minute. He'll be hungry and tired, and he'll be ready to come back. He *was* a little angry, you say, and he *is* that age. Maybe his feelings were more hurt than you thought."

"Well, his feelings were hurt, it's true. I know that. As much by his brother earlier in the day."

"Another thing is it *is* the weekend. That's when children, boys especially, might take off on some adventure. To join the circus or something. They get an idea into their head. And there has been this warm weather."

"Well, the weather has been different."

"At the same time, I'm going to go ahead and get some stuff out on him, have people looking for him."

"You think he'll just come back?"

"Well, I hope so, Mrs. Wells. I'm concerned, I'll tell you, that he apparently didn't take anything with him, and that he had no money. So, I'd really like you to keep checking. And I do need to talk to your older son."

"I don't know why he isn't out here," Claire says.

"Mrs. Wells, listen. It *is* Sunday. So there's no reason why your son would *have* to come home. It's very possible he's camping out in an abandoned house or something, to sort of teach you and his brother a lesson because he feels upset with the way he felt he was being treated. Do you understand? It's possible, even, that he's having the time of his life."

Claire is on her way down the hall. At the closed bathroom door, she hisses, "*Matt, you come out of there right now! What in the world is wrong with you?*"

When she returns this time, the man says to her, "When's the last time Eric saw his father or heard from hm?"

"Oh, over eight years ago."

"No calls or letters?"

"Nothing. Not a Christmas card or a birthday card to either of his sons. He's—he's missed some of the most wonderful things in life, which has been to see his sons grow up."

"He could have changed, Mrs. Wells. He could have realized something like that and come back. And picked Eric up."

"Not him. Not anyone who would go off and leave two wonderful little boys without even any money to buy food or clothes."

Matt appears then, and the policeman says, "You're Matt. Do *you* have any idea of your father's whereabouts?"

"My father?" Matt says. "No—"

"When did you last see your brother?" the man says.

"When I left yesterday," Matt says.

"When was that?"

"About noon, wasn't it, Mom?"

"I understand you were with a friend. What's his name?"

"Cormac."

"Who Cormac?"

"Cormac Hughes. Cormac's his first name."

"Where does Cormac live?"

"Over here, on McDonough."

"Where were you yesterday, until you came home?"

"I was in town."

"By yourself?"

"I was with Cormac."

"What did you do?"

"We just hung around, went to the movies."

"What movie did you see? At what time?"

"Well, we saw, it was about this kid who went back in time. *The Time Machine*, or something like that."

"At what theater?"

"The Cinema."

"What showing?"

"Well, the one that started at about five, I guess."

"Then what did you do?"

"Went to the Mall. Just hung around."

"What time did you get home?"

"About nine thirty."

Returning his pad and pen to his pocket, the man says then, "Mrs. Wells, there are a couple of things I'd like you to do. I'd like you to write down the names of anyone you knew who was at the Legion Hall when you were working. Anyone, best friends included. *Anyone*. And I'd like a recent picture of Eric."

"I'll have to look," Claire says, knowing in a flash they have ordered no school pictures in some time, perhaps years.

"Fine. I don't mean to alarm you. These are just some precautions I think we should take. I still think chances are Eric will come strolling in any time."

"You want us to keep looking for things he might have taken with him?"

"Absolutely. I'd like to know if he stopped here after he left the Legion Hall. Check on any kind of camping gear or sleeping bags, too. Flashlights, anything like that. Matches. Even cans of food. Can opener."

"Okay," Claire says.

"And give me a call," the man says, nodding, pausing before opening the door and leaving.

In the man's sudden absence, Claire and Matt stand in something of a vacuum. Claire says, "Why didn't you come out when I told you to?"

Matt doesn't reply.

Going into the kitchen, Claire is asking herself if Warren really would come back. *Would* he? she wonders. There's just no way, she tells herself as she thinks how that policeman seemed to think differently. He just thought she was a typical stubborn woman who couldn't see reason, and maybe she was, in part, where Warren was concerned; still, he didn't know Warren the way she did.

She comes to herself again, as if sensing and then realizing that something is wrong. Stepping back through to the living room, she says to Matt, "You know, maybe Eric has run off because of the treatment he's been getting around here. I can't say as I'd blame him."

"Oh, Mom," Matt says.

Claire goes on, against her better judgment, "Well, you have been *mean* to him," she says. "You were mean to him yesterday!"

"My gosh, nobody'd run away over something like that."

"How do you know? How do you know how he feels? Has anyone ever picked on you the way you pick on him? Have they?"

"Oh, Mom."

"Just your dad I guess is the only one who's picked on you."

"Mom, don't say that," Matt says. He has started to break.

"It's true!" she says.

"Don't," Matt says. "Please don't say that."

Claire cannot help beginning to cry, too. "What in the world is happening?" she tries to say to him.

"I don't know," Matt cries. He draws in air, as he bawls. *"I don't know."*

FOUR

THEY ARE DRIVING, going nowhere. At a loss for what to do, Vernon feels like a criminal. He feels like he did when he once played hooky from elementary school, in California, and went into a church and stole some candles. He felt lost and haunted in his heart, all that day and the next, in fear of being caught. The fear stayed with him even after they left California. It was with him still, in him now.

The boy is beside him as before, covered to his waist with the sleeping bag, neckties around his wrists and ankles. They are driving west on Route 4, a two-lane highway. They are just driving. Burning up gas, Vernon thinks. There are open fields, woodlots, house trailers, houses that are slightly out of balance. There is a building supplies store, closed on Sunday morning. Everything is quiet, except for the trucks going by. A few cars driving under the early angle of sunlight. Snowmobiles stand next to outbuildings. Smoke puffs from metal chimneys. The boy whimpers again, "*It hurts.*"

Vernon drives. He thinks how he'd rather be in his room, studying, or on his way to the library. Going to see his friend. But he can't just go ahead and do any of these, because he cannot think of what to do with the boy. If only he weren't hurt, he thinks. He can't just let him off hurt. Because—even if he did promise not to tell—someone would make him do it. The question was if they would be able to trace anything? Would they care?

How he'd like to take a bath, he thinks. It's so awful, feeling dirty, wanting to brush your teeth. Being so tired. Everything is a problem. Using a bathroom. Eating. Buying food. How is he going to get gas? Maybe he'll have to tie the boy to something and leave him somewhere. He could put him in the trunk, he thinks, although it would be horrible to be locked in a trunk.

Bathing him, he thinks, glancing at him. That's what he'd like to do. Wash him in a shower or in a bathtub. Wash his hair and ears. Wash between the legs as his mother washed him when he was a child. He could do anything he wanted, he thinks. How could he stop him?

They roll along in silence. The boy's faint sniffling and gasping is the only sound above the sound of the car.

"I wanted to buy you a bicycle and be your friend," Vernon says. "It's your fault that you feel hurt. If you weren't hurt, if you didn't act like that, I could take you back right now."

When the boy doesn't reply, he says, "Do you hear me? At least you could talk."

"*You fairy!*" the boy suddenly spits at him.

Vernon keeps driving. Stung, he doesn't say anything. As the highway opens before him, offering a passing lane, he goes on to pass an oil truck with a low belly, thinking to try to argue his case, to explain that the charge isn't fair, but lets it go and continues to feel unliked, which feeling is familiar and has always made his jaw sink, his words disappear.

The town is Northwood, a widening in the highway, a gas station or two, a small diner, some white houses. He decides to turn away from this westward direction, maybe turn south, not to get too far away from where he might escape his dilemma, Portsmouth.

He pulls in then on the all-but-empty blacktop stretching before a country supermarket. It's a sudden decision, and he sits here with the motor running. The boy, he knows, is alert. Vernon thinks how they would both like to be back close to the ocean where the highways are lined with drive-ins for fried clams, soft ice cream, hamburgers, or on the beach itself with waves unrolling and birds darting around. Don't stop here, he thinks then. Everyone will notice you if you're the only stranger.

He turns off the motor, though, and takes out the keys.

"This is a test," he says. "I'm going to get some food in there. You just sit still here. If you do anything, then I'll know I can't trust you. So don't move."

Coming back out of the store in only a minute, he can see that the boy is partially through the door on his side, struggling like a seal. Vernon runs to him, snaps at him, "*What are you doing?*" The boy has shifted, pulled the door lock—which is in the armrest—and opened the door a foot, in order to start pawing his way out to the blacktop.

Reaching a box of doughnuts to the back seat, Vernon lifts the boy, presses him back inside, and slams the door. "*Help me! Help—,*" the boy shouts as Vernon hurries around to the driver's side. Jumping in, he turns on the radio, but it gives off no sound; fumbling wildly for the keys, he gets a key into the ignition and quickly has both motor and radio going loudly, as he pulls around to leave.

Driving along the highway then, as before, Vernon is trembling. The radio snapped off, the boy is gasping tears but saying nothing. Vernon is surprised at how shaken he feels. Rejection, even shock, is in his eyes once more and he doesn't know what to say.

He keeps driving.

"I can't believe you did that," he says at last. "I can't believe you did that."

He drives on, drives into the unusual morning light crossing the highway through the trees, as if into some new plane of existence. "How can I ever trust you?" he says to the boy, almost in tears himself. *"How?"*

FIVE

THE ARE THE CITY'S three ranking police officers. Dulac, who has done most of the talking so far, and the captain, a man named Adam Sloan, and the chief, Pat Emery. They sit at the round table in the chief's conference room before empty styrofoam cups. The chief, a short, blocky man with the manner of a school principal, was hired out of Providence half a dozen years ago. Adam Sloan, the captain, ever harsh-throated and red-faced, a large man like Dulac, has been around long enough to be considered homegrown, and is not, like the chief, on his last tour before retirement.

Called from their homes, the chief and the captain are also dressed casually. Maybe they are in a hurry to return home, Dulac isn't sure. Contrary to his lecture earlier to the police cadet, they are not entirely eager, and the captain has just suggested for the third time that regular procedure be followed, that the twenty-four-hour rule be honored, to allow the boy time to return home.

"You realize," the chief says, "no one is going to hassle us if it turns out this boy *has* been picked up. The right thing's been done so far. In fact, we're above and beyond so far. Officially, he hasn't even been missing a dozen hours yet."

"He's been missing since six forty-five last night," Dulac says. "It'll be eighteen hours roughly at noon."

"Still, he shows up in school in the morning and we'll look a little foolish with fliers all over the place. You know what I mean?"

"We can survive that," the lieutenant says. "The thing is, we're going—"

"Gil, I know we can survive it," the chief says. "We have to. The next time, though, people are going to say wait a minute now."

"We can explain ourselves," Dulac says, "if it comes to that. We can

98

simply say we didn't mean to put up a false alarm, it just looked real at the time. No one's going to make a deal of it. We did it five times, okay. Not once."

"I'm for the procedure," the captain offers from the other side in his raspy voice.

"Gil, you're convinced about this?" the chief says.

"It looks like what it looks like," Dulac says. "That's all I'm saying. Not a thing missing. Not one thing."

"You'd put money on it?"

"I don't want the kid to be abducted," Dulac says. "I'd just as soon go home and read the Sunday paper. But it *looks* like that to me. It *feels* like an abduction. The kid never made it back home and his mother is certain he didn't have more than twenty cents in his pocket. That he didn't have money is why he was badgering her. She's a nice simple woman who is worried to death. In my judgment—as I see it—something is wrong. He's been gone overnight. He's twelve years old. He's on his way home to watch a movie on television. It's something he wanted to see. It's not like he was wandering around. He was going somewhere. Someone got in the way. We *have* to figure he was picked up. Don't we? The longer we wait, chief, as far as I'm concerned the worse we'll look in the long run."

"You believe that?" the chief says.

"Of course I do. I know I could be wrong. I hope I am. Jesuschrist, this city's been getting weird lately, let's face it."

"Now, now," the chief says.

"I'm still for the procedure," the captain says.

"Isn't the best bet the father's got him?" the chief says.

"I thought that," Dulac says. "Now I'm not so sure. The mother's *so* certain on the point, and the guy has never so much as written a postcard. Over eight years."

"Well, okay. Legion Hall has to be the place to start," the chief says. "When's the mother coming up with her list?"

"As soon as we're done here I'm going to pick it up," Dulac says. "And a photograph of the boy."

The chief pauses, taps a knuckle to the side of the table. "Okay," he says. "Okay, this is what we'll do. Go ahead and have your fliers made up. We'll cover just that end of town. Work up the description and so on for radio and TV. Only, we'll ask them to hold it until the six o'clock news. The boy comes walking in by then, you can make a couple of calls and cancel out. In either case, we'll say 'Portsmouth Police decided to move quickly in the case of a missing boy, et cetera.' You see what I'm saying? Adam?"

"I'll go along, if you say so. We should call up a file of known sex of-fenders, to see if any of them come in on the mother's list."

"It's being done," Dulac says.

"Tomorrow," the chief says, "if the kid hasn't shown up, we'll put it out to the newspapers and to the networks in Boston. What about the budget, Adam?"

"It's going to be a problem, just calling in people today. I'd say keep the crew as lean as possible. Neil Mizener, say, to assist. Then, two uni-formed officers to do a neighborhood search and canvass; they can call in a couple of cadets to help with that. How's that sound?"

"One other thing," Dulac says. "How about Shirley Moss coming in at five, to set up a base operation here? She can do a central clearing thing, deal with the phone, build the file, and so on. Keep an eye on the cadets. Shirley's good at that."

"Okay," the chief says. "You could get a bunch of calls. Shirley can handle that. Use 4022."

"Okay," Dulac says. "Good. Only two uniformed isn't enough. Four is more like it."

"Two," the chief says.

"This, then," Dulac says. "We run it on the six o'clock news. Say it gets to be eight or eight thirty, and the kid is still out there somewhere—how about asking the Boston stations to run a nine o'clock spot on a boy missing in—"

"No, that's out," the chief says.

"They'd never do it anyway," the captain says. "Not this soon. You know something else, Gil? You put out a blitz like this, you're going to scare the shit out of whoever is holding that kid. They could get nasty with the kid."

"Aren't chances just as good they'll let him go? Chief, what's your feeling on that?"

"Well, gee, chances are of course, if he's been abducted, it's someone known to him or in his own family. As you know. And that they've taken very few steps to cover themselves. Chances are, of course, if it is an ab-duction, that he's dead by now. That's the way it usually goes. You know? Anyway, of course you're going to scare whoever picked him up, if that's what happened."

"I'll still put my money on the father," the captain says.

The chief is backing away from the table, taking up his empty cup. "Tell Shirley to keep me informed," he is saying. "Regular updates. I'll be home all day and all evening. I'm not going anywhere."

Dulac takes up his cup, too, and the metal ashtray as he has used. He brushes his hand over his area of the table, before heading back to his cubicle.

Detective Sergeant Mizener—Neil—welcomes the call. "I'm about to take my oldest kid's head off," he says to Dulac. "It's just as well I get out of here."

He is not a close friend and Dulac doesn't know if his oldest is a son or a daughter. He believes the man has four children. They have never clashed but have always stayed more or less aloof from one another.

Shirley Moss is less willing. Her husband's sister and brother-in-law are supposed to stop by. "What the hell," she says.

Dulac explains the case. "Shirley, you were my recommendation," he says. "And it looks a little scary to me. This boy's been missing since yesterday evening."

"Who is it?" Shirley says.

"I'll tell you when you get here. It's a little boy—nobody important."

Dulac makes other calls. He confirms Claire Wells's account with the bartender Smitty. "Claire is just a good soul you can always count on," the man says. "I had an idea it wasn't any small thing when she said she had to leave even though it did leave us shorthanded."

"Anything unusual happen before or after?" Dulac asks.

"Nothing," the man says. "It was just another Saturday night."

When a false note rings for the first time Dulac almost misses it. It comes in a phone conversation with the older son's friend, fifteen-year-old Cormac Hughes. "I'm sorry," Dulac says to him. "You say you and Matt split at about five thirty? He left the movie theater?"

"Yah," the boy says.

"How did he leave—why did he leave? Was the movie over?"

"The movie wasn't over. He just left. He got up and walked out."

"What do you mean?"

"He was acting weird, that's all."

"How so, weird?"

"I don't know. It was like he was mad."

"About what?"

"I don't know," the boy says.

"What did he say?"

"Nothing. He just said he was leaving. Said he'd see me in school."

"He never acted like that at other times?"

"No. Never."

"You see him after the movie or any time since?"

"Nope."

"What time did you leave the movie theater?"

"I don't know. Six thirty or so."

"Okay," Dulac says. "Listen. I don't want you to talk to Matt or to anyone else in the meantime about this. Not even to your parents. We're going to stop by and get a statement from you. So you stick around until we get there. It'll be within an hour."

"What's happening?" the boy says.

"I'll tell you when we get there," Dulac says, and concludes the call.

He pauses to think a moment then over the yellow pad on his desk. The hours match up. He sits staring away. "Jesus," he says aloud. "His brother . . ."

SIX

CLAIRE IS IN THE CHILLED crawl space looking inside cardboard boxes. She knows too well that there is no recent photograph of Eric here, or anywhere; still she keeps looking as if there is. She has put aside a collapsing shoe box filled with photographs she is going to take out to the kitchen table in a minute to inspect. They are old, though, she knows, and will provide nothing showing what Eric looks like now. In the meantime, she is looking wherever she can think to look, on that huge detective's suggestion or insistence on the phone that some Instamatic or Polaroid snapshot might have made its way home and ended up *somewhere*, that a photograph is important.

Backing out, getting to her feet in the living room with the old shoe box, she starts to the kitchen. "I can't find anything," she calls down the slight hallway to Matt. "Can you?"

There is no reply.

Shame is what is bothering Claire as she places the box on the table. It is shameful, she believes, not to have any recent pictures. Her sons growing up so fast and changing so much. It's as if, without pictures, their life adds up to nothing.

The handful of old photographs she lifts from the box begins to touch her all at once, however mixed and confused they are in time and place. There is Helen, her sister, who lives up near Bangor still. There are Helen and Manse. Warren in his army uniform. There are her mother and father in separate small photographs with disintegrating, scalloped edges. There, everywhere, is time passing. Shooting stars.

It is a pet, though, her childhood dog, Bonnie, that strikes her with loss. She had forgotten Bonnie. She never thought of her at all anymore; she's been dead now some thirty years. In the photograph, however, the dog calls up all that had ever been right in her life.

She continues. There is Warren and the boys. They are so small, such disguises of themselves, and they are innocent while Warren, in retrospect, is not. She sees into him here, although she hadn't seen into him at the time. She experiences wisdom she has never experienced before. What keeps stabbing her in the photographs is the foreshortening of life. In perspective, it is all so misunderstood.

She lifts and sorts. Altogether, there are hardly a dozen pictures of Matt and Eric, together or alone, and she knows even as she sets them aside that they are useless to her present need. Nor does she know why she has sorted out both when of course it is only Eric's picture they are coming to pick up.

She looks over the dozen. None will do. All are too old. Too young. Or they are blurred, some of them, so they look like old black-and-white pictures taken from a speeding car.

Here's Eric. He's in those little tan swimming trunks he had, standing ankle-deep in the lake near Bangor when they visited her sister. Sunlight is in his eyes. His head angled one way, his eyes squinting. It was several summers ago. Three? Could it be four? She knows it's her most recent picture of Eric. She *knows* this but isn't ready to admit it to herself, as if to do so will say the intervening years have not quite happened.

She kisses the photograph. She thinks to call Matt, to see it, but doesn't.

The background of the picture is filled with those giant pine trees up there. It was that time, she recalls, that same day that Manse took them out at the crack of dawn in his pickup truck and they saw a bull moose and two cows standing up to their bellies in the water of some pond or river. Boy, did they think that was something, especially Eric. Riding those dirt roads in the back of that old wreck of a truck. The way they enjoyed telling and retelling of seeing the moose, trying to decide if one was the calf of the pair, as Manse, after a time, said it was, when Matt or Eric asked something about there being two females. The image of the moose family, standing deep in the water, surrounded by the great dark trees, was the high point of her trip, too, however secondhand, for the way it thrilled, the way it enchanted her sons. It was a vision. It was the reason she had scraped and finagled to take her two sons north, even if she hadn't known her mission exactly before it happened.

She comes back around. Eric was nine in the picture, she thinks. Did he weigh fifty pounds? She knew from a health card sent home from school just a few weeks ago, as she had told the detective, that he now weighed nearly a hundred. Did the card say ninety-three? Ninety-five? She signed it, to be returned to school, and now she cannot remember. Maybe it was ninety-seven?

That big detective, she thinks. She hopes he is the one who comes after the picture and the list she'd made. He seemed to be a nice man and she did not think he would say anything about her not having school pictures. The young policeman who was here last night, who said to her, "You mean your son was on his own all this time?" She could imagine him saying, *You don't have any school pictures? Are you serious?*

Walking into the hall, she is going to call to Matt, to see if he has had any luck, but there he is coming toward her. "You find anything?" she says.

"Any what?" he says.

"Pictures! My gosh, Matt. They're coming to get a picture. I told you!"

"Mom, you know we don't have any pictures."

"Well, where can we get one? Wouldn't someone have one?"

"How should I know?"

"Well, you've got to know. You've got to help me, Matt. What are you doing? Where are you going?"

"I'm going out to look for Eric."

"To look where?"

"Anywhere. Places we used to hide. Maybe—I don't know—maybe he got locked in or something. I don't know. I'm just going to look, on my own, that's all."

He is upset, too, Claire sees, and she pauses as he takes down his jacket and slips it on.

"Matt," she says. "Do you want something to eat? We're going to have to eat."

"Not now. I'm just not hungry now. Maybe I can find him."

The door closes and he is gone. Claire thought he was starting to cry, again, and the emotion brings tears to her own eyes. She hears him go out downstairs, and she stands, afloat it seems for the moment, in the new emptiness of their apartment.

Their home, she thinks. She'd never quite appreciated it before this moment. This is their home; it is something, one thing, they have.

In the kitchen she looks once more through the photographs. None will do. There's no reason to have them out. Still, she is thinking to show them to the detective, as if to verify something.

Her feelings of shame stir up again. *We just haven't had money for school pictures*, she hears herself trying to explain. *It was that, it was come up with four or five dollars for those pictures, or money for lunch. It was worse than that—if you want to hear the truth. I'd have two dollars in my purse, if I was lucky. I'd give them each a dollar for lunch. There just wasn't any money for pictures. Is that so hard to understand?*

SEVEN

"LISTEN NOW," Vernon says. "We're going to stop for gas. I've been thinking about it. I have to buy some gas and we're going to stop."

Time has skipped again for Vernon. Here he is driving, recognizing that he is south now, near Plaistow, near the Massachusetts state line, and recognizing that his gas gauge is on E, but the experience of getting here seems to have vanished.

Pulling into an unopened gas station, he lifts the doughnuts from the rear seat and opens the box.

"A doughtnut?" he says.

The boy remains in a slump, looking away, refusing to speak.

"You see," Vernon says, "I can forgive you for doing something. Why can't you forgive me?"

The boy gives no response.

"There are cinnamon, powdered sugar, and plain," Vernon says.

The boy says nothing.

"What kind do you want? Vernon says.

"Cinnamon," the boy says.

Vernon places one of the cinnamon doughnuts in the boy's hands. Watching him take a bite then, with his wrists tied together, he feels a rush of sympathy for him.

"I only wanted to be your friend," he says.

The boy is taking another bite of the doughnut. He doesn't look at Vernon, and no new expression comes to his face. He pays no attention, either, to the doughnut crumbs which fall to his lap.

"I know there's a self-serve gas station along here," Vernon says. "That's where I'm going. I just hope you don't make me put you in the trunk. I will, though. You make any fuss, like you did before, I'll just drive away, and I'll put you in the trunk. I'll gag you, too. Then I'll go back and buy the gas. Do you hear me?"

The boy sits there.

"I want you to say so," Vernon says to him. "I want you to say you understand or I'll just take you and put you in the trunk anyway. Do you understand?"

The boy doesn't respond.

"Say it," Vernon says. "Say you understand or I'm going to do it."

"Okay," the boy says.

"You do understand?"

"Okay," the boy says.

"You want another doughnut?" Vernon says. The boy shakes his head. With no appetite for doughnuts himself, Vernon reaches the box to the back seat.

Returning to the highway, he drives along. "None of this would have to be," he says. "If you wouldn't act like you have. You're the one who makes things awful. Do you know that? I could forgive you, and give you a doughnut—after what you did. Why can't you be like that with me?"

The boy ignores him, keeps staring away.

"You could be driving the car," Vernon says. "If you were nice, I could be teaching you how to drive. If you were my friend."

Turning to him, the boy says, "You're not my friend."

Vernon loses his breath for an instant and has to check himself or it seems he will start to cry. He continues driving. "Thank you," he says.

Approaching an intersection—a sign says STOP AHEAD—he begins to grow increasingly tense, as if, again, already, he is going to cry. Slowing down—only one other car is in view, at a distance—and not quite stopping, he accelerates, as if unnoticeably, and passes through the intersection.

He drives on. His hurt passes. Stores, drive-ins, and fast-food outlets line both sides of the highway here, and he sees from a gun law sign that they have crossed into Massachusetts. The boy seems too subdued now to try anything; still it makes Vernon tense to be around so many cars and people.

Intentionally, he drives past the Gibbs Self-Serve, to look it over. The gas station looks workable to his plan; if he pulls in on the outside of the furthest row of pumps, no one should notice the right side of his car, where the boy is seated. A quarter of a mile along, he turns around to start back.

"I'm going to turn in here," he says. "You don't have to be my friend if you don't want to. But don't forget what I said." As he slows down and his directional signal flashes, he adds, "There's no reason why you wouldn't be able to get out and pump the gas, you know, if you weren't so mean."

Rolling into the station, Vernon sees that another car is pulling in directly behind him and he panics for an instant, until he sees the car turn away to another row of pumps. Pulling up outside the far row, he parks at the first pump then, so no one can park behind him. He turns off the motor, leaving his hand on the keys. "You do anything at all," he says. "You do anything, and I'm going to jump back in, go some place, and put you in the trunk."

Removing the keys, stepping from the car, he leaves the door ajar. But after four or five steps, he turns to walk back.

He gets into the car and slams the door. He sits there.

"You were going to try something, weren't you?" he says. "I know you were."

The boy glances at him but doesn't speak.

"I'm going to do it. I'm going to put you in the trunk." Vernon is returning the keys to the ignition.

"I didn't *do* anything," the boy says.

"You were going to!"

"No, I wasn't. I wasn't."

Vernon inserts the key, starts the motor.

The boy is crying. "Please don't do that," he says. "I didn't do anything."

"How do I know you won't try?" Vernon says.

"I won't," the boy cries. "I swear I won't."

Vernon holds. "Do you really promise?" he says.

"Yes, I do," the boy says. "I do."

"How do I know you mean it?"

"I said I won't do anything," the boy cries.

Again, Vernon turns off the motor. Then he says, "As soon as I can trust you, I'll take you back home. Don't you know that?"

He gazes at the boy, into his eyes. It occurs to him that neither of them knows anything of this, of what is happening, and a shiver passes over him.

Removing the keys, stepping from the car and closing the door, Vernon walks directly to the glassed-in booth. Removing his wallet, he takes out a ten-dollar bill. He is deciding to attempt to trust the boy. A trial run, he is thinking.

At the window, as a man steps away before him, he slides the ten-dollar bill through the opening, and says, 'Five dollars' worth, lead-free, right back there."

A large girl takes the ten to make change. Vernon looks back at his car's windsheld. There is the boy's face, down low, under an upper glare, unhappy, looking at him. Raising a hand, Vernon waves. The boy shows no response. The girl says, "Thank you."

Five dollar bills in his hand, Vernon walks back. The boy keeps looking away, will not meet his glance.

Gas pumped, on the driver's side, where the boy is not in view, he re-hangs the pump and reenters his car.

In a moment, driving back along the hamburger offerings, he says, "Because you were good, I'm going to buy you something more to eat. A hamburger. Maybe some french fries. Are you hungry? Would you like that?"

"Yes," the boy says.

Vernon presses his directional signal for Burger King just ahead on the right. He feels a small thrill, a slight sense of well-being. Maybe things will work out.

Pulling around, they join a line of two cars, immediately one. "You don't even know my name, do you?" Vernon says. "Do you?"

The boy shakes his head.

"I'm not going to tell you either," Vernon says. "That way, even if you wanted to tell on me, you wouldn't be able to, would you?"

The boy sits there.

"If you can be nice, in a while I'll untie you," Vernon says. "And just take you home. It's as simple as that. If you promise not to tell."

They wait. Then Vernon says, "All I wanted, in my heart, was to do this. Take you out places. Buy you hamburgers. Teach you how to drive a car."

Glancing around, through his misted eyes, Vernon sees that the space next to the intercom-menu is vacated. He downshifts, rolls ahead.

"Everything on your hamburger?" he says to the boy.

The boy nods, as if to say yes.

"French fries?" he says.

Again the boy nods.

"Would you like a milkshake, a chocolate milkshake?"

The boy nods again.

Turning, rolling down his window, Vernon is greeted by a static voice saying, "Your order please?" and on the edge of his vision he is aware that the boy has turned his head to watch him, and he thinks it might be a good sign. With new hope, he speaks to the glass sign, to place their order, food they will eat together, he is thinking, beyond which their problems will no longer exist, on which thought he adds, "And two hot apple pies," and turns to look at the boy, to see if he has generated the slightest expression of approval.

EIGHT

THE PHEASANT. It was right here, Matt thinks, although there is before him now the cinder-block backside of a warehouse. Sprague Oil, he knows, is in the other direction, beyond the fences, near the river. Everything is changing.

The tall bird was a shock, the way its color stood out in the field. They were on the paved street and the bird was standing in the crushed, bleached weeds looking like one of those paintings they sell near the traffic circle, and Eric was whispering beside him, *"Don't stop! Keep walking! Keep walking!"*

Thirty yards along, past some trunks of dead trees, Eric took over like a sergeant, whispering all kinds of instructions, and Matt went along with it, he remembers, even though he was older, because Eric had all the ideas. And—even though he'd admitted it only that once, sort of—because he was a little scared of the big bird back there in the weeds. What if it went for your eyes?

Shifting to the far side of the road, even into a ditch, as instructed by the Marine sergeant, his little brother, he made his way back past the pheasant, and returned across the road to the driveway beside a house, on the other end of the field. Raising his arm, he opened his fingers, but did not wave, in the signal the big-game hunter had told him to give.

Eric started toward him, carefully. Going to his toes, being quiet, Matt watched the glossy bird—which hardly moved, except for its neck—and he watched Eric beyond the bird, entering the field one step at a time, as if he were playing statue.

What was so amazing was that the dumb bird did almost exactly as Eric said it would. Standing there, watching, Matt saw things about his brother he had never seen before. He saw that they were different. Eric had more nerve, Matt saw, although he had known at once it was nothing he'd ever admit to anyone.

The bird's head cocked then and held, alert to something. There were its green colors, its red face and the white ring around its neck, its green-blue oil-on-water feathers. It stood like a full-sized jewel, a glossy vase, in the sand-colored weeds. On tiptoe, Eric took one step and then another.

The bird took off! It half flew, half ran suddenly, flicking its toes, opening its wings, gliding fifteen or twenty feet, and down, out of sight.

Eric, holding a moment, took another step. And another.

The bird's head came up. There was its deep, dark eye. Periscope up, Matt thought, his heart racing; he remembered thinking, too, how dumb the bird was not to fly all the way away, into some other country, at least across the wide river into the State of Maine.

Eric took more slow-motion steps. One step at a time. You dumb bird, Matt thought. He's going to get you.

Eric crouched, out of view, and Matt wondered what he was doing. He must have found a path, he thought, and was duck-walking or sneaking along on his stomach. The bird stayed in place, still periscope up, looking around so its red jowls jiggled. A minute passed. All at once, twenty feet closer to the bird, Eric's face lifted into view, looking so intent, so like an Indian brave from a movie screen, that Matt would have laughed were he not so impressed.

Eric continued crouch-walking. Matt could see him and the pheasant. One step at a time. The pheasant stood in place. Then, on a step, the pheasant also took a step. Eric froze. Nor did Matt breathe, as he watched.

Eric exploded all at once, and the bird exploded. Matt was startled. There was the dark pheasant, sailing right past him, over the driveway, and down out of sight behind the house. There, too, was Eric, saying, *"Couldn't you get him?"* as he ran by.

Matt went after him to catch up. Behind the house, in a yard of cut grass, Eric was looking all over and saying, "He came down right here. He's gotta be right here. Look down there, before he takes off again."

Eric found him. "Here he is!" he called. "We got him!"

He was crouching under the steps of a small porch at the rear of the house. Joining him, looking through the square openings of the latticed side of the steps, Matt saw the pheasant.

Slipping under the porch, crouching, they had a better view of the bird in under the steps, closed in by the latticed side walls. "What a stupid place to go," Eric said, as if to the bird.

"What if somebody comes?" Matt said.

Eric ignored this; as he was in charge, Matt ignored it, too.

The bird was three or four feet away. He crouched near the second-to-lowest step. There was his deep shiny eye on one side. There, less lighted, were his oil-on-water colors. The ring around his neck. His spotted rust-colored body. His bouquet of tail feathers, a foot long and drooping.

"We have to kill him," Eric said.

"What?" Matt said.

"We can't take him home alive," Eric said. "If we're going to have him for dinner, we have to kill him, and clean him."

"Oh," Matt said. But then he said, "What if he goes for your eyes?"

"Mister Pheasant, you made a real mistake," Eric said.

"Let's let him go," Matt said.

Eric ignored this, too. "Let's get some rocks and zonk him," he was saying. "Stay right here. Don't move."

Crouching back under in a moment, Eric had his shirttail in front filled with rocks, stones, and pebbles, which he let tumble to the ground. "Okay," he said. "We are going to have pheasant dinner. Mom will go berserk."

Eric threw and missed half a dozen times, the rocks banging off the underside of the steps, before Matt said, "Let me try." At least he could throw better, as he was always a better athlete.

Using a sidearm, with Eric out of the way, he whipped around and fired a rock which ricocheted sharply off the unpainted wood. On his second shot, with a *thunk,* he hit the pheasant in the body, but it was Eric who made a sound, saying, *"Ouch."*

Matt drew his arm back to fire again, and Eric said, "Maybe we should let him go."

Matt fired. This time, he clipped the bird somewhere about the head, although in a glancing shot.

"Maybe it's not fair," Eric said.

"What's that mean?"

"Maybe it's not fair," Eric said. "He doesn't have a chance."

"It was your idea!"

The bird blinked an eyelid.

"I think you got him," Eric said.

"Well, what did you expect?"

Crouching, Eric duck-walked a step closer. "Let's help him," he said.

"You better watch it, he might go for your eyes."

"I think he's tame," Eric said.

"Tame?"

"He could be somebody's pet. I bet he understands what we're saying."

"Hey, Mister Pheasant," Eric said to the bird. "Come on now, we're not going to hurt you anymore. Come on now."

"Better be careful!" Matt said.

Crouching, reaching in, Eric gripped the bird all at once in his hands. "See, he's tame," he said, backing out with him.

"Jesus, keep him away from your eyes," Matt said.

Out from under the porch, holding the pheasant away, Eric walked back in the direction of the field. Matt followed. "You're going to be fine, Mister Pheasant," Eric was saying. "You're going to be okay now, so don't worry. Hey, his eye's bleeding."

In the knee-high weeds, Matt stood next to Eric to study the bird's eye. A droplet of blood, as dark and thick as a drop from a girl's bottle of nail polish, had appeared on the surface above his eye.

"You think he'll die?" Matt said, for this, too, was Eric's territory.

"Nah," Eric said. "It's just a nick. Or his eye wouldn't blink." And Eric said, "He's tame. I can tell."

The bird's face became familiar. They stood looking at it.

Then Eric said, "Here you go, you dumb bird."

He gave the bird a launch into the air. Its wings came up and flapped and caught and it sailed over the weeds a distance and settled in once more, out of sight, fifteen or twenty or thirty feet away.

"There goes supper," Eric said then.

"Let's go," Matt said.

"You wouldn't believe how oily his feathers are," Eric said, wiping his hands.

"Come on, let's go," Matt said, and it was the first time, he sees now, he had ever asked anything of his brother. Always before—and since—he told Eric what to do.

As Matt rides, pedaling block after block on the wobbly bike, from street to sidewalk and back again, Eric slips to the rear of his mind. Vanessa Dineen returns to the forefront. Maybe she has been close by all along, for the experience of last night has not really left him for a moment, in spite of all else that has happened. A feeling of her has remained as close around him as his shirt.

He peddles on.

On Maplewood, coasting back into downtown, he decides to call her. It seems a new decision and he feels new boldness making it.

In town, at side-by-side telephone stalls, he leans the old five-speed onto the ground and decides to gamble with himself on remembering her number. If he remembers it, it will mean they may be together again soon—today?—like they were last night. If not, he will only lose a dime.

He dials. A telephone rings.

"Dineen residence," a woman says.

"Vanessa there?" Matt says, pleased with himself.

"Just a moment," the woman says.

Matt glances over an adjacent parking lot. There is a restaurant called Tortilla Flat, and something, he isn't sure what, clings to his mind. There, at the sound of the receiver being taken up, is her voice, which affects him in his neck and shoulders, along his spine.

"Hi," he says.

"Hi," she says, after a pause.

"How are you?" he says.

"Okay, how are you?"

"I been thinking about you," he says. Staring at the pavement, he seems to be seeing the sky. "A lot."

"Have you?"

"Oh yes."

"Well. What have you been thinking?"

"That was really something."

"What was?"

"You know."

"Okay. I thought so, too. It was nice."

Matt glances to the blue sky; he is smiling but doesn't know what to say.

"Don't get any ideas, though," she says.

He laughs. "I like you," he says.

"Well," she says. "It's a nice day today." Her voice is direct. He laughs some again.

"You know why I did that?" she says.

"Did what?"

"That which has made it a nice day today," she says. "Don't be so slow."

"What—why?"

"It was what you said about my fingers."

"Was it?"

"Don't bother saying it again, though. It won't work a second time."

He laughs. "Was that your mother who answered?" he says.

"Yes, that's my mother. She's an Air Force brat, too; that's why she talks like a secretary."

"You won't believe what's happened," Matt says. "Police and everything. I've been out looking for my brother."

"What?"

"My brother's missing. My little brother. I been out looking for him. It's kind of scary, like he ran away or something."

"What are you saying?"

"I have a brother, twelve. Eric. He's been gone since last night, and I've—"

"He's missing? You don't know where he is?"

"No. The police are—"

"He's twelve?"

"Yah."

"Gee. Did he run away?"

"I don't know. I guess he could have."

"He was gone all night?"

"Yah, but I been looking for him," Matt says.

"That's serious. You better keep looking," she says.

"I know," he says.

"In Texas, once," she says, "well, there was this boy who lived in the same building where we lived. He was missing. He was twelve."

"What happened?"

"He was killed."

"He was?"

"This man, a major, asked him in to help him paint or something. And he killed him. In a bathtub."

"Why?"

"I shouldn't have told you that. I didn't mean to scare you. Your brother is probably just hiding out. But I'd go look for him if I were you. That's what I'd do."

"Why did that guy kill him?"

"I don't know. He was crazy or something. Go look for your brother. Jesus, get off the phone."

NINE

"I'VE CAUGHT THE BROTHER in a lie," Dulac says to Mizener, as they are pulling away from the police station in Dulac's unmarked car.

"What do you mean?" Mizener says. "How old is he?"

"The brother's fifteen," Dulac says. "What's interesting about his lie is that it covers *precisely* the time the little brother came up missing. He said he was with his friend, at the movies—that's what he told me—at the same time he was acting pretty strange. I was there a good ten minutes before he came out of the bathroom, even though his mother called him. Then he said he was with this friend of his at the movies in town, and returned home at nine thirty. Now his friend says that wasn't so. His friend says it was five o'clock, about, that the movie had *just* gotten underway. The older brother—unlike anything he'd ever done—got up and walked out of the theater. All he said was that he'd see him in school on Monday."

"So he lied about where he was during that time?" Mizener says.

"That's right."

"That sure sounds like something, doesn't it? Are we going to pick him up?"

"In just a minute. We're going to stop first and get a statement from the friend, just to be sure."

"Well, Jesus, Gil, not to tell you how to run your business, but if it was me I'd pick him up first. That sure sounds like something to me. What if he takes off?"

"I'm not too worried about that."

"I don't know. It really sounds like something to me."

"Like what?"

"I don't know. Some kind of cult stuff, maybe. Jesus, the stuff that's going on anymore. I mean around here. All these people moving in here. My daughter tells me that some of the beach areas are so weird now that the ordinary kids don't go there anymore, because they don't know what's going on."

They race along. The town is small and in just another moment they are turning onto the street where Cormac lives. "This won't take long," Dulac says. "It could tell us what's going on with the brother. I mean he could have the simplest reason for lying."

"Initiation stuff," Mizener says. "Kids that age get into stuff like that. The little kid could be tied up somewhere. A lie doesn't sound good to me. Not at all."

"But it's not a good lie," Dulac says. "Is it? If something was going on and it was serious, wouldn't he come up with a story which wouldn't cave in half an hour later?"

"Could be. But maybe not. It still sounds like something to me."

"Well, we'll pick him up in a few minutes," Dulac says. "I'm not real worried about him taking off. Although I'd have to admit, he did act pretty nervous."

TEN

WRISTS REMAINING UNTIED after eating his hamburger and drinking his drink, the boy sits looking mainly down the front of his shirt. Turned to face him—they are parked in the furthest corner not of the Burger King lot but of a closed Dairy Queen further along the highway—Vernon is no more than a foot away. The windows are rolled up and the doors locked. Sometimes the boy turns up his eyes, to glance at Vernon. He does so when Vernon calls on him to guess his age, and tells him that he could be eighteen, or seventeen, even sixteen, but he isn't going to tell him exactly, so he won't be able to tell on him even if he wanted to.

"His name was Sal," Vernon says. "His regular nickname—what I came to call him—was Uncle Sally. He was a friend of my mother's, one of her boyfriends, the only one really, who came over to eat meals with us. He brought food over, and for a long time I thought he was the nicest man. In the end you could see how it was all a scheme he was working out, that he really was just out for himself, but it was some time before that became clear.

"I liked him, in the most genuine way, which, I believe, is why the whole thing hurt and left scars when it was finally over.

"What happened to tell it exactly, is he seduced me before he really seduced me, if you know what I mean. I mean he talked to me, and acted like he was my friend, brought me presents and things, brought my favorite foods, ice cream, things like that.

"Then, this one night when my mother was working. It was one of the first times I was left alone—when I was about your age. I was just falling asleep and I heard someone come in the house downstairs, and this voice called out not to be scared, that it was just Uncle Sally coming to see if I was okay.

"What was odd about this was that I think, deep down, I really knew what was happening and did my own share, you know, of participating. He sat on the side of my bed, and rubbed my foot and leg while he talked to me, and I certainly felt aroused before anything actually happened.

"Of course I liked him. He was always fun to be around, and this was no exception.

"He was rubbing me elsewhere by then—up over my thighs, over my belly—teasing me in the way he circled around. If I said I didn't want him to go ahead and cross the line, I wouldn't be telling the truth. It felt nice. I was twelve years old, and—well, believe me, it was nice, it was exciting.

"What he did then, he wanted me to show him where the bathroom was, because that's what he said he had to do was use the bathroom. Of course he knew where the bathroom was—just down the hall, on the way to my mother's bedroom—and it took me a while before I realized what a turn-on it was for him to stand at a toilet and have someone there, I guess, to look at him.

"I went along with this game. My little thing, it was sticking up just like a branch inside my pajamas, and I went along, down the hall, and turned on the light inside the bathroom door, just like he told me to.

"He finally touched me where I, of course, was longing to be touched. Passing into the bathroom, he said something about having known for some time what a little devil I was, and when I said, meaning what? he said, meaning this, and he reached down and felt me with his fingers through my pajamas and made some joke about keeping a flashlight there. He had me come inside and close the door, and standing at the toilet, he let himself out of his pants, and it wasn't to use the toilet at all, I realized in time, it was just to stand there while his thing got hard, and then he had me stand next to him, and so we ended up holding each other in our hands and rubbing together, you know.

"That's what always happened. I mean he took me back to my bed and did all kinds of things to me that were sensational, to be sure—although he didn't do anything or make me do anything, at least for a while, that hurt or that I resisted.

"For a while. He came over all the time after my mother had gone to work, and I think I really liked it for some time. Because I had this secret, and this secret friend, although he would get a little angry and pushy with me sometimes if I didn't want to play the games he liked to play or do things he wanted me to do. Still, it was a special thing for me, and even though he'd hurt my feelings at times, I always looked forward to him coming over after my mother had gone to work, and I was disappointed if he didn't.

"What happened then was he took too many chances. He came over this one Saturday when my mother was working lunch and was due to get home any minute. He had me go into the little downstairs bathroom with him and we were standing there and had to hurry out and look innocent as my mother came into the house.

"She wasn't fooled. I don't know if he knew it at the time, but I think I did. What happened then, it got to be another Saturday and he came over early again, and there we were in that little bathroom, playing dirty like that, and suddenly there was this knock on the bathroom door. I think my heart just fell all the way through me.

"It was my mother. In this real calm voice, she said, 'Sal, please come out here.'

"He walked out and I never saw him again after that. Not ever. Not even accidentally.

"When I went out, finally, what my mother said to me—well, it was awful—she called me a little fairy, and she said I had no idea how much she resented me, how much I was ruining her life. That was bad enough to have to hear, and know—and you know things like that, if you want to or not—but there were other things that were actually worse. Because she was there, even if she did feel that way about me. What hurt more, though, and hurts still, was being used and betrayed by someone I liked and admired—and being abandoned. I mean I knew by then that it was his own gratification he was after—even as a twelve-year-old I knew that—but what was hard to handle, endlessly after that, was not having him as a friend anymore. Because—if he was out for himself or not—he liked me. And I liked him. He cared about me, cared who I was. He wanted me to be someone special. When he was there, life had something.

"Which *isn't* to say that that's some kind of excuse. It's only to say that that's what it is. That's all."

ELEVEN

AT THE KITCHEN SINK, Claire is separating and rinsing icy chicken parts. She will start the chicken frying in the skillet as soon as she has the potatoes boiling. Perhaps she is a little angry. She isn't sure. She is going to fix a meal though, if anyone comes home to eat it or not.

It is something to do, and she has another reason. It is a notion which has entered her mind—Sunday afternoon dinner may be all that is needed, traveling on its aroma, to call things back to normal. It had worked before somewhere in her life. When feelings were confused and tempers loose from their stalls, mashed potatoes and chicken gravy seemed more effective than anything else at coating over the rawness.

To believe or to not believe? This is the issue with which she is struggling as she begins opening and closing refrigerator and cupboard doors in her preparation of a Sunday meal. Is something awful happening? Is something terribly wrong? Why did those detectives ask so much about Matt? What was that all about? What in the world is happening?

She can't believe anything. She won't, she decides. She will not let herself accept that something is wrong. She starts the burner under the potatoes, turns the chicken where it is draining. Faith. In itself, she thinks, faith may help them. Help Eric. It has to be real, though. She has to believe. If she can believe, her belief may be the force which will do the job, will save Eric, whom she knows by now, at this odd Sunday hour, to be the center of her everyday life, the mere reason she lives. She knows this as she unwraps a stick of Blue Bonnet margarine. Her faith alone, and the chicken, may be the force which will bring him running up the stairs any minute, running into the kitchen hardly out of his jacket, which will wake her from this dream as the screen door, which he never closes quietly, at last, finally slams, because no one else ever takes those steps so quickly.

The margarine is melting. Believe it! she is saying to herself. Do your best. Do better than that. Believe.

Dinner's under way, she'll say. *But it'll be a few minutes yet. Watch TV for a while. Do you have homework to do?*

She adds some oil, guides the melting margarine around with a fork. Where *is* Matt? Why *did* he take off like that? No, she thinks. Don't let yourself get carried away. Matt's a good boy. He's a fine boy. He'll be here any minute. They'll both be here. We'll eat dinner. In the servings of fried chicken, of potatoes and gravy, this nightmare will slide away, disappear into clouds of memory as a lesson against taking their love for granted.

She'll never work nights or evenings again, she thinks. She tells herself this as she adds tablespoons of flour to a mixing bowl, as she reaches for salt and pepper.

Matt, come home and help me, she says to herself then.

She turns the chicken. It is browning on one side. There *is* a call in its aroma, she realizes. There *is* something there; it is almost comforting.

On a sudden urge, she opens the kitchen window three or four inches. Let it go out, she thinks, even as the air pouring in is chilly. She raises the window another several inches, imagines the smell of frying chicken traveling throughout the neighborhood, between houses, behind garages.

She sets the table. Something stops her, though. An instant of hesitation. Two places or three? Three, of course, she tells herself. She directs the other thought to the back of her mind. She will never do otherwise, she is telling herself, as she places the three plates and three silverware settings on the table, as she moves around and the chilly outdoors air is passing over her legs, as she tries to ignore her moment of hesitation, her moment of not believing.

TWELVE

MATT HAS AN IDEA. As he pedals down Miller Avenue, coasting, sailing along for stretches at a time, a decisive feeling, a heroic feeling is rushing through him, through his fear, telling him where Eric is, telling him that he is going to discover him and set him free from a fallen beam, a jammed door, a collapsed floor that has him trapped. It's an old barn, as they knew it the previous summer, a semi-abandoned one-story outbuilding out along Little Neck Road, and pedaling hard now over the pavement, Matt finds himself increasingly filled with a sense of mission.

They kept a stack of skin magazines in the outbuilding and it was where they went, throughout the summer, to look at the photographs and pictorials, to joke, to masturbate. They talked of the girls they would give anything to have join them there, although the closest they ever came to launching any of their schemes and dreams was Cormac calling across a street once to two girls—did they want to go to an old horse barn?—the several of them laughing wildly at the uninformed expressions on the girls' faces.

Matt pedals on. Eric could really be here, he thinks. It's a perfect place to hide out. It's where he'd go, if he wanted to hide out. But something will have gone wrong. Matt will spot him through a pane of dark glass. He'll signal him. Eric will signal back. *Tap-tap. Tap-tap.* Using a log, using his strength, he will hoist and shift and pull; he'll set his brother free. Eric will be happy, as he leads him home. Maybe he'll ride him on the bike's handlebars. He can hear his mother exclaiming already, *Then here they were, coming down the street, both of them on that old bicycle, Matthew pedaling and Eric* . . . Vanessa will be there on the sidewalk. That big policeman will be there. *No big deal*, Matt will say. *I had an idea he'd be there.*

The outbuilding, though, when Matt arrives, shows no sign of having been disturbed. Leaning the bike against the front, lifting up the sliding door, as they always did, to slip in under, Matt can tell that no one has been here in some time. Within the old smell and the cool air inside, where there is only partial light from two filthy side windows, his heroic feeling disappears.

There is the familiar musty smell and he wonders if the magazines are still there. He shouldn't even look, he knows, yet he wonders if they are there.

"Anybody here?" he says.

It is a smell of earth, and perhaps of oil. The hiding place for the magazines was down between two upside-down oil drums. He thinks of Vanessa, imagines her at home or out in the air with her friend, Barbara.

His arm is trembling some as he reaches between the oil drums to where they kept the magazines. They always joked about rats being in there, but it is not in fear of rats that he is trembling.

He is taken with the feelings of last summer.

Gripping the three-inch stack in his hand, he has to turn them sideways to extract them from between the barrels. He places the stack on one of the barrels; dim light from a window is at his side. The magazines are familiar. Some things you never forget, he thinks, and from the covers he knows the contents of each. He is taken. The magazines themselves give off another familiar smell. Then he sees something he had not noticed before. On the cover of a magazine called *Swedish Exotica*, one of two naked women is black. He had not fixed on her before, but he does so now. Her breasts look almost streaked, as if dusted with beige powder; her nipples stick out like black fingertips. Even his hair feels aroused. He is taken.

THIRTEEN

THEY SEE THE BUILDING and slow down. A red bicycle is leaning there, against the front, and they don't stop at first. Almost soundlessly they roll by, to take a look at the unexpected object. From behind the wheel, Dulac has taken up the mike to radio the station. Mizener is looking back over his shoulder.

Dulac gets Shirley Moss on the line and says, "We missed the older boy at the house. We're on Little Neck Road now, at the mother's suggestion. We've spotted a bicycle. Looks like a regular ten-speed boy's bicycle. Red. Not new. Call the mother, Shirley, will you, and get right back to us. See if they own a bike. Over."

Coasting yet, passed by a car, Dulac checks his mirrors to be sure they are out of view of the old building. He avoids raising the car's brake lights until he sees that dips and curves in the road are in the way; then he turns around in silence in the two-lane road. They start rolling back slowly, waiting for the reply.

There is no sign of life about the building as it returns to view. The red bike remains in place. A pickup passes the other way. "Several kids involved in something would make more sense," Dulac says.

"Like what?" Mizener says.

"A game. Something that got out of hand. Who knows? The brother could be locked into not letting it out no matter what."

"Still wouldn't explain his lie," Mizener says.

"Oh, I think it could," Dulac says, irritated this time with Mizener being disagreeable.

As they pass the building, looking it over, Shirley Moss is back on the radio telling them that the older brother apparently has the missing brother's bike; the mother went down to the garage to check and the bike isn't there; she feels certain it was there when she looked last night.

"We're going to pick him up then," Dulac says. "This is probably him. You know our location; we need assistance, we'll let you know."

Off the air, forty yards past the building, Dulac coasts across lanes to the left shoulder to park. He turns off the car's motor and looks around through the rear window at the building. "Let's be careful," he says. "World gets stranger every day." As Mizener is removing, checking, and replacing his .38 police special in his shoulder holster, Dulac adds, against his better judgment, "Be careful with that, too. These are only kids."

Opening the door on his side, Dulac says, "You take the window on the side; I'll take the door there."

Leaving the car, not slamming the doors, removing their pistols and directing them skyward, they step back along the shoulder and approach the building. "Check the back," Dulac whispers. "See if there's a door there and let me know."

Mizener slips away then to step through weeds to the side and rear of the building. Dulac takes a position next to the large door in front, positioning his ear to pick up any sounds from within. He hears nothing. He looks over the bike, sees how battered and rusted it is.

Coming around the corner of the building, Mizener, pistol still in hand, has a smirk on his face. He whispers, "You won't believe it; this kid's in there jerking off."

"He's what?"

"Is there a back door?"

"I didn't even look. Doesn't look like it."

"Did he see you?"

"I don't know. I might have shadowed the window."

"Well, go back, and keep an eye on the rear, too. I'm going to call him out."

Dulac waits several seconds, as Mizener is gone. *Jerking off?* he thinks. Is he serious?

Firmly, to project his voice into the building, he says, "You. Inside. This is the police. Stop whatever you're doing and come out. Right now! Matt, do you hear me?"

When there is no reply, Dulac says, "Is that you, Matt? Tell me that you hear me. Right now!"

"I hear you," a voice says from within.

"Come out right now. Keep your hands up and in full view."

Still nothing happens. Dulac shouts. *"Now! Come out of there!"*

"I have to push this door," the voice says.

"Okay, push it! And come out!"

The door lifts outward and there is the boy, crouching to squeeze through, straightening as he is free of the heavy door and looking slighter and younger than Dulac remembers him looking. There, too, is Mizener reappearing as Dulac, returning his pistol to its holster on his hip, is saying to the boy, "Turn around, hands against the building, legs apart."

Matt complies, although he says, almost cries, "What's the matter?"

Dulac frisks him. "Straighten up now," he says. "Put your hands behind your back. Here, turn around."

Dulac handcuffs him, and turning him, almost spinning him back around, he says, "Matt, I'm going to read you your rights now."

"I didn't do anything," Matt says, with little strength in his voice.

"Matt, just listen to me," Dulac says. "You have the right to remain silent. You have the right . . ."

"I didn't do anything," Matt says, and he is beginning to cry.

"You're in there jacking off and your little brother's missing?" Mizener says. "Cut out the shit."

"Do you know where Eric is?" Dulac says. "Matt, do you know where your brother is?"

"*No,*" Matt says. "I don't know where he is."

"Matt, I'll ask you again. Do you have any idea at all where your brother is?"

"*I don't,*" Matt cries. "*I said I don't. I don't.*"

"When did you last see him?"

"Yesterday," Matt says. "Just like I said."

"How do you explain being here, doing this?"

"I don't know."

"Why're you out here jerking off in this building?" Mizener says. "Answer the question!"

"I don't know. I just was. I just was, that's all."

"Anybody else in there?" Mizener says.

"No."

"Was your brother in there?"

"No. You mean now?"

"Now—or yesterday? Was your brother in there?"

"No," Matt says.

"Would you be willing to take a lie-detector test?" Dulac says.

"*Yes,*" Matt says. "Yes. I haven't done anything."

"Matt, we're going to take you back downtown, to ask you some more questions. I just want you to tell me again if you know anything at all about the whereabouts of your brother."

"I don't."

"If you know anything, Matt, you better tell me right now."

"I don't," Matt says. "I really don't know anything. I don't."

"Sergeant Mizener saw you in there masturbating. Why were you doing that?"

"I don't know. I just felt like it. There're some magazines in there, that's all."

"Where were you last night, Matt, from six to nine thirty P.M.?"

"I don't know."

"You don't know? I guess you don't. Is anyone inside this building, Matt?"

"No."

"Okay. Neil, let's call somebody to keep an eye on this place. On the bike, too, and the door. We'll have to call the state police lab people. Come on, let's go; this way, Matt."

"I was just with this girl, that's why I lied about last night," Matt says.

"We'll talk about it downtown, Matt. Just come on, so I can get somebody out here. Neil, look through the windows while I go call. Don't touch anything. Just try to be sure there's no one else in there. You can prop that big door open to throw some light in there, but don't walk in; leave it all as clean as possible."

"There's nothing in there," Matt says.

"And you said you were with your friend Cormac last night," Dulac says.

"That's the only lie I told," Matt says. "It was because I was with this girl."

At the car, guiding Matt with his handcuffs into the rear seat, Dulac radios in, calling for a patrol car to come out and stand watch on the bike and the outbuilding. Then he radios the New Hampshire State Police in Concord, telling them he needs a lab crew to check out an old wooden building in the missing child case on which they have already received a bulletin.

With time to wait then, seeing Mizener walking back toward the car, Dulac looks at Matt in the back seat and says, "Matt, listen, let me give you some friendly advice. If you know anything, just come clean. You'll make everything a lot easier on yourself. Whatever it is."

"I don't know anything," Matt says. "I swear I don't."

Dulac keeps looking at him. "Your brother's missing," he says. "Something strange is going on, and I don't get it."

"Neither do I," Matt says.

FOURTEEN

VERNON'S DECISION is both spontaneous and a climax of all that has been running through his mind in these hours of driving here and there, parking to nibble food, sitting in the car, circling. He is so exhausted his bones and muscles ache and there is a sign preceding an intersection with a blinking yellow light: a right hand turn will take them east, in the direction of the ocean, of Portsmouth, of some possible resolution to this situation he has found impossible to resolve. A return, he thinks, to where it started, to the way things were.

He makes the turn. Portsmouth lies ahead. He is driving in the direction of the boy's home.

He glances to the boy, to see if he is aware of what has happened.

He drives along and glances again. The boy only sits there; he shows no change.

"Portsmouth is this way," Vernon says.

The boy looks around some, appears to give this some thought.

"We're going back to Portsmouth," Vernon says, and he adds, when there is no response from the boy, "What do you think of that?"

"You going to let me go?" the boy says.

"I want to," Vernon says. "And I will—as soon as I'm convinced you won't make trouble."

They roll along, as if in a momentary vacuum in which Vernon is waiting for confirmation. "You won't, will you?" he says at last.

The boy shakes his head. "No," he says.

"Are you hungry?" Vernon says.

The boy shakes his head in the same deliberate way. "No," he says.

Vernon drives along. The day is turning now. Evening is coming on. Vernon's eyes burn some, from lack of sleep, as he blinks them. He has to take a chance, he is thinking. He has to. There is no alternative. He has to trust the boy enough to let him go. There is no alternative, he tells himself.

FIFTEEN

THE INTERROGATION ROOM has white walls and ceiling, and one-way glass in the door; the room's lights are also white. There is an old wooden table without drawers, and several chairs. A tape recorder on the table is revolving soundlessly. Matt, waiting as if in a hospital for this to begin, sits in a straight-backed chair on one side of the table; Dulac is on the other side and Mizener is angled far enough away that he has to extend more than an arm's length every other moment, on every other question, to tap ashes into a metal ashtray from which gold paint has all but disappeared.

Matt sits with his hands between his legs or shifts them to the tops of his legs. He makes little eye contact. He looks mostly at the tape recorder.

Dulac says then, "Matt, tell me this. Have you had any of what might be considered to be sexual problems?" They have asked him about his father and school, their family move to Portsmouth eight years ago.

"What do you mean?"

"Let me rephrase that," Dulac says. "Have you had any bad sexual experiences? What would be considered to be unusual or abnormal sexual experiences? With men, say? Have you been accosted by men?"

"No."

"Relations with a girl?"

"I don't know."

"You don't know? How can you not know that?"

"I guess."

"Matt, I don't mean to pry into your private life. Really. I just want to get some ideas. About your sexual orientation. This whole business is strange and I'm going to find out what's going on. Now, when you have sexual relations with a girl, you either do or you don't, it's either yes or no. Have you?"

"Yes."

"Okay. Other than with a girl? How about men?"

"*I said no!*"

"Any men ever make suggestions to you, proposition you?"

"No."

"What about your brother?"

"Not that I know of."

"He ever tell you about anyone putting moves on him?"

"No!"

"Why is your face so red?"

"I don't know."

"You don't know?"

"No, I don't know."

"Okay. Do you have a girlfriend?"

"No. I don't think so."

"What does that mean? Yes or no?"

Matt hesitates, shifts or squirms. "No," he says.

"You'd like to have a girlfriend? There's someone you like?"

"I guess so."

"If you had a choice?"

"I guess so."

"You don't consider yourself gay?"

"No—heck no," Matt says.

"Okay. Let's move along then. Tell me, what were you doing—why?—in that building? I don't get it."

"I was just there," Matt says. "I was looking for Eric."

"Go on."

"I found those magazines."

"So?"

"I got carried away, that's all."

Dulac pauses. "You got anything so far?" he says to Mizener.

"Let's get to the witness," he says.

"Witness about what?" Matt says.

"Matt, we know you lied to us. Your brother is missing, and we know you lied to us about the time he came up missing. We've talked to someone who—"

"Cormac," Matt says.

"Right, Cormac," Dulac says.

"I told that one lie," Matt says. "That's all."

"Just one?"

"Yes."

"Which one? Explain which one."

"Just that I said I was with Cormac, yesterday, or last night, and I wasn't."

"Where were you?"

"I was with this girl. I said that's where I was."

"Okay, Matt. What girl? Where?"

"We were at the Mall; then we went to her house."

"What time?"

"I don't know. I guess from six thirty or so. We had a Coke, and then we went to her house."

"You had a Coke at the Mall; then you went to her house? Until when?"

"Nine. She had to go in at nine."

"In? You said you were at her house."

"Well, we were outside her house."

"Outside where?"

"We were in the garage."

"In the garage? Until nine o'clock? What were you doing in the garage?"

"We were just messing around."

"Okay. What did you do then? At nine?"

"Nothing. I just walked home. Then my mother called."

"What time did you get home?"

"About nine thirty, I guess."

"Okay, we'll get back to that in a second. You say you were with this girl from six thirty until nine. In the garage. What is this girl's name and address? Did you see her parents?"

"She won't be questioned, will she?" Matt says.

Dulac looks up at him, catches his eyes. "What do you think we're doing here?" he says. "Do you think this is a joke? She'll be questioned all right. Hell yes, she'll be questioned! We've caught you lying to us, okay? We've caught you in that building, playing with yourself. We're not here on a fucking Sunday afternoon because we don't have anything better to do. You say you lied because you were with this girl. You lie because you're with a girl! I think you'd better wake up. That's not a reason to lie. You think you're talking to the fucking parish priest? You think this is a chat with your fucking school counselor? Your brother is missing. Right now you are a suspect."

"Vanessa Dineen," Matt says.

"Where does she live?"

"Woodlawn Circle. I don't know the number."

"What did you do all this time?"

"We just messed around. In her garage. Like I said."

"I see. Okay. What about from five or so until you met her? From the time you left the movie theater?"

"I just walked around."

"Why did you leave the theater?"

"I was ticked off at Cormac, that's all."

"Why is that? What did he do?"

"He's just a jerk. We ran into this girl earlier, and she was with this friend of hers named Barbara, and I wanted to do something with them and he didn't want to. That's all."

"Did anyone see you, at this girl's house?"

"I don't think so."

"You were in the garage for *two hours?*"

"We were in the car there, her mother's car."

"Her people were in the house?"

"I guess so. There were lights on. We sort of sneaked in, then I sneaked away."

"Did you see your brother at any time throughout this time?"

"No."

"Do you have any idea where he is? Do you think he would have run away?"

"I don't know. I don't think so," Matt says.

"You don't think he'd run away?"

"No, not really."

"Well, where do you think he is?"

"I don't know. I was looking for him. I thought he might be hiding or something. Or like camping out, because he likes that kind of stuff."

"Why did you lie to us?"

"I don't know."

"That's not good enough," Dulac says.

"She's black," Matt says.

Dulac pauses, looks at him. "She's black?" he says. "This girl is black?"

"Yes."

"That's why you didn't go *in* the house when you went to her house?"

"Yes."

"They live on Woodlawn Circle?"

"Her father's in the Air Force, like a colonel or something," Matt says.

"Matt," Dulac says. "Listen to me now. Do you know anything at all about your brother's whereabouts?"

"I don't," Matt says. "I wish I did."

Dulac leans back. "Neil," he says, "why don't you go ahead and check out the girl. Double-check with her family, too; be sure this checks out. I'm going to take this guy home, then I'm going to get on those fliers. You have anything to add?"

"Not right now," Mizener says, taking up his pad and pencil. "Maybe later."

Dulac remains sitting, as Mizener leaves the room. He sits looking at Matt. Then he says, "Where would *you* go? Suppose you ran away. You know kids used to run away to join the circus or the Merchant Marine. Things like that. Where would you go; what would you run away *to*? You know what I'm saying?"

"I think so. But I just don't know. He likes the Navy and all that, but he's only twelve."

"Yeah. What about Florida, Disneyland, or something?"

"I just don't think so. He's not like that."

"Not like what?"

"I don't know. He's like—well, he doesn't go for kiddy things like that, like Disneyland. I don't think. He likes things like . . . the Marines."

"You like him, as your brother?"

"Sure," Matt says. On a gasp, then, he has to check himself against crying.

Dulac watches. Then he says, "Matt, is there anything at all you haven't told me?"

"No," Matt says.

Dulac shrugs. "It's okay to cry," he says then.

"Is he going to be okay?" Matt says.

"Let's hope so," Dulac says, getting to his feet.

Moments later, as the tape recorder is turned off and they are walking out to the car, Dulac says, "There's a chance he'll come walking in any minute. Especially if he's resourceful like you say, if he's the kind of kid who likes to camp out and so on."

Matt is nodding.

"In the meantime, anything you can think of about where he would go, however off the wall, I'd like you to let me know."

"Okay," Matt says.

"Try not to worry."

Matt nods.

"Don't worry about what color your friend's skin is, either," he says. "That's no big deal."

Matt nods, keeps walking next to the man.

SIXTEEN

HERE WHERE THEY have pulled up, in Hampton Beach, darkness looks to be falling quickly over both the horizon and the ocean. The line between the two is no longer distinguishable. Nor are there any other cars in this parking lot at water's edge, but a couple times Vernon has seen people pass on the wide expanse of sand, has seen their colorless shapes as they walked by. He is so tired by now, he feels he could fall asleep in seconds if he allowed himself to do so. He doesn't. He keeps stirring himself awake, and he says now to the boy, "You're part way home. Do you realize that? That's where you're going to be, in no time, if things work out."

"I won't tell," the boy says.

Surprised he has spoken, Vernon looks at him through the dimness. He had been so quiet, he had thought he might have fallen asleep.

"Do you know where we are?" Vernon says.

"No. By the water," the boy says.

"You don't know where we are?"

"At some beach," the boy says.

Vernon is looking through the windshield. For a moment now he hasn't seen anyone walking on the damp sand over which water and sky seem to be spreading a darkening haze. "I want to take you back," he says, "because I have other things to do."

"I won't tell," the boy says again.

This only makes Vernon disbelieve him, and he says, "How can I believe that?"

"You can, because it's true," the boy says.

"Would you meet me—if I asked you to meet me—on Friday night?" Vernon says.

The boy takes a moment. "I don't know," he says.

Vernon looks back to the gray dimness of sea and sky; a single chop of water looks unusually white. He likes the boy's answer. "Let's walk on the beach," he says. "I'll untie you—we'll walk down the beach and back—and if you show that I can trust you, then I'll take you home. I'll even buy you something to eat before I take you home. Are you hungry?"

"No," the boy says. "I'm not hungry."

"You have to be," Vernon says. "So don't lie."

The boy doesn't respond.

"We'll walk on the beach, as a test," Vernon says. If he takes off, Vernon is thinking, he'll just let him go. If he doesn't, all the better; he'll buy him something to eat and let him off in town. He'll take his chances.

Reaching, lifting away the sleeping bag, he unties the boy's ankles. "We're going to go walk on the beach," he says. "It's going to be a test to see if I can trust you. Just wait now, until I come around to your side of the car." Reaching past the boy, he pulls out the lock.

The boy sits there.

Getting out of the car, extending his legs, standing within the mist and odor of the ocean, the sound, a hundred yards before them, Vernon goes around to the passenger side of the car. This is all a game, he thinks. It's all a contest of wills, of deceptions, to see who will have his way.

"Okay," he says, opening the door, the dome light flashing on again. "Let's go. Do exactly as I say."

The boy turns his legs and starts to get out, to shift his weight to his feet, but he winces in sudden pain and his hand reaches to the car door. Still he pulls himself to his feet, is standing, and as if he understands the implications of his being hurt, says nothing, makes no complaint.

"Does it hurt?" Vernon says.

"No," the boy says.

"Let's walk then," Vernon whispers, closing the door as the boy takes a step and is clear.

Vernon moves a few steps along and watches, through the darkened, sound-filled air, to see the boy come with him. Trying, managing some steps, the boy cannot help grimacing, gasping almost silently in pain.

"You can't, can you?" Vernon says.

"I can—yes," the boy says.

Vernon holds, watching the boy, who also holds in place. Something is sinking in Vernon, as he says, "Forget it; you're just going to make it worse."

"I can do it," the boy says, moving over to him.

"You can't," Vernon says. "You can't. Just get back in the car."

"I just need to try!" the boy says. "That's all. *I can do it.*"

"Just get back in the car," Vernon says. "It's okay. You'll feel better in a while. Just get back in the car."

"*Please,*" the boy says. "*Please let me go.*"

"*Get back in the car!*" Vernon says.

SEVENTEEN

DULAC IS ON ROUTE 1, finishing up. He hits his directional signal still again, this time to turn into a Cumberland Farms grocery store–gas station. He has taken Route 1, while Mizener has covered busier coastal Route 1A, which passes near the beaches. Starting with businesses close to the boy's home, they have stopped to leave fliers where they have guessed a twelve-year-old boy might show his face—gas stations, mom-and-pop stores, pizza, donut, and hamburger counters, and supermarkets, almost anything that is open on a Sunday night in February.

This will be Dulac's last stop. Earlier, while two uniformed officers and two cadets looked into and around garages, dumpsters, yards, and cellar holes, he and Mizener canvassed neighbors, in the house where the boy lived and in several houses in each direction. They came up with a total of nothing, and within the past hour Dulac has been taken with doubt himself over the amount of activity he has initiated, and over the mere reality of the case. Is someone really missing? Is something really wrong? Momentum of a kind has kept him making his rounds. Even at six forty-five P.M., when twenty-four hours had passed since the boy was last seen and everything became altogether official, he found it difficult to acknowledge that they had a missing child case on their hands. Here—in Portsmouth. Everything seemed the same. Life, so far as he could tell, simply moved along, paid no notice.

Parking, turning off the motor and headlights, he takes a flier with him as he shifts out of the car. Ten minutes to eight. At eight o'clock another public announcement will be made, by radio. At that time, he thinks, as the news goes out and the case continues to become real it will have its impact. At eleven o'clock, if nothing comes in to change their plans in the meantime, an announcement will be made on channels 6 and 9, the two more or less local television networks. In tomorrow afternoon's newspaper then, the announcement of a missing child will be front-page news. Again, if nothing happens in the meantime. If the boy isn't in school in the morning, Dulac has thought, there won't be any question. A missing child. In its way, it's new here, and Dulac has no wish to explore the curious implications of newcomers and change. Theorizing makes for poor police work anyway, as he well knows.

The man behind the counter is elderly and frail, visibly frightened as Dulac identifies himself and begins his explanation. As he has cautioned Mizener, they need to pinpoint the attention of the people they talk to and get them to pass on the same concern to those who relieve them. Dulac uses the word *emergency.* He also says, "It's crucial that we have your help."

The man nods in the midst of his trembling.

"The photograph here is a problem," Dulac says. "You'll have to look closely at any boys this age. It's an enlargement from a class picture, was the best we could do in a short time. Will you look closely now?"

"Oh, yessir," the man says.

"Good. Now be sure anyone who replaces you is thoroughly informed."

"Oh, I'll do that."

"Good. It's not unreasonable at all that this boy, alone or with someone, might stop here. If you see him, or anyone who looks like him, you call that number."

"Yessir, I will do that."

Dulac glances at the flier, Scotch-taped now to the very top of the counter. There is the blurred photograph of Eric Wells and the line above his image, which says, HAVE YOU SEEN THIS BOY? "You see anything at all suspicious," he adds, "be sure and write down any license numbers."

"You bet. I will certainly do that."

"Thanks very much," Dulac says.

Returning to his car, shifting his elephantine legs into place, Dulac has the keys in the ignition and the motor running before he realizes that he has to decide what to do next. He is tired out, he knows that. And angry. Unsettled. That boy has been picked up by someone, he thinks. That's what it is. Some sonofabitch has picked him up. Has sexually assaulted him. Perhaps killed him by now. That's what they have to face up to, that something of the kind has come to town.

Dulac turns off the car motor. Returning the key to ON, he turns on the radio. He will sit here and listen to the news, he thinks. He will just sit here and think for a moment. Then, no, he will not be able to go home. He will have to do some time at the station first, to see if any calls come in and to be sure that things are set up for the night.

He sits staring through the windshield. Glancing to the side, he notices cars going by as usual. Things are going on as always. A blue Cherokee pulls in, parks next to the pumps; a woman in a brown vinyl jacket leaves the car to enter the store. The car is two-door, New Hampshire plates.

On the radio, he listens to a Ford commercial. At last—there it is, as the lead story:

> *Portsmouth police have no clues tonight concerning the whereabouts of a missing Portsmouth youth. Twelve-year-old Eric Wells of Cabot Avenue was last seen Saturday evening leaving Legion Hall on Islington Street where his mother works part-time as a cocktail waitress. He is four feet ten inches, weighs about one hundred pounds, and has brownish blond hair. When last seen, the sixth-grade student at Little Harbor Elementary School was wearing blue jeans and an orange-colored windbreaker-type jacket. Anyone with any information concerning the whereabouts of twelve-year-old Eric Wells is asked to call the Portsmouth Police Department at 421-3859.*

"Cocktail waitress," Dulac thinks, sitting there. Newswriters seem to think in such clichés, but otherwise okay. Let's see what happens now, he thinks. As he starts the car and backs up, though, he sees that the Cherokee is gone—he hadn't seen it leave—and the blank space next to the pumps sends a feeling of futility through him.

Backing around, pulling out, and heading downtown, he thinks how unsympathetic he could be to the person or persons who picked up the little boy, how cold-hearted. Because that's what it has to be, he thinks. That's what they have to face up to.

EIGHTEEN

FROM THE LIVING ROOM, Claire hears music—rock and roll—coming from the bedroom, where Matt has gone and closed the door. She thinks to ignore it, to force away again the suspicion that keeps coming up in her.

In the kitchen, without turning on the light, she stands at the window to look out. She wishes time would stop passing, that the world would stop its turning. It seems to be the first time she has ever looked out over housetops and trees and known that the world and all its life just kept going and would not stop, could not be stopped no matter what, on Sunday or on any other day.

Like the music down the hall behind the closed door, it went on. And on.

In the living room, she turns the television back on and sits down once more to watch—to stare at anything. She doesn't take in what she sees, however, for her thoughts are on the telephone. Will she hear it if it rings? Should she sleep out here, spend the night out here, to be certain she will not miss it if it rings? How can Matt hear it, she thinks, with that music playing? Does he even care? If he cared, would he sit in there or lie in there listening to music like that?

Maybe she should make some more calls, she thinks. And let Matt use the phone, too. But since that policeman told her to keep their line free and to stay alert for a call from Eric, she has stayed off the phone, and kept Matt off it, too, except when his friends have called, when she has ordered him to tell them that he cannot talk.

Going along the hallway, her thought is only to speak to Matt about anything at all that comes to mind. What she says to him, though, rapping on his door and walking in, is, "Do you have to play that so loud?"

"What?" he says, lying on his bed.

"Turn that down!" she says.

Reaching, he turns it down.

"My God, just turn it off!" she hears herself say.

"Do what?"

"*I said turn it off!*"

Silence follows. He has pressed a button; the music has stopped.

"Eric is missing and you're in here listening to that?" Claire hears herself say.

Matt doesn't say anything, nor does he look up at her.

"You've got to help!" she says to him.

"What're you doing?" he says then. "You're in there watching TV!"

"You want me to slap your face?" Claire says to him.

He looks back down.

She stands there. Then she hears herself say, against her better judgment, "Matt, there's something I'm going to ask you. And you have to tell me the truth."

Matt only lies there.

"Do you hear me?" she says.

"I hear you."

"Well?"

"Well what?"

"The way you're acting, I'm not sure you even care."

"Care about what?"

"You know exactly what I mean."

He lies there.

"Do you care about your brother or not?" she says.

"You don't think I care?" he says.

"I don't know if you do or not."

He lies there. He makes no move, gives no sign.

"I'm going to ask you this," she says. "Do you know anything about this, about what is going on?"

After a moment he says, "No."

"You don't know anything about what's going on? Matt, I do know some things. I'm not a fool."

He has, she sees, begun to cry. Against the hurt she feels, she hears herself say, "Matt, you have to tell me."

"I don't know anything," he says, crying.

Claire stands there; her own eyes are full. "Have you and Eric been doing anything you shouldn't have been doing?"

"No," he cries.

"Matt, if you have, you can tell me. I don't care what it is."

He only lies there.

"Well?" she says.

"There's nothing," he cries to her. "There's nothing."

She stands looking at him through her own tears. All at once she believes him and trusts him again, and she doesn't know what to say. Time, she sees again, in the space between them, keeps happening.

NINETEEN

THERE IS MOVEMENT. Sound. All at once, something is happening. They are at McDonald's. They are under the canopy, at the pick-up window. Vernon is reaching a five-dollar bill to the stainless steel window coming toward him, opening like doors to a bus; there is a McDonald's boy in a cap leaning forward, and a sound is screaming into him—"*Help me! I'm being kidnapped! I'm tied up! Help me!*"

He jams the gas pedal. He loses the five-dollar bill. The boy is trying, he sees, to open the door. The car is swerving, skidding, roaring all at once against its turned wheels. He will not know for an instant that he is simultaneously pressing brake and gas pedals in his frantic attempt to gain control of the car. The car hits and jumps a McDonald's side curb and slams as it slows down—as he sees that the boy is halfway, two-thirds out of the door, as he knows he has heard a squeal, a cry, a thunk.

Reaching, grabbing waist, pants belt with one hand, he pulls the boy back—as the car is rolling again—grips jacket and shirt to pull him in, hears another cry and sees *blood blood blood*, wails himself as he reaches past the boy to slam the door, wails and cries as he presses the accelerator again, as the car skids on over soggy grass, down over another curb, righting itself to a degree as it bounces onto the paved shoulder and swerves into the street lane, into the flow of traffic, and on, as he presses the gas.

He cries out, "*My God!*" And, "*My God!*"

He has to roll up his window but doesn't know how to use his hands.

He has to shift gears, but everything seems impossible. The car is laboring madly in first gear and everything seems impossible, but then he coordinates his arms and legs enough to shift the handle to neutral, then to third . . .

He rolls up his window.

He is afraid to look. He drives on, looking only ahead. He is afraid to look. He knows the boy is lying over in the seat. He knows he is bleeding. He knows the boy is bleeding. Everything is wrong. Everything is wrong. He can only cry, bawl out tears, and cry out then, "*How could you do that? How—oh God!*"

He moves to roll up his window again but it is already done.

"*I'm so mad at you!*" he cries out.

"*I'm so mad at you,*" he cries.

Vernon drives on, holding the steering wheel in both hands. There has been, he knows, no response from the boy. It is a head injury, Vernon knows from when he touched the boy to pull him back into the car. It is a head injury. *"My God, oh my God,"* he wails to himself as he drives along.

Vernon is resting now. The boy, slumped in the seat beside him, seems to be resting, too. In the Portsmouth Hospital parking lot, Vernon has parked and turned off lights and motor—in a flock of cars, at a distance—where he can see a single red neon sign, EMERGENCY, over an entryway, but he has not left the car.

The boy's breathing has settled—he has even spoken a few words, has mumbled *oh* and *no*—and the bleeding from the gash in his skull, above his ear on the left side, has stopped, and Vernon's own panic has settled back down from the unmanageable pitch it had reached earlier. Using a rag from under the seat, no matter that it isn't clean, Vernon has wiped at the boy's neck and behind his ear, as well as the vinyl seat, and he has pressed and wiped, lightly, at the stickiness in his hair around the wound.

However settled, Vernon remains nervous and has an idea in mind that he should not allow himself to fall asleep. Driving here because of the boy's injury, turning at several blue signs in the small city, then approaching carefully, circling at a distance as he entered a complicated patchwork of adjacent and lower and upper parking areas, he has since decided to just wait and see how things develop. Maybe it's a minor cut, he has thought. An amount of blood, but in need, finally, of little more than a Band-Aid. Nor is anyone going to bother him here, he has thought. The other places where he stopped and spent time—dirt roads, unused parking lots, the public lot at Hampton Beach—were places where the police cruise by and look things over. Not here, he guesses. Doctors, nurses, kitchen workers, and visitors; people never stopped coming and going at a hospital day or night, and its parking lots would not be on the rounds of the police.

Time passes. Vernon cannot help relaxing more than he feels he should. There is little activity. An occasional car enters and parks and someone walks to one or another doorway to disappear into one of the window-lighted buildings; an occasional woman or pair of women in white shoes and stockings emerges, appears all at once, and reverses the sequence of car doors slamming, motors starting, cars pulling out and away.

Vernon watches the boy. When he speaks to him, when he says, "Do you hear me? Listen to me!" the boy gives off a moan which seems to say he is taking in words in some dreamlike way.

Leaning to look more closely at the boy, though, and seeing that his eyes remain closed even as he seems to be breathing steadily, Vernon guesses he hasn't been heard at all. Vernon watches him. He decides he will not let himself fall asleep. Whatever it takes, and even if it isn't his fault that the boy is hurt, he will watch over him, and if he needs help, he will carry him to the emergency room. At whatever cost, whatever risk to himself.

At the very least, he thinks, he will place him at the door, and knock or ring a bell, and go on his way.

PART THREE
Police Work

MONDAY, FEBRUARY 16, 1981

AT MINUTES PAST FIVE A.M., Dulac telephones the special number at the special desk. He is standing barefoot downstairs in the kitchen, in his underwear, just as he turned his bulk from bed moments earlier. There is nothing. The officer on duty runs down seven calls that came in after the eleven o'clock news last night. Six are reported sightings of the boy, without identification or knowledge of present whereabouts, and one is a call from a man, refusing to identify himself, reporting the underground formation in the Seacoast area of a Men Who Love Boys chapter.

"Individual declined to provide any other information," the officer says as if reading from the log.

Dulac stands there, thinking he will start the coffee perking and return upstairs to shower and dress. But on a yawn his tiredness speaks to him, and he thinks he should return to bed to see if he can sleep another hour or so and to leave behind the weariness he feels. Sitting on a wooden stool in the near darkness, as if to think, he seems only to stare at the floor.

A sadness comes up in him. Age has become a presence in his life in recent years, and sitting here, staring at the linoleum floor, he wonders if this is what life has come to. This feeling of insignificance. This feeling of small successes adding up to overall failure. It seems not to be the missing child who is on his mind even as he is thinking that this could be where children would save your life. Children and grandchildren. They have none, will never have any, and in this moment he misses that part of life. A child's love at this time, this age in his life, would be life itself, he thinks.

To his surprise, he nearly weeps.

Life seems all at once to have handed him a massive deception, and he holds the fingers of his hand to his eyes, not to cry. What he'd like is to have some potting soil, and plants and clay pots to work with, to have something upon which to focus his attention.

He hears Beatrice and knows she is coming into the doorway. "Gil," she says. "What is it? Are you okay?"

He is more relieved than embarrassed to be caught in this way. "I'm just sitting here," he says.

"You are?" she says.

"Come on in," he says.

"Is it that little boy?" she says. "Are you upset because of that little boy?"

"Oh, I don't know," he says. "I don't think so. I just felt this rush, and I started to cry. Sitting here in my underwear. I think it's old age."

Beatrice doesn't say anything to this; she stands there in her nightgown, what little morning light there is coming through the doorway behind and the windows beside her.

"What it is," Dulac hears himself say then, "it's a feeling that life hasn't turned out the way you thought it would." He and Beatrice seldom if ever speak so seriously, and he takes a breath and proceeds carefully. "I *was* thinking about that little boy. I called in but there's nothing new. You have to wonder where he is at this time of day. I was thinking, too, wondering all at once, what I'd ever done with myself that meant anything. It came to me that if we had children, or grandchildren, and if they loved us—if I were a father and a grandfather—then I wouldn't have been sitting here in my underwear with tears in my eyes. Is that strange or not?" he adds in a different voice.

"No, of course it's not strange," she says.

"I guess not," he says. "But it seems that way. A person's life shouldn't be predicated simply on the basis of having children or grandchildren. Should it?"

"I don't know, Gil."

"Well, me neither. Are you up? I guess I'll start the coffee and go in early."

"I'll do the coffee," she says.

"I am kind of tense," he says. "I've been awake since a little after four."

"Let's just get up," she says.

Back upstairs in the bathroom then, where he and Beatrice circle and shift past each other at such times in a hippo and elephant ballet—using

144

sink, steamy mirror, tub shower, and toilet—Beatrice says. "Why does it have you tense? Is it because it's a little boy?"

"I don't know," Dulac says. "It has me upset, I know that."

They seldom mention or discuss his cases. Only when they are special and in the news, like this case, and then—usually—only indirectly. It's a habit they established years ago, when Beatrice realized that details of his work could place her in lingering states of anxiety and depression. Talk thereafter of work was usually of her job, the Con Merilees Real Estate Company where she worked at a desk, of property and prices, but mainly of the people who bought and sold. Dulac's work, like their inability years earlier to have children, was something both present and important, but seldom mentioned.

Now Dulac says, "The idea this kid is going to be in school this morning has bothered me all along."

"Was it your idea?" she says.

"I guess Adam started it," Dulac says. "But I passed it on to the mother and now she and who knows who else thinks the little guy is going to come walking into school this morning."

Beatrice, in her robe, is ready to leave the bathroom. "You don't believe that?" she says.

"What?"

"I said, 'You don't believe he'll be in school?'" she says.

"I wish I did," he says. "In which case I wouldn't feel so goddamn charged up. I'm so angry, I feel like hurting somebody."

TWO

VERNON OPENS HIS EYES, comes out of sleep, in a foul mood. He aches in his shoulders, in his back and neck, and in his hips from sleeping under and next to steering wheel and gearshift. He is chilled, and hungry. A faint watercolor wash of daylight is in the dark sky through the windshield; he needs to stretch and he needs to urinate, and he panics for a moment, feels himself giving in to a stomach and mind seizure, a paralysis of partial loss of control, partial madness, in his inability to extricate his trapped body and trapped self from the situation he is in. "Oh God," he cries aloud to the boy, raising no response, wanting to strike at him, disliking him for the first time. "Wake up!" he hisses at him. "Open your eyes! Why did you hurt your head! God almighty, you are ruining my life."

There is still no response from the dim form, the boy there in the seat beside him, and Vernon wonders if he has died. He doesn't touch him, though, as he twists around to try to extend his legs and back to relieve the cramped and trapped sensation. Nor does he strike him, as his feeling of panic gives way to mere anxiety and depression. Reaching a hand under the sleeping bag to the boy's chest, feeling his warmth, his life, he withdraws his hand and realizes it is disappointment he is feeling that the boy is alive. Vernon's face falls some as he sits there, as it crosses his mind that he felt love for the boy yesterday, and last night, while it is hate he feels for him this morning.

"This is your fault," Vernon utters to him. "I hope you know that."

To his surprise the boy makes a sound, takes in a breath at least, as if in response to being spoken to, and Vernon looks down at him. There is no other response though, and Vernon says nothing more.

Nor does Vernon urinate on the pavement outside the car, as he feels an urge to do. Urinating outside, even in the woods, is something he has almost never done and he restrains himself from doing so now, even as daylight is only partially covering the sky. And he thinks of the time, at summer camp, when he followed the trail through the woods at daybreak, to the bathroom-shower, and met the boy there his age and size who spoke to him of going to parties, who spoke to him of other things in life. Settled some, Vernon positions himself and starts the car's motor. He turns on the headlights. Have to get back to normal, he says to himself. He rolls out of the parking place, heads for the exit from the lot.

He will go back to the cottage, he is telling himself. He will wait for his housemates to leave for their classes, and then he will take the boy inside and feed him and clean him up. Then, when the boy is good as new again, he will somehow return him and put an end to all this. For he must put an end to it; he has no choice. No one can live like this. He will return him to where he picked him up or return him here to the hospital.

And go on his way. Take his chances that nothing will happen. How could it, he asks himself, if the boy doesn't even know his name? How could it?

What he has to do, he thinks, driving along, is return to normalcy. It's Monday now; the weekend is over. Weekends are fine for passion, for new experiences. For both, he thinks. But now he has to return to his studies. For that is what he truly loves. He has to extricate himself from this situation he has gotten himself into, and he has to guard against panic to do so. He has to use judgment, he thinks. He has to return things to normal.

"The weekend is over," he says to the form beside him. "We're going back to the real world."

THREE

AT HIS DESK, as seven o'clock is approaching, Dulac is reading and studying the special log for himself and considering ongoing steps in an investigation. In an hour or so, to look around and to be there when the principal and the teachers arrive, he will drive to the boy's Little Harbor Elementary School, to at least allow the school idea its chance, he thinks. Then he will place things in motion.

Returning the special log, he sees that the officer on duty is the same one who took the call on the Men Who Love Boys chapter alleged to be forming in the area. "Yes," the officer said, "it did seem like a local call."

"Tell me exactly what was said," Dulac tells him.

"Well, this guy said, 'Are you people aware that a Men Who Love Boys chapter is forming in the Seacoast area?' I said, 'Sir, could you give me your name, please.' He said, 'No, I won't do that. I just think you should be aware that one of these groups is starting up here, and that they do work to recruit young boys.' Then he hung up."

"He said 'work'?" Dulac says.

"Yessir, that's what he said."

Moments later, when Sergeant Mizener comes in, Dulac tells him to check out the group. "Check with Boston, but also Portland and Concord," Dulac says. "See what they can tell us. Explain our situation, that we have a twelve-year-old missing. Mainly, see if they think there's any connection. Make up a little report for me. Make sure you get the names of people you talk to, because we'll probably be following up on known sex offenders. What do you think? Does this make sense to you?"

"None of this shit has ever made sense to me," Mizener says. "It sure as hell is out there, though. I don't know why it wouldn't come here. Everything else is."

Well, Mizener isn't going to be much help, Dulac is thinking, even as he hears himself say, knows it is coming from his exhaustion, his lack of sleep, "Neil, goddamit you sound like some old reactionary cop. It looks clear now that this boy has been picked up. If we're going to get him back, or if we're going to avoid having some other kid picked up, we're going to have to play a little smarter game than that."

Mizener, reprimanded, appears stunned. "Why does it look clear?" he says. "I thought everyone expected him to show up this morning at school." Mizener is staring at him.

Dulac is surprised himself at his little outburst, which seemed to run away on its own. "Listen, I apologize for barking," he says. "I'm tired. But do you really think the little boy is going to show up in school this morning? You really think that?"

"You obviously don't. That's the word that came down, that's all I know."

Dulac pauses, checks himself from barking again. Then he says, "Shirley Moss will be here any minute; she can help with the calls coming in."

"She's going to screen the calls?" Mizener says.

"Right. You do the phone stuff, and we'll work together on other things. Right now, today—this afternoon and evening, too, when the paper comes out—is going to be our best time. Our most important time, if this little boy has been picked up. Somebody *has* to have seen something. Pass that on to everyone. Someone *has* to have seen something. The calls are important."

"Lieutenant, I think you are tired—if you don't mind my saying so. Maybe someone else should take on this case."

"*What?*" Dulac says.

"It's another case, Lieutenant, is all it is."

Dulac stares at him. "I know exactly what it is," he says.

Mizener makes an expression, dismisses the question.

"I'll be at Little Harbor School," Dulac says. "Anything comes in that looks halfway promising, I want to be called. Even if it's questionable, I want to be called."

Dulac starts to turn away and turns back. "I mean what I say about this being the best time. I don't want any screwups on that. I want people listening—carefully."

Going on then, he says to himself, Jesus, you are in a state of mind. At his desk, though, fixing his cuffs to his belt, slamming shut a drawer, still in debate with Mizener, he imagines saying to him, *Someone better take charge of you, because you sure as hell won't ever take charge of anything, because you're a fucking loser is what you are, a fucking reactionary cop.*

A moment later he is looking for Shirley Moss on his way back through the building—he'd like to have any kind of exchange with her, as a person he likes—but she seems not to be in yet. He goes on, strides along the driveway to his car at the rear of the building. Easy now, he says to himself.

FOUR

CLAIRE IS IN THE KITCHEN sipping coffee. The telephone is there on the wall. The cord is straight, the receiver down; nothing might interfere with its ringing. The telephone itself has become so alive for her it could be a squirrel clinging to the wall.

She is passing time, waiting for Matt to come around. She has no feeling to call him or to nag at him in any way this morning. She thinks he may have been awake as much during the night as she was herself. Let him sleep, she thinks. At least one of them may be rested and quick. She needs him too much now to have things deteriorate like they did last night. Still, he did act funny and if he'd only—just stop it, she tells herself suddenly. Just stop it.

She'll have Matt stay home from school, she thinks. It made no more sense for him to be in school than it did for her to be at work, and there was no way in the world she was going to spend her time packing boxes while Eric was missing.

The telephone rings and so startles her she can hardly speak or hardly hold the receiver as she moves it to her ear. It is her friend, Betty, who says, "Claire, what in the world—we heard this about Eric on the radio—what in the world is going on?"

Claire tries to explain what has happened and when, explains that the police believe he might show up in school this morning, that she did not call yesterday because she didn't want to tie up the phone, that the police told her not to tie up her phone. She promises she will, she will, as Betty tells her to feel free to call on them for anything, anything in the world. "Don't you hesitate a second," Betty tells her. "I mean that."

Claire is relieved to be off the phone, to clear the line, and at once wishes she could have continued talking to her friend. She will call her

149

later, she thinks. She can hear herself explaining to Betty how happy she was that Eric was back in school where he belonged, so relieved there was no way in the world she could bring herself to be angry with him.

She and Matt can call in together, she thinks. When he comes out— any minute now—and when people are in their offices, around eight, they'll both call in. Well, she'll make the calls, she thinks, even as the thought raises her old childhood fear of having communication with people who stamp grades and give orders.

Well, Matt, she thinks. Come on now. You can't just stay in bed like this. I have to rely on you. You have to help me.

Stepping over, she looks down from the kitchen window, as if— again—to see something on the sidewalk. Cars are parked along the curb down there as usual. The sky is overcast this morning. It looks more like February, she thinks, but she turns away from a thought of the temperature dropping.

She calls in. At seven fifty, as she knows her shift is under way, she calls to tell the time clerk she will not be in this morning and maybe not all day. "My son is missing," she says, feeling she is taking advantage of something to get out of work.

"You're not calling in sick?" the man says.

"Well, no," she says.

"Will you be in tomorrow?" the man says.

For a moment, envisioning the pencil-thin clerk, Claire doesn't understand. "What?" she says.

"Will you be in tomorrow?"

She tells him she'll let him know, and a moment later, glancing from the kitchen window again, she realizes he did not take in or did not care what she had said about Eric.

Does anyone care? she wonders. Why should they?

Eight o'clock. Eight oh five and eight ten. She wishes Matt would come out, but he doesn't.

Calling the high school then turns out to be easier than expected. A woman with a Southern accent repeats her message. "Matthew Wells will not be in school today?"

Time passes. She is building, she knows, to another telephone call— the call to Eric's school—even as she wishes they would call her first. Why should they? Was Eric so important? If he went to school, and went to his homeroom like he should, why would anyone call to tell her so? She will wait. When homeroom is under way, after eight forty, she will call and ask if someone will check Mrs. Dubois's room, to see if Eric Wells is there this morning.

Eight twenty-five. Almost.

"Matt," she says, at last, after standing a moment in his bedroom door. "Maybe you better get up now. I didn't want to wake you, but I thought I should—even if you don't go to school. Which I don't think you should do."

"What?" he says.

"Matt, just please get up," she says. "I need you to talk to."

Claire realizes in a glance that only one of the two small beds has been used. Matt, turning to extend his feet to the floor, is as subdued as she is, and she feels stricken in this moment over being suspicious of him yesterday. She can see, she knows very well, that he is only a boy. He's older than Eric, but he's only a boy himself, his hair pressed sideways with boyish sleep.

In a moment, in the kitchen, hearing faucets running in the bathroom—full blast, as Matt always runs them—she wishes she had left him alone. She had only wanted his company, and now she isn't so sure she does.

Eight thirty-five. Really, eight thirty-six. Okay, she thinks. She can find out now. Here in a simple phone call, she can find out what she has been waiting to find out. Maybe the news will be good, like the one policeman suggested. She can have a smile for Matt when he comes into the kitchen. Eric's in school. And get Matt off to school, too. Get herself off to work.

Her call to Eric's elementary school surprises her. A woman who answers says to her at once. "Oh, Mrs. Wells, the message is just going out on the PA system. We are so concerned. Can you hear that?"

The sound of panic in the woman's voice kindles Claire's panic. Over the phone she hears, ". . . *to the principal's office immediately. This includes anyone who may know or have heard anything at all of Eric Wells's whereabouts. Report to the principal's office immediately.*"

Claire holds the phone, chilled. She hears movement and talk over the receiver, but they seem to have forgotten her. Should she hang up? Her question has been answered; should she just hang up?

She waits. At last, as the receiver is picked up, another woman says to her that she is Mrs. Berry, the assistant principal. "Mrs. Wells, we'll do everything we can," the woman says. "We all know how you must feel, and we'll do anything and everything we can. Lieutenant Dulac is here right now and is going to talk to Eric's class. He believes someone might know something and feels the children could know more than they think they know. Mrs. Wells, we just pray that Eric is all right. We just pray that he'll be back in school tomorrow, or this afternoon even, and that everything will be all right."

Waiting for Matt to appear, Claire sips more coffee. She doesn't want to tell him. The new fear at school has frightened her so oddly she feels afraid that in telling Matt the news she may break apart, like glass.

A curious thought comes to mind. Of all the children in his class who would help find someone, it was Eric who would do the best job. Eric would know what to do. Where to look. How can it be that he isn't there? His love for her is too strong, too natural, she thinks, for him to leave her feeling hurt like this.

As Matt walks into the kitchen, she says, "I called Eric's school. He's not there."

Matt nods. He continues to the cupboard.

"The police are there right now," Claire says. "Matt, it scares me so much, my heart is just stopping."

"I'm going out and look some more," Matt says.

"I think you better stay in, since you're not in school."

"No," Matt says. "I'm going out. I am. I don't care what anybody says."

Claire doesn't say anything. He has never spoken to her in such a way.

"I'm the one who knows where he could be," Matt says.

He has removed the gallon of milk from the refrigerator, a box of Wheat Chex from the cupboard.

"Where are you going to look?" Claire says.

"I don't know. Everywhere. I'm just going to look."

"Well, let me fix you some toast, so you'll have something warm," Claire says.

Matt eats standing up and in hardly a moment, it seems, he is gone and Claire, cleaning up the table, rinsing his dishes, is missing him. His sudden manliness has called up some strength in her, though. Thank God for Matt, she says to herself. Forgive me for doubting him. Be strong, Matt, she says to herself. Bring Eric home.

She stands at the window again to look outside. But nothing is happening out there. There is only gray stillness. It seems the world is not moving, but she knows it is.

The telephone rings behind her.

She turns, stepping to it, realizing at once that something is wrong. It is the timing; there is no second ring.

Silence.

The telephone doesn't give its second ring.

It holds to the wall, refusing in its smugness to ring again, to set her free.

FIVE

VERNON IS STANDING in his bedroom, when someone taps on the door. "What is it?" he says.

Duncan opens the door, leans in. "You're here!" he says.

"I'm here," Vernon says.

"Your car's not here. What's going on with you? Did you just come in?"

"I parked down the road a ways."

"Why'd you do that—if you don't mind my asking?"

"The morning sun will warm up the car."

"Even when it's overcast. And where were you all night—if I might ask that?" Duncan is grinning as if in anticipation of a punch line.

Vernon tries, on a near smile, to accommodate. "Am I being cross-examined?" he says.

"You *do* have something going, don't you?"

"Who knows?" Vernon says, managing the faintest of grins.

"I knew it!" Duncan says. "I knew it! You weren't in bed here, you had to be in bed somewhere."

Vernon only looks, as if slyly, as Duncan says, "Well, that's good, more power to you," and closes the door on a laugh, adding, "See you later."

Vernon resumes waiting. The deception allows him relief, but only for a moment before the anxiety he has been feeling so endlessly is in him again. Well, it's safe to go out and use the bathroom now, he thinks, while they are preparing to leave; still he remains reluctant. He has no wish to face Leon and risk the questions which might be thrown in his face.

He waits, listening for the sounds which say they are slipping on coats, taking up books. One or two of them—he is not sure which—have nine o'clock classes on Mondays, which will have them leaving between fifteen to and ten minutes to the hour, for their frantic ride to school. It's how they do it.

At last the back door opens and closes. Someone has gone outside. There is movement in the voices—from sink to doorway to kitchen table. A car motor coughs and starts. Then the door opens again—but its closing doesn't follow.

Vernon listens carefully. At last the door is closed, and there is a stillness and he believes he is alone. He listens another moment. Opening his bedroom door, he sees no sign of anyone. He hears the car backing around then and, at the window, sees its exhaust twirl as it goes down the gravel road, past his car where it is parked off the road in something of a clearing, and out of sight. He stares at the front of his car, which looks like the chrome face of an animal in the trees. The face holds there. It makes no sound or movement, as it seems to him it could if it wanted.

Moments later, having used the bathroom, having brushed his teeth and washed his face, he is hurrying out and along the gravel road in his shirtsleeves. He hears the sound only of his own feet on the gravel, the jingle and click of his keys as he opens the car door. Inside, door slammed, he hears moaning all at once behind him.

"Eric," he calls out. "It's me. Are you okay?"

There seems to be an answer, a sound, but he doesn't know what it is or how to respond to it. Starting the car, Vernon feels some relief. The boy is there, and he may be conscious again. At the same time, of course, there is pain in whatever he had tried to say.

Pulling out, Vernon slips back along the road to to the cabin and pulls in next to Duncan's car, as always. Quickly, at the back of the car, he unlocks the trunk and its lid springs into his hands as he lifts it.

The boy is squinting at him. His face is right there, and he is squinting—his eyes filled and swollen—at the same time he is gasping to cry. "Oh, let me out of here—," he is crying.

"I am," Vernon says. "I'm letting you out. That's what I'm doing. Everything is going to be okay." At the same time he feels anger and impatience with the boy for asking him to do anything.

Lifting the sleeping bag from on top of him, Vernon begins untying the necktie from the boy's wrists, as he continues to cry, as he pushes out his legs, which are also tied at the ankles.

"You're going to be okay now, so no more crying," Vernon is saying as he works on the necktie at the boy's ankles. "I'm going to fix you some breakfast and get you washed up—and then you're going home. Do you understand? You're going home, and you're not going to say anything to anybody! Do you understand that?"

Vernon reaches an arm under the boy's shoulders, to lift him out of the trunk. There is a small dark spot where his head had lain. Nor does the boy help, as if he has no strength or has gone back to sleep. Vernon looks at his face. His eyes are only partially open now and he looks but semiconscious; a gasp comes from his mouth as he is lifted and his eyelids move.

"Come on," Vernon says, turning with him in his arms. The boy's face reacts some to this. "Come on, no more crying," Vernon says to him.

The boy cries, "I can't . . . lift my legs."

Vernon kisses his cheek. The boy makes no response to this. Walking with him, Vernon says, "Some warm food and a bath and you're going to be fine. I'm going to take you home then. Your legs are just cramped."

Making his way to the cottage door, feeling with his fingers to find the doorknob, Vernon is saying, "We're going to get everything straightened out now. You're going to be fine, aren't you?"

The boy doesn't say; his eyes still do not appear to open all the way as Vernon carries him inside. "Aren't you?" Vernon says.

The boy's eyes roll yet again; they appear and roll away, and he doesn't respond.

SIX

DULAC FEELS A LITTLE stage fright. He is at the front of Eric Wells's homeroom, waiting for the children to settle and to be introduced by the teacher. They are merely children, he thinks, as a thought of Men Who Love Boys crosses his mind. Some are quite small, some bigger; they are the singular investments of their parents, he thinks. All things to their parents, more important than houses or jobs or cars. More important than anything. Was it true that they gave life its final meaning, as he had feared that morning?

While the teacher tells them about Eric, and explains who he is, he feels a little like a child himself, about to have to stand before the class and give a talk. When he has taken his place before them, though, and has said, "I'm here to ask you guys, you girls, too, to be my eyes and ears," and sees them staring back at him, his stage fright gives way to other concerns.

Smiling, afraid they might be intimidated by his bulk, his general homeliness—thinking it is a job better done by Shirley Moss—he takes in a breath, like a child doing a report before class, and gives them his heartfelt pitch. Only true urgency within will create the same without, he has told himself.

"Listen now," he says. "Listen to me, boys and girls. *Someone knows something.* Someone had to *see* something. Or they *heard* something. No matter what has happened to Eric, or where he is. Someone saw something. If he ran away—which we don't think he did—or if some person or persons picked him up, probably in a car, or if someone got him to go into a house. *Someone. Saw. Something.* Eric had to walk, or he had to ride. Willingly, perhaps, but maybe there was a struggle. Someone knows something—because someone saw something or heard something, and police work has to do with getting through to what that person saw and heard—"

"What if nobody did see anything?" one boy asks.

"Even if the person doesn't know it," Dulac says, "they did. Someone *saw* something. It's always that way, believe me."

"What if he just ran away?"

"We don't believe he ran away—" Dulac says.

"Why not?" one or two children ask.

"Well," Dulac says. "He didn't take anything with him. No possessions. No money. No extra clothes or food. Nothing. Which indicates to us that he probably did not run away. Do you understand?"

"All that Green Beret stuff he liked," a boy calls out. "He even wrote—once—that they go in the woods—with nothing—and eat snakes to stay alive."

The children hoot and laugh some, as Dulac says, "Wait, though. Those guys have knives and weapons. It isn't as if they don't have anything, do you see?"

"Green Berets have all kinds of stuff!" another boy calls out.

"Still," Dulac says, "that's the second or third time now I've heard that Eric has a special interest in military—"

"It's just about all he ever writes or reads about," the teacher says. "If Eric has a story to write, it's about a man with a parachute, jumping from a plane. When we used reference materials, he looked up the history of hand grenades—really. In art class, I know, what he's been drawing have been soldiers shooting rifles . . ."

The teacher has them all smiling, Dulac included, and he smiles again moments later, as he finishes his drive downtown and turns into his parking space behind the police station. He pauses. If the boy was that interested in the military or in survival, he wonders, couldn't it mean that he is off somewhere testing himself?

No, he thinks. No, he'd still have taken things with him. A flashlight. A pocketknife. A rope.

Matches! he thinks, going into the building. Make a point to ask his mother to double-check if any matches are missing. Then he thinks, these were just children. Eric is one of them, and they are children, and aren't they just about capable of anything? It is then, in a flash, that Dulac believes he understands why someone might steal a child, to give meaning to his life, a thought which suddenly frightens him.

Through the swinging gate, walking to the special desk, he is confronted—all at once—by the cadet on duty, by Shirley turning from a computer console a dozen feet away, by Mizener entering from the corridor, and he has to hold up his hands to sort them out.

From the cadet he learns that the boy's brother is back in the squad room. "He has an idea where the boy might have gone," the cadet says.

"Okay," Dulac says, imagining he is going to hear about something crucial at last, as he turns to Shirley Moss.

"I've studied the newspapers for the past four days," she says. "Like you said. The only thing I've found is a movie—it's a triple X movie—called *Children in Bondage*—playing in that state-line place called The Sex Barn."

"Children in Bondage?"

"That's right. I called to see if it's *still* playing, but there's no answer."

"We'll check it out," Dulac says, turning to Mizener.

"We've got a guy," Mizener says. "Called in, says he offered Eric Wells a ride outside Legion Hall Saturday night."

"You're kidding. Say that again."

"What I said. This guy called, says he heard the report on the radio this morning. He remembered leaving the Legion Hall on Saturday. At about six forty-five. He says he offered the Wells boy a ride! He says he knows him. Says the boy turned him down."

"I bet," Dulac says.

"Can you beat that?" Mizener says.

"When did he call; did it just come in? Where does he live?"

"He called at eight twelve, so he checks out on that okay—right after the news."

"Why wasn't I called? Eight twelve? I hadn't even left here by eight twelve."

"It's okay. The cadet who came on thought it was routine or something."

"It's *not* okay. Our cadets are *too fucking polite!*" Dulac says. *"Goddam it!"*

"I've checked the guy out," Mizener says. "He's single—has no record. I was just going to pick him up and wanted to know if you want to go."

"I do," Dulac says. "But I can't. I have all these things to get rolling. No, I'm going to go. Just hold on a second. Let me see what the brother has to say—"

In the squad room, where Matthew Wells is sitting at one of the long wooden tables, Dulac says, "What's going on? Come on in my office; I'm in a rush, I'm afraid. I'm glad you're here, though. I was meaning to call

157

you. I want you to make a list for me of all your adult friends. Men you and Eric would know. Coaches, Sunday school teachers, neighbors, family friends—anyone like that, okay? Anyone you've ever known."

In his office, where Dulac motions to Matt to sit down, he says, "What is it? What's cooking?"

"I thought of something," the boy says.

"Okay, go on. What is it?"

"Well, this might sound kind of dumb, or something, but you said— you told me, you know, to try to think of things that someone would run away over, or run away *to*. You said, like kids used to run away to join the circus—"

"Right."

"Well—I'm not so sure about Eric—but what a person would run away for . . . would be a rock band. You know, to be the sound man or something. The equipment man. Just about anybody I know would take off if they had a chance like that. I would," he adds.

Dulac is watching him, taking in what he is saying. Okay, he says to himself. That makes sense. "Okay, Matt," he says, deciding to use his name. "That makes sense. Have there been any rock groups around; was anything like that around on Saturday?"

"Not that I know of."

"What about the high school?"

"I don't think so."

"Okay. We'll check it out. It's a good idea. It's a smart idea on your part. We'll check it out and I'll let you know. Okay? You check it out, too, okay?"

"I know why, too," Matt says then.

"You know why about what?" Dulac says.

"Well, why you'd take off with a group like that."

"Why is that?"

"It's so you'd be part of something. So you'd belong to the group, instead of just watching them. You'd be on the inside."

"On the inside of what?"

"Everything."

"As opposed to being on the outside?"

"Yeah."

"Is that how you feel—on the outside?"

"I guess I do."

"You have your family. Your mother and your brother."

"I know," Matt says.

Dulac looks at him, notes to himself that the father's whereabouts is unknown, has been for eight years. Then he says, "Matt, your idea is fine.

We'll check it out. You have any other ideas, be sure and let me know. And do that list for me, too."

As the boy leaves, Dulac holds at his desk for the moment, looking for something elusive to fall into place, and goes on his way when it doesn't, thinking what a pathetic thing that was for a kid to say, what an unfortunate way to feel, to look to a fucking rock band as a place to which to belong.

SEVEN

VERNON IS AT THE STOVE, stirring a package of chicken noodle soup into lightly bubbling water. The boy is across the room, lying on his side on the ratty couch. With a warm washcloth, Vernon has cleaned the head wound. Thinking now to cover him, Vernon turns the gas burner down to a blue circle and goes to his bedroom to retrieve a blanket.

The boy lies there; he gives no sign of consciousness, although it is clear, in his faint periodic gasps, that he is breathing steadily. Vernon chooses to believe he is asleep. Now that they have settled in and Vernon has had some coffee, he feels less frantic and less frightened.

"How does your head feel?" Vernon says to him.

There is no response. Vernon leans forward, to look once more at the head wound. While he washed the wound and the surrounding hair earlier, the boy's gasping had increased and he seemed once to all but wake up—which allowed Vernon to continue to believe he was merely drifting in and out of sleep.

"I wish you'd wake up," Vernon says now.

There is no response. Vernon looks at him. Pulling the blanket to his shoulders then, leaning down, he kisses his cheek. Then he gets to his feet.

He stirs the soup. What are you going to do? he asks himself.

The wave of fear, familiar by now, comes back up in him.

He glimpses the impossibility of everything.

His worry lessens, though, as he stands stirring the soup. Turning off the burner, he goes to the couch and uses a pillow to prop the boy into a partial sitting position. With a coffee mug a third full, some milk added, he returns and sits beside the boy.

The soup works. He tries a partial spoonful, and although part of it runs over the boy's chin, a taste gets down and—to Vernon's amazement—the boy's eyes move and he begins to come around. "Here you are," Vernon says, as the boy's eyes continue to open groggily and close again.

"Another little taste now," Vernon says. The boy takes in the warm liquid from the spoon. His eyes seem to roll some but return to center as he continues to take the sips Vernon lets slide into his mouth. Vernon's hopes are coming up again, trying to take hold.

"There you go," Vernon says. "Now you're going to be okay. This is better. Now you're going to be okay."

Finishing the third of a cup of soup, Vernon goes to the stove for more—adding another dash of milk—but when he returns, the boy's head has rolled back to the side and he appears once more to be dozing. Vernon puts the soup down and leans close to feel and hear the boy's breathing. It seems more even now. He's resting, Vernon thinks. He's resting. Of course he's tired. Who isn't tired?

Back at the stove, however, taking spoonful sips of soup himself, he feels his relief interrupted again by waves of fear. With sudden clarity, options cross his mind. He can return the boy home. Or he can take him to a hospital. He will have to do something. He can't keep him here.

He may have to do something more drastic, he thinks, as if on the sudden passing of a breeze.

In the next moment, as if he is another person, he raises another spoonful of soup to his mouth. You are going crazy, he says to himself. You have to get this over with. You have to. You should be in school.

He hears something. His scalp tingles. Looking to the door, to the windows, he sees nothing, hears nothing. His heart had stopped, is thumping now. He tries again to listen.

He exhales and inhales but seems to have lost his strength. Checking to see that the boy hasn't moved, he steps to the windows which are close to the door. Trying to look out from beside the windows, he sees nothing. Moving into the entryway between doors—where it is cold—he looks along the driveway-roadway, and to that side of the house, but sees nothing there either. The sound was right here, he thinks. Well, it could have been an animal, he thinks, deciding to step outside. Even a bird.

Outside, he startles nothing. There is only the stillness of the overcast air. He looks around, down over the pond, which is as gray once more as the sky. A wooden boat is upside down on the bank there, where it has been all year.

Nothing. There is nothing around but the depressing color of ice, here and there. The chilled air and gray sky. His life; this impossible situation.

He looks to the trees and above the trees, in the direction of the university. He is missing two classes this morning. He is missing his time in the library, too, hiding at a desk in the second floor stacks where he usually spends much of the day writing papers or studying or daydreaming. Mainly studying. His life, as he has known it, is not going on as it had before.

The fear which passes through him then affects his eyes. What is all this? he asks himself. Dear God, what is all this? Does he really think he can just walk away from this?

EIGHT

MIZENER DRIVES. As he has arranged, they meet the man at the main gate to the Portsmouth Naval Shipyard, and he seems only too willing to return with them to the police station. Dulac's thought is that an innocent person would want only to make his statement, and turning to look at him in the back seat, he says, "Mr. Nagy, you're not going to lose pay for this, are you?"

"I'm on the clock," the man says.

In a moment, Dulac glances back again, as Mizener drives. The man is about forty, with a bony face and thin blond hair; that steak sauce guy on television but harder-looking, Dulac thinks. "We need to make a list of everybody who was in Legion Hall," Dulac says. "It'll take a little time. And we have some photographs we'd like you to look at. And we want your statement on tape. That is if you don't mind."

"Photographs of what?" the man says.

"Known sex offenders," Dulac says, glancing back. "Right now you're the last person we know of to see Eric. Maybe one of these people was at Legion Hall. There's always a possibility, too, that you saw something you don't know you saw."

Dulac doesn't especially like the man. He sure as hell knows they're after more than a statement, Dulac thinks, and he's sitting on it, being coy about it back there. Being coy about something. "You're single, Mr. Nagy?" he says.

"Divorced."

Eyes front again, Dulac sees Mizener side-glance at him, but reads nothing in his glance.

At the station, in the interrogation room, they hear from the man how he noticed Eric Wells walking on the sidewalk, recognized him as someone he had seen a number of times at Legion Hall, and pulled over to offer a ride. The boy shook his head and said, 'No thanks.' That was it. No one else was around. And no, he had not talked to Eric Wells at Legion Hall, and he wasn't sure if he had seen him there or not, although he thought he had. He was certain he had seen him at other times, usually around the pool tables.

Down the hall then from the interrogation room, where they have the man making up his list, Mizener confides to Dulac, "Lieutenant, this guy seems pretty straight to me."

"Meaning what?"

"Just that he doesn't look like anything other than a good citizen who has come forward with some information. I don't see why we should give him a hard time."

"Neil, we're going to read him his rights, and we're going to polygraph him."

"*We're going to what?*"

"The guy is thirty-eight years old. He lives alone. Saturday night, by his admission, he stops to offer a ride to a twelve-year-old boy. If I did *not* verify someone presenting that kind of pattern, man, I'd be derelict in my duty."

"And he called in to offer help."

"As you know, it would not be at all unusual for a person to attempt to be close to an investigation of his own crime. That's nothing new. It's consistent. It's *not* contrary. It's *consistent.*"

Mizener looks at him, the faint smile on his face not friendly.

"The guy may well be what you say he is," Dulac says. "I can see that. But we have to clear him. We don't have any choice. I'm going to have the brother polygraphed, too, because he's not out of the woods yet either, as far as everything is concerned."

"You still think the brother's a suspect?" Mizener says.

"No, I don't," Dulac says. "But it's not a runaway anymore. Kid's been gone *two* nights now. He did not show up in school and what we have, we have to admit, is a probable abduction. This is where we're supposed to earn our pay. We'd never be forgiven if we did not polygraph the brother. Certainly this guy. We'd really be small-town if we just took this guy at his word."

"Whatever you say," Mizener says.

"I'll be right there. There's something I have to do before I forget."

Returning along the corridor to the front of the station, Dulac crosses to the special desk set up for the case and motions to a second cadet who is on duty there during the day.

"You guys, listen to me," he says, getting the two together. "A call came in this morning, at eight twelve, on a man *admitting* he was the last person to have seen Eric Wells. Admitting he *offered* Eric Wells a ride. For some reason I wasn't notified about that call. I don't know why I wasn't notified. My guess is that some people don't quite believe this is for real, and I'm up to here with that number.

"We've got to get sharp. If somebody has picked up this kid, he's not going to be a goddamn green-eyed monster with scales. Okay? He's going to be somebody like you or me. And somebody like you or me *has seen* something or *knows* something. If we're lucky, and *listening,* that person is going to tell us what we need to know.

"I don't mean to be mad at you. But you have to stop being so fucking *thoughtless.* At the slightest whiff of anything, from now on, you call me. Call anybody. Ask any question. Call the governor if you have to. Wake him up. Wake me up. Wake anybody up. That's your job. You want the world to make fools of us? Well, I don't either. So let's do what we're here to do."

On a glance, Dulac turns and heads back along the corridor to the interrogation room. Entering, closing the white door with its one-way mirror, he says to Mizener, "Did you tell him?"

"More or less," Mizener says.

"Mr. Nagy, listen," Dulac says. "We're going to read you your rights, and we're going to take your statement from you again. And I want to ask you right now if you would be willing to submit to a lie-detector test."

"This is what I get for trying to be helpful."

"Well, we appreciate your being helpful," Dulac says. "We do. All I can do, I guess, is ask you to understand the position we're in. Okay? Now, would you be willing to take a lie-detector test?"

"I don't care. If those things are accurate, I don't have anything to hide."

"Fine. Mr. Nagy, would you like to have an attorney present? Right now, before we go any further, we can—"

"Look! Let's just get on with it. I don't need any goddamn lawyer, because I haven't done anything. Except try to help."

"Neil, finish up here, will you? Read Mr. Nagy his rights. Take his statement. On tape. Make an appointment for a polygraph this afternoon. Mr. Nagy, thanks very much for your cooperation. We're sorry to inconvenience you. Again, I ask that you understand the position we're in. We simply have to clear you, because you are the last person to see Eric Wells. Thank you."

Asshole, Dulac thinks of the man, walking to his cubicle. Once there, however, lifting his glass ashtray, as always, from the top of a notepad left on his desk, he adds to himself, and you're being an asshole cop, too, so cool it a little. Chances are nine out of ten the guy is doing exactly what he says he's doing.

Dulac has things to add to his list, others yet to check. He adds *Rock groups* and *Children in Bondage—Sex Barn. See Shirley,* he writes after one, dittos it for the second.

He adds *Media,* meaning he wants to think it out for himself, and discuss with the chief and with Shirley Moss, too, the effect that afternoon of the story appearing in the newspaper. If the boy is being held, what are the risks of the story in the newspapers? After *Media,* he writes *Press conference?*

On another line, he adds *Weather/Explore,* to indicate that he needs to think out and discuss with others, too, any implications of the unusually warm weather they had at the time the boy disappeared. Ships in harbor, he thinks. Stowing away. Sailboats. Swept out to sea.

He returns to the first entry on the list, one he has yet to cross out. *Father. Warren R. Wells. 48. Believed to reside in New Orleans. No record in New Orleans 2/15/81. Believed to be alcoholic.* Pondering this a moment, he adds, *Desertion? Effects?*

He dials Shirley Moss's extension then, to ask her to come back to his cubicle to talk. "Shirley," he says.

"The Sex Barn," she says at once. "That movie. Gil, I just got off the phone to someone there. A real jerk. Refused to give his name. He refused to even say if the film played there on Saturday. A really nice guy. I told him we have a child missing. You know what he said? He said, 'That's your problem.' I couldn't believe it."

"Shirley, I'll take a ride out there in a while," Dulac says. "I have some other things I need you to take on—and some things I want to talk to you about. I'll come out there," he says as an afterthought.

Dulac replaces the receiver. Standing, he takes time enough, after slipping on his suitcoat, to light a cigarette, take a puff, to check his hardware under his coat flap. Then he takes up the notepad to leave with Shirley on his way out, to have her check and ponder. Slow down now, he adds to himself then as he recognizes his own insistent heartbeat. Slow down. You never will beat the sonofabitches if you go at things like a madman.

NINE

THE BOY'S EYES ARE OPEN. Returning from the bathroom, from washing and shaving, seeing him propped on the pillow, Vernon says, "Well, look who's awake."

The boy's eyes move some, otherwise he gives little sign of recognition. He looks like a child awake but still partly asleep.

"Let me get you some more soup, and some milk to drink," Vernon says.

The boy remains propped in the same place when Vernon settles in again on the couch beside him. The boy does not look frightened or startled now; he appears distant and exhausted.

He opens his mouth to take in the lukewarm chicken soup, and he tips his head to accept swallows of milk. "That's the way," Vernon keeps saying. "That's the way."

In time, the boy shakes his head, however faintly, to say he has had enough. Vernon reaches the soup mug and glass to the table. "It's not actually my milk," he says, but the boy gives no response.

"Are you tired?" Vernon says. He is thinking that he wants to like the boy again.

The boy hunches his shoulders slightly, to say he doesn't know.

"Do you know where you are?" Vernon says.

The boy seems only to look at him from his distance, his chin more down than up.

"Do you know where you are?" Vernon says.

The boy shakes his head slightly, to say no.

"Does your head hurt?"

The boy shakes his head slightly again.

Vernon keeps looking at the boy, who merely stares back. He wants to ask if he knows *who* he is, but doesn't let himself do so.

"Don't fall asleep," he says, as the boy's face is dipping once more.

His eyes open again, but in a moment begin lowering as before.

"Well, go ahead and sleep," Vernon whispers, and settles him back down.

Getting to his feet, Vernon looks on the boy for a moment. He is drifting away. His head bobs slightly, as he either inhales or exhales, and Vernon wonders if he is hurt, if he has suffered some kind of concussion. He is thinking, too, that the way to get out of this awful situation is to make things right again, to like the boy and return him home.

The kitchen clock says ten minutes past twelve. Vernon rinses the dishes in the sink. Two o'clock, he thinks. He will have to be out of here by two, to be on the safe side. If any of them comes in before that, he will say the boy is his cousin. His aunt was going to Boston, he will say. She had to go to a doctor there. A specialist. Women's problems. His cousin wasn't feeling well, so she left him here.

He sits on the bench of the picnic table watching the boy. The corner of the boy's mouth is open and the slightest bubble keeps coming up there. A small stain is under his mouth on that side. He is hurt, Vernon thinks then. He has had sexual contact with him and has hurt him. People go to jail for such things. For years.

If only he could not remember who I am, Vernon is thinking. If only he has experienced some kind of amnesia or developed a blank spot. He could take him home. Drop him off. Come back and go to his class this afternoon. Even if someone wanted the boy to tell, he wouldn't be able to. He'd worry about everything for a while, for sure, but then it would fade. It would be forgotten. An incident long ago. Everyone must have such moments in their lives.

He thinks of Anthony. This at least has pushed Anthony from his mind. At least for a while.

Reaching, he squeezes the boy's shoulder to wake him. The boy sleeps on. Vernon shakes him some, until his eyes open and he is looking at him.

"Eric," he says. "Do you know what's happened to you?"

The boy only looks back at him, as if he hadn't spoken.

"Do you?" Vernon says. "It's very important. Do you know where you are or if anything has happened to you? Or what?"

The boy stares at him. He seems to shake his head.

"Yes or no?" Vernon says. "It's important."

"What?" the boy says.

Encouraged that he has spoken, Vernon says, "Do you know what's happened to you?"

"What?" the boy says.

"*Do you know who I am?*" Vernon says. "*Do you? I want to know! Do you know my name?*"

The boy, looking at him, shakes his head.

"*Say it!*" Vernon says. "*Say it!*"

"No."

"You're not lying are you?" Vernon says.

The boy shakes his head.

"*Say it!*" Vernon says.

The boy only shakes his head some more, looking as if he is about to cry.

"*You're lying, aren't you?*" Vernon says.

"No," the boy says in a whimper.

"*You are!*"

"No," the boy cries.

"You don't know who I am?"

"No."

"You don't know what's happened?"

"No."

"Nothing *has* happened, has it? *Has it?*"

"I don't know, I don't know," the boy cries.

"Do you want to go home?"

"Yes," the boy cries.

"You're sure you don't know who I am?"

"I don't," the boy cries.

"And nothing's happened to you, has it?"

"No," the boy cries. "No."

Vernon takes a breath. He pauses, staring at the boy. "Okay," he says. "I'm going to take you home. I'm going to clean you up. I'm going to give you a bath is what I'm going to do, and then I'm going to take you home. And you aren't going to say anything at all about anything happening, are you—because nothing has happened. Has it? Nothing has happened."

The boy whimpers, utters, "I won't."

"Okay, I'm going to do it," Vernon says. "Let's see you walk. Come on. Come on, get up."

The boy moves his feet to the floor and stands, reaching a hand back to steady himself.

"Are you okay?" Vernon says.

"I'm okay. I'm just dizzy, a little."

"Let's go, this way," Vernon says, placing his hands on the boy's shoulder and arm to guide him to the bathroom. "I'm going to clean up that little cut on your head," he says. "Then you'll feel better."

He guides the boy along, but then is pushing him and stops. "What's the matter?" he says. "Are you okay?"

"I just can't go so fast," the boy says.

"Fast? That's not fast. Aren't you okay?"

"*Yes,*" the boy cries. "*I'm okay.*"

"If you're not okay, I can't take you home."

"It just hurts a little," the boy cries.

"Where does it hurt?"

"Here," the boy cries, reaching his hand to the back of his leg.

"What happened that it hurts there?" Vernon says. "Did you fall down?"

"Yes," the boy cries.

In the bathroom, Vernon is going to have the boy sit on the toilet seat while he dresses the wound in his head, but trying to sit, the boy cries out in pain. Having him rest on his knees on the bathmat, Vernon separates the hair around the cut in his scalp and uses a damp washcloth to clean away more of the dried blood in the immediate area. Each time the boy cries or begins to wail, Vernon says, "I'm not going to hurt you." Nor does he put a Band-Aid over the cut as he had planned to, as it passes through his mind that he might leave his fingerprints there.

Helping the boy to his feet, he begins unbuttoning his shirt, saying to him. "Everything off now. You're going to take a bath and then I'm going to take you home. Turn this way."

The boy doesn't resist. Stripped, though, as Vernon says, "Use the toilet now, before you get into the tub," he says, "I don't have to."

"Use it," Vernon says. "Look how filthy your underpants are. Use it!" Turning away, Vernon sits on the floor to start the water running in the old tub. Looking back, though, there is the boy sitting on the toilet crying, his toes just reaching the floor. "My God!" Vernon says.

"I can't go!" the boy cries.

"Why not? Look what you did in your pants!"

"I just don't have to," the boy cries.

"You haven't gone since last night!" Vernon says. "I know you haven't."

"I just don't have to," the boy cries.

Getting to his feet, Vernon stands over him for a moment. "Does it hurt?" he says.

"Yes," the boy cries.

"Okay. I'm going to go out of the room," Vernon says. "You see if you can go then—okay?"

"Okay."

Turning off the faucets in the steaming tub, Vernon leaves the room and closes the door. Walking into his own room, he looks around. He has walked out and is in the kitchen looking outside when he hears the toilet flush.

"Did you go?" he says, reentering the bathroom.

"Yes," the boy says.

"Really?"

"Yes."

The small naked child is standing there, and Vernon feels momentary embarrassment looking at him and realizes again that he doesn't like him anymore. At the tub, he tests the water with his hand. "I'm going to help you get in," he says. "This is going to make you feel a lot better. Then

I'm going to take you home. When you're feeling better. And you're not going to say anything, are you?"

"No," the boy says. "No."

Holding the boy's smooth arms and shoulders, he helps lift and guide him into the tub of water and helps him sit, then lie back, in a way which is not entirely painful. "There's the soap," Vernon says, standing upright. "Soak a little first if you want to. I'm going to wash out your underpants is what I'm going to do. That's a sign of real friendship, isn't it, to wash someone's soiled underpants? Wouldn't you say?"

The boy is lying in the water, looking ahead; he doesn't say anything.

At the sink, Vernon runs hot water on the boy's underpants and scrubs them together to loosen the sediment. Rinsing them again, he lowers the stopper and fills the sink with several inches of water. Adding hand soap to the fabric, he squishes and squeezes and rinses. "See," he says then, turning to show the clean garment.

The boy doesn't look; he continues staring ahead, as if he has come more awake.

"See," Vernon says.

The boy still doesn't respond.

"It doesn't really matter to you, does it?" Vernon says. Vernon looks down at him. "Nothing I do matters to you, does it?" he says.

Upon a pause, without expression, the boy says, "You fairy."

Vernon stands with the sopping wet underpants in hand. Something like a bubble comes up into his face. "Why do you say that?" he says. He would say more to the boy, but for the moment has lost his ability to speak.

TEN

ROLLING IN ON THE BLACKTOP outside The Sex Barn, Dulac turns off his motor and looks around for a moment. There are five cars and two pickup trucks parked here, an eighteen-wheeler along the side. At least two cars are parked down behind a cinder-block addition to an old barn. Looking over license plates, Dulac takes a breath and exhales. The complex is, he realizes, a former orchard.

Apple red—although fringed with flaming orange—the main building could still pass for the roadside orchard sales barn. The portable electric sign—bright yellow—doesn't say *Fresh Cider, MacIntosh,* and *Pick Your Own,* however, but *NonStop XXX Movies, Peeps, VCR Exchange,* and *Adult Novelties.*

Take it easy now, he reminds himself, leaving his car. Keep the lid on.

Only three men are present within the immediate room. Two are customers, studying cellophane-wrapped magazines, while the third, clerk or proprietor, stands behind a counter on a raised platform, reading something on the counter. This man, Dulac notices, doesn't look up. He notices also, realizes, an immersion he is undergoing into the explicitness all around. Flesh is everywhere. Hard-core. There are nipples the size of finger joints reaching between leather straps, massive penises within and without various openings male and female, penises ejaculating, breasts the size of football halves squeezed in the hands of women with tongues signaling. He has to admit a degree of unintended response. And a degree of anger.

And something unclean in the air, Your Honor. Other people's sweat. A sticky floor. Staleness, although I'm not sure if it was physical or moral.

At the counter, Dulac removes his ID wallet. The clerk, he notices, is glancing at him, lifting his eyes. The clerk does not have ex-con written in his face, as Dulac had expected; rather he looks like a weathered farmer, come in from the cold. Neither helpful nor friendly, the man says, "What do you need?"

"Lieutenant Dulac, Portsmouth PD," Dulac says anyway, still hanging out his shield. "I just need some information."

"Always thought Portsmouth was in New Hampshire," the man says.

"I think you're right about that," Dulac says. "If you like, I can have the Maine State Police stop by in a few minutes."

"Maine State Police don't bother me," the man says.

"From what I understand, they're very pleased with the business you have here." He and the clerk both turn their heads to see one of the men who had been browsing slip away through the front door. "I think they'd like it a lot if I called and told them how cooperative you are." At once the other man leaves.

"You're just scaring away the customers," the man says. "If you've got a police car parked out there, you're gonna scare away more."

"I wonder why that is," Dulac says.

The man returns his stare directly.

"You don't have to make this any more difficult than it has to be," Dulac says. That's the way, he says to himself. Be cool. "All I want is some information."

"Let's have it," the man says.

"In your theater there, you were showing a film called *Children in Bondage.*"

"It's not illegal."

"I'll tell you what," Dulac says. "You listen to what I have to say. That way we can get done with this."

The man stares, doesn't speak, and it occurs to Dulac how much he wants the man to defy him.

"A twelve-year-old boy has come up missing. In Portsmouth. Saturday night. We're trying to find him and we don't have much to go on. It's possible, given the subject matter of that film, that someone could have left here and gone looking for a victim. It's remote, I know, but we're checking it out."

"So what do you want from me?"

Dulac, glancing at the man, reminds himself again to cool it. "A couple things," he says. "I want the times the film was shown. I'd like a description of the contents of the film. And I want to know if anyone was here to see the film—I'm especially interested in Saturday before seven P.M.—who might have aroused suspicion in any way. I'd like to know how many days the film has been shown, and if anyone, that you might have noticed, came to see it more than once. In any way called attention to themselves. I may also want to see the film itself, have it viewed by some experts, to see what they think it might suggest to certain persons."

"Can't give you the film," the man says. "It isn't mine, for one. For another, it's not here anymore. It's a rented film and it's on its way somewhere else as of this morning. I'm not even sure where right now."

"Did it just go out?"

"More or less."

"Let me say this again," Dulac says. "A local twelve-year-old boy is missing. It'll be in the paper today. It's not a TV show. He may have been abducted for sexual purposes, which is the story these days. I'm asking for your help as a citizen. On the outside chance this film could be related to his disappearance."

"I'd like to help," the man says. "Far as I know, though, it was proved in Denmark long ago that this kind of stuff doesn't have anything to do with what you're talking about. In fact, they say it does the opposite."

"Well, I wasn't there, so they didn't prove it to me. Not yet. So why don't you answer my questions, so I can get on my way."

"There's nothing new under the sun," the man says then.

"You're pretty sure?" Dulac says.

"Okay—whatever good it will do," the man says. "Film played here a week. Six days. Saturday was the last day, 'cause we don't open on Sunday. When it ran, it was continuous showings. Evenings, five P.M. until midnight. Saturday, ten in the morning until midnight. That's it. All within the law."

"What's the content?"

"Well, I'm not so sure I know. Standard stuff, I guess."

"Did you see the film?"

"Some of it. Not much."

"What is standard stuff?"

"Regular bondage stuff, like it says in the title. On the soft side."

"Which means?"

The man hunches. "Just a make-believe world," he says.

"The title says children, too."

"Well, that too. What it is, people are tied up, given a few swats and so on. People get off on it. It's their business."

"Any other violence, besides being tied and swatted?"

"That's it."

"By people, you mean children?"

"You could say that was the idea."

"What else could you say?"

"They're like actors acting like they're children. Otherwise it wouldn't be legal."

"What about actors with false birth certificates?"

"Anything's possible."

"In the film—how many children? What ages were they supposed to be?"

"Two children. They're supposed to be just coming into their own, whatever age that is."

"Male or female children?"

"One each."

"What happened to them? What's the story?"

"That's about it. They get tied up and swatted."

"How tied?"

"Well, their hands and feet are tied."

"Necks?"

"Yah, I think so."

"How are they swatted? With what?"

"Well, a switch, I believe. Maybe there was some leather."

"How hard?"

"Oh. Enough to raise small welts. That's it."

"Did you see or notice anyone in particular on Saturday? In the way of customers?"

"Nope."

"Are you sure?"

"I'm sure."

"Did you see anyone come to see the film more than once?"

"Nope."

Dulac takes in a breath, looking at the man. Then he says, "You the owner?"

"That's right."

"Didn't this use to be an orchard?"

"That's right. That's what it used to be."

"Family farm?"

"That's right."

"Your family?"

"That's right."

"I think your forebears would be really proud of you."

"I make a living," the man says.

Turning, walking to the door, Dulac leaves.

Outside, in the cooler air, he pauses to light a cigarette. At his car then, he stands—touching the opened door as if it were a fence rail—smokes slowly and looks around. Three of the cars and both pickups are gone. Must be a side exit, he thinks. Realizing how little information he has gathered, how the man did not actually cooperate, he feels anger in his neck again and cautions himself to take it easy. He wonders why he is so angry, why something in this has become so personal. He thinks it may be his age. He may be turning a corner in life, while others are taking things for granted.

In the driver's seat, the door shut, he has yet to start the motor. He continues to pause. It isn't likely to lead to anything anyway, he thinks. He knew that in the first place, and if he had had anything better or more promising to do, he wouldn't even have driven out here. Still, he is angry. Disappointed. He might have just lost money playing cards. Or been ridiculed. And lost time on his case besides. He should be in his office. Until he is cleared, the father has to remain their primary suspect. The man who offered Eric a ride is also a primary suspect, until he is cleared.

In the next moment, however, Dulac is climbing back out of his car and walking back across the open space to the door he just left. He walks in. The man looks directly at him this time as he enters.

As he reaches the counter, the hair on Dulac's neck is a little alive. The counter comes just above his waist as he leans forward to speak softly. "Your answers are unacceptable," he says. "I want you to start over and I want you to cooperate this time. Just in case there is a connection."

"Are you threatening me?"

"Maybe. I'm not leaving this time until I know you're being straight with me. I didn't drive all the way out here to play a little game. Is that threatening? Call the police."

The man stands in place.

"I don't care what you do here," Dulac says. "It's your fucking life."

The man only looks at him, without expression.

"Where's the film?" Dulac says.

"It's in Portland," the man says.

"Where?"

"It's not there yet. It's on the way."

"What is the name of the place?"

"It's called The Playground."

"That's neat. How is it transported?"

"Parcel post."

"What else didn't you tell me?"

"There's a little violence in the film. They draw blood on the girl."

"Real blood?"

"I believe so."

"Just on the girl."

"Yes."

"What else?"

"That's it. I don't deal in child porn."

Dulac stands looking at him.

"There *was* a guy here," the man says. "For whatever it's worth. He asked for kiddy porn; he went to the movie."

"Describe him."

"He's a young guy. Mid-twenties."

"White?"

"Yes."

"How tall?"

"I don't know—average."

"Five ten?"

"About that."

"How was he dressed?"

"Sort of clean-cut, as I remember. I'd forgotten him until a minute ago."

"A working man?"

"I don't think so."

"White-collar?"

"I don't know; I couldn't say. More like that."

"Clerical?"

"Maybe. It's hard to say."

"Glasses?"

"No."

"Hair color?"

"I don't remember. Brown maybe."

"Long hair? Short?"

"Average, I'd say."

"The guy went to the movie?"

"I saw him go in."

"What time?"

"Between one and two—about that time."

"What was the movie's playing time?"

"About fifty-five minutes."

"What time did he come out?"

"I didn't see him come out. I never saw him again."

"Did you see what he was driving?"

"No."

"He *asked* for kiddy porn? What did he say?"

"I don't know. 'You sell young stuff?' Something like that. It's not un-usual."

"Blue jeans?"

"I didn't notice."

"Heavy, thin?"

"Average."

"Muscular?"

"I don't know. I couldn't tell. Average."

"Was he a bad-looking guy? Homely? Scary?"

"Just an average guy. I didn't look that close at him. I saw his face, but that's about all. They come in all the time."

"He was alone."

"I think so. One thing I remember. His cheeks were sort of reddish. Ruddy, whatever you call it."

"You noticed that?"

"He stuck his face up close, when he asked for kiddy stuff. I noticed his face."

"His cheeks were reddish?"

"They had color, the way some people do."

"Anything else you remember about him?"

"No. That's it."

"Eyes?"

"No."

"Okay. Thanks. I may ask you to look at some mug shots."

"Okay."

"Thank you."

"Look, it's a living," the man says. "I did two tours in Vietnam."

"Why tell me?" Dulac says.

"I'm owed," the man says.

Dulac walks away, leaves through the door without responding.

ELEVEN

MATT IS IN A CHAIR against the wall. His mother is to his left, near the desk where the detective sits. The detective—Lt. Dulac—has his suit coat off and his tie loosened. He is talking, but Matt is listening only in part. There is a file cabinet behind the man. He looks as wide as two file cabinets put together, Matt thinks, although mainly he is thinking of Vanessa. And of Eric. This is what Eric would like, talking with the police, he thinks. But then Eric never knew what it was like, when something was really wrong. When it's you. To Eric, it was like seeing something on television, Matt thinks, and he imagines telling him this when he sees him.

In fact, when it's you, Matt thinks, it doesn't feel good at all. It isn't fun. It's like being in a waiting room, going to see a doctor and not knowing what he might do to you with his knives and needles. It isn't fun at all.

"Does that bother you?" his mother says, turning to him.

"It simply should be done," Dulac is saying. "We had intended to ask you to do one, too, Mrs. Wells, but we've talked to half a dozen people already who are certain that you were in the Legion Hall dining room throughout the entire evening, so it isn't necessary."

They are talking, Matt knows, about his taking a lie-detector test.

"It's just another thing I'd like to move on right away," the large man says. "It isn't that I feel Matt is a suspect in any way. I want you to understand that. It's regular procedure for *all* family members. If an outside inspector came and reviewed the steps we'd taken so far, he'd say what about a polygraph for this family member? What's going on here? And so on. You have to start as close to home as possible and go from there."

"Well, Matt?" his mother says.

"I don't care," Matt says. "What's it like, though?"

"It's just some diodes and a printout. It's nothing much, believe me."

"Do you feel anything?"

"No. Nothing."

"Well, does it make you say things you might not want to say?"

"Matt, what is this?" his mother says.

"I don't care," Matt says. "I'll take it. My gosh, can't I say anything?"

"That's okay, Mrs. Wells. Matt, it's not like a truth serum, if that's what you're thinking. It doesn't probe. If you cheated on a test at school, it's not going to tell on you or anything like that. The questions will only have to do with Eric, and with anything you might know about his whereabouts. That's it. The idea is just to *clear* you, not to implicate you."

"I can't believe you're carrying on like this," his mother says to him.

"I said I'd do it!" Matt snaps.

Dulac lights a cigarette. Matt, not looking at him, knows he is being looked at. He still doesn't look back at the man. It will show in his face that he is withholding something, he thinks, even if he isn't.

"As I was saying," the broad detective says, "we want to move quickly on this and on several things we're suspicious about. I've called you both in, at the same time, to ask you some more questions. Some direct questions, to which I want direct answers. Again, you see, someone knows something, even if they don't know they know it, and the most likely candidates are you. Someone you know. Something you heard. That kind of thing. Okay? It's always kind of difficult to interview family members in a situation like this, but it has to be done. Eric's been missing almost two days now. This means things have become quite serious."

Matt, keeping his eyes down as he listens, feels his face burning with confusion. He hears his mother say something about the police finding Eric in their regular work.

"This *is* regular work," the detective says. "We don't know where to look unless you give us some clues. Okay? Mrs. Wells, listen. I don't mean to be insensitive. Or rude or anything. We have to move quickly on this, on what we have so far. Things are critical. They're bleak, I'm afraid. You need to know that . . . it's my job to tell you . . ."

She doesn't know it, Matt is saying to himself. She doesn't hear it or believe it because she just doesn't want to.

"Chances are," the detective is saying. "You both need to know this. Chances are there is some kind of *sexual* motivation involved in Eric's disappearance. That's usually what it is."

"A *little boy?*" his mother says.

Jesus don't be so dumb, Matt says to himself.

"Mrs. Wells, listen now," the detective is saying. "Let's not be naive. Eric may be having a wonderful time camping out somewhere like Huck Finn. I hope he is. For our part, though, we have to assume other things. Things which aren't so nice. It's important that you understand what I'm saying."

At once, Matt is feeling bad for his mother, as if a friend in school were being reprimanded by the teacher for not being able to understand something. She doesn't think bad things, he wants to tell the detective.

"The unfortunate truth," the detective is saying, "is that immediate family members, as statistics prove, are the most likely perpetrators where there is foul play of any kind, including that which is sexual. Okay? After family members, we have to be concerned about relatives, friends and neighbors, teachers, friends' parents, acquaintances at work, and so on. Persons known. If Eric got into a car with someone, chances are it's someone he *knows*. Okay? I don't mean to seem hard, but it's Eric we want to get back and we can't do that if we don't take a hard look at things. Don't worry; we're not going to implicate anyone in any way—we're careful about that—and no one is going to know anything about what is said in this room. Okay?"

His mother doesn't respond, and Matt glances over at her. She just won't hear it, he is thinking.

"If Eric is being held," the detective is saying, "we're hoping—because he seems like a resourceful little guy—that he'll get away."

His mother still doesn't respond.

"At any rate," the detective says, "we have to get down to specifics. We're assuming at this time that Eric has been picked up. Our first suspect, Mrs. Wells, even as we know you have grave doubts, is Mr. Wells."

"Oh no," Claire says.

"Well, we hope to clear him as soon as we can."

"I don't believe he'd be sober long enough," Claire says.

"People do reform," the detective says.

"He hasn't sent either of them so much as a birthday card—for eight years!"

"That doesn't mean he couldn't have changed. It could be the reason he would change, if you see what I mean. Anyway, he has to stay on our list until we clear him. The problem is, we haven't been able to locate him. We're checking New Orleans right now, because the people in Maine—where he is still in arrears on the support payments—don't have any idea where he is."

"I can't believe Eric isn't okay," his mother says.

The detective looks up at her, Matt notices.

Then he says, "At the same time we're working to clear the man who offered Eric a ride. That is, it looks like he will be cleared because we've found someone who can verify his whereabouts for a part of Saturday night. And because, Matt, you're certain he never did or said anything unusual when you've seen him around. We've also been informed of two or three other suspects, or other leads, we're checking out. One is a report from two young girls who do not know Eric that they saw someone resembling him get into a car, with two men, on Market Street at about that time on Saturday night. We've also learned that a man was in the general area on Saturday afternoon attempting to buy child pornography, and that this person viewed a pornographic film about children. And right now—this is on your advice, Matt—authorities in Burlington, Vermont, are interviewing the members of a rock band which played at a beach club near York through Saturday night, on the chance, remote or not, that Eric might somehow have joined up with them or been taken on by them in some way. Another thing, the Coast Guard is conducting a general search throughout Portsmouth Harbor, just in case Eric is stowing away there."

Pausing here, lighting another cigarette, the man says, "None of those is real promising. We're checking them out, but I'd be less than honest if I told you I thought they'd lead to anything. Which is another way of saying we don't really have much, or anything substantial, to go on. So we need your help. I'll say it again: People know things, even if they don't know they know them."

Pausing once more, the man says, "Which brings us just about up to date. A police cruiser is going to pick you up about six this evening, Mrs. Wells, to take you to a television studio in Portland. If I'm not there, someone else will be—although I'm going to try to make it myself. The idea will be for you to speak directly to the camera as if you're talking to Eric. If someone is holding him, we want to be careful not to antagonize them or trigger something in them in some way. Since we know we can't *predict* such a person's behavior, our thought it to keep it strictly between yourself and Eric. 'Eric, we miss you. We want you to come home.' Anything like that will be enough. A number will be given for anyone to call who has something to report. At the same time, could you each have your lists of names ready by then, when the officer comes to pick you up?

"As for these lists, do them separately, and if you don't know a person's name just say, for example, the man at the candy counter at such and such a location. Or the assistant coach on the soccer team two years ago. The plumber who fixed the sink in January. Put down if the person ever gave Eric a ride anywhere. If he ever called or talked to him on the telephone. Anyone who ever gave Eric any kind of present or money, or even attention. And don't worry, again, about putting down the names of your best friends, or relatives. We'll be very careful, believe me."

Matt has looked up and the detective, pausing, is glancing his way. Matt looks down again, blood rushing once more into his neck and face.

"Has Eric ever told you of anyone being fresh with him? Touching him, taking liberties? Suggesting things?"

"No," his mother says.

"Matt?" the detective says.

"No," Matt says, shaking his head, wondering why he feels so responsible, so guilty.

"Anyone offering him a ride?"

"Gee, no," his mother says.

"I can't think of anyone," Matt says, more to the floor this time.

"If you do, put the person on your list," the man says.

"He knows not to go with strangers," his mother says.

"How does he know that, Mrs. Wells?"

"He just does. He's not dumb."

"Who would he regard as strangers?"

"He'd know," his mother says. "I know he would."

"Mrs. Wells, you know—I don't know if it's quite like that. A person offering Eric a ride wouldn't necessarily be unusual, you see. Or a dirty old man. He could be an attractive, even an appealing person. Friendly. Intelligent."

"Why would someone like that want to pick up a little boy?"

She really doesn't know, Matt thinks, looking away. Nor does the detective say anything more to her on the subject. Rather, he says then, "Today's paper will be out in about an hour. That may bring in something. And your appeal on TV tonight. We have hopes for that, too. One other thing. What about enemies? Have you ever had any problems—any bad blood with anyone?"

"There was the bank, when we lost our house," his mother says. "There was some bad feeling there."

"Oh, Mom," Matt says. "My gosh."

"It's true, isn't it?" she says.

"That's not what he means," Matt says. "My gosh, you sound like a broken record. That's not what he means." Matt is about to break into tears, without knowing why.

"What's *wrong* with you?" his mother says.

"That's all you ever talk about," Matt says.

"Well, it had a lot to do with our lives," she says. "A lot more than you'll ever realize."

Matt is looking down, trying not to cry. Nothing is said for a moment.

"What about personal enemies?" the detective says then. "Problems with anyone. Like at work? In school? Feuds with anyone? Neighbors? That kind of thing?"

Neither Matt nor his mother responds.

"About the foreclosure, Mrs. Wells," the detective says then. "How would you see that as being connected with Eric?"

"I'm sure Matt is right," she says. "I guess it's just one of those things I'll never get over. The bank—well, the bank was mean. They wouldn't give us a chance. I mean they gave us ten extra days. After Warren left us three months in arrears to begin with. It just all came down all at once and the best I could do right off the bat was custodial work over in Somersworth—"

"Oh, Mom," Matt says.

"Anyway, Eric has always said that when he grew up he was going to get us a house like the one we lost. Matt's just tired of hearing about that other house."

"I just don't think it has anything to do with this," Matt hears himself say, remaining close to tears.

"His teacher said Eric is shy," Dulac says then. "How shy would you say he is?"

"He's not so shy," Matt says. "Not when you get to know him. He's shy at school maybe. Or with grown-ups."

"Okay, one other thing," the detective says, "and then I'll get you a ride back home. What about coaches or adults? Has there been anyone, in any role like that—coaches, scoutmasters, teachers—who has taken a particular interest in Eric?"

Matt and his mother both sit there. Neither responds.

"You know, Little League teams and clubs, things like that?" the detective says.

"He didn't do stuff like that," Matt says. "Neither of us did. Because—well, it cost a lot of money."

Matt looks up then, and looks at the detective. The man offers the slightest expression, as if to say he understands. "I think it's why he was shy in school, too," Matt hears himself say. "The kids who aren't shy are the ones who have a lot of money. It's always like that."

"Oh, Matt," his mother says.

"That's okay," Dulac says, "I know what he means."

"Kids whose fathers have good jobs get to do a lot of things that other kids don't," Matt says.

"Matt, my gosh, why are you saying these things?" his mother says.

"They're true," Matt says. "I'm saying them because they're true."

"I know what you're saying, Matt," Dulac says. "It's okay, Mrs. Wells. I understand what Matt is saying."

Matt has to look down then. Even so his eyes fill, and he feels taken in by the man and adopted, and only when another minute has passed, and his mother happens to be talking, is he able to look up and be himself again.

TWELVE

DRIVING YET AGAIN, Vernon has a hollow feeling in his heart. He thinks of the time, when he was twelve and they had just moved east from California, when he felt the same kind of hopelessness. His mother already had a boyfriend, who had taken them to a lakeside beach, and what happened left him so lost as a new child in a new world that for the first time in his life he had wanted to die.

He was in the water, while his mother and her boyfriend sat on a towel on the beach. He was not swimming, because he did not know how, and overweight at the time, was keeping all but his head underwater, to use his fingers on the bottom to pull himself around as if he were swimming. Slipping through the water crocodile fashion, among other children, mainly younger children, there occurred in him all at once a desire, or a capacity, to do to others something of what he had imagined doing with the two boys in his secret magazine.

Using his hands underwater to shift directions, he approached a boy sitting in the shallow, sudsy water with his legs in a V. Gripping the boy's toes first, pushing to and fro like a tethered boat, a smile ready on his face and rubbing himself upon the sandy bottom, he reached underwater to caress the boy, to squeeze lightly a slight caterpillar between the boy's legs, to say "What's that?" only to have the boy shift away to play at another angle.

Sliding back around, he pulled up to a young girl, smiling at her and reaching in to touch and feel between her legs, too, feeling little more there than something like rubber but eliciting some flat-handed splashes from her. Sliding out in the water the length of his arms, and sliding back, he reached in once more to search for the center of the girl, or for the center of himself as he rode upon the sand and his senses thrilled, only, suddenly, sharply, to have the girl snatched out of the water, snatched into her own heart-stopping scream, and to look up into the face of a woman in a one-piece bathing suit, holding the girl, seeing her spit at him, *"You little shit, you keep your hands to yourself!"*

A scene. The world stopped. Sound stopped. He wanted to melt. He wanted to withdraw into himself. He knew his mother was watching. He knew his mother was sitting next to her new boyfriend and, like everyone else, both were watching. He knew, too, that she would merely watch, that she would not come to him, and turning away, in his childlike stroke, pulling himself into somewhat deeper water, he wanted to slip in under the surface and never, as long as he lived, lift from the water or walk before the eyes of anyone, or ever be seen or spoken to again by his mother. He could not melt, though. Nor could he live forever within the water. Or die. And in time—however much time passed and however far along the beach he managed to move—he had to lift his overweight child's body from the water, had to be seen, endlessly, as he circled, eyes down, and sat on a towel at his mother's side, away from the man, sat with plum-colored lips, shivering, while his mother continued to talk to the man, sat until dusk without a word, for his mother was hiding, too, he knew, sat until the sun on the horizon could be looked at as directly as a lampshade and the beach was all but deserted, and his mother addressed the subject for the first and last time, in saying to him as she stood and gathered things, "Are you coming?"

The same hopeless feeling is in Vernon now, driving the car next to the silent boy. Vernon glances at him. "It's easy to call people names," he says then. "Anyone can do that. It's always done, though, by people who don't understand. If they did understand, they wouldn't do it. Simple people," he adds, taking another glance at the boy slumped beside him, "have simple answers."

Driving on, Vernon takes a longer look at the boy, fearing he has fallen unconscious again. With his right hand, keeping his eyes on the road, he reaches to find the boy's hair, which is silky clean now in places. He moves his fingers gently over the boy's forehead and down to his nose, and lets them pause upon his partially separated lips. There is the give and take of breathing, and its warmth, and Vernon wonders if he is bluffing. He returns his hand to the steering wheel. He drives along. "You are ruining my life," he says then, while his voice and the lower part of his face tremble.

"*Goddamn you!*" he cries.

There is no response and Vernon doesn't cast a glance in the boy's direction. Thinking clearly is difficult for him now, as new thoughts and images keep landing in his mind but take off before he can absorb them, only to be replaced by others. He is near Route 1A, south of Portsmouth—he had circled this way, he is telling himself, to return the boy home—and he is having thoughts, half-formed, of getting rid of the boy.

Vernon drives along, "I know you're bluffing," he says. "You think you're so smart." For the moment Vernon imagines the boy lying there as if asleep, plotting an escape.

At an intersection, taking the way to the ocean, an idea which he is thinking of as devious is taking shape in Vernon's mind. He will *let* him escape, he is thinking. That's what he'll do. He'll let him get away, and then he'll return to school, to his life and classes, and try to forget any of this ever happened.

Rolling along in silence for a moment, Vernon finally says, as if more to himself than anyone else, "I shouldn't do it, but I have to stop along the beach here to make a call. Can I trust you? I guess I'll have to, at least for a few minutes."

Following the blacktop road over reaches of saltmarsh, he sees water and sky come into full view on one side. At this afternoon hour, under overcast skies, the water is a faintly muddy green, showing many small whitecaps lifting and disappearing, and Vernon feels soothed by them, or by the expanse. He turns into a public parking lot and pulls up facing the sky as much as the water. Two other cars are parked there. He turns off the motor. Saying nothing more, as if quietly, he slips from the car, closes the door, and steps up to the slight rise before the car, between wooden posts the size of fire hydrants, to look down upon the littered beach. He sees someone, to the left, running with a dog where the sand is wet. It is a man, in a blue jogging suit. Vernon imagines the boy peeking over the dashboard at the moment behind him. Well, he says to himself. Here's your chance. I don't ever want to see you again. You can go call someone else names.

He is walking through the loose sand, on an angle, making his way to the ribbon of sand that is firm with water. Once there, he walks along, and as he does so he imagines the boy opening the car door, slipping out, moving, even limping, away. In just a few more minutes, Vernon thinks, he'll return to his car, head out the way he came, and return to his life.

Even if the boy wanted to, he is telling himself as he walks in the thickening sea air, he could not identify him or tell where they had been. Would anyone even care? Oh, he'd be nervous for a while all right, in fear of being caught, but days would pass and things would fade and soon all would be left behind.

He walks along, watching the water roll in on the beach in its mis-angled waves. He watches the whitecaps, some flapping like gulls' wings, some snapping here and there like towels over the pale green surface, and he begins to feel hopeful. All at once, though, a woman passes him from behind, striding hard on the wet-packed sand with a German shepherd moving and sniffing here and there as if at the end of a rope.

The woman marches on. Vernon hesitates. Well, time enough, he tells himself. Time enough. Turning, he starts back, looking down at his own footmarks now as the wind rushes over him.

Moments later he is driving once more over the blacktop causeway and the boy is beside him as before. The boy appears not to have moved, not yet, and Vernon's anger with him now seems as confused as the mix of thoughts in his mind.

"Aren't you hungry?" Vernon says, close to tears. "Don't you want to wake up and have something to eat?" He hardly glances at the boy, though, but looks to the windshield close before him, and a little to the roadway he is following, as if he is going mad.

THIRTEEN

DULAC HAS PULLED OVER and is sitting in his car on a side street. Dinnertime is approaching and he is between the police station and home. Except that he feels down, he isn't sure why he has stopped. He has decided to drive Claire Wells to Portland himself, to have her appeal videotaped for the eleven o'clock news, and leaving the station he thought he would stop at home for a bite to eat. Beatrice will just be getting home from her job, however, and he knows he isn't very hungry. Maybe he isn't hungry at all.

What is on his mind, more or less, is porn. It's been there throughout the day. As policemen they were given a policy that seemed to presuppose an attitude, his attitude, but all along he knows he hasn't been sure. The war, its endless hangover—that had been all around them, too. Everything they did as policemen had changed in his time and he had never been comfortable—he had always been upset—with the implication that a policeman was not a good or humane person.

Of porn, all he can say—he sees in this moment—is that it makes the air around it different. It creates an air in which life has a different value. Less value. Uninspired. As a policeman, it put him between the devil and the deep blue sea. The goods do seem educational, he thinks. What are they teaching? Are they teaching something new?

FOURTEEN

CLAIRE, in the apartment alone, is thinking of searching through Matt's belongings. The idea has been in her mind for several minutes. She is standing at the stove, heating a small amount of canned stew she has spooned into a saucepan. Matt has gone to the grocery store for milk. There seems something terribly wrong in the idea, and more than once she has told herself it is something she will not do. No way. Still, she keeps returning to it.

Trust is what it is. To make such a search would say she doesn't trust her own son. She has read notes in his pants pockets before, and taken looks here and there, but she has never gone looking for something out of pure suspicion.

Turning off the soup, she senses herself like another person, walking to their bedroom. Something is attracting her. It is his dresser drawers, spaces between T-shirts, under shelf paper. Within pairs of socks.

She pauses, considers returning to the kitchen. She makes no move to do so.

In the closet, crouching—when she has looked through his clothes on the rack and found nothing—she looks inside his old shoes, and inside Eric's, too. She looks into and between boxes. Standing, returning to the clothes on the rack, she even checks watch pockets, inserting a finger and touching corner to corner.

Pulling up a chair to stand on, searching under and between sweaters and old clothes on the shelf, at last she removes something which clearly has been hidden. It is on Matt's side, under his sweaters—a book.

Taking it down for better light, she can tell with her fingers that things are inserted between the book's pages. Her pulse and her temples are working. Dear God, she has found something.

The book, she sees, stepping down from the chair, is a Hardy Boys

186

mystery that she remembers Warren giving to Matt years ago. Opening to the first object between pages, she sees a Christmas gift tag. On a short red string, its message is, "To Matt With Lots Of Love / Dad."

She holds a moment. Then she sits down on the chair. Other inserts in the book, she sees, are other tags and small gift cards. There is one from Eric, which says "To Matt / Happy Birthday / Eric." She recognizes the last one, which is hardly two months old. It says, "Merry Christmas To A Wonderful Son / Mom." They are the gifts of Matt's life. A handful of words, all they had ever given him.

Closing the book, Claire sits still and cannot hold back the hurt welling up in her. She sits and holds her face in one hand, as the universe spins within her.

FIFTEEN

STUDENTS' CARS ARE OFTEN towed from the Shop 'n Save parking lot during morning and midday hours, but seldom this late in the afternoon. Still, as most students with cars know, spotting them parking in the supermarket lot while they go to classes is one of the favorite activities of the town police. For this and other reasons, turning into the lot with the boy slumped yet in the front seat beside him, only partially covered by the flannel-lined sleeping bag, Vernon drives to the main concentration of cars, to conceal himself there at the same time that he flirts with the risk of someone seeing them or seeing the boy, or having the boy cry out to signal someone.

Turning off the motor, Vernon sits a moment. The anxiety or nervousness he feels is in his throat. He's far enough from the supermarket, he thinks, so most people coming and going will not walk past his car, but close enough for the danger of what he is doing to be real.

He wonders what he *is* doing. All he can determine is that he doesn't know. He is drawn to taking this chance, he can see that, but he doesn't know why. Does he think that someone is going to come up and take the boy away and everything will return to normal? Is he here because this is home to him and he doesn't know where else to go? Is it in his mind, in his fantasies, that Anthony will walk up any minute and tap on his window, and not be exhausted or muddled, and tell him in his superior way exactly what to do to extricate himself from this otherwise impossible situation?

Or is he simply here to be caught, to put an end to things?

He doesn't lock the car door. Getting out, closing the door, not caring, he turns and starts across the parking lot in the direction of the university, away from the shoulder-to-shoulder stores to whom the parking places belong. Stop me, he thinks. Tow my car. It's what I want you to do.

Nothing happens. He reaches the street and crosses.

In the library, walking aimlessly, he imagines running into Anthony and begins to look for him. He has no reason to think Anthony would be here at this time, but given the flow of students it isn't out of the question. He makes his way to the third floor, where he has done much of his studying, and sits and broods for a time at a window overlooking the campus.

Between the trees, lights are already on in the windows of other buildings, and in his loneliness and exhaustion, Vernon rests his face in his hand and stares away. This is the lonely floor. He has always liked it here. Now he loves it, as if more than any other place this—this carrel beside a window—is where he has been most content. He actually speaks aloud then, saying, "Please somebody—"

Nothing happens.

Moments later, in the third floor men's room, a man exposes himself. Vernon is standing at a urinal, preoccupied with his fears. The man, who does not appear to be a student, is standing two or three urinals away. Glancing, seeing the man lift his eyebrows, but not comprehending a signal, Vernon realizes then that the man is pivoting enough to reveal an erection. Vernon thinks of Uncle Sally, but remains unaffected. In a moment, avoiding any eye contact, he is making his way out and then along the carpeting to the stairway.

He sees a photograph. He is walking back along the small town's main street and there is a photograph of a boy on the front page of a newspaper. The boy, he realizes, is the boy he left in his car; he realizes, too that something in his bowels has forsaken control and that he is in a state of shock. The paper is in a blue wire rack before a luncheonette.

He is walking on, he knows.

BOY, 12, MISSING, the headline said.

He shifts to the store side of the sidewalk and stops. He feels he could slide to the ground. People are passing in both directions. He stands there.

Something has him step back to the luncheonette, whose windows are steamed over. He looks again. There is the boy. It is the boy he left in his car. It isn't a good likeness; you'd have to know him to recognize him, he thinks. His hair looks darker in the picture. His features are not very clear. You'd have to know him to recognize him.

Another paper in the wire rack—a more local paper, Vernon realizes—shows artists' sketches of two men, both bearded, under a headline saying, "POLICE SEEKING 2 MEN." Looking closer, Vernon reads, "Police today issued a warning to area residents concerning two separate incidents of sexual harassment that occurred within the past week."

Two other papers in the rack are *The Boston Globe* and *The New York Times*. Each of the out-of-state papers, Vernon notices, has a front-page story starting with the phrase "Post-Vietnam . . ." Vernon looks over the papers, trying to think that nothing matters, that in the newspaper or not, it will go unread, unnoticed. Or will it? Time seems for the moment to tumble through his chest and stomach like a video game.

Inside, at a glass counter, he places a dollar on the surface and says, "*Portsmouth Herald.*" It is a paper he has never bought before; his thought is that if he asks the price, everyone will turn to him and they will know he is the one. He takes up coins in change.

Outside, folding over the copy without looking at it, he carries it in his hand. Realizing he still has his change in his left hand, and that his palm is sticky in spite of the cool air, he releases the coins into his pocket. As he walks, he glances to the sky. It is heavily gray now. Perhaps it will rain, he thinks.

Reentering the small shopping center, he looks down over the rows of parked cars. People are walking back and forth here, too, and he doesn't see anything unusual. Still, he walks along before the rows of stores, trying to spot his car—he cannot seem to locate it—and turns into the supermarket.

On his way out, he goes through a checkout line to pay for a single purchase. The store is busy now—dinner hour is here, students are buying food—and even in the express aisle there are four or five people ahead of him. The boxed pastry he has picked up is expensive—$1.98—but remembering how little the boy ate of the soup, his thought is to tempt him with something special. And to drop him off at a hospital emergency room, he thinks. Or do something else with him, get rid of him, he thinks in this moment, allowing this forbidden thought at last, going along in the line of customers.

"You get the paper here?" a young woman says, ready to poke a key.

Vernon is looking at her but doesn't know what is being asked.

"Our newspaper or yours?" she says.

"Mine," he says.

She places some coins in his hand and sacks his single purchase. You don't have any idea what I am thinking, he is thinking as he takes the bag from the woman's hands. It seems he could tell her, too, could tell her something in this moment, as he has been able to tell himself, of the enormity of his thought, but she has already shifted her attention to the next customer, and he is left to go on his way.

Everyone is so busy, he thinks, walking along. Oh, God, he wants to cry out.

Through the pneumatic door, into the cool air, he strolls along the curbed pedestrian walkway before the stores until he can spot the front of his car. A van is parked next to it, blocking most of it from view.

He pauses before the window of a hardware store. Could it be the police hiding in the van? he wonders. Ha, he thinks. They wouldn't be so clever.

Nor, he thinks, if they found the boy would they leave him there as bait. They'd take him away, he thinks. They'd take him away and there'd be six police cars pulled up by now, surrounding his car with lights flashing.

Carrying the newspaper and grocery sack, he walks in an adjacent aisle past his own car. When he is opposite, he glances over to see if the boy is still in the front seat.

He sees in a glance that he is.

Circling, he comes into the aisle behind his car. Nothing appears unusual. On a burst of nerve, he turns in between the van and his car, opens the door without rushing, slides in behind the wheel, and closes the door.

He takes a breath.

"Got you something to eat," he says.

The boy actually stirs, makes a sound, in response to his voice.

"Pastry," Vernon says. "Apple something. Pastry."

The boy seems to breathe audibly and move in response to this, although he doesn't make any other sounds.

Vernon reaches the sack to the floor behind the passenger seat but holds on to the newspaper. He had had no feeling to read the story when he first saw it, nor as he carried it through the store; here, all at once, he is anxious to see what it says. As if to glimpse life's meaning.

Holding the paper for light from the fading sky, he reads:

> Police say they have no clues in the disappearance of a 12-year-old Portsmouth youth who's been missing since Saturday. The boy is Eric Wells, who is in the sixth grade at Little Harbor Elementary School.

"This is not looking like a routine missing case," said Detective Lt. Gilbert Dulac of Portsmouth. "The boy had no money or wallet on him and this may be a giveaway."

Mrs. Claire Wells, the boy's mother, said he left the Legion Hall on Islington Street at about 6:45 p.m. Saturday. Mrs. Wells, a divorcée, works as a barmaid there on weekends.

Police said school officials describe Eric as an average student with a good attendance record.

He is 4 feet 10, weighs about 100 pounds, has medium-length dark blond hair and blue eyes.

Persons with any information that could help police locate Eric are asked to call Portsmouth Police Department at 421-3859.

Vernon sits still then and knows that he is again in shock of a kind. There is something in the paper that makes things more real than they seem to be here where he can actually touch them.

Moments later he is driving out of the small university town on a two-lane paved road. He has the car's headlights on; carefully, he passes a jogger, then another jogger, then someone on a bicycle. He will be careful not to break any laws, he thinks. Only greater laws, he thinks. Darkness falling so rapidly, light leaving the sky, seems both the end of the world to him and a promise of cover.

Driving along, he says, "So your mother's a barmaid?"

Expecting no response and receiving none, he says, "So is mine."

SIXTEEN

MATT SITS IN THE KITCHEN in the lowering darkness. His mother is on her way to Portland with the lieutenant. Before he turns on any lights, however dim the apartment has grown, Matt gets himself to telephone Vanessa.

Answering the phone herself, she says to him, "They talked to me, you know."

"The police?"

"That's right. Real neat."

Matt doesn't know what to say. At last he says, "What does that mean?"

"Humiliation city is what it means."

"Are your parents there?"

"They're not listening."

Again Matt doesn't know what to say. Then he says, "I'm sorry. I had to tell them."

"Yeah, forget it," she says.

Matt has no idea what to say.

"I have to go," she says.

"Will I see you in school?" he says.

"Probably."

SEVENTEEN

IT IS CLOSE TO NINE when Dulac has returned from Portland and from taking Claire Wells home. Her appeal and its taping were fine, he thinks. Something about her image on camera would command viewers' attention, at the same time that it would not be confrontational. So he believes, or hopes. "Eric," she said to the camera, "we love you. I do. So does Matt. We miss you. Please come home. Or please call up. If you are with someone, we just want you to come home. We hope that person will let you go. Everyone misses you at school, too."

Who knows what is confrontational? Dulac thinks. And what isn't?

He butters a roll. Claire Wells's words keep playing in his mind. Their tone, the implications, the effect on viewers, the effect on someone holding the woman's twelve-year-old son? Anything could set such a person off, Dulac thinks. Who knows? There are cheesy noodles, broccoli, and pork chops on his plate, and he eats methodically, chews over one thing and another. Unless, of course, the boy is already dead, he thinks. Like the chief said. As others have said. As he doesn't wish to believe.

"Thinking about your case?" Bea says, across the table. Unlike other times when he has come in late, when she usually continues watching television, she is sitting with him now.

"Yeah," he says.

"Everyone at work is talking about it," she says.

"Are they?" he says. Talk of this kind is off-limits, of course, according to their old pact. Still he adds, "Just from the radio?"

"And TV," she says.

He nods. Then he says, "The fliers, too, I guess."

"A couple people did mention those," she says.

"That's good," he says. "Wait until tomorrow, with the papers out this evening. And of course, the mother's appeal tonight on TV. But I think the papers get the biggest response."

"You're not still feeling upset?" she says.

"No, no, I'm fine," Dulac says. He continues to eat, to sip from his glass of ice water. She brought it up, he is thinking.

"What's she like?" Beatrice says.

Dulac pauses, as if to finish a mouthful. Then he says, "You sure you want to talk about this?"

"Well, everyone is asking me questions."

"What kind of questions?"

"Well, what does Gil think has happened to him? That kind of thing. What they want to know, of course, is if I know anything. At the same time everyone's a little afraid, you know. Certainly those who have children."

Dulac hunches his shoulders, chews some more. Then he says, "I don't want you to tell people what I think."

"I won't," she says.

He sips more water. "If it's what it seems to be," he says, "then it's probably sexually motivated."

"You think so?"

"Odds would have it, too, that he's no longer alive."

"Oh."

"I hope he is. Our assumption is that he is. That's why we're trying to be careful."

"A twelve-year-old boy. It's sad."

"There's a risk in what we're doing. If he is alive and being held, we're putting pressure on the person holding him."

"Meaning?"

"Well, put yourself in the place of someone holding him. Here's all this pressure, a lot of people despising you, looking for you. What would you do?"

"I'd take off, I guess."

"After you did away with the evidence. Buried it. What would you do if no one seemed to be looking for you or seemed to be mad at you?"

"I don't know."

"Neither do I. But chances are it would be neither of the above. That's the risk, you see. For me."

Bea doesn't say anything then, as he continues to eat. The reason they banned such dinnertime conversation has entered the air; his own food taste is affected. "Don't mention that to anyone," Dulac says.

"I bet you're tired," Bea says after a moment.

"I am. I know this is just getting started, too."

"Do you have any good leads?" she says.

Dulac looks over at her, surprised again. "Not really," he says, continuing with his chewing. "The problem now, the chief told me a couple hours ago—with the papers out—could be in keeping the pressure from ourselves."

"From yourselves?"

"From the press and so on. The media. To answer that question you just asked. Do you have any leads? What's going on? If the press takes it on, the chief says to watch out for the politicians—city, state, and so on—and of course he thinks the press will take it on."

"Politicians?"

"That's what he says. If it's action, if it's carried by the papers, they're going to want a piece of it."

"Does that make sense?"

"I don't know. It's what he says. He says we'll spend half our time on the case and half justifying ourselves."

"You've had big cases before," she says.

"Not like this, though. It's almost fashionable."

She nods; once more he turns back to his food. "So how did things go with the mother on TV?" she says.

"Fine, I think. I think she did a fine job. We told her to keep it simple and direct. To imagine she was speaking only to her son. Directly. To just ask him to come home. You'll see."

"What's she like?"

"The reason I think she was effective is that she just spoke clearly. And slowly, too. I mean she wasn't slow, but the TV people, you know, their voices are so quick, and here was this woman who just says, 'We love you Eric. We miss you. Please come home.' It shot me through for a minute, you know. I think it did everyone who was there."

"She works at Boothbay?"

"Yeah, she's just an ordinary person who works. Lives in an apartment with her two boys. A single mother. The touch in the paper calling her 'a divorcée who works as a barmaid' was inaccurate. The newspaper people amaze me. I guess that kind of thing sells."

"She's a nice person?"

"She's a fine person. She's been working as a waitress on weekends, working two jobs just to keep her family together. Then this happens."

He doesn't say any more. Nor does he eat any more, although he has food left on his plate, and he never leaves food on his plate. "I'm going to have a drink," he says. "You want a drink?"

"No, thanks."

While he is up then, Bea says to him, "What should I say if people ask me things?"

"Say," he says, "that you and your old man never discuss his work."

"It's so sad, isn't it?" she says. "In a little town like this."

EIGHTEEN

VERNON SLIPS BACK to his hiding place in the hospital parking lot. He has driven here on another thought of laying the boy at the door of the emergency room. And going on his way. Going back to the cottage, doing his school work, returning to his life. Taking his chances.

He sits in the dark car, though, looking over the tops of cars. It is quiet; visiting hours are over.

A car is entering then. Pulling into the lot, it parks in the crowd of cars close to the building. Vernon watches. He feels distant, even absent. Nothing happens to the car for a moment, until a man emerges, closes the door—no sound comes to Vernon, as if there is an overall drone of generators—and walks away, into the overlapping buildings. Vernon feels he has a vantage point, all at once, on existence itself, here in his hiding place.

A woman is coming from one of the buildings. She is on a sidewalk, where she pauses under a floodlight. She wears a dark coat and does not appear to have on white stockings or white shoes, like so many others. She slips into a car in the main concentration of cars, and in a moment, soundlessly, the car's exhaust lifts into the darkness. Her headlights come on; as she pulls around to drive away, another car is entering.

"Wake up," Vernon whispers to the boy, as he looks at him.

Then it comes to him that he doesn't really want the boy to wake up. If the boy would join him, and make a game of imagining why people are coming and going from the hospital, it would be wonderful. It would be all he ever wanted.

But he won't, Vernon thinks. Not now or ever.

He settles back and looks up through the windshield as if it were a skylight. No stars are visible. Low clouds look pink in the darkness as they reflect light from below. A capability is in him, he sees, and he is merely waiting. He is merely waiting. It has come to this.

NINETEEN

MATT IS STANDING. He has no feeling to sit down. The news is almost there. He stands behind the couch where his mother is sitting. What if Vanessa sees his mother on television? he thinks. Would she ever speak to him again? Everyone will see his mother, he thinks.

"Mom," he starts to say.

"Shh," she says. "Don't talk now. Let's just watch this."

"It's only a commercial," he says.

"I said be quiet! Why don't you sit down?"

He was only going to ask how long she thought she'd be on. He stands there with his hands on the back of the couch, as a couple is shown at a desk. Anchorman and anchorwoman. The woman leads off, saying something about nuclear disarmament talks breaking off or starting up. The man returns a headline about missing POWs, and then the woman says, "Meanwhile, in Portsmouth tonight a mother appeals for the return of her missing twelve-year-old son, whose whereabouts remain unknown."

Matt stands there. He seems to think, okay, that wasn't so bad. Other headlines are given, followed by commercials and then the man is talking about Southeast Asia. Matt doesn't take in any of the words. Then—all at once it seems—the woman is talking about Eric Wells, who is twelve, who lives in Portsmouth, who was last seen Saturday evening . . . and the words are ringing, striking into Matt's mind, going by too quickly.

There is his mother. He is shocked by her looks. She is pale, small, and old in comparison to people on television. She speaks so slowly. "Matt and I both love you," her voice says into their living room. "We want you to come home."

Matt feels lost. He feels as he did once when he saw a man and a woman fighting, physically, on the sidewalk. For moments afterward, he felt lost. So does he also miss the following, quickly spoken stories now; they fly past him. *Matt and I both love you*, he hears again. Is that all there is to life? he wonders.

"What did you think?" his mother says, turning to look at him at last.

"About what?"

"Well, what do you think?" she says.

"I don't know."

"*Was it okay?*" she says. "*Did you think it was okay?*"

"Sure."

"My gosh, is that all you can say?"

"What do you expect me to say? I thought it was okay."

She is looking to the screen again, and Matt wanders into the kitchen. He looks around there, feeling he doesn't know what to do. Does he love Eric? he is wondering. Does he? What is love? He had thought it was the amazing feeling he had had for Vanessa Dineen. Yet he thinks and sees—in this moment—that he feels something, too, for Eric. It's like the ground or the air, he thinks. It's not rainbows and flash floods. It's the two of them talking in the dark at night in their bedroom when they were supposed to be going to sleep. Or walking somewhere. That's what he misses all at once, what appears to be gone in this moment.

Love for his brother. Where is he? Why isn't he here? Why would some man pick him up? How could anyone be interested in a little kid like Eric for something like that?

Matt stands next to the sink in the kitchen. His eyes are confused with everything. It comes into his head that he has to say it aloud, speak it out, declare it, if it's going to do any good in bringing his brother home again.

He listens to the sounds of their life. The refrigerator hums. Other things hum. A weather report is spilling from the TV in the other room; a man is chirping—"low pressure . . . cold front . . . chance of precipitation . . ." Matt imagines his mother watching, imagines Eric gone from her mind.

It must be said aloud, he knows, and he utters, "Rockport, come on home, man. I love you."

Time pauses.

"Did you say something, Matt?" his mother says.

"What?" he says.

"I said did you say something?"

Wandering back into the living room, he leans on the couch behind her, keeping his eyes on the screen. "What's the weather?" he says.

"It's not very good," his mother says, sitting there under him.

TWENTY

DULAC IS IN THE BATHROOM when the call comes. Beatrice, coming to the door, tells him the duty officer is on the phone.

Getting himself together, going to the phone in the hall, he hears the officer explain that they have a call from a man who says he will speak only to the lieutenant, because he knows from the paper that the lieutenant is in charge of the case. Also, this guy says that *he* has to do the telephoning, because he will not give out his number. "Maybe he's a crackpot," the officer says.

"He wants my home number?"

"Right. He's going to call back in a minute to see if you'll give it out."

"What did he sound like?"

"Sort of arrogant, maybe. He was—"

"Local?"

"It was a local call."

"Give him my number. Tell him to call right away. Tell him I'll be waiting."

To Beatrice then, who is in the bedroom watching the *Late Show* and waiting, Dulac knows, he says he's going downstairs to take a call, and he slips back into his shirt and pants.

"You mean about the little boy?" she says.

"I'm not sure," he says. "Maybe." He has no wish to tell her, no wish to build up hopes.

Downstairs in the kitchen, he has fixed a cup of cocoa—tearing a packet, heating a splash of water from the hot water faucet—before the telephone at the cookbook desk rings.

"Hullo," he says.

"Lieutenant Dulac?" the man says.

"That's right."

"I just thought I should call," the man says. "But I'm *not* going to identify myself. I want you to know that at the outset."

"Okay," Dulac says. "Can you tell me why you're calling?"

"I saw it in the paper," the man says. "About the missing boy. Then I just saw the mother on television."

"Okay. Do you know the mother—or the boy? What is it you have?"

"Well, I'm reluctant to say. I don't mean to be evasive. I just can't afford to get involved in anything myself. I mean I want to help, but there are other considerations."

"Okay," Dulac says. "Okay. Just let me know what you have. We'll talk about it."

"I just want to be a good citizen," the man says.

"Sir, do you have someone to report? A suspect?"

"That's exactly what I have."

"Do you know this person's name?"

"Not really. I don't think so. That is, he gave me a name, but I have a feeling it wasn't the truth."

"What name did he give you? Could you be more specific?"

"Let me back up a little if I can. Again, I'm sorry to be evasive."

"Okay," Dulac says.

"I'm gay," the man says. "And I'm a professional. If this were to come out, it could cost me dearly. Financially. Professionally. At the same time, I want to be a good citizen, like anyone else. Am I making sense?"

"I think so," Dulac says. "At the same time, you wouldn't need to worry about your identity being disclosed by me; I don't work like that."

"That's fine," the man says. "It's not a chance I'm willing to take, though. Sorry."

"What is your profession—would you mind telling me that?"

"Come on, don't play games now."

"I don't mean to play games. Tell me about this suspect."

"Well, I don't know much. It's a person I met."

"Who is the person? When did you meet him?"

"I'm not going to tell you where I met him."

"Sir, listen. I understand your concern. About your identity. I appreciate that. Okay? If you have some information, though—and if you *do* want to be a good citizen—then I have to ask you to be a little more forthcoming. We do have a twelve-year-old boy out there somewhere—if he's still alive—and to tell you the truth, we need all the help we can get."

When the man doesn't respond, Dulac says, "*Why* are you suspicious of this person?"

"I just want it understood that the so-called gay community is *not* irresponsible," the man says. "Do you hear what I'm saying?"

"Loud and clear. Now please tell me what you have."

Dulac listens; there is nothing.

"In a gay bar," the man says then. "Saturday. Early evening. Happy hour. I picked up this young guy. It came out in conversation—he was interested in boys. Young boys, I believe, although I'm not sure he was even gay. He was different. I took him to my place, but nothing worked out. He became upset. Visibly upset. He just took off. It was perhaps six forty-five when he left. The paper said the boy disappeared about seven."

"Were you within ten minutes' driving time of Islington Street—near downtown?"

"Yes," the man says.

"Really?" Dulac says.

"Yes," the man says.

"Would it be out of the way for him to end up on Islington Street?" Dulac says.

"Not at all."

"Really?"

"It's exactly on the way. That's why I'm calling."

Dulac pauses. "Listen," he says. "If we should lose this connection, be sure and call me back. What I want you to do right now—and I'm going to be taking this on tape, too, which I hope doesn't bother you; it's only for recall purposes—what I want you to do is give me a full description. Everything you can think of about this person. Did he have a car?"

"Oh, yes."

"Did you get a license number?"

"No, I'm afraid not."

"Was it in-state?"

"I think so. I'm not sure."

"Make and model?"

"I'm not sure of that either. It was silver. Or gray. A recent model. Fairly recent. Small. A coupe. Like a two-door coupe. As for the make, I just don't know. I'm not into cars."

"Were you *inside* the car?"

"No. He followed me."

"Okay. Start with him. With a description. This may take some time, but it's important that we do it right away, so we can act on it. Start with a physical description of this person. Start with his age, please. How old was he? Did he say? Did he indicate his age in any way?"

As the man talks then, even as his tape-recording device is running, Dulac scratches around with a pencil, making notes of details such as *early to mid-twenties, childlike, emotional, seemed educated*. Some fifteen or twenty minutes later, when he has covered everything he can think of and has persuaded the man to telephone him at his office number at nine o'clock in the morning—"to maintain contact," Dulac tells him, "because this sounds promising and I'm sure I'll think of something between now and then I forgot to ask you,"—Dulac thanks him and immediately telephones the special desk, to put out a general alert on a small silver car. He telephones the chief at home then, waking him, tells him that they have what sounds like a possible suspect and that they need to meet first thing in the morning, to come up with some way to protect the identity of the man who called. "I need to get at this guy, get more dope from him, get him to rack his brains, help with a composite, and so on."

The chief is less frantic. They do have a secret witness program, he explains. On the books somewhere. Although in a small town like this, not many things would stay secret very long.

"Eight o'clock," Dulac says. "We'll pull it out. I want to have it ready by nine, when this guy calls back."

At several minutes after one, when he has told himself not to get worked up—it may prove to be nothing—Dulac turns off the lights and returns upstairs. In the dark bedroom, when Beatrice says, groggily, "Well?" he says, "Knock on wood. It's all I can say right now. It sounds possible. Knock on wood."

Lying in the dark, though, lying on his side and seeming to stare through the house, through the walls and out over the countryside, he finds his thoughts keep returning to the implications of time and place, of motivation. Then again, his thoughts run over the implications of time and place, of motivation. And then again, as he lies there.

PART FOUR

An Act of Cowardice

TUESDAY, FEBRUARY 17, 1981

ONE

SOMETHING AWAKENS HIM, in terror. An alarm has gone off in his heart and is now quiet, in terror's aftermath. During the night he awakened again and again, but not to alarm. Straightening now, in the driver's seat, feeling the cold from the windshield and side window, he sees there is nothing out there to have alarmed him. Anxiety-filled already, realizing he has unfolded some of the sleeping bag to cover himself, *knowing* the boy is still there, he tosses it back. *Don't move, don't say anything!* Vernon imagines snapping at him. He sees there is some light in the sky. Another day. Goddamn you, he thinks at once, still not touching the boy, nor even looking at him to ascertain that he remains alive. I have to get rid of you.

He sits still. His jaw is clenched and he wonders if what has crossed his mind was a passing thought. He doesn't know, could pursue it no further in his mind it seems if he wanted to, as he is looking over the parking lot, cars, buildings, questioning again what it was that awakened him to such a frightened feeling. All looks still, and he wonders if a car went by and tooted its horn. Stupid cops, he says to himself all at once. Stupid idiot cops. Why is it so easy to outsmart them? How can anyone be so stupid? Why aren't they here?

He touches the boy then. Reaching, finding his arm, he shifts to his uncovered wrist, turns it upside down and with two fingers searches for his pulse. He searches and searches, without concern. He finds it then, feels its message of life telegraphing through to him.

Life and death. They are that close. Odd disappointment is in him. As the faint pulse under the boy's skin keeps lifting, Vernon knows it was an end he was looking for, not a continuation.

He drops the boy's wrist and returns his attention to the sky. What to do? he thinks. What to do and where to go? There seems a continuous sound of ocean in the air; otherwise there is stillness. There is both sound and stillness. Another day. Moments to be counted. This is what it is to be alive. Counting moments. Then when the telegraphing stops, life is over; who knows what part of it has been a dream and what follows thereafter.

Nothing follows thereafter, Vernon thinks. Nothing. A thought stirs in his mind and loins to have sex with the unconscious boy; he tells himself this is ludicrous even as he marvels at the egocentricity of his libido. A cock has a mind of its own. A hard-on has no conscience. He feels new desperation. He could do it, he thinks. He isn't going to, but he could. The horrible psychology of it excites and angers him, until he gets himself to look away from the idea in even more anger.

"I could take you to the door of the emergency room and drop you off," he utters to the boy. "I could do that, but I'm not going to because I'd get caught then and I don't want to be caught. Do you understand how angry I am with you? Do you?"

Where a high span of horizon is visible between buildings and trees, he discerns the faintest washing into the sky of daylight. A watercolor sweep along a straight line. Day is breaking. Vernon has a feeling that something from the heavens has spoken to him, in the moments before daybreak, has spoken of life and death and of the revolutions of planets through the universe.

No one counts, he thinks. Or ever has. Even as some names linger longer than others, all simply disappear into nothing, carry less weight than particles of sand washing up on beaches down through the ages, through eons. Life is a passing moment. A momentary gift. A brief pleasure in seeing something and thinking something, afflicted entirely with a need for love. A cruel paradox.

A car entering brings him back. The car's headlights pass before him; he watches the car pull into a parking space. Its lights go off. In a moment, doors on both sides open and close and two women appear, walking in the direction of the hospital buildings. Going on duty, Vernon thinks. He decides in this moment to move out of here, to attempt to do something. It seems a moment of clarity, a span in his own anxious horizon, although he doesn't know what to do or where to go. To go on duty. He has to get out of trouble, he thinks. He has to get away from this trouble. He has to do what has to be done. He has no choice anymore.

Another car enters, then another. The headlights follow in, one directly behind the other.

Maybe, he thinks then, the boy will come around like he did yesterday. Maybe if he gives him something warm again to drink, he will regain consciousness and be okay. Reaching, as if he hasn't already done so, he holds his fingers over the boy's opened lips, feels the warmth of his breath. Why don't you wake up? he thinks to beg of him. Can't you understand anything?

Sitting up behind the steering wheel, Vernon turns the keys to start the motor and is startled by the sudden sound. Yet no one is running at him.

Not waiting, he pulls out, without knowing where he is going or what he is going to do. Another car with headlights on is entering the parking lot as he approaches the exit, and he pulls his car's light switch, not to be different.

Pulling up at the exit, he watches the light, early-morning traffic passing in the street. He pauses. At least he doesn't have to decide immediately which way to go. No one is pulling up to press him from behind. Before him, cars keep going by and it is clear that the small city on the ocean is starting a new day. Going to work, he thinks. People are going to work, taking all things for granted.

What day is it? Is it Tuesday? Was it only Saturday that all of this started? This grief and fear. It seems it has been with him all his life, all his mornings and nights, that it may never go away.

An added moment slips by as Vernon watches the thin parade of morning cars. It is only when the headlights of a car suddenly turn into view behind him, that his anxiety jumps back into place.

He presses, manipulates the car's pedals to escape, rolls, accelerates, brakes, rolls again as he looks to his mirror to see the aggressive headlights still coming on. Unsure which way to go, he accelerates again, into a long space between cars and is surprised that the other car does not roar after him. Driving on, following the traffic, he is surprised at the new uncertainty he feels, to be on the loose once more, to have to do things, to have to decide what he cannot decide.

He drives to the police station. Following traffic, it happens that he sees a milky white sign with blue letters and an arrow, POLICE→, and he turns nervously, as if instructed to do so. There is an old stone building which looks like a town library, police cars with insignias and dome lights nosed up quietly along its side, and a sign on the front door: ←USE SIDE ENTRANCE.

Passing, he pulls over, looking to park, and does so, paying no mind to parking signs. He doesn't know what he is doing or going to do. There is a thought in his mind to walk into the police station and say he is the person they are looking for—he sees in this moment why such surrenders often happen—and as he turns off motor and lights and sits there, he tries to consider going that way.

He gets out of his car. That a policeman might be watching him frightens him less than it seems an odd attraction, a dark magnetic pull. The sky appears altogether gray and overcast. As he steps around to the sidewalk, though, a curious thing happens. There is a strong smell in the air of bread baking. Bread, pastries, cookies—something of the kind. Dimly lighted windows just along the sidewalk, he sees, belong to a bakery. The smell is warm. Stepping along to look in the windows, he sees that the main lights are to the rear—in the foreground are several small tables and chairs—above a long work surface where several women, five or six, are working with pans and dough, mixing pots, spatulas. Behind them is a complex of black ovens, with many doors and handles.

Vernon stands there watching. The women wear head scarves and long-sleeved shirts; all appear to be working industriously, looking to their work and not to each other. The setting looks like a stage set, the women like actors in a play. There are so many women and no men, and Vernon is increasingly affected by the warm baking smells and by what he sees. They are all hurt and wounded, he thinks, working together for salvation, baking, of all things, expressing vows of some kind; as he notices two glass-bulb coffeepots on a heater, on a glass-top counter, next to a cash register facing the customer side, one full, the other half full, cups, cream and sugar there, too, for self-service, it seems another remarkable step in a sequence. His anger feels tempered.

The heavy door opens under his hand. He is inside and however slightly, life is appearing possible again. As he steps to the counter, though, none of the women look up or seem to have noticed him. They continue to work, and he tries to contain the excited adoration he feels, as if they will save him as they are saving themselves.

What can he say? How can he ask for help? He wants to cry out to them that it is a miracle to him that they are open, that he has happened to stop here.

He will be a customer, he decides, on a rush of feeling. To think, he thinks, that being a customer might be so meaningful. Clay mugs are upside down on a tray, next to Styrofoam cups and plastic lids; fresh-baked loaves, one of them cut, are along the old glass counter. He turns upright one of the clay mugs and as if he has been adrift at sea feels he might weep with joy at the sustenance being offered. He pours steaming coffee into the mug and still no one comes to him. "I need help," he says then, and adds, less certainly, "I need help."

A woman who is taller than the others speaks softly over the worktable and a younger woman puts down her work and walks over. The young woman's face is round; her eyes resemble horse chestnuts under her lightly flowered head scarf. "The coffee is self-serve," she says. "I will cut the brioche if you like. This is walnut. This is blueberry. This is pecan. Excuse me one moment."

The young woman seems to recite, as if just learning to speak; standing there, Vernon watches her step back to confer, in whispers, with the tall woman. Returning, her skirt so long it nearly reaches the floor, the young woman, eyes wide and glassy, says, "Each slice costs ninety cents."

"I need help," Vernon says. "That's what I need."

The girl looks at him as if perplexed; with hands raised she presents the first brioche, which has been cut. With her eyebrows she inquires if it is his choice.

"Okay, yes," he says.

As he watches, she cuts a great five-inch thickness weighing perhaps a pound, from which syrupy walnuts ooze, which she turns over onto a small plate. As he offers to pay, she makes an expression like a mute, steps away once more to whisper to the tall woman, and returning, says, "You may pay now or after."

He hands her two dollars. He steps to one of the small tables, places his coffee and brioche there, and steps back to the cash register, where the young woman has shifted. As he holds out his hand to receive his change, she places a fistful of coins on the counter next to it, uncounted, and returns to her place in the rear.

At the table, Vernon devours the warm bread-pastry in a moment and sits looking through the window at his side. More cars pass; others turn in at the police station. He sips the coffee and thinks of how little the boy out in the car has had to eat and drink. The thought surprises him, as if remembering something he had entirely forgotten. He looks back to the women in head scarves and sees how they resemble unopened flowers, looking down all the time, saying so little. Work may set them free, he thinks. Work and companionship. But not really, he thinks then. Not really.

He is startled all at once, hearing someone enter, to see a uniformed policeman at the counter saying, "Let me have a piece of that bread." The young policeman has no stripes on his dark blue uniform, nor is he wearing a hat, and he is hardly older than Vernon.

As Vernon looks, the policeman turns, looks at him, and says, "That your car outside?"

Vernon says nothing, gives no sign, freezes.

"If it is, you better move it before the traffic starts up," the young policeman says. "That's a no parking zone."

In a moment, as Vernon glances through the window, the young policeman is striding back across the street, and he is wondering if the older detective, the large man whose picture was in the paper, would miss him so easily. He wonders, too, if the young policeman was lenient because he felt some kind of kinship or sympathy with the women and their bakery.

Vernon is back at the counter, next to the cash register, when he feels he is going to break down and cry out for his mother. "Could you help me, please?" he says.

The taller woman looks and comes over; it is clear she has read the appeal in his voice. "What is it?" she says. "What do you want?"

"Can you give me a job?" Vernon says. "I'll clean up, wash everything, I'll sleep on the floor, I'll do whatever has to be done. I'll never go away. Never."

The woman is looking at him. "I'm sorry," she says. "We have no such position."

"I'm in real need," Vernon says.

"I can tell that," she says. "I'm very sorry."

"I'm in trouble," he says.

She continues to look at him. "Don't you have a family?" she says.

"No, not really," he says.

"No, not really?" she says, making an expression of having heard this before. "I'm sorry," she says. "We're just a bakery."

"I'm desperate," he says.

"Sir, I'm sorry," she says. "We're just a bakery."

Vernon looks down, as if reprimanded by his mother. As always at such times, his mind stops turning and he doesn't know what to say.

TWO

MATT IS UP EARLY. There is plenty of time to get ready for school, but he doesn't know if he will go. Unlike most other mornings, most of his life, he has an urge today to go to school. He wants to be there. He wants things to be as usual. If he could go back and start over, he thinks, he would do it right this time. He would be good in school, and happy, and

210

Eric would not be missing but would be here this morning, also getting ready for school.

The bathroom is quiet. Matt has walked in and walked over to stand at the window without turning on the light. Barefoot, he stands on the cool floor, beyond the new blue rug. His mother is in her room, asleep he imagines. There is no pushing or jockeying for toothpaste or for the sink or toilet this morning, even if it is early. It's so quiet. It's hard to believe that he would prefer the pushing and grabbing and their quick tempers to this stillness and aloneness.

The lower half of the window is bubbled. He stands where he can look through the upper half, beside the old manila-colored window shade. He sees chilled air, first light coming into the gray sky.

He looks back to the sink, thinking to see Eric's toothbrush gone. Eric's toothbrush is not gone, though. It's there next to his own, in Eric's chosen color of blue. It means that Eric is gone against his wishes, and that he is hurt and cold out there somewhere. Matt stands next to the window and realizes that he just doesn't know what to do. He is never up early like this. He has no idea what to do. None. In the only such appeal of his life, he thinks, says to himself, God, if you exist please let Eric come home. He feels no hope as he stands there, though. He feels little more than guilt, and this new desperation which will not leave him alone.

THREE

Across the street from the bakery, in the police station, Dulac is in the squad room, drawing his first cup of coffee. The shift change is under way, but the activity is at the other end of the room. Dulac is early—it is just after seven—and feels somewhat groggy for lack of sleep at the same time that he is possessed of an eagerness, on the new lead, to get things under way. He especially likes being here early, for a feeling of confidence it gives him, a feeling of being ahead of the other side; carrying his coffee to his cubicle, he winks, as if to say, *I'm going to get that sonofabitch.*

He wishes Shirley Moss were here. It is to her especially that he wants to say, *It looks like we have a real suspect.* Or perhaps he will say, *We have a suspect—did you hear?*

Sitting at his desk, he explores possibilities. That the suspect is young, he thinks, could explain an apparent ease with which the boy went with him. Where he wouldn't go with the greaseball from the Naval Shipyard, he might trust a much younger man. Also, the time and place details, and the possible motivation, could explain the absence of anything like a pattern in the boy's movement, the role of chance. How else was a twelve-year-old boy picked up? A child might have a pattern on school days, but not on weekends. An encounter, an accidental crossing of paths takes place; an abduction occurs on impulse. An opportunity presents itself; action is taken. Thus an anonymous abductor.

Sex, he thinks. If the suspect was sexually frustrated—therefore, conceivably, sexually alert or on—would this or whatever he might say be stimulating to the boy? Was a twelve-year-old boy subject to such stimulation? Certainly, Dulac thinks, he would be subject to sexual stimulation, but would he respond to a young man in circumstances of the kind?

Would depend on the young man and depend on the boy, Dulac thinks. And on what the young man might do or say or present. Dirty pictures? Might the boy be sexually aroused, persuaded to go somewhere by being shown dirty pictures? Words? Could such a young man come up with just the right words that would work on such a boy?

Whatever or however, Dulac tells himself, he likes the looks of the lead. What he likes especially is the way it falls together so neatly, without inconsistencies—so far as they know, he tells himself yet again. Yet again, too, he wishes the chief would get here, so the secret witness program could be set up, and wishes Shirley Moss would arrive, too, so he could convey to her this charge he is feeling, the anticipation over this possible real break in the case. Nor is it only because he has a long-term, low-key crush on Shirley Moss that he is eager to see her; he desires her judgment, wants to see if her gut feeling on the new suspect is the same as his own. A kind of entrenched secretary, she has usually understood the implications of things more quickly and more accurately than have most others to whom he has turned. Of course, it is one of the reasons he likes her.

Or does he turn to her so often because—? he wonders.

She knows. She knows that he knows that she knows. He knows, too, that her feelings are more or less the same. They have a thing. At the same time nothing has ever been articulated or consummated or acknowledged. Both seem to know—he has imagined—that the attraction may be sustained, may remain endlessly stimulating, so long as it is not admitted. They do not go to lunch together, nor does she enter his cubicle and close the door; they never discuss anything but business, and on various social occasions, each may chat with the other's spouse in the most genuinely affectionate way.

The sweetness of fantasy, he says to himself now. An endless caramel available to his tired heart, an aid in bed, also, with Beatrice.

By seven thirty, though, Shirley has yet to arrive and he goes looking for the chief, to see if he has come in early. He has, as Dulac learns at the special desk, where he pauses to take a call himself and fill out a tip sheet. Standing next to the uniformed officer, who is on another phone, Dulac hears a fifteen-year-old high school girl, her mother in the background offering too much advice on what to say, tell of having seen a boy "forced into a car" on Saturday evening. Taking down her name, address, and telephone number, he asks if she knows Eric Wells; she does not, although his brother, Matt, although not a friend, is in her grade, she tells him. He asks her to describe what she saw.

What happened was, the girl tells him, this car pulls up, down on Congress Street, and it stopped beside this little boy who was walking on the sidewalk. This man got out on the driver's side and went around to the sidewalk, where he sort of talked to and sort of forced this boy into the back seat of the car behind this woman who opened her door on that side.

"How did he force him?" Dulac asks.

He sort of pushed him and held his arm, the girl tells him, the mother in the background saying, you said he pushed him hard.

"What did the woman do?" Dulac says. "Was it a two-door or a four-door car? Did she have to lean forward, out of the way, for the boy to get into the back seat?"

Yes, yes, the girl tells him. It was just like that, and the boy looked like the picture of Eric Wells in the paper.

Dulac asks if she was alone, and looking up sees Shirley Moss entering through the main door, waves at her, winks a little, hears the girl say no, she was with her girlfriend, and hears the mother say, tell him her name.

Writing down the girlfriend's name and address, telephone number and age, Dulac asks the girl if she knows what time it was that she saw the boy get into the car. The girl is able, as it turns out—on a couple more questions—to say almost exactly when it was because she and her girlfriend had just left Daddy's Junky Music Store as it was closing at six o'clock. Did they stop anywhere else? No, the girl tells him. She's absolutely sure of that? Dulac asks, reminding himself for the first time this morning not to close off his mind because they may have a suspect. They looked into windows, that was all, the girl explains, and together, the mother helping some more, they calculate that it was two and a half blocks later that they saw the boy being forced into a car.

Dulac asks several more questions, mainly about the car and about the description of the boy, and then he thanks the girl and tells her she will be contacted if any more information is needed. Still leaning over the desk, he completes the tip sheet, entering a C in its priority space— meaning no follow-up is required and places it in the wire tray next to the computer where it will be double-checked, entered in the computer file on the case, and the sheet itself filed in a drawer.

This done, mentioning to the chief's secretary in passing that he will be right back, he goes looking for Shirley. Finding her at the coffee maker in the squad room, where Mizener as well as two uniformed officers are also gathered with styrofoam cups, he can tell at a glance that she has already heard the news. "Shirley," he says, "there are some things I have to talk to you about right away, before I see the chief."

As she follows to his cubicle, he says, "We need to set up a press conference for ten thirty or so. In the squad room. So we can make this afternoon's paper. Anyone who calls, from the media, give them the message; call anyone who hasn't called, and ask them to attend."

"How *real* is this suspect?" Shirley says.

"I'm not sure; he looks real to me. I'll know more as soon as I talk to the witness again. Which is what I have to see the chief about. Do you know anything about our secret witness program?"

"I guess I don't. Why does it have to be secret?"

"The guy is gay, the witness; he's afraid it would hurt his job if it got out."

"Poor thing. What else do you have? Is that it?"

"Is that what?"

"You said you had several things."

"Well, this. We could have something here. If we do, and if the witness is good and cooperates, we could have a full description, even a composite, to put out at the press conference. Question is—what I wanted to ask you—if this *is* our guy, and if he is holding the boy, what do you think the effect on him would be, the impact, of a composite, a blast of info on him in the papers and on TV?"

"Gil, what are you saying?"

"The risk, you see. If we put out a blast of publicity, it seems a good chance that he'd snuff the boy, dispose of the body, and if we picked him up at all, assuming he didn't take off, claim not to know anything about anything. The critical thing would be forcing his hand. Assuming the boy is still alive."

Shirley is looking at him. Pausing, she says, "You think he's still alive?"

"We have no reason to think otherwise."

"Gee, I don't know, Gil. I'll tell you what I think. I think the little boy was picked up by some creep Saturday night, and he never saw daylight again."

"That's your gut reaction?"

"I guess it is," she says.

In his disappointment, Dulac glances down to avoid looking in her eyes. He feels stabbed. Is he being naive? Usually it's women and children who believe in the impossible. "I have to see the chief," he says.

As she starts away, he goes with her a step but turns back to his desk, as if he has forgotten something. Standing there, he feels once more as if he is going to break somehow. A faint anger comes up in him then and he goes on his way.

FOUR

VERNON IS WALKING on campus. In his state of mind he knows he has parked again, left the boy again, in the Shop 'n Save parking lot. He had thought to look for Anthony but is not looking for or at anyone. His nerves are so pinched that when someone calls his name his heart leaps up and wants to run.

There is Duncan, closing on him. "Quiet Man," he says. "What in the world is going on with you?"

Vernon is unable to say anything to this.

"Leon says you're pouting because he's been so insulting. I said you have something going." About Duncan's face is an urge to smile.

Vernon is unable to respond, and Duncan says, "Well, what is it?" still appearing eager to smile.

"I'm in trouble," Vernon says.

"Trouble—what do you mean?"

Vernon only looks, glances at him; he cannot say.

"What kind of trouble?" Duncan says.

"Life or death," Vernon says.

Duncan does more or less smile now. Then he says, "What does that mean?"

Again Vernon cannot say, even as he is trying to think of something.

As with all else, a conversation appears hopeless. There is a flash in his mind of the town police towing his car, discovering the boy there, putting A and B together. Was it happening right then? It would be the moment in his life, he is thinking, beyond which nothing would ever be so bad. The worst would be over.

"Tell me," Duncan is saying.

They are approaching a Y-intersection, where it seems to Vernon they will part to go in different directions. As he steps to the side, however, to let other students go by, Duncan stays with him. "Tell me what that means," Duncan says.

"It doesn't mean anything," Vernon says.

Duncan is shaking his head. "Vernon, you don't look real good, you know that?"

"I'm not good," Vernon says. "I'm not."

"What's the problem? Where are you sleeping?"

"In my car."

"In your car? Jesuschrist—is it Leon? Where are your books?"

Vernon doesn't say, cannot remember, although he is trying to think of something.

"Tell me you're not sleeping in your car because of that fucking Leon," Duncan says.

"I'm not," Vernon says.

"If you are, goddamit, I will not stand for it."

"I'm not," Vernon says.

"You're sure?"

"Yes—yes," Vernon says.

Duncan is looking at him. "Vernon, listen," he says. "If you're having problems, personal or whatever, why don't you talk to me about them. Okay? That's what friends are for, you know."

"Okay," Vernon says. "I will. Later, though."

"You get back tonight or later this afternoon, we'll talk over whatever the problems are. Will you do that?"

"Okay," Vernon says.

"I mean it. I don't care what the problems are. However personal, you understand? Nothing's so bad it can't be talked over and worked out. Okay? Do you need money?"

"Money?"

"Are you fixed okay for money? I can loan you some right now if you need it."

"No, no, I don't," Vernon says.

"You be back later?" Duncan says. "I want you to say you'll be back. We'll talk things out. Tell me you'll be back?"

"I will," Vernon says.

"Okay," Duncan says. "Good. I have to go to class. But I'll see you later. I mean it now."

Vernon nods, as if in agreement.

"Don't forget now," Duncan says.

"I won't," Vernon says.

Duncan nods and goes on, taking the leg to the left. Vernon waits another moment before turning back in the direction from which he came. Maybe he could blurt it out to Anthony, he is thinking. Maybe even to his mother, even as he knew she would not help him go undetected, or help him get away, or call a lawyer for legal assistance, that she would simply rage at him with insane anger, with accusations, would scream at him *why? why? why?*

At last though, or down deep, she would understand. Duncan would not understand, he thinks. Not ever.

He reverses direction. Acting out the slightest role of having forgotten something, he turns to go in the direction he had been going in before running into Duncan. He doesn't wish to return in the direction of his car. Why don't they catch him? he thinks. How can he just walk here like this?

He leaves the overcast air in a moment and turns into the library. Passing through its initial smell of overshoes, he discovers as if for the first time—beyond the long circulation counter—its dryness.

Warm air and carpets. Peace and quiet. No cars or loud voices. No cruelty here. Why had he never seen that this was life, too? Why had he been so lonely so much, looked so much to others with whom to spend time? Could he stay here forever? he wonders. Would they let him live here, in this building with floors the size of parking lots filled with books?

Might he trade his life in this way, as payment?

FIVE

MATT IS SITTING at the end of a wooden bench in the locker room. He is waiting for the rush of boys to change into gym clothes and disappear into the gym—which they are doing, quickly, in the midst of a near-constant slam-slamming of locker doors. Matt likes the feeling of being here—it's more like being home than home all at once—but he has no feeling to put on shorts, T-shirt, and sneakers and run around in the gym. He doesn't *have* to be here anyway, he thinks, so it doesn't matter if he misses gym. Or anything else. For an instant, however, he thinks of his mother at home alone, and his eyes close on him. It's all so weird, he thinks.

He looked to see Vanessa earlier, coming into the building, and he looked for her after his first class, and missed her both times. He doesn't even know yet if she's in school today. And he can't go look for her now, even if he does know her room, because of the rule against anyone being in the hallway during classes without a pass. She is what fills his mind, though, he thinks. Eric is there, too, sort of, but not like he was earlier, and his mother comes up in flashes. Vanessa has a grip on him. She seems never to be far away.

He could just take advantage, he thinks. Given the situation, who would hassle him? No, he tells himself, it wouldn't be right. The thought of taking advantage of things makes him feel cheap.

Still, a few minutes later, when he has walked throughout the empty locker room and has wondered again if what is happening is happening to him, he finds himself in an empty hallway, walking along. He isn't sure what he is doing, knows only that he is tending in the direction of Vanessa's classroom.

He catches her eye, but it takes several long minutes. Looking through the glass half of the door on an extreme angle, she finally—in a movement of her head—sees him. She shakes her head once, as if seeing double. She smiles faintly, and looks back down. God, she is actually beautiful, he thinks. A real person sitting in there. He guesses he loves her, as it occurs to him that he'd do anything to be with her.

When she looks his way again, however, there is something like a warning on her face as if to send him a message of another kind. He feels something of a fool and feels cheap again, but he doesn't know how to get out of it either, and so he stands there, nearly against the wall, watching her, waiting for her to look up again.

She doesn't.

It's the racial thing, he thinks. She feels funny letting it show in public that they know each other.

He does leave for a minute or two. Walking to one of the recessed drinking fountains, he leans down for a mouthful of lukewarm water. And he hears one of the hallway clocks click and looks to see its hand jump. Nothing makes sense, he thinks. Lost in space. That's how he feels.

From his angle again, he watches her. She doesn't look his way and he wonders if she looked for him in the moments he was gone. When she comes out, though, when the class ends and the room begins to empty, and there she is with her friend Barbara, a moment later than it seems she should be, she says to him, too directly, *"What are you doing?"*

He doesn't know what to say. So surprised that she is critical, so dumbfounded that she has seen right into his taking advantage, he feels too humiliated to speak, even as he does walk along the hallway beside the two girls. "Well, I was just going to say hello," he manages to say, as neither of the two girls has said anything more.

He is slowing up to turn away, and Vanessa has a new expression on her face. "Okay," she says. "You want to meet us for lunch?"

"I have second lunch," he says.

"I know what lunch you have," she says. "That's what lunch we have. So meet us for lunch."

"Sure," he says, "okay," knowing already, in the humiliation he is experiencing, that he will not.

"Anything new about your brother?" Vanessa says, as he is moving away.

"No," he says. "Why should there be?"

Getting turned the rest of the way around, saying no more, he keeps going, with no idea where he is going. He moves along, thinking of the main door just ahead when a hand grips his shoulder and tries to stop him.

"I'm sorry," Vanessa says.

"That's okay," he says. "No problem." She seems to fade, and getting his back turned a second time, he continues on his way.

Near the main door, though, there is Cormac, and another boy, and Cormac says to him, "Matt—hey, what's going on? Have they found your brother?"

"No," Matt says. "No, not yet."

"Jesus, how's it going?" the other boy says.

"All kinds of rumors are going around," Cormac says. "Even Mr. Kazur talked about it today, when he wasn't saying nasty things about Reagan."

"A bunch of kids, I heard, are going to be given lie-detector tests," the other boy says.

"Who said that?" Matt says.

"I could get one myself, because the police did talk to me," Cormac says.

"I heard it could have something to do with drugs," the other boy says. "That your brother hit on somebody's supply line and they took him hostage to teach him a lesson."

"Or knocked him off," Cormac says. "That's what I heard."

"Somebody else said they think the police might be in on it themselves because they control all the drug traffic and what happened is your brother accidentally discovered their network—"

"Who said that?" Matt says. "I haven't heard any of that stuff."

"I think that's all bullshit," Cormac says. "Who ever heard of something like that in some little town like this?"

"They did pick up somebody," Matt says. "This guy who offered Eric a ride. But they let him go. I do know that, because the police showed me his picture and asked me all kinds of questions about him."

"Wow—did they really?" the other boy says. "What kind of questions?"

"Oh, nothing, really. I'm not supposed to say," Matt says, and sensing the feeling of cheapness coming up in him again, moves away, saying, "I gotta go; I'm supposed to go in and answer some more questions myself."

You liar! he is thinking, passing through the door, walking into the air. *Stupid liar! You make me sick.*

All it is, he says to himself as he turns on the main sidewalk and hurries along as if to escape—all it is is you're more concerned with *her* than you are with your own brother. That's why you came here. Because you're a total zero. And she knows it.

Leaving the curb, Matt breaks into a run, to get away from himself. Along the street, angling to cross, he slips between parked cars and lopes on, the air in his eyes.

He feels an urge to go to the police station. That's what he'll do, he decides. Go see Lieutenant Dulac. On whatever pretext, he'll go see that one person—he is realizing as he jogs away from himself, as his feet hit the sidewalk one after another—who understands things, who knows what is going on, who heard the things he had to say and didn't look at him like he was crazy.

The idea seems so right, so appealing that Matt increases his pace. A glow comes up in his eyes.

SIX

DULAC IS OUTSIDE, walking, going to meet the witness. The man called at nine, as agreed, and upon a brief exchange, as he declined to come to the police station, however casually or carefully, Dulac suggested they meet two blocks down the street at Fisherman's Pier, near the wide river and away from any activity at this time of day.

Walking out on the pier now—the restaurant is closed and there is only the choppy seawater around the pilings below, not to mention an occasional squawking gull or a fishing boat motoring by out in the river—Dulac is trying again, or still, to sort out his thoughts and questions, the possible moves and implications concerning both the suspect and the man he is about to meet.

He is finding the air pleasant here, away from the confusion of phones and voices, almost away from the pressure itself of being directly responsible for the case. In the near shadow of the old Memorial Bridge, he waits next to a bleached wooden post and looks out over the green water lifting toward him in its massive way. Dulac is trying to think things out. There are a dozen things, it seems, to consider all at once, not least of all the possibilities of something inconsistent emerging to eliminate the suspect altogether, to have his tip sheet priority dropped from A double plus to C.

His license plate has to be familiar, Dulac thinks. It has to be. Maine, New Hampshire, Massachusetts. Anything else would have spoken loud and clear, even if it was only seen in a rearview mirror. There's no way a strange license plate would go unnoticed. Would it? Even on a short drive to sex?

No. The license plate would be noticed. It was daylight. The plate had to be familiar. He'd bet on it.

The details they have, he thinks. Two cheers at least for a gay witness. The suspect's exact height. Five nine and three-quarters. Green eyes. Brown hair. Clean fingernails—well cared for—so he isn't likely to be a laborer. Clean toenails, too, of all things. What does that mean? If the witness was as good with details as he had been so far on the phone, they should be able to come up with a composite approaching a photograph.

And, of course, a name: Anthony. Alias or not, it could tell them something. Even as an alias, it might be known to others. Yes, Your Honor, we learned that the suspect had used the name Anthony in half a dozen different places, four of them alone on the day the Wells boy disappeared.

Was there any reason the secret witness would be putting them on? Of course, Dulac thinks. Main reason: he had picked up the boy himself. Another reason: a wish to protect someone. Protecting someone was not terribly remote, either. Clever, but not unique. The world of up-front sex. A companion (Dulac has difficulty with the term *lover*) commits a crime. A clever person might come in, be close to an investigation, attempt to turn it away from the actual offender.

Still, Dulac thinks, there's nothing to suggest the witness is lying. Nothing about him seems deceptive, and nothing he has said so far suggests he is anything other than what he has said he is.

He'll see, Dulac thinks. In about two minutes now, when he can see the guy's face as he talks, he'll see.

Use good judgment, Dulac reminds himself. Don't be an old bull in a china closet. Be alert. *Think.* You can have the sonofabitch in hand by tonight. After the news. After the papers are on the street. Go with full disclosure, strike with everything. That's probably the way to do it. Act quickly then. Listen carefully and act quickly. Avoid mistakes. With a little luck then, and another good break or two, you'll have him. And the boy will be okay. A little worse for the wear, but okay.

Hearing footsteps on the wooden dock, he turns to see a man walking toward him. As if casually and not immediately, Dulac slips his hands from his pants pockets, where he had held them for warmth. The man is keeping his eyes on him, coming directly. Looks like an ordinary businessman, Dulac thinks. That Boston newscaster. No glasses. Receding hairline. That congressman from Maine, Your Honor. As the man is within a half a dozen steps, Dulac says, "Hullo there."

"Hi," the man says.

"You're—who I think you are?" Dulac says.

"Probably. Lieutenant Dulac?"

"Right," Dulac says, shaking hands, continuing then to show his shield, to verify his identity and to be official. "Your name?" he says.

"Can we wait on that?" the man says.

"Okay for now," Dulac says. "I understand your concern," he adds. "As I told you on the phone, I'll do all I can to preserve your anonymity. I don't see and my chief doesn't see, right now, any reason why you'd ever be called to testify in this, although the chief says it isn't out of the question, if we should end up in a strictly circumstantial situation. At that time, of course, you'd have the option to testify or not. Or you could be subpoenaed. Okay? For now, you can simply be a secret witness which is no different, really, from someone telephoning in a complaint and leaving the burden of proof up to us. If there was a reward, you'd be eligible for that, under this program, but there isn't any reward. So far at least."

"I'm not here for a reward," the man says.

"Fine," Dulac says. "That's fine. The thing I have to get across to you, right now, is the time pressure we're under. Frankly, we should have done this last night, or at five or six o'clock this morning."

"You believe the boy is still alive?"

"Well, we hope so," Dulac says, surprised. "If we can get any kind of lead on this guy, from what you have to tell us, our hope is—my hope is—we can maybe flush him out, or have someone identify him, without the boy getting caught in the crossfire."

"I'll do what I can," the man says. "That's why I'm here."

"Good. What we need first of all is to have you work with one of our officers, to come up with a composite. I'd like this in this afternoon's papers, which means it should be ready to be handed out at a press conference, which is scheduled for just about an hour from now. Okay?

"Then, I need to dig more deeply into your statement and get it on tape, to come up with *more* details, more information. As for you being *seen*—because all this needs to be done at the police station—my thought was to have you put on glasses, say, and a hat, for purposes of coming and going. You could even do a false mustache, if you wanted to. There's a little shop down here, it's like a head shop, where you can get such things—I can go in and get them, at our expense—so you wouldn't be identifiable even to a clerk, it if came to that."

"Lieutenant, aren't we wasting time?"

"We are. But I have to cover these things. Something else I need to know is how to get in touch with you, by phone, any time, day or night. Also, I want you to understand: first of all, this is admirable of you to come forward and take time like this to help. I want you to understand I will do all I can to protect your identity, but the thrust of all this, the purpose—my first responsibility—is to see if we can walk out of this without losing the life of a twelve-year-old boy. So, you see, you *have* to help, you see, irrespective of risk to you, simply because it's your responsibility, because this boy's life, if it isn't lost already, is almost certainly at stake. Okay? There's where we stand. I can't guarantee your identity."

Dulac looks to the man, trying to catch his elusive eyes; he adds, as the man doesn't say anything, "I could lie to you."

The man lifts his eyes then. "Lieutenant," he says, "I think you're sort of emotional about this."

Dulac says nothing, looks back at the man as if he, Dulac, is a rock, as if he is not emotional at all.

"An appeal to my humanity," the man says. "It's what I've been waiting for all my life."

"Good," Dulac says. "Good. That's fine. That's good. Now we're talking. What we have so far. We've ordered up printouts of every sex offender, first name Anthony or Tony, in the three-state area. What I want you to do, first off, is look at what photographs we *do* have, in case this guy wasn't just using Tony as an alias." Turning, Dulac has started walking back along the pier.

"I'm sure it is an alias," the man says, walking beside him, "I used one myself. I always do in situations like that."

"Okay," Dulac says. "Okay. I understand. Still, it could tell us something. I'd like you to work right off, with an officer, to come up with a composite. Then, the questions, from two or three of us, to see what other details about this guy we can dig out of you."

"I *am* going to pick up some glasses," the man says. "And a hat, which I have in my car. Why don't you go on Lieutenant, and I'll catch up with you."

Dulac pauses over this. "You're not gonna take off on me, are you?" he says.

"No, Lieutenant, I'm not going to take off. I don't want you to see my car, okay? I have an Indiana Jones hat in there, which I've never had the courage to wear, and if I'm going to go incognito, I might as well look neat, you see."

"I'm not too crazy about letting you out of my sight," Dulac says. "Not right now. You're the key to my case, you know."

"Lieutenant, you appealed to my humanity; it worked."

"I said I'd need to be able to get in touch," Dulac says. "Why don't you give me some numbers now and at least a first name. In case you get hit by a car."

The man is removing pen and notepad from an inside pocket, saying, "To get in touch with me—you mean to ask more questions? For what purpose?"

"That, follow-up questions, and maybe to look at a lineup or listen to a recorded voice maybe. I'm not sure. For example, a young man was reported to have visited a sex store, Saturday afternoon, to have viewed a film called *Children in Bondage*. The clerk there said this young man, who had an unusually reddish complexion, not only viewed this film but also asked if he—"

"Red cheeks?" the man says, glancing up from what he is writing. "Red cheeks—that's what he said?"

"That's right," Dulac says.

"The guy I picked up had red cheeks," the man says. "Did you ask me that? Did I say that?"

"The guy you picked up had red cheeks?"

"He certainly did. I'd forgotten that. He did, though. They reddened, you know, when he got embarrassed or excited—but that's what he had. Red cheeks. It's true."

"Apple-colored?"

"Apple-colored is absolutely right," the man says.

"Jesuschrist," Dulac says. "This guy tried to buy child porn. That's what the clerk says. Between about two and three. He went into the movie then. *Children in Bondage.* Which lasted fifty-five minutes."

"I met him at five thirty," the man says. "I bet it's him. He was trying to buy child porn? That's amazing, absolutely amazing."

"Get your stuff," Dulac says. "Come right back. Let me have that."

"My name is Martin," the man says, as Dulac takes the slip of paper from him.

"Tell the cadet you're there to see me," Dulac says. "He'll ring me."

"I'll be there in five minutes," the man says, as he moves away to the left.

Dulac, watching a moment, goes to the right, slipping the paper into his wallet. Already his mind is on the consequences of the press conference. It has to be him, he keeps saying to himself. It has to be him. Red cheeks. Kiddy porn. A wayward missile looking for a target. It has to be him. He feels certain of this, if it's good police work or not.

He strides along. He has to be local, he is thinking. There's the license plate—and only local yokels would know about The Sex Barn. No, no, that's not true, he thinks. There'd be networks. When it came to sex, there'd be networks.

You better slow down, Dulac says to himself as he turns the corner to the police station. You could still be wrong about this. This rosy-cheeked guy in his gray car could show up and clear himself in ten minutes. You could be wrong all the way around and end up looking like a world-class fool. And you're going to endanger the boy, you'd better recognize that. If he isn't already a statistic, like Shirley said. If the guy isn't already in Miami, on the beach, or in Montreal. Or looking for another child to pick up. You're going to tighten the screws on this sonofabitch and that's going to endanger the boy.

You have to do it, you have to use it at the press conference, Dulac says to himself, reaching the door and entering. You have no choice, really. You have to do it because it has to be done. It'll scare the shit out of the guy, for sure, if he's still around. At the same time someone is going to know him. A neighbor, at least, or a coworker or landlord or gas station attendant is going to know exactly who he is. A mailman. His wife or parents. His boyfriend or girlfriend. No question—with all they have to go on, one person at the very least is going to call in, and if they are lucky, if they can somehow slip up on him or make contact with him—if it isn't too late—the little Wells kid is going to come walking out. As in some child's game in darkness, he's going to be home free.

The odds have to be fifty-fifty. Don't they?

SEVEN

ON THE THIRD FLOOR, Vernon is sitting at a carrel next to a window. A chill is reaching from the glass to his side but there is little or no sound up here. There are no voices. He hears the wind come up now and then like a distant airplane in the gray sky. Then he doesn't listen. Perhaps he thinks. The partial enclosure of the metal desk provides some privacy within the privacy of the seldom-used floor. It's a place to hide, here above the world, and he is hiding. Resting. Trying to rest. Calm down and think, he keeps saying to himself.

No one would look here, he thinks. If only he could stay here. If only he could close off something like a corner for himself on this side of the third floor and stay here forever. There was heat. Running water. Books to read—a window from which to watch life go on, to watch it change out there as it passed by, year after year.

Time passes. He stares out over buildings and treetops. The sky remains gray, painted-over gray. Under the sky, in the parking lot a few hundred yards away, there remains something, a small space, significant to his mind. Will someone make the discovery? Will they trace his car and trace him—appear here in a moment to take him away?

At the same time there is a feeling of some safety in this hideaway corner. No one would think to look here, he keeps telling himself. Even if they had found the boy and traced his car, they wouldn't look here. They'd go to the cottage. They'd question Duncan, and Leon and Wayne. Placing his head on his arms on the desk, thinking, Vernon stares away at nothing. In time his eyes close, and he dozes some. Coming around in a moment, he feels troubled again. Something is out there. Everything is wrong. The terror will not go away.

This is Tuesday, he thinks. Only last Friday, even Saturday, his life was okay. He was miserable over what was happening with Anthony, but it wasn't like this. He was unhappy and helpless. So it seems now. But it

226

was nothing like this. This is like death. It is death. The tremor within him is the tremor of death. His heart knows it, feels its nearness.

If only they would catch him. If only the progession of fear within him would stop. Would someone listen to him? He'd tell everything. Would they let him explain? Would anyone listen? What a godsend it would be if merely one person in the world would listen, would hear his explanation, if they understood him or not.

EIGHT

WALKING INTO THE POLICE STATION, telling the cadet on duty that he is there to see Lieutenant Dulac, Matt is directed instead to a woman working next to a uniformed policeman at a long table, in a far corner of the room. Both the woman and the policeman are holding telephones to their faces, listening and talking; inviting him with her eyebrows to state his purpose, the woman then covers the receiver with her free hand. She says to him, "Wait just a minute, please," and Matt retreats a step and a half and stands looking around while she turns her face down and finishes her call.

"You're Matt, aren't you?" the woman says to him.

"Yes," Matt says, pleased to be known.

"The lieutenant's busy right now," the woman says, keeping her eyes on him. "What did you want to see him about?"

"Oh, nothing," Matt says.

"Nothing's ever nothing around here," the woman says. Again, there are her eyebrows extending an invitation. "If it's an emergency—," she says.

"Oh no," Matt says. "No, it's nothing."

"I don't mean to pry," she says. "We're all working on your brother's case. The lieutenant's in the interrogation room right now, but he's going from there into a press conference. I'm going to tell him you stopped by, and he's going to ask me what it was you wanted. You see?"

"I just wanted to see him," Matt says.

"That's all—nothing in particular?"

"No, that's all."

"Okay. That's fine. The thing is, he's really busy right now. After the press conference he has to go meet with some expert at the university, because this guy doesn't have time to come here. Who knows when he'll have lunch."

"I understand," Matt says.

"How old are you?" the woman says then.

"Fifteen," Matt says.

"Tenth grade?"

"Ninth."

"You're home from school today?"

"I went," Matt says. "Then I left."

"You felt out of it."

"I sure did."

"Well, it's a hard time. Is your mother at home?"

"Yeah."

"You feel out of it there, too?"

"Yeah."

"I'll tell the lieutenant you were here, that you wanted to see him. Because you're feeling out of it. Okay?"

"Okay," Matt says, feeling better, smiling some.

"Where can he reach you?"

"I don't know."

"Okay, I'll pass on the message. I know he'll want to see you, so you check back in, okay? This afternoon."

"Okay," Matt says.

"I mean that," the woman says.

Matt looks at her.

"You look after your mother, too," the woman says.

"I will," Matt says.

Head down into the wind, though, as he walks along Marcy Street close to where the wide river begins to open into the harbor, it is not the care of his mother which is on Matt's mind but an idea all at once of yet another place to look for Eric. Only a block and a half ahead, over a causeway, he can climb down the rocks and search the shore around Pierce Island, a semi-forbidden, uninhabited island attached to downtown where he and Eric have explored before. Perhaps he will find him there, he thinks, as his hopes become airborne again. That will show Lieutenant Dulac, he thinks. It will show them all.

He imagines Eric in a cave. Waiting to get aboard a passing ship. Maybe caught in the rocks. For however off-limits the sandy-rocky beach was to their mother, the water was one of those places toward which Eric was always tending.

Down over the barricades and fifty yards along, however, Matt has a sense of being wrong. He will have to go all the way around the island, however, just to be sure. Something called him; he can take no chances, even if the weather here is wetter and windier. What if Eric was near the tip of the island, his foot pinned by a rock?

Vanessa keeps flashing into his mind, too, but he looks away from thinking of her. There is the choppy cold water, its whitecaps coming up. And the Naval Shipyard across the harbor; trying to spot ships over there, especially subs, lying in the water, was one of Eric's favorite activities. Could he have gone over there, trying to drive away a submarine?

What happened between him and Vanessa never happened at all, Matt thinks then. It was a dream. He'd show her, too. Still, it is the big cop who holds the center of his mind, the big cop's smile.

What if Eric just came walking along the beach? he thinks, pushing through weeds to another stretch of sand. It seems so possible, Matt looks ahead over approaching rocks, to see if he will appear, experiences disappointment as an empty stretch comes into view.

He recalls the submarine story then and how Eric was always so taken with it. Its log showed, so it was said around town, that during World War II a German U-boat had slipped into Portsmouth Harbor and lay in overnight, near the Memorial Bridge, watching the Naval Shipyard. The Coast Guard operated a steel-mesh fence across the mouth of the harbor, and when it was opened the next morning to let fishing boats and lobstermen go out to sea, the submarine slipped out underneath them. Matt liked the story, too, although he always insisted to Eric that it wasn't true. Eric wouldn't have it. "Can't you just see it?" he liked to say. "Its periscope on the shipyard all night—then this big, long, black thing goes along under the fishing boats. Think how you'd feel if you looked down and saw it! You could blast it with a hand grenade!"

At last, near the tip of the island, Matt spots something dark red in gray rocks. Pushing closer in the breeze, though, he can see that it is only a rag, a cloth or a shirt, caught on the rocks. An image stays with him, though, as he pushes on through loose sand.

Other things disturb his mind, too. One is a man's upturned brown shoe, caught in a tangle of dried seaweed. Another is the carcass of a fish, lying in the suds. For the first time an image of a body comes into Matt's mind. The body lies on its side.

Matt tells the image to go away. He pushes on, as if it is his duty. His spirit leaves him, though, and doubt comes up in its place. Did he make a fool of himself, going to the police station? It seems he did. It did not seem that way then, but it does now. That woman, asking him all those things. They'd probably laugh, he thinks, when she tells the lieutenant of his wandering in and asking to see him. He's the one who told him to do it, Matt thinks, all at once close to tears. He didn't just come up with it on his own.

NINE

"IT'S NOT A REAL IMPORTANT THING," she says, "but I believe the brother is developing a kind of fix on you."

"You believe what?" Dulac says.

They are entering his cubicle, as he has just stepped away from the press conference—some reporters are literally jogging with their machine-copied composite sketches—and Shirley is coming to give him an update of calls and callers.

"You had children, you'd see it in a second," she says. "He's turning to you. You're the strong figure in this thing. He's in need and there's no father. He's a kind of lonely kid anyway, it seems to me."

"What about his mother? What are you saying?"

"I don't think his mother is the one he wants to be around right now. And I'm not saying anything. All I'm saying is that it's something for you to be aware of. He's fifteen. That's young. This is no small thing for him, even if he won't know it until later. And he probably doesn't know he's gravitating toward you. With his mother he probably feels that *he* should be the responsible one. I just thought you should know, that's all. There are other things to talk about."

"Did he say that?" Dulac says.

"No, Gil, of course he didn't say that."

"Should I do something? I have to leave here almost at once, to talk to this guy at the university. And I have to call the secret witness—told him I'd only contact him in an emergency—to see if he'll go with me. And I'm going to ask him to take a polygraph, too, which is going to piss him off, I'm sure."

"You're taking him where?"

"To see the expert guy at the university. State Police delivered the sex film. Expert's going to give us a critique, say if the film could suggest behavior. The secret witness I'd like along because he *knows* the suspect, and because he's a very astute guy. Now you're making me feel bad because I don't have any time for the brother."

"Take him along. He'd be thrilled."

"I can't do that—not to talk about a sex film that could have implications about his brother."

"Implications? Do you believe that?"

"I don't know what I believe. I know the guy saw the film. Then he went to a gay bar. From which he went home with this guy. Where, as they say, he hit on soft times. Then, if he's the one, he picks up Eric Wells. There's something of a sequence there."

"You're going to polygraph the secret witness?"

"Well, think about it. The guy is involved in sexual hanky-pank, for one. He calls up, gets himself involved in the case, so we have everyone looking for a person he has described, driving a car he *cannot* identify. He's a smart man. It's one of those things. I'm not that quick, but I'd never be forgiven if I didn't check him out. It's the car, mainly. I don't like that he can't identify the car. I have to have him polygraphed."

"Which is going to piss him off?"

"I think so. Especially if I ask him to offer an opinion of this film."

Shirley is nodding, starting to leave. "Concerning the brother," she says. "I could get a hold of him, try to, and tell him you want to see him later today—something like that?"

"Fine, that's a good idea. I'll be back, I don't know, this afternoon. Bring him in here, let him hang out in my office if he wants to. Or in the squad room. They're people around. I'll be back then, and I'll talk to him."

Sitting at his desk, Dulac is trying to sort things out. As nothing seems quite willing to fall into place, he decides simply to do some things which need to be done, and he removes from his wallet the slip of paper on which the secret witness jotted down two telephone numbers. Stop trying to do too much at once, Dulac reminds himself, as he is thinking there is something he has to touch base with Shirley on before he leaves, and thinking, too, that he has something for Mizener, something which seems important—what is it?—which came to him exactly as he was standing with the chief and the others in the press conference and someone was talking. One problem, he thinks now, is that his concern with Mizener being too inflexible, *not* being really helpful in the investigation, keeps getting in the way of whatever it is he has on his mind to ask him to do. The car, he thinks. Isn't it something about the car? Mizener's sort of a handful, he thinks. A pain in the ass. He's too bitter, really, to be a good cop.

The number is dialed. At least some number is dialed, Dulac thinks as he realizes he is listening to a telephone ring and the slip of paper belonging to the secret witness is on his desk before him. Now he has the brother to worry about, too, he reminds himself. It's too much.

The man answers. It's his voice.

"Lieutenant Dulac here," Dulac says softly. "I know I agreed to call only in an emergency. Are you free to talk? This is important."

"More or less," the voice says. "Not altogether."

"I have a favor to ask. A couple of favors."

"Go on."

"What?"

"I'm listening. Go on."

"I'm leaving here in ten minutes," Dulac says. "To go over to the university, to see some of that sex film I told you about—*Children in Bondage*—and to talk to an expert there on child abuse. What I'd like is for you to come along. Share your knowledge. Your insights."

"Knowlege of *what?*" the man says.

"Well, you're an expert in a certain area. Okay. The general idea—I mean I don't expect much—the general idea is to see if the film could give us some clue about anything. I have to do this myself. I'd be interested in your opinion. It takes time and all, I know, but it would be a help."

"Well, I'm not sure about that," the man says.

"As a citizen," Dulac says.

On a pause, the man says, "Fine. Okay, I'll do that. I'm not getting anything done here anyway."

"You'll do it?"

"Yes. That's what I said."

"Good. Oh, yes, there's something else I have to ask you. It's a little more awkward. But official."

"I don't like the sound of that."

"I have to ask if you'll agree to a polygraph. As policy."

The pause this time is longer, before the man says, "I don't think that's fair."

"Let me try to explain," Dulac says.

"Please do," the man says.

"It isn't what it sounds like," Dulac says. "You see, I don't believe you have any involvement in this. Still, it wouldn't be the first time a person who was a perpetrator became involved in the investigation of his own crime. You see? It's a Freudian number I know, but it *is* a way that people return to the scene of the crime. It *is* well documented as a pattern—a syndrome. So it's rather like policy. At the same time, personally, if I thought you were involved, I sure as hell would not ask you to go talk to this professor guy with me. Okay?"

"Okay what?" the man says.

"Why don't you just say you agree, and let me set it up. It's all confidential. A State Police expert does it. I can have the guy here waiting for you when we come back, say at four. That way it won't cut into another day."

"If I decline, you'll think I'm involved."

"Let's just say that if you do it, it'll remove any doubt."

"How long would it take?"

"Thirty to forty minutes."

"Okay. I have nothing to hide. The next time I'll think twice about trying to help."

"Come on—try to understand."

"I said I'd do it."

"Fine. You want to drive over here, to the parking lot then? We'll go over to the university in my car."

"You mean wait outside?"

"It's just your cover I'm concerned with. That way no one will see you. Come inside if you want to. It's okay with me. Wear your hat."

"I'll wait outside. And I'll park where I wish to park."

Moments later, coat in hand, Dulac tears the top sheet from the notepad on his desk to take out to Shirley. He has just added the four P.M. appointment with the State Police polygraph specialist—and snuffed out a cigarette which was so long it may have been lit for no more than two or three seconds. He's smoking too much, in addition to other failures he is commiting in life, he tells himself. Well, it's a special time, he thinks. One of these days he'll have to quit. Cold turkey. Not today, though.

Shirley has words of her own, which he allows into one ear as he tries to look attentive. Thirteen media people were at the press conference, she is telling him. Four were photographers or cameramen, the rest reporters. To her mind, given some calls that came in, they made two mistakes. Too many of their own people, clerks and cadets and patrolmen, came and stood around and took up copies of the dope sheet. You'd think they were programs at a theater. Then, too, there were too many bosses up front. The chief, the captain, Mizener—it looked like everybody was trying to get into the act. Bad impression. When the lady reporter from Portland asked if any one person was in charge of the investigation, she wasn't asking a question, she was offering a criticism.

"Where *is* Mizener?" Dulac says.

"He's out; he's checking out some high-priority tip."

"What tip is that?"

"I'm not sure just offhand. I didn't see him go, and he doesn't report to me."

"Don't we have a prime suspect?" Dulac says.

Shirley only shakes her head, makes an expression.

Leaning in over his sheet then, Dulac checks off the items there, from informing the New Orleans police that Warren Wells is a fugitive, as he is in arrears in excess of twenty-six thousand dollars in child support payments, to checking with the Department of Motor Vehicles on the number of silver-gray cars in the four models named, to checking with the MPs at the air base to see if the suspect's length of hair exceeds their standards, to making an appointment with the State Police now, to polygraph the secret witness at four P.M. "Something else," Dulac says. "But I can't remember what the hell it is."

Shirley says something then, while Dulac is trying to call up what he thinks he has forgotten, and he says to her, "What was that? I'm sorry."

"The squad room," Shirley says. "We'll be getting a lot of calls and I think that for tonight at least we should shift this operation to the squad room."

Dulac nods, agrees, as he is trying again, or still, to call something into focus.

"Should we do it right away?" Shirley says.

"Yes, sure, do it right away," Dulac says. "It's a good idea."

"And I'll try to track down the brother," she says.

"Fine," Dulac says. "That's fine."

It is in the squad car at last, with the secret witness, that Dulac sees what has been eluding him. It is the lies. The range of deception in such an encounter. "Tell me," he says. "If this guy, as you are so certain, lied about his name—if Anthony is a lie—he'd lie about other things, too, wouldn't he?"

"Well, yes, he would; I'm sure he would. I did."

"You did?"

"Oh yes. Small things."

"Such as?" Dulac says.

"I said I was a lawyer. I'm not a lawyer."

"What did he say he was?"

"He didn't. But he did say what he wasn't. I told him I thought he was a student. He said he wasn't."

"Which means he might be, if he was lying?"

"That's right."

"What do you think?"

"Well, I thought he *was* a student, right off. That's what I said to him. Maybe it's why I approached him, because there was a clean-cut student look about him."

"What else did he say? Did he say that he wasn't from this area, for example, which might mean that he is?"

"I'm trying to remember," the man says. "It is something you say, but I just can't remember if that's what he said. I don't believe I asked him where he was from. In fact, I more or less told *him* it wasn't the thing to do to pry."

"Great."

"Sorry."

"His name *could* be Anthony then? If he was so inexperienced?"

"Could be, but I don't think so."

"Was he gay? What's your judgment on that?"

"Is this the knowledge you wanted me to share?"

"You told us everything he said and did. You didn't say if you thought he was gay."

"You didn't ask."

"Okay, I'm asking."

"I thought he was. Then I thought he wasn't. People do mess around. Young people especially. They experiment a little. Finally, I'm not sure. I'd say yes and no."

They are approaching a stoplight, and seeing someone familiar, walking away to the left, Dulac realizes it is Eric's brother, Matt Wells. At first he isn't going to disclose this to the man beside him, but then he says, "That's the older brother. Walking there. That's the little boy's older brother."

"What's he doing walking there?" the man says.

"I'm not sure," Dulac says.

"Are you going to stop?"

"No," Dulac says, going on with some uncertainty as the light changes. "I wish I could; I just don't have time."

"What's his problem?" the man says.

"I was going to polygraph him, too, but I changed my mind," Dulac says.

"What happened to policy?" the man says.

"It got changed, in that case," Dulac says, driving on. "As for his problem. His brother's been abducted. There's no father. And generally speaking, no one quite has time for him, even though he has needs that he doesn't understand himself."

TEN

Up the painted cinder-block, steel-pipe stairwell, Vernon enters at the sixth floor and walks along the hallway. There are its familiar smells. In a small doorless room, two ironing boards with cast-iron footings stand unused. As always. Someone is suddenly passing; Vernon takes a look to be sure it isn't Anthony.

There is the door, heavily varnished; a feeling is in him that this is all wrong, another mistake. He takes a breath, hesitates. Get out of here, he tells himself. Go somewhere and die. He taps the door with his knuckles in the old way. He will be told to go away.

Nothing happens. He hears nothing. It's mid-afternoon, he thinks. Is he here? Was he here before at this time of day?

Vernon taps again. He hears something this time—he is certain. A chair scaping, a bed squeaking. He waits, inches from the door.

"Someone there?" a voice says.

"It's me," Vernon says to the door.

Gradually, the door is opened. On the other side of the chain is Anthony's youthful face. "I was working," he says. "What do you want?"

"I need to talk," Vernon whispers. "Please let me in."

Anthony only looks at him, before turning his face downward.

"I need help," Vernon says. "I'm in trouble."

"Aren't we all," Anthony says.

"It's serious," Vernon says.

"What is it?" Anthony says.

"I can't just say. Please let me in."

Anthony still makes no move to unchain the door. He looks at Vernon, looks away, looks at him again.

"Are you alone?" Vernon says, as if this is the problem.

"No, but you are."

Vernon only looks through the opening, without understanding.

"That was supposed to be funny," Anthony says.

Vernon still only looks; he has a glimpse of what he often felt like before in Anthony's presence, when he did not understand. "You've got to help me," he says.

Anthony makes an expression. "Vernon," he says. "Listen to me. I'm going to tell you something for your own good. When we were together, it was okay for you to come to me with your problems. It's not like that now. I know that may seem awfully cold, but the sooner you face it, the sooner you're going to begin to feel better about yourself."

Vernon is looking at him. "I'm in serious trouble," he says. "It's life and death."

"What kind of trouble?"

"I can't say—out here," Vernon manages to say. "It's personal."

"Vernon, I have news for you. You are so naive. *Everyone* is in personal trouble. Do you understand? *Everyone. Trouble is what life is.*" The door is closing. "I'm sorry," Anthony is saying. "I have work to do. I'm sorry. Just go away, will you. Try to grow up."

The door closes, catches.

Vernon needs a moment to turn and start away. Then he knows, as if someone else is possessing him, as if time is slipping again, that he is walking down the hall. And he seems to think that he feels better now. It was what he wanted. To ask, and to be turned down.

ELEVEN

RESEARCHER AND WRITER, psychiatrist and professor, recognized authority in the general field of human sexuality and in the subfield of sexual aberration, R. Marc Miller has a personal method of outlining occasions to himself, while they are happening, using brief captions that he records in his mind. This late afternoon, retreating to his home on Old Colony Cove Road, overlooking a corner of the Great Bay, he sits back and relates the day's events onto tape cassettes to be typed by a departmental secretary. His thought is that almost everything is grist for the mill—the mill being the publication of the monographs, articles, and books which have in the past and will in the future continue to enhance his name and increase his national visibility in his chosen field.

At the same time, he yearns privately for added degrees of recognition. His professional dream, he doesn't mind admitting, is to publish a book that would reach an audience of the size attributed to Stephen Jay Gould or Carl Sagan. His private fantasy, he doesn't mind admitting either, is to be retained as story consultant for a dramatic television series given to case studies in criminal sexual behavior, based on his experiences, in which offenders are traced not by a mere detective, but by a plainclothesman who is also a psychiatrist. Its title, he likes to mention to friends over dinner: *The Psychcopatrist.*

Running through a sex film with two investigators from Portsmouth, he makes the following captions and mental notes to himself:

SITUATION. *Viewing and critiquing porno film with two individuals from Portsmouth Police Department. Date: Two seventeen eighty-one. Lieutenant Dulac, in charge of investigation of missing twelve-year-old Portsmouth boy. White. Sixth grader. Lives with mother, brother fifteen. Father's whereabouts unknown. Mother works full-time, minimum wage. Part-time Saturdays as waitress. Tenth grade education. Family rents Portsmouth apartment.*

Other individual with Lieutenant Dulac not introduced. Reticent, but observant. Keen listener.

Film called Children in Bondage. Running time approximately sixty minutes. Color. Played through previous Saturday night state-line adult theater called The Sex Barn.

Prime suspect in case white male, early to mid-twenties. Clean-cut in appearance. Believed to be educated. Suspect known to have viewed film Saturday afternoon, thereafter in gay bar to have articulated interest in sexual relations with boys. Age of boys not specified. Suspect believed new to gay scene. Described as extremely nervous, intense, something of a loner. Unable in homosexual encounter with patron of gay bar to function sexually, meaning unable to achieve erection or to become aroused. Highly agitated following unsuccessful, unfulfilled homosexual encounter.

Portsmouth investigators pursuing suspicion—layman's suspicion it should be pointed out—porno film stimulated individual to act out urges in abduction of missing Portsmouth youth in attempt to reenact scenes or story from film. Main questions to me: Does film suggest pattern of behavior or sequence of action, and/or does film reveal profile of offender in relation to alleged abduction of Portsmouth youth?

SEX FILM. *Porno film, Children in Bondage, story of two would-be children, boy and girl, who appear prepubescent but obviously shaved, needing to be eighteen or over to satisfy legal requirements, and probably about that age. All characters in film Caucasian.*

Boy and girl, seeking shelter from cloudburst, wander into dim, semirural Victorian mansion where inadvertently they observe various sex games between two adult males and one very buxom adult

238

female (oh my), mainly sadomasochistic binding and birch rod and cat-o'-nine-tails switching of nude female's buttocks.

Boy and girl become aroused, in supposed youthful innocence, and begin to engage in what is portrayed as initial sexual experience. (A little something for everyone in this film, as the two are not children and not innocent.) Of course their sighs and moans soon—but not too soon—give them away and the two adult males step over to open the door and to say aha, what do we have here? and so on, continuing an undercurrent of satire in the film.

To be sure, the so-called boy and girl are taken into the larger room where it is decided they must be punished to teach them a lesson for peeping at the door. The two are therefore stripped and bound, wrists and ankles, with the two bindings loosely tethered together to permit hands-and-knees postures, for the moment, but little mobility.

Joined by the adult female, who has been untied, who is naked but for black nylons and black garter belt, the two adult males also strip in part, to reveal their genitals, and any number of sexual activities in the general categories and themes of sadomasochism and suppressed pedophilia are carried out. Mainly, buttocks are switched and spanked, breasts and male genitals are tied with strands of leather to exaggerate presentation, followed by what is portrayed as forced oral, anal, and vaginal penetration, in all possible combinations, the main theme of the activity being the transition of degrees of pain and punishment into erotic seizure, excitement, and ecstatic climaxes.

Film begins to conclude as adult captors become so engrossed in erotic excitement they untie their victims and beg to be bound themselves, to receive the same treatment. Boy and girl comply, of course, and when the three are tied togther, they slip away, as if mischievously, to make their escape from the old mansion. Film actually concludes as the camera pans along a country road, then off the road tracing weeds to two bicycles leaning against trees, and down into the weeds where the girl is performing fellatio on the boy who says, this is great, if only we'd discovered it sooner, and the film concludes as he climaxes over her mouth and face.

Final scene inconsistent with themes addressed throughout film, although maintaining something of the pedophilic theme of experiencing initial sexual contact. Film fairly standard of its kind, above average in production quality, and not ineffective in its erotic appeal to both a particular and general clientele.

GENERAL DISCUSSION. *Missing Portsmouth youth described as ordinary twelve-year-old with older brother who would appear to be typically dominating of the younger boy, who is believed to be the mother's favorite in a one-parent household. No knowledge or evidence of any sexual proclivity in boy, this in response to detective's question of the boy being subject to some form of sexual enticement by his captor.*

Portsmouth detective Dulac himself serious, interested, and polite as we discuss effects of the film. Basic layman's questions. Could viewing of film generate sexual response? Sexual need and/or frustration? Could viewing of film generate consciously or unconsciously imitative behavior?

Answer yes, of course, to these questions, pointing out that responses differ in all people, creating entire spectrum of possible reactions, all in likely relation to previous sexual experiences, especially in formative childhood years. In reply to specific questions, could film create desire for similar sex with a child, yes but not probable, depending on prior sexual makeup. Could film bring to mind or cause an attempt to pick up a child, answer yes, but not probable, again depending on previous sexual repertoire being triggered or not. Could film in certain individuals quote stimulate or cause forced abduction of a child unquote, answer yes, possible but not probable.

Citing here of studies showing violent sexual behavior not necessarily a consequence of viewing similar pornographic materials, more likely pornography serving as sexual outlet, et cetera, leading to masturbation. Detective apparently amused here, noting that his response to stimulation through photographs is to seek out wife and get her to bed, wanting to know, the old question, why sexual arousal through porn would lead to masturbation rather than sex with others. Answer that it isn't that arousal from pornography doesn't lead to sex with others, but that it doesn't lead to or create an imitation of violent sexual behavior or aberrant behavior, except so far as it may occur in a person's mind in the form of erotic fantasy.

Detective interesting individual, polite and courteous throughout. Other questions having to do with pedophilia and homosexuality in general, wishing to affirm that male adult attracted to male children, especially prepubescent children, may not be homosexual or attracted to sadomasochism or other sexual aberrations. Discussion of general definition of pedophilia and attraction to children.

What to look for, detective wants to know, which might indicate relationship of missing child to film, answer that only direct imita-

240

tion might verify relationship, such as wrist and ankle burns, or switch marks or cuts, or anal or oral penetration, but even then these likely to be in reference to early childhood experiences.

Finally, any predictable actions or directions or tendency to look for at this point, assuming prime suspect is harboring missing boy, answer that nothing in film would suggest a particular action which might be predictable, remarking to detective at this point more forcibly that aberrant behavior is not created by pornography, to which he replies that it does create an air of suggestion and approval, if I would accept at least that, to which I reply that as a professional researcher in the field I accept only what may be scientifically verified.

ADDED POINTS. Discuss also in conclusion possibility of cult or religious practice possible in abduction of Portsmouth boy, replying that taking and holding of a child deprived parents of most valued possession and therefore inflicted dearest punishment, allowing kidnapper to experience feelings of satisfaction and omnipotence over parental figures. Examine photo of missing boy, with little comment to make as photo is very poor, except that prepubescent age constitutes particular syndrome for certain individuals usually having to do with successful nonthreatening sexual experiences in their own childhood.

Portsmouth detective something of a paradox as typical police officer involved in criminal investigation. Unusually large man, six-four or six-five and two hundred fifty or sixty pounds. Wearing a wool outdoors-type shirt jacket over a shirt and tie, carrying his service revolver on left side where it may be detected under his jacket but not showing in any way. Some policemen like to show their guns, as if inadvertently, to hold their coats back with their thumbs to put their weapons on display like they're exposing their penis, so everyone can see how powerful they are, but this officer respectful and courteous even as he is large, strong-looking type physically. Showing photograph of missing boy sensed it was like his own son missing, in the face of which he was remaining under control, because he had to be aware that poor quality of photo rendered it nearly useless, merely the blurred image of the face of an ordinary-looking preadolescent boy. All else about this man suggests him to be well-seasoned police veteran and one who is streetwise and capable of not having to take anything from anyone. Fairly open-minded, willing to accept views of experts but wanting complex issues explained in layman's terms. There is some anger here under a smooth exterior.

Other gentleman makes little impression through to end of seeing pair to door to say good-bye. Not introduced even, or identified in any way by name. Would guess he may not be policeman, but social worker or case study person having something to do with family or perhaps welfare agency.

FOLLOW-UP. *Case itself of general interest. Make note to discuss related issues and psychodynamics of criminal sexual behavior with this and other law enforcement persons, for the particular experience, interpretations, and preconceptions they bring in from the street.*

TWELVE

AT THE MALL, as school kids his age have begun to join the flow, Matt leaves to walk back downtown. He doesn't know why he doesn't want to be around school kids, but he doesn't. Maybe it's because, all at once, they seem frivolous to him. He'd like to see Vanessa, though, and for the exact reason it occurs to him, that she isn't like that, although she makes jokes and has fun. After what happened in school, though, he wonders if he should ever look for her again or ever call her.

Some of his problem disappears at once, as her mother answers the phone. Called from somewhere, by her tone Vanessa cancels the rest of his problem. "Matt," she says. "What are you doing; where are you?"

"I'm in town, just walking around," he says.

"You haven't seen the paper?" she says.

"What do you mean?" he says.

"Today's paper. This afternoon's paper. You haven't seen it, have you?"

"No," he says. "I guess I haven't."

"You should. The whole front page practically is about your brother. And this scary guy—does he ever look weird. I'm surprised you're even out walking around."

Matt doesn't know what to say to this, then says, "What guy do you mean?"

242

"This suspect," she says. "There's a picture of this guy—a drawing. Eric's picture is there again, too, and so are these detectives. It's almost the whole front page. They know everything about this guy. Almost everything. It says they think he's here somewhere, that he comes from here, lives around here, that he drives this small gray car, he's educated, in his early twenties—all this stuff, it is really scary. I can't believe you haven't seen it. What are you doing; where are you?"

"Nothing," Matt says. "I'm not doing anything."

"They haven't asked you about this guy? It says he uses the name Anthony, which they think is false. I can't believe they haven't asked you about this guy, because my mother says it's probably somebody you know. Wow—it *is* scary, believe me."

"I'll have to read it," Matt says.

"Are things real heavy at home?" she says.

"Oh, yeah, they are, but I'm not there. I mean I haven't been there."

"Oh."

"I just been walking. Looking for my brother."

"Really."

"I was thinking about you. A lot."

"Well, we been talking about you—you know. Even Mrs. Sims."

"Oh."

"About your brother, you know. Mrs. Sims says she doesn't think it looks real good. Because he didn't take anything with him."

"Yeah," Matt says, as the significance of the detail shoots once more through his mind.

"Aren't you scared, being out?" she says.

"Well no," Matt says, as fear also checks into his mind.

"I'd be," she says. "I am as it is."

"You are?"

"Heck yes. Shouldn't you be home? I mean, is your mother there by herself?"

"I guess so. But I have this thing," he adds.

"What's that?"

There it is, coming up in Matt. "About you," he says.

"Meaning what?"

For a moment he doesn't say. Then he says, "Don't you know?"

"I don't know," she says.

"Yes, you do."

She pauses. "Matt, listen," she says at last. "Come on, you've got other things to worry about right now. Okay?"

"God, you're always doing that!" he says. "Always like you're the boss or something!"

"Hey, I'm sorry," she says.

"Forget it," he says. Hesitating a second too long, he replaces the receiver.

Hesitating a second too long a second time, he lifts the receiver back up, to have her back—only to hear the buzz which says the connection is discontinued. He hooks the receiver back into the cradle. Turning, he hits the palm of his hand upon the aluminum wall. He walks away, keeping his eyes open, holding against even a blink. What a total jerk you are, he says to himslf. You are a total jerk.

Nor does he walk to the police station, as he had planned. What for? he thinks. Lieutenant Dulac would just tell him to get lost. At least that's what he should do, Matt thinks, walking through town. He should tell him to grow up. He should tell him he's a total jerk, because that's what he is, and that no one likes him or ever will, because why should they, why should anyone like anyone who is just a total nothing?

Matt doesn't walk to the police station, but he walks by it on his way down to the river, to the park along the water there, and he is on the end of a pier, in the brisk sea air, before the mask into which he has set his face begins to break and give way, and he takes in a gasp of air, into his throat and chest, and turns his face down not to be seen even by some passing, squawking, ignorant seagull.

THIRTEEN

VERNON IS WALKING on the campus. He has not returned to his car. Not yet. He has circled close enough to be across the street from the parking lot, close enough to believe he can pick out the silver-gray top of his car among the several hundred others packed around it. Is the boy still alive? he wonders. Is he still lying there, still unconscious? Has no one noticed his hair under the sleeping bag? Has no one tapped on the window— opened the door? People are so stupid.

Vernon doesn't cross the street into the parking lot. He turns back into the campus and walks wide-eyed. There is in him now, after his seeing Anthony, an odd feeling that nothing he does will matter anymore. Is that what he wanted?

In the library, up on the third floor, he makes his way to the men's room, which is empty and heavily marked with gay messages. Standing at one of four or five urinals in a row, he reads marked and scratched messages. In a moment the door opens and someone walks in. The person crosses the tile floor and stands at a urinal. Vernon stands where he is, looking ahead. In another moment, Vernon realizes, the person is shifting to the urinal beside him. Vernon only stands there. All along the wall is the message: Show It Hard / Get It Sucked.

Vernon stands there. The person is beside him and he knows what is happening, knows it on the periphery of both his mind and his vision. The person next to him is presenting himself.

Vernon looks down, watches the boy manipulate himself near the base of his penis, which is reaching straight out. The boy shifts his pelvis a little, to offer himself in Vernon's direction.

Vernon is thinking of Uncle Sally long ago. Uncle Sally's game, his thing, he thinks. He sees at last why it was something Uncle Sally always wanted to reenact. There is reluctance in him and in his hand, but he reaches down and grips the boy's penis.

No eye contact has occurred.

The boy whispers, "In a booth."

Vernon doesn't say anything. He thinks to say that he wants shame, he wants degradation. He wants whatever it may take not to be what he is. If depravity will allow him redemption, he wants it. Holding the straining turkey neck in his hand, however, he doesn't say anything.

"Come on," the boy whispers, withdrawing, slipping over and into one of the stalls.

Vernon obeys. It is clumsy squeezing inside; the boy is closing the door, sliding home the latch. The boy's penis is higher now than it was outside.

"*I want it in the ass,*" Vernon says.

"*What?*"

"*I want it in the ass. I want to die.*"

"*Jesuschrist,*" the boy says.

"*I want it to hurt,*" Vernon says, and is crying. "*I want to die.*"

The boy is climbing onto the stool, presenting himself. "*Suck it!*" he hisses.

Vernon stands there crying.

"*Suck it—you fucking weirdo! Here! Suck it! Suck my cock! Do it!*"

The boy fucks him in the mouth, as he stands there. He takes it. His tears continue, his breathing made up of gasping and choking. Nor does he shift away as the boy's pumping grows erratic—as the boy keeps hissing at him, *"Suck it hard! Suck it hard, goddamn it!"*—and cannot shift away then as the boy is gripping, holding his head with a hand.

Vernon stands choking, crying, spitting into the toilet as the boy, down from his perch—has someone come in out there?—is zipping. Pulling the latch opening the door, the boy says, "Thanks, fag," and is gone.

Vernon leans to the wall. He spits into the toilet and in a moment sits there, and holds his head, and cries, and it is as if he is a child again and has closed himself in the bathroom to weep in confusion and heartbreak while his mother ignores him. Hers was a resolve that he could never break. He knows now that he has to do what he has to do. He has to, because there is nothing else he can do. It reverberates, keeps reverberating in his mind. He has to get rid of the little boy. Forever.

FOURTEEN

WHERE HAS THE TIME GONE? What's happened to the brother? Did his meeting with him get lost in the shuffle? All he seems to know for sure is that Shirley went home for dinner. Is she coming back? Did she say she was bringing him something to eat? Where is that key call, that key person? Why doesn't this thing break?

Using his shoulder to keep the telephone to his ear, Dulac lights another cigarette. Too many butts, he thinks. His thick glass ashtray, which he has carried to the squad room, is packed with stubs. He lifts his eyes to the wall clock as the man on the other end of the telephone keeps talking, talking like water moving in a stream. Twenty to six. Jesuschrist, he thinks, is everyone having dinner? For of the three lines set up for calls, one is standing idle.

The man he is talking to—listening to—goes on. His dime, Dulac thinks, even as he is growing anxious. The man, calling from Boston, a Dr. Abel, a research psychiatrist with a special interest in criminal behavior, he has said, has been making some interesting remarks, and things are quiet enough for the moment—or Dulac would have cut him off, however rude he might have seemed to be.

Still, being an audience to the man's rambling lecture is testing his patience. He would feel impatient in any case, but he knows that Mizener, at that very moment, is rounding up some bodies for a lineup in the interrogation room, and that the secret witness—for whom he is responsible—is due to return yet again to do the lineup. As the voice continues into his ear, Dulac lifts his eyes once more to the clock on the wall.

Five fifty.

Something the man said has caught his attention, and he interrupts. "Doctor, excuse me," he says. "Excuse me. Just back up a little there, would you? Something you just said, about persons reacting violently, might be pertinent to this case. You see, what we—"

"The kinds of violent reaction," the doctor says—not reluctant to interrupt him, Dulac notices. "Of the—"

Dulac interrupts back. "Doctor, listen to me, please," he says. "I'm sorry, I just don't have time to hear all that you have to say. Okay? I'd like to ask you some questions. A profile and—"

"Well, you need a foundation," the man says.

"Could be, could be," Dulac says. "But I don't have time for it right now. I appreciate your calling, Doctor. But I am pressed, we are pressed for time. If you could give me some responses to what we're actually dealing with—"

"I'll try. I only want to help. That's why I called. I felt it was—"

"Doctor, hold on a second. Let me ask you something. You were talking about different kinds of violent reactions, acting out anger and so on, transference and hostility and all. Let me ask you this: Is there anything we might put out, over TV or in the paper, a kind of subliminal message, or a direct message, an appeal, that might *stop* someone from hurting the little boy in some way, if he hasn't done so already? Do you know what I'm saying? If we said, 'Please let Eric Wells go because . . .,' I don't know, because he's supposed to help his mother clean house or he's supposed to be in the school play? He has to feed his kitten. You see what I mean? I'm afraid we might be scaring the shit out of this guy. Is there any way we can intercept his emotions—redirect his behavior—do you know what I'm saying?"

"Certainly," the man says. "However, I don't know if it's very possible, what you're suggesting. Your alleged abductor is probably a pedo—"

"He may not be alleged, Doctor. We've got eyewitnesses. It's real."

"I see. The individual, in any case, would be a pedophile, which would mean you are *not* dealing with a person who is given to violence as an end in itself. You see, there are—"

"Just stick with this guy, Doctor, please."

"Lieutenant, I am trying to do just that. Now, this individual would be *after* what he has been unable to get from adults, because his own personality would be underdeveloped and he would have grown fixated on children. Or remain fixated on them. Do you see? He isn't being motivated by hostility in itself, although he may be acting out hostility toward what the child represents—childhood itself, and the love and attention perhaps that he did not receive himself when he was a child. So here he is, seeking a substitute for that which was denied. Of course, one of the most pitiful offenders is the elderly widower—"

"Do you believe he's homosexual? We have reason to believe this person went to a gay bar just an hour or so before the little boy was picked up."

"He could be homosexual," the doctor says. "Not necessarily, though. It could be anyone, you see, as far as there being triggered in them a fixation on children. We've treated lawyers. High-ranking military officers. Physicians—with very successful practices. And we've also treated plumbers and construction—"

Dulac is looking at Mizener, over in his doorway, something of a smile on his face, waving for him to come over. Dulac says into the phone, "Doctor, excuse me—I'm afraid I have to go. Someone is motioning to me right now. I appreciate your—"

"I'll hold," the man says.

"You'll do what?" Dulac says, although he has heard clearly.

"I'll hold. If you don't mind. There are just a couple other things I need to say."

"Doctor, I'm awfully busy."

"It will only take a minute or two. If you'll just do what you have to do, I want to sort out some thoughts on the question you raised."

Against his better judgment, Dulac agrees, although placing the receiver on his desk, getting to his feet, he mutters, "Jesuschrist," to himself. "He's going to hold," he says to no one.

Mizener, a file folder in one hand, grips his elbow with his other hand. "This guy is something else," he says.

"You got a lineup?"

"Just about. We've got three suspects. This first guy, though, is really something. Listen to this."

"What?" Dulac says, pulling up with Mizener along the hallway.

Mizener has the folder up to read. "Just listen," he says. " 'Sadler's residence, a four-room, first-floor apartment, is a filthy wreck. There are dirty dishes, garbage, dirty underwear strewn on dirty floor. Forty-five-pound punching bag suspended from living room ceiling by chain.' "

"He's a suspect?" Dulac says. "You have him here? I don't understand."

"Right. He's in the interrogation room. But listen: 'Arrested March

11, 1980, June 7, 1980, and November 19, 1980, by Hampton Town Police for indecent exposure. November 19, 1980, apprehended for walking on beach and sidewalk naked. Contacted this date'—this is this evening—'at residence, in response to anonymous tip, Mr. Sadler answered door stark naked. Undersigned'—that's me—'identified himself to suspect as police officer, at whch time suspect told undersigned to remove his "fat ass" from his door.' "

"Neil, what is this?" Dulac says, growing impatient all over again lingering here in the hall.

"Just a second, Lieutenant, there's more. Listen to this: 'Suspect advised undersigned he holds doctor of philosophy degree, University of Chicago, was formerly instructor Mount Holyoke College, but presently unemployed.

" 'Suspect advises he spends fourteen hours a day working out, or walking the streets with his knapsack full of rocks and carrying a sledgehammer to build up his wrist strength.

" 'Contacted former live-in companion of suspect now living in Newington. She advised she has known suspect approximately two years and lived with him four months, with her son by a previous marriage, until last Thanksgiving when she moved out after she learned suspect was attempting to have sexual relationship with her son, who was eight at the time. She believes suspect capable of violence.' "

"Neil, he sounds weird, this guy does, but *is* he a suspect?"

"Well listen—"

"Neil, I don't want to listen! Is he a suspect?"

"Well, come on, and take a look."

Going along to the one-way window of the interrogation room, where another plainclothesman and a uniformed officer are watching, Dulac says, "Is this a lineup?"

"That's coming," Mizener says. "Where's the witness?"

"He'll be here any second."

The men at the door titter, and shift aside as Mizener and Dulac approach. Mizener behind his shoulder, Dulac looks in. There is the man standing naked in the corner of the small white room. A pile of clothing is on the old wooden table there. The man's hair is dark and he is balding slightly. "He won't leave anything on," Mizener says behind him.

Dulac turns back. "Neil," he says. "Step over here, will you."

Three or four steps away, Dulac turns to face him. "Neil, that man is thirty-five or forty years old," he says. "My God, don't you understand that we have a suspect? What are you doing?"

"He looks like a suspect to me, Lieutenant."

"He's a mental defective. That's what he looks like. Get him out of here! Get him dressed and get him out of here! What in the hell are you doing?"

"Lieutenant, look—"

"Don't lieutenant me; don't say another word. Do as I say or I'm putting you on report."

Reentering his office, squeezing his temples in one hand, Dulac swings around into his chair and lights another cigarette. He sits, pulling his forehead in his fingers until he realizes the telephone is lying on its side. "Jesuschrist," he says, and reaches to take it up.

He exhales. "Doctor," he says. "I have only a minute now, so you have to make this quick."

"Okay, fine, it's an idea I have," the doctor says. "A scheme. Use the truth. In a direct appeal. Broadcast a direct appeal, in which you say: To the person who picked up so-and-so, this twelve-year-old boy."

"Eric Wells," Dulac says.

"Right. Say: We know you are not happy in the situation you have gotten yourself into. We know you would like to return this young boy to his family before anything worse happens and so you may receive treatment so you will not commit this kind of act again. We ask you to please put an end to the horrors you are causing yourself as well as your captive, and telephone the following number. Et cetera."

"Doctor," Dulac says. "I don't think we could make a public offer of treatment. That's something that has to be decided by a court. Besides, we don't even know if the boy is still alive."

"Well, to understand is to sympathize," the doctor says.

"Fine, but my own sympathies right now are elsewhere," Dulac says.

"To succeed, though, an appeal needs to be nonthreatening."

"Fine. I understand that. It also has to be legal. I declare this guy is in need of treatment, it implies he's mentally deficient. The worst lawyer in the world would get him an acquittal in half an hour. We are instructed, Doctor, policemen are, to not even say something like there's a 'weird' person out there, or an 'animal,' because that kind of remark implies a perception of mental deficiency. Besides, if I offered this guy treatment, I'd be run out of town the next day. As I should be. This is not theory, Doctor, and it's not alleged. The truth is, this guy could pick up another little kid."

"Well, lieutenant, if your suspect is a true pedophile, as I suspect he is, he would have acted out of love to begin with. Desperate love, certainly, but love of a kind nonetheless. You offer understanding of that in some direct or subtle way—I think direct would be most effective—you might get him to come in. And it must come from you. As the authority figure, with your picture in the paper, the person in charge. He'll know you by now, you see. Don't turn it over to a policewoman or to the boy's mother because you think they'll be less threatening. Make an expression of concern for this young man."

"Doctor, listen, I'll think about it. Thanks very much for your help."

"This person—listen, my friend—this person is *not* happy with what he has gotten himself into. Unless he has done this before, and gotten away with it, he is probably terribly confused right now."

"Doctor, I don't think anyone is happy when they commit terrible crimes."

"Well, this is an epidemic, isn't it? It's everywhere, isn't it? You must try to understand that."

"I've been trying."

"It's a new pathology, you know."

"It is?"

"Absolutely. It isn't surprising to me that this is happening. Children as sexual objects have been literally advertised for years now. This is not surprising. Not in a society where the moral climate has been exhausted."

"A new pathology?"

"That is my belief."

"Okay, Doctor, thanks again. I'll think about making an appeal, like you said."

"Another thing, you see, is that the pedophile is quite convinced he's doing the child a favor by giving him or her the care and affection he or she doesn't receive at home. We are no longer a child-oriented society. Not at all. Children are considered a nuisance, an expense. A man here, convicted of molesting children, said he picked out his victims by looking over a schoolyard to see which children looked lonely or unhappy, not well cared for, inadequate clothing and so on. Such children, he tell us, make up a significant percentage. What the pedophile does is capitalize on that vulnerability—that's why this pathology is new. Television advertises general approval, parents are busy elsewhere; moral authority is being subverted—"

"Excuse me, Doctor," Dulac says. "I don't mean to be rude—don't you ever stop talking? I have other things to do."

"On this subject, no, I don't stop talking," the doctor says. "These phenomena need—"

"Doctor, I have to go. Call back sometime."

"You put it that way, okay, Lieutenant."

"Thanks, Doctor. I have your name." Dulac replaces the receiver, gently. Following, he places his arms on the table and his head on his arms. He doesn't close his eyes, however, and in a moment lifts his brow to read the clock.

Shirley. She is entering the door, under the clock, and he forgets the time, for the moment. She glances at him; he glances at her. Relief—a wave—passes over him. In a moment, he knows, as she hangs up her coat, she will join him at this first long table set up here for the investigation. Now two of the three phones are in use—his extension makes a fourth—and getting up and stepping over to the coffee maker, he looks back to see Shirley returning to the table he just left. Asking her with a glance and a pointed finger if she wants coffee, receiving a nod, he draws two cups and carries them back, one black, one with cream and sugar.

"Have you eaten yet?" she says, as he sits down.

"Not yet," he says. "I thought you were bringing me something."

"Don't be fresh," she says.

Confused by her remark, he lets it go. Fresh? "Did you contact the brother?" he says. "It slipped my mind; things have been hectic."

"It's not that busy though, is it?"

"No, it's not. I expected more, to tell you the truth."

"I talked to Claire Wells," she says, "but I didn't want to tell her we thought the boy, the brother, was being overlooked, so I said you wanted to talk to him about some things. I said we'd call back, that it wasn't important. What's going on here?"

"Nothing real hot has come in. I just talked to this professor guy, from Boston, who said he thought a nonthreatening pitch, from me, as the boss, might get the guy to turn himself in. I'm just thinking about it and it sounds like a not-too-bad idea; I'm thinking of doing it. Have it on the eleven o'clock news. Problem is, I'd have to drive up to Portland and back, and it would take two and a half hours altogether."

"And you don't think we can manage things if you're not here?"

"Sort of. No, the truth is, I want to be here."

"Anything comes in, I can call you."

"Yeah, I know."

"I mean I don't know about what you're saying, but we can look after things here, I do know that. You can take the boy with you, the brother, stop and get something to eat."

"This doctor suggested what I should do is dangle some kind of therapy, in exchange for the guy turning himself in. I told him we couldn't do that."

"The suspect?"

"Right, the suspect. What he said, though, what did make sense, was that as the officer in charge I would be known to this guy by now. Assuming he's still around. That I would be the person he's afraid of. That if I offered something like a little understanding—as opposed, say, to an appeal by the mother—that it could possibly do the trick. Just possibly."

"Maybe you should go ahead and do it," Shirley says.

"You think so? Nothing else seems to be working. There are so many opinions flying around you get a little shell-shocked."

"I'll help you set things up. I'll call Matt Wells, too. Take him with you. Stop thinking everything's going to collapse without you. Jesus, get a pizza or something. Anything comes in, I'll have it to you immediately."

"You think I should?"

"I do. I'm not so certain Eric Wells is still with us, to be saved, but if you think there's a chance, you should do it. What else can you do?"

"Call him," Dulac says. "Call the brother. Tell him I'll pick him up in ten minutes. I'm going to call Portland."

"Way to go, Gil," she says, taking up the telephone on the table. "Use your office phone," she adds.

Who the hell's in charge here anyway? he says to himself, going on to use his office phone.

FIFTEEN

SIX O'CLOCK. They are always late, and it is no different this evening. In The Union, a five-story building built into a hillside as the crossroads of the campus—doors and ramps coming and going everywhere—Duncan McIntyre settles into a vinyl couch in a TV lounge to wait for the arrival of Leon and Wayne, to walk out to Leon's car, parked on a side street, for the ride back to the cottage. This is assuming they will triumph over the urge to detour to one or another of the underground or aboveground town pubs, a tug-of-war they face every evening, in fact or in jest, depending on money, papers or exams, lingering hangovers, Celtics or Bruins games on TV, or the force of persuasion, of one or another of them, for or against the magnetic pull.

Although a large color television set, mounted on the wall, is playing across the room, Duncan makes his choice of a couch because of the presence of an apparently discarded newspaper, the *Globe*, he would hope, its sports section remaining more or less intact. Otherwise, even as it may be television news time, on the network channels, he would sit and watch one of the *Star Trek* or *All in the Family* reruns playing forevermore on whichever cable channel the television seemed always tuned to—to the apparent satisfaction of the scattering of students, mainly boys, who sit or lie, stare or snore, from the collection of other vinyl armchairs and couches.

The initial disappointment for Duncan, as he places his books down and takes up the paper, is that it is local rather than the *Globe*. The second disappointment is that it is the front section, which as he knows does not contain sports. So it is, by happenstance, that Duncan looks at the newspaper's front page, and so it is that an unexpected process begins to occur within him.

Two-thirds or more of the top half of the front page is given not to a national or international news event but to the case of a local missing twelve-year-old boy and the suspect being sought in the case by the Portsmouth police. There is a picture of the boy, a photograph so blurred it looks like something from a spy movie, and a black-and-white composite of the suspect, a young man who looks threatening and ominous, missing only, it seems, some kind of tattoo or scar, and a picture of a large man standing beside a computer console next to two other men, captioned, "Police Lt. Gilbert Dulac, left, in charge of the investigation of missing Eric Wells, believes a computer may help return the Portsmouth boy home unharmed."

The photos and composite sketch mean little to Duncan in themselves, nor does the text of the article, except that it is something to read, more or less casually, as he checks his watch again to see how late Wayne and Leon are running tonight. Nor is it the case itself which is addressing his mind—such a case seems almost generic in newspaper offerings—rather that it is taking place in nearby Portsmouth, the neat little city over on the water which it seemed he like other students was always planning to visit.

Duncan smiles then, even snickers lightly, as a couple of details in the article—a silver-gray car, a man in his early twenties with a reddish complexion—make it sound, of all people, like their strange and needy housemate, Vernon, who has been following the weirdest schedule lately. Vernon, he thinks. Dear God, of course, he had promised to hear him out tonight, to help him with his problem.

With new curiosity and a tingling about his ears, however, Duncan finds himself looking hard at the composite, to see if there is any resemblance. There seems little. The hair looks black, of course, and the face appears too hard, too evil, to belong to anyone like Vernon. Glancing up then, seeing Leon and Wayne headed his way, Duncan misfolds the newspaper, lays it back where he had found it, and gets to his feet. Taking up his books, turning to join in procession with the other two, knowing he will make no mention here of the curious coincidence concerning the already much-maligned fourth in their household quartet, he joins, too, in a ragged ongoing exchange having to do with someone's charge, somewhere, that amnesty amounted to repudiation of the charges against those who had escaped to Canada. . . . He will always remember, though, and will relate any number of times, the unsettling presence, a silent blinking light, which seemed to be signaling him even then from a remote corner of his mind.

SIXTEEN

THE CALL COMES as they are shifting telephones, switchboard, paperwork, and computer from one part of the squad room to another. The tip sheet will be marked 1825 hours, but Shirley Moss knows—will have noted—that it was closer to 1828. Dulac has left to pick up the brother to make the run to Portland, and a young officer named Benedict, assigned to the task force for the night shift, takes the call at one of two tables as Shirley and a cadet are lifting the other, which is stacked with two-story wire trays holding tip sheets.

Shirley lowers her side of the table to the floor and indicates to the cadet to do the same. She heard Officer Benedict say, "You *saw* the boy?" She holds, continues to listen to the uniformed officer's questions. "They turned right?" the officer says. "That's an easterly direction? The color of the car? Your name please?"

As the officer replaces the phone, even as he continues to fill in spaces on the form, Shirley says, "Someone *saw* the boy? Is that what they said? When?"

"I'm getting it down," he says. "Just a second."

Shirley holds—bristles some—watching him make added notations too slowly. "Well?" she says when he pauses.

"One second, please," he says.

Again, she holds. He takes up the paper then, hands it to her. "There," he says. "You want to file it?"

"File it? Is it a sighting or not?" she says.

"Are you in charge here?" he says.

"Just answer my question."

"Aren't they all?" he says.

"What are you saying?"

"I gave it an A priority. What are *you* saying?"

"It's a sighting? Someone *saw* the boy?"

"That's what he said. But it's two days old and it's a kid making the call."

"Who said what?" Shirley says. *"Kindly stop fucking around!"*

The officer appears to freeze. "Easy," he says.

She glares.

"Sunday evening," he says. "Four P.M. McDonald's—in Dover. This boy, he's sixteen—he says a boy shouted that he was being kidnapped. From a car. At the pick-up window."

"Shouted what?"

"Screamed is what he said."

"Screamed what?"

"For help. That he was being kidnapped."

"Then what?"

"That's it. The car took off."

"The boy screamed, and the person driving the car took off?"

"That's what he said."

"What about the driver?"

"No one he knew. He just said it was a man."

"How old?"

"He didn't say."

"You didn't ask him?"

"Hey—look—"

"What kind of car?"

"A gray coupe—it's written down."

"Did they order food?"

"I guess so. That's what he said."

"Did they pick up the food?"

"Look—if you will just hold your ass—this is probably a prank by school kids."

"They took off? That sounds like a prank? Did they pick up the food?"

"I don't think so."

"You don't think so? Did they pay?"

"No. I believe he said they did not pick up the food. I don't know if they paid. I gave this an A priority. A so-called sighting is supposed—"

"There are sightings and there are sightings," she says, starting to move past him.

"I thought I was the officer here," he says. "You're the secretary."

"Get out of my sight," she says. "Go do some push-ups."

Tip sheet in hand, Shirley returns across the room to the telephone at her table. She can go through the radio switchboard and speak to Dulac in his car, or she can call the TV station directly and have him summoned to a phone. Forty minutes. Forty-five. She decides to try the latter first, leave a message, then see if he can be raised by radio. As it happens, just a moment after she has spoken to a woman in Portland and has turned to speak to a detective about the distance over which they may speak by car radio, her telephone rings and it is Dulac, having just walked into the TV station.

"It's an apparent sighting," she says. "It all seems to fit. The only problem is that it's two days old, it happened two days ago, on Sunday evening."

As he asks questions and she gives added details, he interrupts her, saying, "He was alive and being cared for. That's what this means. It was twenty-four hours after he was picked up and he was alive—and being cared for. It was an order for two?"

"I'm not sure," Shirley says.

"Bring him in. Pick him up—have him picked up and brought in for questioning."

"We'll do it, Gil. Don't worry. Do what you have to do. There are a couple detectives here. And Mizener's around somewhere."

"Don't have Mizener do it. Jesus—Eric Wells was okay Sunday. That puts you in a tough position, doesn't it? If you abducted a kid and you're caring for him. Listen, I'm going to go ahead with this. It could be important. Have this McDonald's boy brought in, right away. Have someone other than Neil Mizener pick him up and question him. I'll check back with you, in a while, to see what you have."

The detective to whom Shirley conveys Dulac's orders is named De-Marcus. As he leaves with a uniformed officer to drive to Dover and pick up the boy—a good ten-minute drive—Shirley sits down with the tip sheet and telephones the McDonald's restaurant, to prepare for the detective's arrival. She asks to speak first to the boy, who is sixteen and named Steven March. A sensible-sounding boy, he says to her. "Everybody thought it was some kind of gag, but if it was a gag, would they leave the money behind—and the food?"

"Of course not," Shirley says. She asks to speak to the manager, to make arrangements to have him leave his job, probably, she tells him, for an hour or more.

"He's supposed to work," the man says. "This'll leave us short-handed."

"Sir, listen," Shirley says. "I think this is far more important right now. A squad car is halfway there already, to pick him up."

"How do I know you're a police officer," the man says.

"I'm not," she says. "The officers coming to pick him up will identify themselves. We're working against time. You can leave him on the clock or charge whatever time he misses to the Portsmouth PD. You can charge it to me personally; Shirley Moss is the name."

"And your position is what—if I may ask?"

"I'm just a pushy secretary, jesuschrist. What else do you want to know?"

A moment later, the telephone back in its cradle, Shirley draws part of another cup of coffee and lights a cigarette. To settle her system, she tells herself. Then she thinks, it does mean he was alive; it's a good thing Gil keeps that in mind because it's something which could otherwise be forgotten. To be alive. For the first time, she feels a flicker of hope.

SEVENTEEN

NEAR THE CAMPUS, in the evening air, Vernon is walking again. All within him feels snarled. Somewhere, on a town street, he turns to walk in the direction of his parked car. It seems impossible to him that the car and the boy will be where he left them, yet he has a sense that they will not have been discovered. Nor—as he walks—does his movement here, his being, seem to be part of reality. Not now.

To his faint surprise and greater dismay, the car is where he left it. He doesn't go to it directly. Students and others pass in the evening air, within streetlights, store lights, car lights. Walking to the curbed, window-lighted sidewalk before the row of stores, he passes shoppers carrying grocery bags, people in a hurry, and tells himself that no one cares anyway, because no one has time to care.

Beyond the supermarket, at a dimly lighted sub shop, he pauses at the door, then enters; he tries to remind himself not to look suspicious. Within, where a thin waiter-cook is placing a long open-mouthed sandwich on a counter, where others are waiting, Vernon stands and stares for a moment at the overhead wall menu, then turns and walks back outside.

A moment later, passing through a dream in which he walked across a parking lot, stepped between cars, and opened an unlocked car door, he is sitting in the darkened driver's seat. He exhales. With his right hand he reaches and feels that the boy is still there. He knew he was there, and he decides this time not to reach under the sleeping bag to see if his body is warm or cold, if his pulse will still speak up to him as it did before. What does it matter?

His mother is on his mind. She may have been lurking at the edges of his thoughts all along, as he was thinking of someone to whom to turn. If he told her everything at last? If he told her of his magazine and of his dreams? If he told her about Anthony, and his fears and his loneliness? Would she help him? Would she understand or try to understand? No, he knows she would not, yet appealing to her is something to do, a last-ditch attempt maybe to put things right. Laconia is only a forty-five-minute drive. What does he care about time or anything else? Why should he?

He starts his car.

He knows his mother will not help him. She will only rage at him. Why why why? He knows he will not be able to confide in her. Yet, he thinks, maybe he will and maybe she will. If he goes close enough, if he sees her, perhaps she will know enough of the world, will see into things in a way that she may come to his rescue.

Elsewhere, later—he knows he is near Concord, near the middle of the state—he stands outside his car in a brightly lighted self-serve gas station, adding seven dollars' worth to his tank. The car had sputtered to him a moment earlier. As he stands outside the car now, it seems alive to him with its particular cargo.

He stands holding the chilled pump handle. The ramp onto north-south Interstate 93, the long way home, is just a minute away. Laconia is twenty minutes north. His mother will be there. She will nearly die when he tells her there is an unconscious boy in the car, but when he tells of the accident, when he explains that he had only wanted to have him as a little brother, she will try to help. She will call a lawyer, he imagines, and the police, and an ambulance. For the first time in days, in years—in all his life, he thinks, as far as his mother is concerned—things will begin to sort themselves out. If she wants to move away, he thinks again, he will understand. And at least if they do send him to jail, he will finally be able to fall asleep. Today will have been the worst day of his life. Tomorrow will be less so, and he will let her go and never make any claims on her again.

Pulling around to leave the gas station, he sees a State Police car go by, headed in the direction from which he has just come. Yes, he thinks, the way to slip through unnoticed is to do nothing suspicious.

Maybe this little boy will just come around once a doctor has a look at him, Vernon thinks, driving. In a day or so, he'll be back in school. With some stories to tell, Vernon thinks. And he could be okay himself, even if he has to spend some time locked up somewhere. Wasn't that the key—to return things to what they had been before? The problem was telling his mother. He'd do it, though; then he'd do his time in jail. And he'll never ask her for anything again, if that's what she wants. He'll tell her that, he thinks. I'll never bother you or embarrass you again, and I'll never hurt anyone again, as long as I live.

He drives. There is little traffic on the divided highway at this dark, evening hour. Another thought he has—to save his mother the trouble—is to turn around and drive back to Portsmouth. Go to the police station there. Just walk in, go up to that detective and say, *I'm the person you're looking for. I'm sorry for what's happened. The little boy is out in my car. He's in a coma but that's because of an accident. I only picked him up because I couldn't help myself. I only wanted him to be my friend. A little brother. I didn't mean for him to be hurt. I've never hurt anyone before in my life, and I didn't mean for this to happen.*

He drives along. Even as it startles him, startles his plans for making amends, he reaches a hand in under the sleeping bag again, at last, to touch the boy's face and forehead. "Maybe we will end up being friends after all," Vernon says aloud. "That's possible—isn't it? Stranger things than that have happened, you know."

As he drives through the darkness then, he recalls what may have been the first sexual experience of his life. At least it was the most unforgettable. It was finding the magazine, as a child himself, some ten years ago. The magazine with its collection of photographs. What a shock it was. The two boys with their genuine smiles, their penises hard in every picture, every scene, one like an index finger and just as pink, the other larger-headed, bluish-colored, like some exotic young plant sprouting at the edge of a pond. The smell alone of the pages, of the ink perhaps, and the taste, for he did more in his fantasies than look at or smell the photographs, came to excite him in time more than anything else he had ever known.

He knew what he was looking for. Climbing through the clothes and boxes and grocery bags filled with newspapers inside the Salvation Army collection shed, he knew. The battered, torn-away hinge and bent tin door of the shed told of the ferocity with which other boys had gained entry in their search for *Playboys* and *Penthouses*. The magazine cover slid into view, from between newspapers, and he knew. There were the two boys on a beach towel, naked, erect, smiling, touching each other, and he knew, from the roots of his hair to his toes, in his center, in the unfolding of his initial sexual seizure, he knew that he was found, that life was beginning.

Laconia is just ahead now, along a stretch of two-lane highway. The sky is dark; there are no stars. What lies ahead is the most impossible thing he has ever imagined doing. Yet it is real. To die seems easier than this. To lie back and be put to death would be easier than making a confession to his mother. Yet it is what he must do. What seems most important is that she give him a chance to explain. He drives on, takes his normal way to their house, knowing all along that he is only practicing stories to himself, knowing more than he wishes to know.

The small house is dark; he is not surprised. Pulling into the short driveway, he turns off the car lights and motor. He sits there. That the house is dark simply means that she's at work, at the restaurant. It simply means that he will have to go there to make his plea to her to save his life. That's all it means.

The restaurant where she works, on the highway in the direction of the lakes, has its name in red neon—Brando's Italian Cuisine / Restaurant and Bar—and a split-rail fence around its parking lot. Pulling up, turning into the lot, Vernon experiences a mixed sense in himself of coming home, as he has any number of times previously. Not often, he thinks, since he went away to school, but enough times to recognize this sense in him of anticipation. Home for Christmas, home for a time in the summer. He cannot help having occur in him a feeling of looking forward to seeing his mother. Even as things might deteriorate in an hour or an evening, there had always been this good feeling in him when he came home after having been away for a period of time.

Now, at once, as soon as he has pulled into a space on the gravel and parked, the good feeling is leaving. He has never come here like this, he thinks. When his mother was at work, he'd just wait at the house until she returned.

Well, here he is, he thinks, sitting behind the wheel. Once more then, he reaches under the sleeping bag, to feel the warmth of the boy, to feel his forehead. He's been unconscious all day, he thinks. I wish you'd wake up, he thinks but doesn't dare say in his anxiety. At the same time, from feeling his face, he has moved his hand over his ear until he has touched a stickiness in his hair and the wound. He pulls his hand back.

Another thought comes to Vernon then, an image passing his mind's eye for the first time. It is of a person out in the middle of Lake Winnipesaukee on a dark and misty night like this, lifting and guiding a child's body over the side of the boat and into the dark water on a mere bubble or two, knowing it will sail and sink for a minute, and two minutes, before ever reaching the unlighted bottom a lifetime below.

It is as he is in the damp air, on the long wooden porch to the restaurant, however, and looking through a window which is tinted amber and contains small bubbles, and an interior doorway, on an angle, to see if he can spot his mother where she might appear there at the end of the bar, that it comes to him that his thought of making things as they had been before is hopeless. He sees her, sees his mother. There she is, carrying a small tray. She does not appear at all as he had imagined, sexy, that is, a smile on her face, her hair fluffed and her uniform blouse unbuttoned a button or two. At this distance, at this angle, she appears an ordinary woman. She looks tired. She gives no tosses to her hair as he has seen her do before; rather she places her tray on the counter and stands there. His mother whom he has always loved, Vernon thinks, and loved to excess, in spite of the fact, or because, she has never been able to love him in turn. He who has ruined her life, as she has told him many times. An ordinary woman. A widow at age twenty-four. The war.

Walking back over the gravel and crushed stone, which he notices now is mixed with slush and water, Vernon returns to his car. There is the flashing gold light of another car entering the parking lot; he pays it little mind.

In only a moment, backing out, he is on the two-lane highway driving back in the direction of the interstate. I did it, he thinks. If anyone ever asks, I can always say I did it.

EIGHTEEN

DUNCAN HAS SAID NOTHING of his suspicion to the others. Nor has he quite said it to himself. In the cottage, in their "whoever cooks doesn't have to clean up" arrangement, he has gone to his room to study while Leon—with Wayne's help, the two *are* one—has assumed the role which will free him, Leon, from the mess made in the process.

It is after they have eaten, and after Duncan has relieved Wayne of any kitchen responsibility—"Go ahead, I'll clean up," he has said to him—that it comes to him. Perhaps he relieved Wayne so he might be by himself to think as he washed dishes. Perhaps he did so because of something troubling clinging to his mind. He has finished the dishes. The table remains dirty, and he is cleaning the counter around the sink. He knows then. As he knows, it is as a balloon collapsing in his chest. Vernon, he says to himself. My God.

He finishes cleaning the counter and sink, in a daze. Rinsing the small sponge under the faucet, he turns to wipe the table, and it is as if, at once, he doesn't know. At the same time all things keep falling into place, again and again, from the beginning.

NINETEEN

BEATRICE NEVER LIKED NORTHERN MAINE, in time calling it The Great Haunted Loneliness. And this *isn't* northern Maine, Dulac admits—they are on the Maine Turnpike, well into the darkness south of Portland—yet he is feeling in himself a strain of the haunted homesickness that unnerved her those times they were on the narrow two-lane blacktop state roads up near New Brunswick, where they seldom saw another car or another person and their headlights highlighted only various thicknesses of moisture and blacktop.

Beatrice. He's missing her as he drives. She would know, would understand the fatherly intent of his voice, his words, to this fifteen-year-old boy. And of course she would help.

Coincidence has it, irony has it, he thinks, that the time he is recalling is the time, a dozen years or so ago, when they received word that Beatrice would never be able to conceive a child and they drove north, over a Thanksgiving weekend, to give themselves a slight if haunting vacation, as if to let themselves know that they and their life were okay.

In fact it was another message that they received. Stopping at a restaurant in Calais, near the Canadian border, and just across an especially wide stretch of the Croix River, they saw, separately, a message printed by finger in the steam on a window near the kitchen, on the way to the restrooms. In moisture lightly bleeding the message said:

> *Thanks be to my mother and father. If Charlene could have had them for parents and not me and if Roy had not lost his life on the other side of the world we'd have something to be thankful for—Rae.*

Later, when they were driving on, crossing into Canada and looking for a place to stop for the night, he happened to say, "I keep wondering what happened to Charlene," and Beatrice said, "I do, too. What an unusual thing to write on a window," and at last, when they had lain sleepless for an hour or more in a cinder-block motel which smelled of disinfectant, and Beatrice began to weep softly in the dark and she said to him finally, "Can we go home?" he said of course, and turned out of bed, and returning to the highway and finding coffee at a misty Dunkin Donuts near the border crossing, he drove all night, and she sat beside him, drifting in and out of sleep, and perhaps they had never been closer before or since, or happier in their closeness, than they were throughout those hours of darkness, looking for the divided highway to begin, and looking for daylight to break out over the Atlantic, and looking for Portsmouth to come into view, their small hometown on the water, and looking for the driveway to their house, on Lincoln Avenue, and looking for the familiar comfort it offered within. Looking for themselves.

"What do you think of Portland?" he says to the boy.

"Fine," Matt says. "It seemed fine."

"There's a place there where you can learn to make wooden boats," Dulac says.

"Yeah," the boy says.

"Not much to see, though, after dark," Dulac says.

He drives along, quiet again. The videotaping crosses his mind. His central message was simple and direct—"We know, I know, that you don't want to do what you are doing, and I want you to know that if you call me, at the number appearing on the screen, I will do all that I can to help resolve this situation"—and he wonders yet again if it will have any effect, if the tone was right, the words right, if they will trigger the willingness to surrender. Of course he will look soft to some, he thinks, especially other law enforcement people, but he can't afford to worry about that.

"I wonder," he says to the boy, "if I should have used the word *please*. What do you think?"

"Gee, I don't know," Matt says.

Dulac is only making small talk, but he tries to be serious about the subject. "*Please* could be a key word for such a person," he says. "It's a word everyone knows, from everyone's childhood. I wish I had used it."

"I see what you mean," the boy says.

Dulac feels encouraged; it is as much as he has gotten out of him, and perhaps out of himself, so far. "What's your gut feeling, Matt, about Eric?" he says then.

"What do you mean?"

"Do you think he's okay? Do you feel positive?"

"I'm scared," Matt says.

Dulac drives along. Bad subject, he thinks, at the same time that he is saying to himself that it is the subject he wishes to address, that it is this boy's feelings and fears he wants out in the open, his strength he wants to encourage, to bolster.

Near Biddeford, he radios in to speak to Shirley.

"We have his statement and he's on his way back to McDonald's," she says. "Everybody thought he was reliable. A good witness. It's a near certainty, Gil, that Eric Wells was in that car, which he says was gray. He thinks it was either a Pontiac Sunbird or a Chevrolet Monza—this kid knows his cars—which means we're on the right track, that Eric was okay on Sunday night. Matt with you?"

"He's right here," Dulac says.

"Is he helping?" Shirley says.

"Oh, he's a big help," Dulac says. "And good company." He glances to Matt, smiles.

"Gil, listen," Shirley says. "I know you're anxious but there's no need for you to rush back. Ya Know? I mean I know you haven't had any dinner. Something big comes in here, I'll be in touch with you. Okay?"

"Okay, Shirley, fine," Dulac says.

Driving on then, Dulac is trying again to sort out how to proceed. There are things he wants to say to this boy that he hasn't been able yet to say, or even to formulate for himself, and he wants, too, to be back in the squad room. How *is* a man an effective friend or father? he wonders. How do you get through to saying what counts, what will be heard and understood?

Oh, it's the same old story, he thinks then. Time. Not having time. The preciousness of time. Needing to be elsewhere. "Matt," he says in the midst of this, "would you like a pizza?"

"Well, sure," Matt says.

"You're hungry?"

"I guess I am," Matt says.

"You'd *like* a pizza? Tell me the truth."

"Sure," Matt says.

For the first time, in a glance, Dulac detects something of a smile coming from the boy. "We'll do it," Dulac says. "I'm starving. And we're going to have a talk about things, too. Okay?"

"Okay," Matt says.

On the car radio then, Dulac tells Shirley that they are turning off at Biddeford. "Pizza stop," he says. "With everything. Matt's idea," he adds. "Matt said if we didn't stop for a pizza, he'd break my arm."

"I'd like to see that," Shirley says.

All three laugh politely, through car and airwaves; Dulac's smile holds as he triggers his turn signal to leave the highway. "I know a place here," he says.

TWENTY

VERNON CONTINUES DRIVING steadily. The university is just ahead now. Its smokestack and gray smoke are visible in the night sky. There are no houses or lights along this last stretch of two-lane pavement before coming to the agricultural and athletic fields, the animal barns and tennis courts. All is dark on this approach to the campus and his has been the only car on the road since leaving the four-lane bypass a mile back; even this absence of people speaks to him of darkness ahead.

A car does appear then, coming down a hill toward him. The car's lights go dim. He dims his own. Still the car comes on, and he fears for an instant that they are going to collide head-on. In a sudden shoulder-to-

266

shoulder flash of lights, however, the car passes. For the moment, he feels safe. In his rearview mirrow, the car's red taillights float away into the darkness, close to the ground, as if to signal the only other boat on the wide lake of the world in the middle of the night.

Vernon keeps going his way.

Up the hill, where the terrain flattens, he is coming opposite the first university building, the field house, and there, of all things, is a campus police car, making a turn through a paved space, around the flagpole, before the vast brick building. The car's exterior paraphernalia is dark on its roof, nonetheless glistening and reflecting under high streetlights, and Vernon is seized with a desire to turn himself in. This is it, he says to himself. Oh God, this is it right now.

He flips his turning signal to send its flashing light to the face of the police car. He turns his steering wheel, turning directly into the extremely restricted university parking space before the field house, thinking how he will do it right now, will confess, say all, and have it done with at last. For the moment, he is not breathing; his car is hardly moving. Here is the police car.

It doesn't stop. Its roof lights do not flash on. Even as he looks to their faces—one and the other—and they appear to look back, they do not see what he is trying to say. The police car simply rolls by. There is its door insignia a foot away, then its taillights are in his side mirror—much larger than the previous car's—and there goes the car on into the street, accelerating in the direction of the town's concentration of beer dens and mom-and-pop take-outs, its gray exhaust disappearing over the pavement surface.

Vernon reverses direction. He doesn't know where he is going.

He kills the boy then within a feeling of time having paused. Back off the road, he parks in the shadow of the football stadium which, overhead, is like the prow of a battleship against a night sky. He had hesitated leaving the restricted parking area before the field house, turning part of a turn after the campus police car, but changing his mind in midstream and turning back into the darkness from which he had come. His actions following seem unbothered with start-and-stop uncertainty.

Motor off, lights off, he acts almost calmly, although a tone has come up and keeps humming in his ears. He believes it is his conscience speaking to him, and would disrupt it if he could; he knows this new capacity has occurred in him now as have other capacities in his life, most of which have been sexual. Crossing a forbidden line. A tone in his ears. Blossoming, feeling serene.

He stands outside the car on the driver's side. There is darkness all around. The tone continues in his ears. He looks to the pavement on which he is standing as something grips him from within; a sensation shoots through him, a meteor disappearing. Stepping to the edge of the football stands, where the sky returns to view, he sees a helicopter fluttering in the distance. Two small lights flash from the chopper, one of them red, as it seems to move closer to the port city over on the water. No rockets are fired. Nor any flares. There seem to be no explosions anywhere unless they are within his chest.

He opens the trunk, which has no working light, and leaves the trunk lid standing. Reaching his hand into the cavity, he runs it over the carpeting. Then, opening the car door on the passenger side, he reaches under to pick up the boy, to move him from under the sleeping bag; stepping back around, he places the boy in the dark trunk on his back. He straightens the boy's arms a little at his sides. He thinks to kiss him goodbye, to kiss his forehead, but doesn't. Taking up the heavy sleeping bag, he folds it over once, twice, and three times, until it has a thickness of a foot or more. Placing this upon the boy's upper body, he lowers the trunk lid and when it will not catch, presses his weight on it. He hears it catch. Lifting away, he wishes he could feel more than he does, while the tone continues in his ears.

Stepping back around, he looks for the helicopter in the distance. Its fluttering sound seems to continue, although he cannot discern its flashing lights.

TWENTY-ONE

THEY SIT OVER A battered tin tray which holds a single slice of pizza. They have eaten. Hunger has been the center even of small talk; energy has been given to chewing. Dulac is ready now to talk of other things, although he doesn't know yet what he is going to say. Time, more than ever, crowds him. Hunching forward, more or less giving up on the last slice, he is trying to think how to start.

"You have that," he says, nodding at the remaining slice.

"I'm sort of full," Matt says.

"You have it; I'm all finished."

"I don't think I have room."

"Really?" Dulac says. "You're just being polite."

"No."

"You don't have to be polite with me, believe me."

"I am full."

"Eat that slice of pizza," Dulac says.

Matt smiles.

"Okay, we'll split it," Dulac says.

"Okay."

"See, you are still hungry," Dulac says.

"So are you," Matt says.

Dulac grins. I like this kid, he is saying to himself, even as he knows this was his predisposition. Using his fork as a knife, he wedges off a third of the slice, which he takes up in a fold in his fingers; he spins the tray around to Matt, saying, "There you go."

Matt follows suit.

"I want to tell you to be strong," Dulac says, coming to the end of his chewing.

Matt looks to him.

"This is a tough thing you're going through," Dulac says. "What I'd like to do is to tell you that everything is going to be okay. I'd like to say that. That I'll intercede for you, take the heat, absorb the hurt and the nastiness, because that's my job. But I'd be kidding both of us. I hope your brother comes home. I hope he comes walking in tonight, and that he's fine. There's a chance of that. You know, he is a tough little kid. Did you know that?"

"I know that," Matt says. "I didn't. But I do now."

"This thing at McDonald's, on Sunday. He tried to get away. That may seem easy in the movies or on TV, but in fact it's not easy at all. It takes courage. It takes imagination. Those are important things, and he has them."

The boy keeps watching him.

"At the same time, you have to know that he is in a tough situation. A dangerous situation. The guy drove off with him. From McDonald's. So it shows that *he's* trying to have his way, too. And he holds most of the cards. Do you know what I'm saying?"

Matt nods.

"This is what I'd say to you if I were your father," Dulac says. "I'd say this may turn out to be rough, and you're going to have to stand up to it. Like a man.

"I mean you're just a boy. You're a fine boy. You're a good person, I can tell. And you shouldn't have to face up to something like this. But you might have to. Do you understand?"

Matt nods again.

"You don't know where your father is?" Dulac says.

"No, just that we heard he was in New Orleans."

"Do you like your father?" Dulac says, which is the question he meant to ask in the first place.

"I guess so."

"I had problems with my old man," Dulac says. "Not impossible problems finally. Problems just the same. At the time they seemed impossible."

The boy keeps watching him, listening to him in the dimly lighted pizza parlor.

"I respected him, though," Dulac says. "I loved him. You know—deep down?"

Matt nods.

"I'll tell you a story," Dulac says. "This time, when I was about your age—a little younger even, maybe Eric's age—I began building this little miniature town in the dirt, next to the front porch. We lived in Quebec City at the time. I really got into this, but what it was was that my dad took an interest in it when he came home from work. So in a way I got into doing it for him. I had little trees and shrubs in the ground, you know. My dad, he put his lunch bucket right there on the porch steps and pretty soon was down on his hands and knees on the ground beside me. It's one of the best memories I have of the old crocodile, you know. Maybe it's the best. There was something he loved, that we loved together. However brief.

"He showed me some more things to do, and it was funny, because he went into the house, got a spool of black thread from my mother's sewing stuff, and she came out after him to see why he was taking her thread, and it was like we were both kids, the two of us.

"He said to her, he said, 'Just let us be now, this is important.' " Dulac lifts his glass as if to drink, even though it is clear that the glass is empty.

"The thread was for telephone wires," he says. "To go through our little town. And he showed me how to whittle twigs with his little pocket-knife. To make telephone poles. Jesus—God—you know, he gave me that knife. Right then. It was because—well, it was because he'd never gotten into something like that, before, with me. And because he liked it so much.

"He came up with a way, too, to make fire hydrants by cutting a yellow pencil into segments and whittling on caps, in effect, by leaving a little of the lead sticking out. They were just perfect.

"Anyway, what happened was I went to work again on the town the next day while my father was at work. He'd shown me a way to line little ditches with wax, paraffin, so the town could have a system of rivers and ponds and the water couldn't seep through so quickly into the ground. Of course everything, all the work, was all the more special now, though, because I was doing it for him. I was doing what he had shown me and doing things of my own, and it was all falling into place, new things just kept presenting themselves, with immediate solutions, and all of it building up to his coming home from work again that afternoon.

"Then—of course—it happened. I don't know what I was doing. I'd gone for a jar of water or something. I came back around the house, and there was this boy—he was maybe sixteen years old—this boy—he was destroying everything. He was kicking it, caught up in a frenzy—kicking stomping, just obliterating everything we'd done.

"I don't think I've ever been so shocked as I was in that moment. Or so hurt. The old man would never see it. We'd never work on it again. Not after that. It was senseless. What I did, at first—because this kid was a lot bigger and older—I cried. I cried, and tried to push him away. But it was halfhearted in a way, and he just held me at bay and kept up this violent kicking of everything on the ground.

"Something happened then. You know there may be some truth in Superman, because I tell you this transformation came over me. Nothing mattered. Not to me. It didn't matter if I got hurt. I took up this garden tool that was there on the porch. It was a hand tool, had three small metal prongs which were quite sharp. I was going to kill him. I was possessed. I was going to end his life, I was so upset.

"I got him once. I got the tool in my hand, went at him. Came around with it, got him just above the waist—cut him in three places. Those were real cuts. He let out a scream then, and he backed off. And I moved after him with that garden tool.

"He ran. He backed away first. I kept after him; I took another real swing at him. He was calling me a little sonofabitch, things like that, but then he took off running, holding his side where I'd gashed him.

"I stayed after him. My anger was still there. Or my hurt. I ran, Jesus, did I run. To say I was just about out of my senses would be more like it. I knew I could outrun him. I knew it. I wanted to hurt him that badly. He could have been Jesse Owens—he could have run twenty miles—and I would have caught him. It was in me. Whatever it was, it was in me.

"He actually ran two or three miles before I got him. There we were, running past houses, through alleys, around corners—this wild-eyed, terrified animal and this determined little kid behind him, with a garden tool, who was crying away and was not going to give up under any circumstances.

"Finally, when he turned between some garages, I came between them myself, and there he was, on the side of one, sprawled on the ground—he was sick he was so winded—and as I spotted him and moved on him, he was terrified and trying to disappear into the ground, into the base of that garage, and begging me not to hurt him and crying.

"He changed my mind. I had him there; I had him cornered and at my mercy. I had that garden tool in my hand. I even had my father's jackknife in my pocket. And I had meant to make him pay, to pay far more than the three cuts he had in his side. Far more. He was crying. Begging me not to hurt him.

"He changed my mind. I didn't do it. I had come to hurt him. And I didn't do it. I didn't spit on him. Or kick him. I didn't call him any names. I walked away. I knew at the time, somehow, I've known ever since, that what I did, what I didn't do, was an act of cowardice. I've never gotten over it. Not completely. I was young. But I don't kid myself, not anymore."

He looks over, sees the boy watching him. "If you were my son," Dulac says, "that's what I'd tell you. So you could learn—from my mistake—that you have to take care of yourself."

He says no more by way of giving advice. In a moment he merely says, "You want anything else?"

"No," Matt says.

"Let's roll then," Dulac says.

TWENTY-TWO

VERNON ENTERS THE COTTAGE almost brashly. An odd intoxication is in him. No one is in the kitchen area, though, and he isn't sure he wants to tell them his big news anyway, whatever that news might be. Has he just won a scholarship to graduate school? Won the lottery? Walked away from a head on collision? Why does he feel so high? Opening the refrigerator, he removes a can of beer and it means nothing to him, pleases him, that the can of beer is not his to take.

He pops the pop top, drops it into the hole so it may swim to the bottom.

"You shouldn't do that," someone says.

It is Duncan; glancing over, Vernon sees that Duncan has come from his room. He see, too, an unexpected distance Duncan seems to be keeping.

"Those things get in people's throats," Duncan says. "You can gag on those things."

Vernon tips back the can, drinks a swallow.

"Vernon, what is going on?" Duncan says.

"What is going on?" Vernon says. "I'm drinking someone's beer."

"I'm not talking about the beer."

"What are you talking about? I'm drinking someone's beer, that's all."

"I'm not talking about beer," Duncan says. "Not at all."

Vernon only looks at him.

"Vernon. You know what I'm talking about."

Vernon just looks at him, seeks to see into his eyes at the distance of the ten or fifteen feet that separate them.

Then, out of the blue, Vernon says, "It's all over now. No need to worry."

"What's over? What do you mean?"

"It's over. Everything's over. I'm drinking someone's beer. I'll pay for it. Tomorrow I'm going back to school."

"Whose beer is he drinking?" another voice says, and there is Leon padding out in his stockinged feet from the bedroom he shares with Wayne, on his way to the bathroom. As his question goes unanswered, he pulls up before going on into the bathroom. "I said, whose beer is he drinking?"

"Just shut up," Duncan says.

"That's my beer?" Leon says, coming over. There is Wayne appearing in the bedroom door, also in stockinged feet, a pencil in his hand, coming to watch.

"Budweiser?" Vernon says.

"Goddamit! That's my beer, isn't it!"

"Leon, just hold it," Duncan says.

"That is my fucking beer!" Leon says.

"I'll pay for the beer," Duncan says. "Okay."

Leon lets up, looks as if he wants to say something else but is holding it back.

"Go to your room, I need to talk to Vernon," Duncan says.

Leon holds, as does Wayne back in the bedroom doorway.

"It's serious," Duncan says. "Please."

Leon hunches, making an expression as he moves on into the bathroom and closes the door; Wayne retreats also, back into the bedroom, closing that door.

Duncan steps closer, as if they may be overheard. "I believe I know what it is," he says.

Vernon looks at him, saying nothing. Then he says, "What what is?"

"Everything," Duncan says. "Everything."

Vernon looks at him. Turning then, placing the full can of beer on the counter, he starts in the direction of the door. "No one knows everything," he says over his shoulder. "It isn't possible to know everything."

Duncan, following after him, is saying, "Where are you going? You better stay here. You better do some talking. You said you'd do some talking."

Vernon, feeling he may be restrained, keeps moving, into the darkness outside, around to the driver's side of his car.

"Vernon, just wait a minute!" Duncan snaps at him in the darkness.

Vernon holds with his hand on the door handle.

"Where are you going?" Duncan says.

"The library. I'm going to the library."

"The library? What are you talking about? Listen—I know. I know!"

"Know what? What do you know?"

"Vernon. I know."

"I don't know what you're talking about. I have to go. I have to go. I have work to do." Vernon is getting into his car, sliding in behind the steering wheel, starting the motor, moving on his way as if he is going to be stopped and held by Duncan, and made to talk, made to tell.

As he backs around, in a flash, there is Duncan's face, highlighted, saying something, calling something unheard. Was he asking him to stop? Was that what he was doing? What did he say before? He said something. What did he say? What was he talking about? He did not hear him. Whatever it was, he did not hear him. He did not. How could anybody be heard in the midst of all that was going on?

TWENTY-THREE

THE CALL COMES to Dulac at home, at six or seven minutes after ten. He is upstairs, where Beatrice is lying in bed watching television; he is reaching to untie his shoes when the telephone out in the hall rings. He knows at once. He simply knows. A fullness, and a restraint is over him as he steps into the hall to take up the receiver. He answers officially, saying, "Lieutenant Dulac."

"Positive ID," the detective says to him from a squad room telephone. "Positive ID. Absolutely positive. A roommate. Our boy is a college student. Can you believe it? Studying some kind of science. Twenty-two years old. Everything fits, Lieutenant. The exact height. Rosy cheeks. It looks airtight. The guy's behavior—"

"What about the boy?"

"Nothing on the boy, Lieutenant. Nothing. Nothing's any different except we have positive ID. The suspect. The roommate believes the suspect knows that he's been made. He was there—it's a cottage in Lee these four students rent—he was there less than two hours ago. Eight fifteen, about. Extremely nervous. Agitated. His name is Vernon Fischer. Vernon Fischer, F-I-S-C-H-E-R. Male Caucasian. Home residence I guess is Laconia. Only child. That's all we know. Quiet guy. No known girlfriends. No known friends of any kind. Honors student. Can you believe it? One of these four students renting a cottage on Wheelwright Pond, in Lee. This is the first call, Lieutenant. Except for the motor vehicle check. Everybody down here is jumping. I tell you. Somebody said, as soon as the Lieutenant walked out, ten minutes ago, the call came in."

"Okay," Dulac is saying. "Okay. Don't let anything out yet. I'll be there in ten minutes. Less than ten minutes. How did the roommate know? Did he confess? What happened? The question is, where is the boy? Is he holding the boy?"

"Saw it in the paper. Says it took him more than an hour to believe it."

"To believe it—really? Did he say anything about the boy?"

"Nothing. Says he saw this Vernon earlier in the day, mid-morning. At school. Says he looked haggard, very upset, sunken eyes and so on. That when he asked what the problem was, he said, Vernon said it was a life or death situation. He says this Vernon guy's behavior has been erratic, very unpredictable for several days now. Since last Wednesday or Thursday. Says he was gone from the cottage much of the time, overnight several times, that he did not return at all on Saturday night, or—let's see—for most of Sunday night, I believe—I've got it written down—and was gone all of the night last night. I've got to check on Monday. Anyway, Lieutenant, this is it. Call came in 2153. It's now 2212. No action's been taken yet. I told the roommate not to move, not to leave; I said if suspect returns they are to act as natural as possible and do nothing to restrain him. That's it, Lieutenant. Motor vehicle checks by the way, so we have the address now, in Laconia. We're waiting for you."

"I'm on my way. Call the state police, right now; call Lieutenant Heon, at home if you have to, tell him we'd like surveillance, undetected surveillance, on the residence in Laconia. Starting as soon as possible. Just in case he shows up there and has the boy with him. Call the attorney general, too; tell him what we're doing, that we will be searching this cottage in Lee, impounding everything there for now, including any and all cars, and that we will be setting up a stakeout on this place for at least twenty-four hours. The same with Laconia. Ask Lieuenant Heon, by the way, if we can have some manpower help, unmarked cars and so on, for the stakeout. Do those two calls; I'll be there in a few minutes. If our luck holds, we'll have Mr. Vernon in no time. Maybe the boy will be home free, too. That's how I want everything to proceed. With caution, in awareness that he is holding the boy. That he was caring for the boy, we know that, and that the boy is in danger. You say he left this cottage at eight fifteen; under what circumstances? Why did he leave?"

"He left in a rush, Lieutenant. Left a full can of beer he had just opened. The reason he left—well, I guess he was being hassled about the beer, but the roommate who called, named Duncan McIntyre, says the reason he left is he was trying to confront him about his suspicion, from having read the paper, and that Vernon left in a rush and was extremely agitated."

"What does that mean about the boy? What do you think?"

"Jesus, I don't know, Lieutenant."

"One other thing. Call the campus police. Have them inform the university provost. Tell them we'll want everything on this guy, right away. On the other roommates, too. We better check them out. Car registrations. Class schedules. Anything like that. Pictures, if they have them. Certainly of Vernon. We'll want pictures of him as soon as possible. I'll be there in five minutes."

Dulac hangs up then. His pulse, he realizes, is at work in his temples; his breathing, though, is calm.

"Gil, is it good news?" Beatrice says from the bedroom.

"Looks good," he says, tying his shoes. "Looks good."

"You're going in?" she says.

"I'm on my way," he says.

"Gil, you be careful now," she says.

276

"I may be gone all night," he says. "We have positive ID."

"Call if you can," she says.

"I'll try," he says, on his way to the stairs, fixing his holster on his hip and looking for his wool jacket as he reaches downstairs.

Forty minutes later, all is in place and they are ready to leave for the cottage in Lee. Dulac is at his desk, checking his list, trying to double-check all that needs to be put in motion or ordered up, while the five other officers who will be going along are either in the squad room checking their gear or close at hand.

Shirley. He wants to call Shirley, to have her there, and knows it is inappropriate that he make the call himself. It is not for personal reasons that he wants her there. Nor is it because she has been in the midst of things all along and might be angry over missing the main event. He wants her judgment. Who knows what might happen? They have positive ID. They have an address. Two addresses. A twelve-year-old boy is being held. What if a standoff of some kind comes up? Who knows what kind of possible escapes the suspect might try to negotiate? Is he armed? What if he tries to take his own life? He wants Shirley there, that's all there is to it. He just doesn't know how to phrase it, or who to ask to do it, since those themselves are tasks he would turn to her to handle.

He looks to his list again. Five minutes and they will roll. Don't miss things, don't go off half-cocked, he is saying to himself. It's time to earn your pay. This is it, he tells himself. This is it. A partial stakeout by the state police is already in effect. Good, he thinks. He just hopes they use restraint, that none of them gets too military, as the state troopers have been known to do. The APB on the car is in effect, through the tri-state area. If he knows, would he try to take off? Would he drive, ditch his car? Switch cars? *Does* he know?

A solution is in his mind all at once to another problem; stepping from his cubicle around the corner to the doorway to the squad room, he calls out, "Hey, somebody call Shirley Moss. Tell her she has to come in. You, Benedict, give her a call. Tell her things are popping and we need administrative help."

At his desk again, he is turning to the next item on his list, the stakeout at the residence in Laconia—we could get pictures there, he is thinking—when Detective DeMarcus steps through his open doorway. "We got a problem with the campus police," DeMarcus says. "The guy's on the line right now. It's been forty minutes at least since I called them, Lieutenant, and they haven't done a thing, except call in this guy. He says they can't cooperate unless they have a court order."

"We don't need a court order to investigate a suspect," Dulac says.

"He's on 2842," DeMarcus says.

Dulac takes up his phone, presses a light. "Lieutenant Dulac," he says. "We're not invading anyone's privacy or violating any laws. We just need to know the addresses, schedules, certainly the home addresses of these four students so we can check them out. We'd appreciate your cooperation. We're not asking for private records or anything."

The man says, "How is it you believe these particular students are involved in something which apparently took place in Portsmouth?"

"What we believe," Dulac says, "what we know, is that one of them is holding a missing twelve-year-old boy."

"Why do you believe that, if you don't mind my asking?"

Dulac takes a partial breath. "Listen," he says, "I am not going to review our case with you at this time. Either provide the information we're after, and do it now, or I will have the state police at the door of the university chancellor in ten minutes; if that isn't enough, I'll have the governor's office in touch with the chancellor in fifteen. And believe me, they will have court orders."

"Listen to me for a minute now—," the man begins.

"I'm not listening to you for a minute," Dulac says. "Or half a minute. *Where in the hell are you coming from? We are busting ass here to save the life of this twelve-year-old boy!*"

As the man begins, "Lieutenant—," once more, Dulac's telephone starts to ring and he cuts the connection by switching to another line, saying, "Dulac here."

"Lieutenant Heon," the person says. "Will we be needing dogs?"

"I hadn't thought of dogs," Dulac says.

"We have two bloodhounds that are really beauties," the state police lieutenant says. "Unless you object, I'll just have them available, along with their handler. You never know in a situation like this. If your boy is holed up somewhere, or if he has moved the little boy around. What you need to do is bring a piece of the boy's clothing. In a paper bag. Not plastic. We've had problems with plastic."

"Okay, fine," Dulac says.

"We'll just have them stand by, in the parking lot there of the State Liquor Store. We need them, we'll call them in. Now, Lieutenant, you got your search warrant in order?"

"We're all set," Dulac says. "A couple last-minute things and we'll be on our way."

"Surveillance at the family home in Laconia is in place," the state police lieutenant says. "What we have there at the present time is a darkened house. A small wooden frame house, two-story, a five- or six-room house, and the corporal there happens to know that the suspect's mother, a woman named Teri Fischer, works as a waitress at a restaurant called Brando's, that she is there at the present time, at work, that she lives alone and generally arrives home between eleven thirty P.M. and midnight."

"Lieutenant, I don't want your guys to get too close now," Dulac says.

"Righto, Lieutenant, we understand."

"What we have now," Dulac says, "is a college student, age twenty-two, a real loner apparently, harboring a twelve-year-old boy. It's necessary that we proceed with great caution."

"Understood, Lieutenant, understood."

"I don't want to get into a conflict of authority on this," Dulac says. "It's important, it's crucial that nothing be done to aggravate the situation or push this guy over the line. What we want to do is bring the boy home."

"Righto, Lieutenant. We copy. That's what we want to do—bring the boy home. My men are well instructed per your instructions; they spot this car, they are to follow, to call in help, to approach with extreme caution."

"A small thing," Dulac says. "We just hit a snag with the campus police at the university. Can you have the attorney general get through to the university chancellor, inform him that the campus police are refusing to cooperate."

"The campus police are refusing to cooperate?"

"That's right."

"Well, my word. What's the problem?"

"Authority, I guess."

"We'll get 'em, Lieutenant. See you at the liquor store, Lee traffic circle, rendezvous 2330 hours."

Off the phone, Dulac returns to his list. Yes, of course, he thinks, the APB should be all New England, and they should put reminders out to the customs people at the border. He'll have DeMarcus take care of that. The photograph, he thinks. Did he mention the need for a photo to the state police commander? He cannot remember if he did or not and reminds himself to mention it in the rendezvous in the liquor store parking lot, before they go ahead and move on the house.

The last item on his list is the phrase and question mark: *Status of boy?*

Was he being kept in the car? Dulac asks himself. Why would Vernon return to the cottage by himself? Was the boy in the car? Tied? Was he harbored elsewhere? How could this Vernon character leave him and be on the campus that morning? Did he have access to some other shelter? A barn? A garage? As he was buying him food at McDonald's, did that not imply an intent to care for the boy? Certainly it does, Dulac says to himself. And given all the signs this suspect has left in his wake, does that not imply that he is *not* a calculating or hardened criminal? Certainly, Dulac thinks. No question there. Is he therefore less dangerous? What is his frame of mind? Does he really know they have a make on him?

Standing, the questions left hanging, Dulac knows without looking at his watch that it is time to leave. Checking his hardware, double-checking the presence in his deep shirt pocket of the warrant and a USGS map on which the cottage has been marked in fluorescent yellow, he takes up not his regular jacket but a flak vest he has checked out, and adds over this a light and roomy, dark blue jacket with POLICE on the back in reflective white letters. And he remarks to himself, this is why you're here, this is the time to do what you're here to do, as he moves across the hall and into the squad room, where the others are waiting in their blue jackets, with tear gas canisters, shotguns, rifle with scope, waiting for his word.

Here Dulac says, surprised at himself, "Listen up, everybody. This may be the moment we've waited for. There's a little kid out there being held. We're close now. Our job is to set him free. Let us be the men this little boy will never forget. Let's do that."

"Right on, Lieutenant," someone says, in relief it seems, as they move to file out.

TWENTY-FOUR

CLAIRE STAGGERS FROM the living room to the kitchen. She continues half-asleep—on the couch, before the flickering TV, she had drifted at last into the bottom of the ocean—as the telephone rings again and calls to her as if in a dream. What is it? Who is she? Where are Matt and Eric? She fumbles the receiver from the hook, stops the ring. It seems that true sleep had eluded her for days, until an hour or so ago.

"Hullo?" she says, getting the receiver into position with both hands.

"This is a true crank call," a male voice says.

"What—who is this?" Claire says.

"People say I am a crank, although I am an ordained minister," the man says.

"What do you want?" Claire says. "Who is this?"

"You may have seen me on television, where I have preached the gospel many times."

"What is this? Do you know something about Eric?"

"Eric? Eric, Eric," the man says. "Of course I know about Eric. Why do you think I've called? Why else would I call? I know exactly about Eric. And exactly about you, too."

"What do you know? What are you saying?"

"Oh, this is a crank call to be sure," the man says. "Those who speak the truth are always labeled cranks. Did you know that? The truth can be most disturbing."

"Please—what do you want? Do you know something about Eric? Who are you?"

"Of your son—I've told you who I am; I am an unacknowledged disciple; I am a *crank*, it is true. Of your son—as you yourself deserted Jesus, as you believed that you could live a life, on this earth, dedicated *not* to the teachings of Christ—did it never occur to you that your child might be taken from you? Did it never occur to you that in the child God created your opportunity for redemption, your opportunity to be saved, that hell on earth might occur in the violation of our children? You know, you know—hear me now—the Lord giveth and the Lord taketh away. Has it not occurred to you, has there not been a voice speaking to you in your heart, as you strayed from Christ's teachings, as you strayed from the needs and welfare of your husband and children, as you elected, elected your path in life to follow into the city's bright and gaudy—"

Claire hangs up. Shaken, she stands there; she doesn't know what to do. Should she call the lieutenant? Forget about it? Wake up Matt? She fears the phone is going to ring right back at her, reach to throttle her with its curious righteousness, but it doesn't. She is bothered then—she hadn't been at first—by what the man said. It was like her parents, her father come alive, to let her know that the fault lay with her. However she might argue, it would not be heard. Nor, she knows, would she hear it herself, for down deep, and in spite of anything anyone might say, she has a feeling that the judgment upon her is true. Her life has been her fault. She made choices, she failed to do what might have been done . . .

She dials the number she almost knows by heart now. The number is on a piece of paper slipped between the telephone and the wall. "I'd say that was a crank call," an officer tells her. "If they call back—"

She hardly hears the rest, as the previous male voice remains more compelling. Dear God Almighty, she says to herself when she has hung up. Is there hell on earth? Sweet Jesus, forgive me if I have offended Thee. Forgive me, please, if I have not been as good, if I have not done all that I could have done. Please let me have my little boy home again. I beg of You. He means everything to me. He is life, he is love; he is the future and the reason to live; I know that he is Your child, too, and that all that is beautiful resides in him; I know this and if You will let me, if You will give another chance, I will dedicate myself to You both . . .

She wakes Matt. She doesn't tell him of the call; rather she sits on the side of his bed in the dark when she has awakened him by speaking his name. She says to him, "Matt, I'm sorry to wake you. I want you to know . . . I'm so sorry I didn't trust you. I did trust you, but then I didn't; I'm so sorry for that."

Matt says nothing, as if he is too much asleep or doesn't know what to say.

"Are you scared?" Claire says then.

"Scared?" Matt says.

"About Eric," she says.

"Yah," Matt says through the darkness.

"I can't believe he isn't here," she says.

Matt doesn't respond.

"He'd come home, wouldn't he, if he could?" she says.

"What do you mean?" Matt says.

"He wouldn't stay away on his own, would he? Because he was mad at us?"

"Mom, they know someone has him. They know that."

"But why?" she says then. "*Why?*"

Matt doesn't respond, as if he is too weary, as if there can be no answer to the question she is asking.

TWENTY-FIVE

AT LAST, as all is in place and Dulac checks his watch—to shift gears—he sees that it is 0220. Okay, he thinks. If they haven't spooked him in the meantime, if he should dare to return here—in spite of the prevailing opinion that he is already long gone to Boston or New York or attempting to slip into Canada—they are ready for him. They will take him.

The appearance of the outside of the cottage, barely disturbed as they took occupation, is normal. The cars driven by Dulac and Mizener remain a couple hundred yards away, out along the long gravel driveway and across two-lane Route 125, in the shadows next to a small closed diner. It is where they parked to make their initial approach to the cottage.

A stakeout is in place. Four cars and ten men are being used. Two cars are positioned at the two entrances to the cottage; another is at the traffic circle half a mile away, through which intersection, the state police commander has suggested, most anyone coming or going, innocent or aware, is likely to pass, and another, already manned like the others, is backed in beside an unoccupied cottage fifty yards away, allowing a view of the target cottage should a car somehow slip unseen past one of the other positions, or should the suspect approach by foot. Inside the cottage itself, two detectives are prepared to take up positions in the dark, to wait out the balance of the night, or until relieved, and to serve as the command post for purposes of communication from without and to the other positions.

Dulac is anxious to be gone from the cottage, to have the lights turned out, even though the roommates have assured him that it would not appear unusual for lights to be on at this hour. For the moment, with the suspect's bedroom and all in the bathroom but the toilet taped off, in case they may wish to call in the state police lab people tomorrow, all present are in the dining room–kitchen area, sipping instant coffee, smoking, sitting and standing, and there exists something of a party atmosphere.

Dulac's position concerning the whereabouts of the suspect and in justification of the stakeout is that the suspect was there that evening, that he had been there on at least two other occasions during the time that Eric Wells had been missing, that something, presumably the boy, kept him from resuming his regular life at the cottage, at the same time that something else—who knew what exactly?—had him making these periodic return visits. Maybe he comes back to change clothes, Dulac has said. To shave, although the report from the roommate had it that as of that evening he had not shaved in two days or more. Maybe he will come back again, Dulac keeps thinking. In response to the argument put forth by the state police district commander—returned by now to Concord— and by Mizener and others, that the suspect, aware that he has been made, would be on the run, Dulac has argued that nothing the suspect had done so far was very rational, that all that they knew indicated an individual entirely new to what he is doing, one who is apparently rattled and confused and who is reported by an eyewitness to have been that very evening in an erratic emotional state. Besides, Dulac has added, alerts are out to block all those more rational and conventional avenues of escape.

They have yet to locate a photograph. In the suspect's bedroom, using the blunt end of a ballpoint, Dulac has picked briefly through his possessions, has discovered a hard-core porn magazine depicting prepubescent boys but nothing which appears otherwise revealing or incriminating, and no photograph.

At last, they are ready to leave. Mizener will be transporting the three roommates to places in town, where they have agreed to stay with friends, leaving their cars in place as part of the decoy and Dulac will be returning to the station in Portsmouth, to check in, to send Shirley home if she is still there, and to be sure that the task force night shift is on top of all that is happening.

"Just a couple more questions," Dulac says then, as the roommates have laundry bags and books and are ready to leave, drawing an expression from Mizener.

"Where do you *think* he is?" Dulac says. "What's your gut feeling? Your immediate reaction?"

"Gone," the larger boy, Leon, says at once. "Boston. The Combat Zone. There's where I see him."

"I have a feeling he's on his way to Miami, Florida," the boy named Wayne says as Dulac turns to him. "That's what I think," the boy adds, as if to apologize.

"I don't know," Duncan says in his turn. "I just don't know. He's an idealistic person, in spite of this. I see him huddled up somewhere. I could see him in the woods, both of them, in a cave, making shelter, something like that."

"Weaving baskets?" Mizener says.

"No, no, let them talk," Dulac snaps at him.

Turning to the three, Dulac says, "Okay, tell me this. Do you think he would *hurt* the boy?"

"No way," Duncan says. "No way. He may be messed up sexually and so on, but I don't see him doing something violent."

"And so on," Dulac says. "What do you mean by that? Did he make advances to you, any of you, or disclosures?"

"No," Duncan says. "He didn't—"

"Come on, Dunc, you can tell us," the bigger student says, drawing a brief snicker from a couple of those present.

"Nothing like that," Duncan says. "Not to me anyway."

To the other two then, Dulac says, "Do you think he would hurt the boy?"

Only the larger one answers. "I have no idea," he says.

"You don't know anyone named Tony?" Dulac says, drawing nothing but stares from the three, for it is a question he has already put to them, separately and jointly, half a dozen times.

"Okay, let's go," he says then, giving a nod.

An hour later, when it is close to four A.M. and Shirley is still there, in the squad room with the night shift crew of three, Dulac is on the telephone in his cubicle speaking to the state police lieutenant in Concord. The suspect's mother did not return home until one ten, the man has told him, as she remained at the restaurant after going off duty and imbibed two mixed drinks. She was up then for twenty-two minutes before turning off the lights. In turn, Dulac has reported the stakeout to be in place at the cottage and has said that he probably *will* be asking for the state police lab people to check over the cottage tomorrow afternoon, to see if there are any hairs or fibers which might tie things even more positively to the boy.

"I'll tell you what my guess is," the state police lieutenant says. "My guess is this Vernon Fischer is trying to slip into Canada right now, if he's half as smart as his roommates seem to think he is. Or he's up in Montreal already, speaking French for all he's worth."

"You think he'd get in?" Dulac says. "With all the alerts we have out?"

"Not in, but around. If he's desperate."

"What about the boy?" Dulac says.

"I'd say a shallow grave," the state police lieutenant says. "Close by. Which may or may not be easy to find. Listen, these things are happening from one end of the country to the other. It used to be drugs. Now it's children. Don't ask me why."

"It's a new pathology," Dulac says.

"Is it?" the man says.

"So I'm told," Dulac says. "Everyone said it was okay and it turns out it isn't."

The state police lieutenant's response is silence; it is a response.

Dulac wishes he had not opened the door he just opened. "We are going to need a photograph," he says.

"Right," the other man says.

"If nothing breaks in the meantime, could your people enter the house there in Laconia? In the early morning, say, at daybreak."

"Of course," the man says.

"Use an unmarked car, say whatever has to be said."

"Of course," the state police lieutenant says.

Moments later, pausing over the replaced receiver to gather his thoughts, and walking out into the squad room, Dulac sees Shirley working at the nearest table with what appear to be tip sheets, and he says to her, "Shirley, what are you doing? You don't have to be here."

"Just checking these tip sheets, to see if anything else might have been a true sighting."

"You don't trust the computer?"

"It's fed by people."

"It's four o'clock in the morning," he says.

"I know."

"I want you to go home," he says. "It's okay if I'm dead around here tomorrow—not you. Good lord, you want everything to go to hell?"

"I need a ride," she says.

"A ride?"

"I'm not going to call Bill at four o'clock in the morning, but that's not the reason."

"What reason?"

"You don't want to know," she says. "It has to do with something called a flywheel."

"I'll drop you off," Dulac says, holding up a hand to say no, he has no interest in the flywheel. "I'm leaving right away. Six thirty's going to come early."

"Lieutenant," Officer Benedict says then, holding a hand over the mouthpiece of the phone he is using. "They just had their second false alarm out there. It looks like that one roadway is something of a lover's lane."

Dulac smiles, nods in turn, however faintly. Going on to his cubicle, giving things a last-minute check and seeing from his desk clock that the time is five minutes to four, he takes up his jacket and slips it on, turns out his office light, thinking over the day's endlessness, and goes on his way along the hall to where Shirley always hangs her coat. She appears, coming from a side office, doing small arrangements with her coat and purse.

For the first time ever, then, they walk from the police station together. An odd contentment occurs in Dulac as they do this. Contentment, casual happiness, are things you forget, he thinks. Of course he is exhausted and this is all innocent, but a feeling of pleasure, the vaguest tingle, continues in him as they walk to his car in the silence, under a sky reflecting only sparsely now the lights still on throughout the small city.

As he drives to where she lives, on a residential side street perhaps a mile from the station, their small talk is also sparse and relaxed, given largely to the depletion and exhaustion, the caffeine tension that afflicts them working in such a situation. "I get too exhausted to sleep well," he says. "Too strung out." As he pulls up before her house then, pulls over to stop and there is a moment of silence, she says, just as casually, as easily, "Go on down another block," and he does as he is told as if he had merely pulled over a block before he should have, even as some other new or lost dimension is opening up in him.

"Why don't you turn right," she says.

He does this, too, turning onto a side street which is smaller and darker than her street, an unlighted street without curbs, and as he follows his headlights to the side without instruction, and parks and turns off the motor and lights, there is depletion in his center, but a falling away, too, of the shutters which have long covered his old heart—for moments of the kind have not been his to know, as a heavy man, which isn't to say that he has been without response—and as she moves in under his arm, and he takes her to him, leans his head to her hair and shoulder and neck, it is with a fondness, with surrender he had forgotten in his life. He does nothing else, however, nor does he speak as they sit and press against each other, and take from the touching what comfort and reassurance and confusion there is to take.

"Gil, I want you so much," she says. "My life is so awful."

He still doesn't say anything and at last he lifts away. Perhaps three minutes have passed. He could turn his face and mouth to her hair, but he lifts away. And at last he speaks. "We better go," he says. Both know—he knows too well—that some patrolman is altogether likely to pull up and shine a flashlight in their faces, and he restarts the car's motor, turns on the headlights, pulls away.

He wants her. He desires her. He circles the block, however, and pulls up once more before her house. "Good night," he says. "I'll see you in the morning."

"Good night, Gil," she says. She leaves the car, closes the door.

He waits a moment, to give her time to be safely inside. He wishes that, like a teenaged girl kept out late, she would blink a porch light, but she doesn't. His life, he can see, was just as limited when he was a teenager as it is now. Here in a world no longer the same. He is, after all, what he is. He had always wanted to change, it seems; now he wishes to remain the same.

Not much later, into the partial sleep he has managed, a sensation comes into his chest of another Portsmouth child disappearing, of the telephone ringing and ringing, of the entry being made again and again in the log, of all eyes being on him, Shirley's eyes among them, of charges pending against him—incompetence, dereliction of duty, evasion, duplicity, inattention as a father—of finding himself unable to stand up against the charges, unable to articulate words in his defense, unable to fashion truth or logic, stricken throughout with an awareness of failure, Shirley under his arm, of not being ready, Your Honor, of not being up to it at all when his turn at the plate came around at last.

Then he is quite awake. The digital clock on the dresser shows five eighteen; hardly an hour has passed since he was sitting in the car with Shirley.

Beatrice is piled on her side, a mountain range of covers, breathing steadily. He wishes she were awake, so they might through a few words be together, but he gives no thought to waking her.

All is wrong and it seems he will never sleep again. He lies with his eyes open, thinking how unfair is the night with its unanswerable exaggeration. If he could only sleep, could drift away from himself and from the inflexible night. He isn't a father, he thinks. He never will be. Nor did he cheat, whatever may be said of his wanting to. He is what he is. His life has been what it has been, neither grand, perhaps, nor frivolous. Things have changed so much, and he has tried to stay apace and alert. And he has done, hasn't he? all that any good policeman might do, if he held Shirley Moss under his arm or not, knows love for her or not; he has only been what he has been, has only undertaken this modest role of policeman, hasn't he? Need he be charged, Your Honor, with all failures in life, all misfortunes in the world, if he has only undertaken this modest role, if he has attempted at last merely to be true to what he sees, to what he believes? Is that why sleep eludes him now?

An Air That Kills

WEDNESDAY, FEBRUARY 18, 1981

VERNON IS WALKING AWAY from the hospital. Overhead, a new day is breaking. He has been unable to sleep. Now and then he drifted. Each time he came around, all things were hopeless.

He turns onto a side street. There are no sidewalks or curbs here and he walks to the side of the blacktop. The sky is blue-black. Few lights are on in the houses. One here to the rear, one there.

What has come to mind is a happy time in his life. One, he thinks, which became unhappy. He was a child then himself. He was twelve years old. His mother had forced him, had literally dragged him to the car, to go to a summer camp in Massachusetts, and stricken with homesickness one morning, even as the two weeks were nearly over (an irony, he thinks, to have been homesick for a home which wasn't altogether his), he lay in his upper bunk, in his cabin, as birds were chirping, determined to go the camp office when it opened, and get his mother on the telephone in the presence of the camp director, and to let loose—it would not be calculated—with the avalanche of tears and heartbreak waiting to hear the sound of her voice.

It did not happen. He had to urinate. Not one to step into the woods, he climbed down from his bunk, slipped outside, and made his way along the dirt path to the toilet, although it was a hundred yards away.

He was barefoot. He had slipped on his cut-offs and wore a T-shirt with a smile on the front. He could remember the T-shirt because one of the counselors had joked with him about it, how different it was from his own face. That smile was ironic, too, he thinks, because his thought at the time had been that if he could die, if he could kill himself, he could leave something to his mother with which she would have to live forever.

Of all things, at that hour, steam was coming from under the bath-house overhang. One side had toilets and a row of sinks; the other side was a walk-in shower room with eight or ten nozzles.

He nearly turned back, thinking it would be one of the hairy camp counselors who would get after him to cheer up. He entered quietly. Using a urinal on one side, he could not resist taking a look into the shower room. And it wasn't a counselor there, but a boy his own age and size, maybe a little bigger, standing with his eyes closed, the flush of water washing over his head and face and body.

The boy rubbed water from his eyes and looked over where he was standing in the doorway. He looked another moment before he said, "What are you doing?"

Coming to take a shower, Vernon told him, and even as he did not have a towel, he removed his T-shirt and stepped out of his cut-off jeans and underpants and stepped over the wet cement floor to the shower nozzle directly opposite the boy, everything in his mind swimming in a sea of excitement. The boy, opposite, had turned the other way and there were his bony shoulders, his spinal line, his shiny cheeks and smooth legs, and it was as if one of the photographs in his magazine, of the older boy, had come alive there, magically, before his eyes.

Turning around and looking at Vernon, looking down at him, the boy said, "Are you always like that?"

Vernon said, "Like what?" although he knew exactly what was being talked about.

"Like that," the boy said, and nodded.

The attention had him even more excited, still he said, "Like what?"

"What are you thinking about?" the boy asked him.

When he said he didn't know—whatever it was he said—the boy said, "You look like you're thinking about going to a party."

"What does that mean?" he asked the boy, and the boy told him that he got like that himself when he thought about going to a party.

"Let's see you do that now," he said to the boy, and his request—as he can see now, wandering along this nearly darkened street—was another stepping across a forbidden line, one which set off in him another blossoming, another capability.

"It feels good to be like that," the boy said to him.

Vernon said to him again, "Why don't you do it?"

"I can do it in a second if I want to," the boy said.

He proceeded to do so. The deflated inner tube took shape, lifted.

It may have occurred to Vernon then how much he liked the boy. As a friend. A person. He was so daring, so direct in his way.

Taking a step toward him, extending his pelvis somewhat, the boy said, "Here."

Reaching, Vernon held the boy with his hand.

The boy told him to use some soap, and when he did this and washed him, the boy told him that what he was doing felt really good. He asked him if he was old enough to get off, and when Vernon said that he was, the boy said, "Make me do it."

He masturbated the boy with his soapy hand, and the feelings within himself were different than they had ever been; as he did this, the boy asked him if he knew how to do other things, and although he knew from his magazine what the boy was talking about, he asked him what he meant.

They went through a game of neither saying what was being talked about. Throughout this time he continued soaping the boy and masturbating him, and the boy had reached down to do the same to him in turn.

"Things that are a lot a fun," the boy said. "If you're not afraid—are you afraid or not?"

He wasn't afraid, he told the boy, but what did he mean?

What did he think he meant?

He didn't know what he meant; why didn't he say what he meant?

How did he know he wasn't chicken?

He wasn't chicken.

How did he know? A lot of kids are.

Why should he be chicken? He sure wasn't chicken, that was for sure.

He just meant if he knew how to do anything else? the boy said. He'd bet he'd never even done anything else, in his whole life, had he?

What did that matter, if he'd done something or not? Maybe he had.

Well, had he—what had he ever done?

Maybe he'd done a lot of things. He sure wasn't afraid, that was for sure.

Did he want to do it?

To do what?

Something else, that was what. He knew what.

Yes, he wanted to do it, he said.

Did he really? He wasn't afraid?

No, he wasn't afraid; he sure wasn't afraid, that was for sure.

Had he ever done it before?

Maybe he'd done it lots of times.

Do it then, if he wasn't afraid, the boy told him. Here, do it. Only don't bite, the boy told him, as he did it. Just do it like that. Only do it harder than that. Yes, like that, do it like that.

Vernon is returned to the present by a car coming around a corner, its lights all at once coming at him. He keeps his face level, walking into the blast of light, which seems to make a sound itself as it comes on, covering him, seeing all, taking forever to pass.

He continues walking. Simply walking, he knows that the steps he is taking are the gifts of life.

Of the boy, he recalls that he only saw him a couple times after that, maybe three times. That night or the next night, when all were led out at dusk for an explanation of the stars, he found the boy, and they went together to sit up on the hill out of view or hearing of the others.

The other definite sighting was a day later. With another boy in the lead, as they carried a canoe down the bank to the lake, there was the boy, the new friend who was on his mind in all moments, coming up the bank, also carrying a canoe with a partner. They glanced at each other. They did not speak. To Vernon, then as now, the exchanged glance was as if the other boy were not only his friend but his brother, even his father, come back from Vietnam to make all things acceptable and safe.

The last time he saw the boy—he wasn't even certain it was him. It was Get Away Day and he was standing along the circular dirt driveway that surrounded the wide parade field and passed before the different cabins. Stuck guarding his duffel bag and suitcase, as were other boys all around the dirt road, waiting for his mother's dull yellow car to appear, he thought he recognized the boy, across the green standing next to a single small suitcase. There was nothing much he could do or knew to do, and in only minutes anyway a glossy purple car drove in through the gate of trees and stopped next to the boy. Two women—he wondered if one would be a sister—got out of the dark purple car, helped load the boy and his suitcase, and backing around on the grass, the car drove away, disappeared through the arch of trees. The car's license plate was orange, and not long after that, as he determined the plate to be from New York, he began to look any time he saw such a car, and he looked still, it was true, to see if the boy was in the back seat of a passing car. He may have looked as recently as yesterday. No, maybe he did not look yesterday. He looked two or three days ago, though, when the future was still his upon which to fantasize.

Another car passes him, this time from behind.

He walks on. There is no hurry.

Glancing here and there, he sees that it is love he has come to know for the small town that is coming into view now under the lightening sky. Love for life of any kind, he thinks.

Nothing is going to save him now, he can see that. Not even death, he can see in the grayness up there, will allow his soul to exist. Not now. He can see this in the sky and feel it in the air.

He moves along. His heart is going out to the tarmac street, to an uneven tarmac sidewalk, to the cracker-box seaside houses, to their small fenced-in side yards and backyards, and to the ocean smell in the air. His heart goes out, too, to the boats wrapped and tied in plastic beside houses, beside garages, to orange basketball hoops, to stacks of firewood on porches, even to a macramé flowerpot holder hanging empty from a porch ceiling. And his heart goes out to a crack of sand making its way along the street with him, as if no one knows that the earth is involved in some hopeless attempt to recover itself, day by day, millimeter by millimeter, even as it must be aware that a road crew will show up in time and refill the crack all the way back to where it started and make it start all over again.

He knows, too, on a sinking sensation, why those who kill so seldom run away. He knows this now. As if you could ever escape, he thinks.

TWO

CLAIRE IS THINKING maybe she should go back to work. She is at the kitchen table, sipping coffee. Matt has left for school, for which she is relieved, and she is wondering if she shouldn't go back to work herself. In the first place, she can't believe she did not ask for sick days when she called in. Everybody used their sick days, no matter what they were doing, going to the doctor or going deer hunting. It meant she was losing pay. Three days now. Dear God. Since she needs all she brings in each week to get along, the loss will be real. In its turn, it will cause its own unbelievable problems. Week after next, when she will be paid for this week.

Of course she'd give anything to have Eric come walking back in. She'd give up a year's pay. She'd give up anything. Still—

At least Matt won't be falling any more behind in school, she thinks. If only she had a way to make up the money—

Claire catches herself. Good God, come to your senses! she thinks.

Money doesn't matter. To heck with money. It will work itself out. The important thing is Eric. Her place is here, waiting for him to call. Her place is looking after him, putting some weight back on him, she thinks, when he comes dragging in like a tom cat that has gotten caught up in more than it could handle.

She sips her coffee. Money comes back to her. Money is like that, she thinks. It's always there. It always comes up. It was something she has sure learned, losing their house like they did, and living all these years on little more than minimum wage. People who didn't know just didn't know. It was the big *if* in everything. People would say no, that wasn't the case, but she knew better. If they'd had just a little money, just a little, Eric would be here right now. Because she wouldn't have been working late like that, and he wouldn't have been left alone. It is what she knows.

Enough of that, she tells herself. She'll get nowhere thinking like that. Nowhere except deeper into a hole.

Then, all at once, two calls she's taken this morning suggest things to her. Betty asked her to come downtown and meet her for lunch. She declined. It seemed like going out to enjoy herself while Eric was missing. Betty told her she'd better do some things and see some people or she'd go crazy. She couldn't just wait there day after day all alone like that. Betty did make it a temptation; still she declined.

Then Lieutenant Dulac called and asked if she could come in around eleven or eleven thirty, to look at some more pictures they hoped to have by then. She said she'd do whatever they wanted her to do, if they thought it would help, and the lieutenant said that was fine. He hung up, though, without saying a police car would come by to pick her up, and she was left wondering if it meant something to the effect that the free ride was over or if he was so busy he forgot to mention it.

Her thought now is that if she can leave the apartment unattended for one thing, why not another? And maybe Betty was right, because it would be a relief to get out for a while and talk to someone, especially Betty, to hear what she had to say, to have Betty hear her out in turn.

Not altogether admitting her reasons to herself, she calls the police department, only to learn that the lieutenant is out of the office. To the woman who answers, she says, "Well, I'll be there at eleven thirty, like he said, so you'll know to pick up on my phone calls." Then she blurts out to the woman, "I was going to have lunch with this friend downtown; would that be okay?"

"I'm sure it's okay," the woman says. "You go ahead and have lunch. You must be getting cabin fever staying there all the time. Is your older son in school?"

"He is, yes. I hope that's okay."

"That's fine. No problem with that. There's a plainclothesman keeping an eye on things in your neighborhood, too, Mrs. Wells, so even if Eric came walking up, we'd spot him. So don't you worry about it. I think we're about to catch that guy."

"Are you?" Claire says.

"I think so," the woman says.

Gosh, Claire says to herself when the phone is back on the wall. She thinks to go look outside from the boys' bedroom window, too, but doesn't. Something else seems more urgent. She is on the phone then, to the paint and wallpaper store downtown where Betty works, to say that she will meet her for lunch after all. Something feels better today, she tells Betty. She isn't sure what it is.

THREE

DULAC, in the pondside cottage, is in a foul mood. It is nine o'clock and even as the state police lab crew is there doing its job, he does not have a photograph. On his call to Concord, he has been told that the state police lieutenant is not yet in his office. They will have to have a photograph sometime this morning, Dulac is thinking, to have it appear in the afternoon papers. He had taken it for granted that this would follow—if something conclusive did not break in the meantime—and now he has begun to wonder. And worry. And right now, too, he'd like very much to see the *face* of the person they are so hard upon apprehending. He'd like to have a look at the face of the person with whom he feels he might have to bargain, in some unexpected way, to gain the release of the boy.

There are other reasons, too. He'd like copies of a photograph transmitted to Boston, to New York, to state police throughout New England, to guards along the Canadian border. Just in case he is wrong. He was wrong in other things; what made him think he had insight in this instance?

He also wants to see the suspect's face to see if he can read anything there himself of the young man's propensity for violence. Can such a thing be read? Is it highlighted in the eyes? The line of the mouth? He especially wants positive confirmation from the secret witness—Martin, contacted earlier at the second number he had written down, is in the university library at the moment looking through yearbooks—and to hear his judgment concerning the questions of escape and violence.

Nor is that all, Dulac is thinking now. A photograph of the suspect, in all that it could do, could actually save the life of the boy. As it would affect time and stimulate action, it could save the boy's life. It's that important, Dulac thinks.

Dulac lights another cigarette, checks his watch yet again. Nine twenty. He should hear any minute from Laconia. How long can it possibly take to have two men enter a house, serve up papers, and locate a photograph? What a terrible mood he is in, he adds to himself, and is just stepping to the kitchen counter, thinking to see if the state police lieutenant is back on the job, to see if he can shake things up, when the telephone rings.

There is Shirley's voice; he has neither seen nor spoken to her this morning. "They have a photograph, a good photograph," she says. "It's on its way to Concord right now."

"Why didn't they call me?" Dulac says.

"They called here—I don't know."

"Jesus, I made it all clear; I've been waiting here forty minutes and I dumped our secret witness at the library."

"You picked him up?"

"I've got him looking at yearbooks—waiting, because I did not give him this number."

"Gil, listen. You better try to ease up. You don't sound real good."

"I don't know why I should sound good."

"Gil, go have some breakfast or something. The pictures should be on their way. They should be here, in no more than an hour or an hour and a half from what they say. A stack of them."

"I have to pick up our witness. I left him stranded."

"I know. You said that. But have a bite to eat; have some coffee. The pictures will be here in an hour or so. Stop worrying about so many things. I'm sorry, you know. You know?"

"Fine—okay. Okay. Shirley, get back to me, though."

"I will," she says.

"Good," he says.

"Have some food," she says. "It'll make you feel better."

FOUR

THERE ARE FEW CUSTOMERS in the supermarket where Vernon is walking now, looking at what the shelves have to suggest to him of one thing and another. There is a woman pausing with a cart. There is another woman. There is a man. Entire vegetable and bakery corners, and aisles of the store, are not populated at all at this hour. Vernon is more or less nervous, and he studies rice for some time. Wild rice, minute rice, brown rice. Why is rice used for weddings? he wonders. Does it have to do with pregnancy, with purity? Is it used because of its capacity to swell up? What does it matter to him? he wonders. Should he feel love for rice, too, over its range of meanings?

In an aisle—at the other end a woman is just pushing out of sight—he sees a child sitting on the floor, among so many cereal boxes. As he sidesteps along, not quite looking at the child directly, he realizes the cereal boxes are being used as building blocks, as things to read. At eight or ten feet, stealing a glance, he still cannot tell from the child's hair if it is a boy or a girl; he glimpses, as the child twists to one side to reach a box, a designer jeans label and the curve of the child's back into its waist.

Vernon walks along the aisle. Around the corner, he places a box of rice he discovers in his hand on a shelf and goes on to leave the store, empty-handed, to return outdoors to the chilled air.

FIVE

IT IS THEIR ONE CLASS together, and he has been tending toward it all morning. Vanessa is there in her seat when he walks into the room, but she doesn't look up.

Nor does she look over, even as he has sat down and is keeping an eye on her. She does turn her head to look outside, through the windows to her left. And she looks to the front again. She doesn't look his way. All the time it takes for the class to settle in and for the teacher to collect homework—he has none to give in and for an instant he feels detached from everything there is to do and know in life—and for the teacher to start the day's work, writing a problem on the board and turning to face them, Vanessa does not look his way, for even a passing glance, and he knows that she knows he is there.

The feeling of being detached from all things stays in him. It's not a new feeling but something he has felt many times in the last year or so, since starting high school. Detached from all things. Maybe, he thinks, it's why he has so taken to Vanessa. To know someone in school. Well, someone besides Cormac, although for the moment, thinking of him, he wouldn't mind having Cormac there to make a joke at, to share the slightest joke over nothing, as they had before.

He determines to look only to the front himself. He has to be strong, he thinks.

In time, though, he glances her way. He can't help it, it seems. All morning he looked forward to seeing her in this room, if only to exchange the faintest of looks. Now this.

He keeps sinking. The feeling is taking in his family, too, his mother and brother and where they live. It's the first time he's quite thought of himself and his brother and his mother and where they live as anything, as any kind of home or family, but that is what he is thinking now. Maybe it's a touch of pride he is feeling, for the first time ever in his life.

She is *black*, he thinks; who does she think she is?

Time passes. Geometry continues and he sits there. He does not belong to geometry; geometry does not belong to him. How they live is the reason Eric was taken. Kids who live in houses and have families, and have cars and money, aren't taken. Geometry belongs to them. That's how it is.

Writing a note to her, he knows, is another mistake. Everything he does with her seems to be wrong. He does it, though, writes *Vanessa* across a folded slip of paper. Leaning across the aisle, he starts the note on its way, whispering "Federal Express," as he has heard other students whisper.

He doesn't look. He sits looking to the front, as if understanding now what the teacher is explaining at the board. His message on the note is simple: "Lunch at Gumps?" it says. He has signed it *M*.

Eating at the same table in the cafeteria is one thing; club or class project might be the cover. Walking several blocks to Gumps—a mom-and-pop store which sells subs and packaged pies—is far more daring. He knows it is a mistake.

His elbow is tapped There is the slip of paper, which he holds a moment and then unfolds on his desk between fingers of both hands. "Not today," it says. That's all. There is no initial.

He keeps himself from looking at her again. When the class ends, he makes his way from the room and along the hall. He seems to be telling himself that he can play hard to get, too. Or is it something else that is on his mind? His hurt is such that he doesn't seem to know what it is that is wrong. Only everything, it seems.

SIX

DULAC DOESN'T STOP for breakfast or coffee. Maybe he is too knotted—the term fits him exactly, he thinks—to have room for food to fit into his body. Maybe, in his stubbornness, he doesn't want food to soften him or relax him as he knows it will. Maybe he wants to remain tightened like a fist.

The secret witness, Martin, is with him now. They are sitting in Dulac's car in the small campus police parking lot, waiting for some records on cars and class schedules to be prepared and handed over at last. Dulac is smoking another cigarette. The two passenger windows are down several inches and it seems clear to Dulac that the man beside him does not like the smoke. He doesn't care what the man likes.

In the library, and taking the yearbook with them, Martin showed him a photo of a group of students, one of whom he believed could be the student, Vernon Fischer. Otherwise he has found no pictures. The photo has meant little to Dulac, except as it shows such a surprisingly young-looking person. Of course a twelve-year-old boy would be easily conned by such a person, he has thought. Of course. Especially if he came on in some sincere way. How strange, Dulac has thought, too, that the capacity to abduct a child might exist within an otherwise attractive person. For even in the eyes of a policeman, it seems to him, it didn't used to be like that. Couldn't you *tell* a child molester?

The witness is too uncertain for the yearbook photo to be used. It may well be, he has suggested himself, a look-alike student. In black and white, the photo shows a line of eight or ten students—a general caption mentions a Student Film Series—looking over their shoulders, apparently on command, most of them appearing surprised at the flash of a camera. The look-alike student, third closest, appears, even as he stands among others, to be alone.

"Does he look homosexual?" Dulac says.

"*What?*" the man says.

"Forget it," Dulac says. He thinks to add *fuck you*, but doesn't.

"My God, Lieutenant, you ask offensive questions. You think people *look* homosexual?"

"It's my job," Dulac says.

"What is your job?"

"Asking offensive questions."

"Really," the man says.

"And it's true," Dulac says. "Some men, who are homosexual, look homosexual. Okay? Maybe some don't but a hell of a lot do. It may not be politic to say that, but it's reality. That's where I work. Reality."

They sit a time. Dulac, lighting another cigarette, feels the campus police may be moving slow in a last-gasp attempt to assert something. Assholes, he thinks. Petty assholes.

As another wave of students passes, Martin says, "It's hard to believe that someone who is a student would abduct a little kid."

"Why do you think that?" Dulac says, thinking how characteristic it is of gay men that their recovery time, upon being offended, is so brief.

"They seem so trouble-free. And so young, at an age when people are usually more generous of spirit than they are later. You know, Lieutenant, I wouldn't be surprised if this Vernon person is still here, even attending his classes."

"I have that feeling myself," Dulac says, "but I'm not sure why. I don't know what he'd do with the boy."

"It's obvious he's a pedophile," the man says. "That indicates a certain kind of motivation. So much, you know, is made of mothers disrupting the sexuality of their sons. I've wondered at times what the effect is, on boys, of their fathers withholding love from them, not being there, you know, when they're needed."

They sit there. In a moment, Dulac says, "What would you do?"

"Is this another offensive question?"

"Probably," Dulac says. "If you knew, from your roommate, that you'd been made. Would you run? Would you harm the boy?"

"I don't think so," the man says. "I can't imagine harming a little boy or anyone else. And like I said, I wouldn't be surprised to see this Vernon attend his classes, as if nothing had happened."

"I don't see how he could feel like nothing has happened," Dulac says.

"Just denial," the man says. "That's all."

In another moment then, when the campus police still have not signaled them, the man says, "You have children, Lieutenant?"

"No," Dulac says.

"Did you want to?"

"We did."

"What happened?"

"I don't know. We weren't lucky. That's all. You didn't really answer my question about running, trying to escape, if you were the suspect and knew you had been identified."

"I thought I did answer it."

"You'd go on with your life?"

"I think I might. I don't know."

"That seems amazingly childlike."

"Well, your suspect may be like that—extremely immature. And he probably isn't gay. About which you keep generalizing."

"Okay," Dulac says.

"Still, you do it," the man says.

Dulac sits quietly a moment. "I guess I do," he says then. "In any case, I've asked your opinion on things because I believed your ideas would be better informed than my own."

"That's offensive, too," the man says.

"I'm sure it is," Dulac says.

"And so smug."

"I'm sure," Dulac says.

"People are different, you know. Even gays. I don't happen to be a child molester. I'm not sure I even understand the impulse. Okay?"

"I didn't mean to say you were a child molester. Although that is a generalization on your part. This is a young boy, picked up by a young man."

"There you go again," the man says. "Putting me in a category. One where I don't belong. I do not go for little boys."

"Okay, let's drop it."

"I think you owe me an apology," the man says.

"Let's just drop it," Dulac says.

"Some men—you know—who are gay are simply biologically so. It's what they *are*."

"I think we should just drop it," Dulac says. "I don't want to hear any more."

"They're not necessarily deviant," the man says.

"I don't know about the biology," Dulac says. "But from where I sit, you see—since you insist—from where I sit, a lot of people who identify themselves as gay weigh in with serious, deep-seated psychological problems. They cause grief. They're aggressive. Selfish. They're nothing but offensive in their demands on my time and attention. The law means nothing to them. I'm sorry, but that's what comes through my door."

"I'm not one of those," the man says.

"Good," Dulac says.

"I'll tell you what rankles me, though," the man says. "It's the positions taken by so-called officials. Like yourself. Lawmakers, and so on. Categorizing *everything.*"

"Why don't you forget it," Dulac says.

"I don't want to forget it."

"Okay. Let me tell you then what rankles me. It's that. Politicking. Demanding. Constant fucking politicking. Blindly. What you're asking for is special treatment. You and *your* concerns, your little weenies. What makes you think the world should stop all the time and indulge your fucking cares and concerns? That is selfishness. That is smug. Who has time for it? I don't. You made your choice, live with it."

"Now I am being insulted."

"You asked for it. I'm not a politician, I'm a cop. I'll tell you some more on the subject, because I'm not finished. And I don't mean to be rude, but it's been a difficult day so far. I am *them,* you know. I've always been *them.* I've always been strong, you see. Always. And I've always been responsible. If things go wrong, I assume it is my duty to help make them right. Okay? You paint a rosy picture of yourself, is what you do. Fine, if it makes life easier, go ahead and do it. But when things go wrong, you blame it on me. That is what is selfish. At the same time, if I didn't think you were a decent person, you wouldn't be here, believe me. But don't give me any more poor-me bullshit about gays. Because, I'll tell you, I've been working almost exactly in the asshole of human nature for twenty-five years, which is where a lot of the guys on your team hang out, and I know better. Reality happens to be one thing I know."

Silence follows for a moment. At last the man says, "I did not mean to say that gays are superior or deserve special treatment. If I implied that, I apologize."

"Fine, forget it," Dulac says. "I'm afraid I'm not in a very good mood. We have this guy, and yet we don't have him. It's beginning to bother me. I apologize, too."

SEVEN

His mother caught him once, in California, without catching him altogether. There was a carport with a partial cinder-block wall, painted an aqua color, and he was sitting on the other side of the wall with his newfound magazine. His mother's voice was suddenly almost overhead, calling his name, and in a panic, he slid the magazine up under his T-shirt. Climbing to his feet, pushing his shirttail into his blue jeans, he paused before showing himself.

He stepped around part way, to speak to her. She was going somewhere; she'd be back in twenty minutes; a man, in uniform, might be stopping. She kept looking at him. She shielded her eyes from the sun and looked more closely. What was he doing? What was that in his shirt? Had he picked up his room? She didn't have time to do it right now; would he go in and pick up the kitchen?

He always believed she saw the magazine cover through his shirt. In the house, before hiding the magazine, he stood before a mirror. The two boys looked visible to him. But then he knew what they were doing. And maybe the sun had reflected in a way that made it difficult to see through his shirt. Still, he always believed she had seen the two boys, and that she had chosen not to acknowledge what she had seen.

That was a long time ago, and he is walking in Portsmouth now, feeling caught and not caught. His car is parked in yet another supermarket parking lot, just beyond the parking lot where he pulled in and removed the boy from the trunk and placed him on the ground. The move only took him ten or fifteen minutes altogether, going to the hospital to get into his car, picking out the place along the way, and deciding all at once to leave his car in the parking lot of a supermarket that was just a couple hundred yards down the road. All happened on impulse, it seems, and he still feels it was something generous to do. Now they can take care of him. Perhaps as he walked past one or another funeral home the thought had come to him that the little blond-haired boy had to be taken care of. Otherwise, well, otherwise it would be different. Now it would be done.

Maybe, too, he thinks, they will take care of the boy and not worry so much about him. The boy is what they wanted, isn't it? Could they even associate the boy with him, now that he wasn't with him? It's something of a relief, anyway, not to have quite so much to worry about. To feel caught but not caught. To walk here, to feel this curious freedom.

EIGHT

THEY ARE SITTING YET IN THE CAR when word comes in from Shirley Moss on the radio. "Gil," she says. "I'm afraid I have bad news. The body of a young boy has just been found. It looks like it's Eric. Near a parking lot—the Norton Office Supplies building on Islington Street."

"It's close to his house?" Dulac says at last.

"Yes," she says. "It is."

"The clothing matches?" he says. He is checking himself against a shifting of the world around him.

"I'm afraid it looks that way. Red jacket is all we know right now."

"Red jacket."

"That's all we know so far," she says.

"Who found him?" he says.

"A man pulling in there to park. It looks like it just happened, not long ago."

"You took the call?"

"Two minutes ago."

"Is Neil going over?"

"He's just leaving. Several people are."

Then Dulac says, "Okay. I'm on my way. The stuff here isn't ready yet anyway. Get Neil, will you, tell him to be sure nothing is disturbed. Tell him to block off the site."

"Anything else?"

"For the autopsy, the medical exam, call Dr. Miller again, from the university here; ask if he'll attend. Has his mother been told?"

"Not yet. She is in the building right now, but she doesn't know anything. There's no actual identification yet."

"Can you keep her there? Tell the chief, too, so he'll know what's going on. I don't want to ask her to do the identification."

"There's the brother."

"He's too young. I'll get back to you. Call Neil. He should know better, and he'll be offended, but call him anyway. Tell him I said to rope off the entire area. Call Concord, too. Tell them we'll need their lab people there right away, probably for several hours."

Pulling out, entering the street, Dulac reaches to flip a switch to activate the car's siren—it seems to come up as always like a cyclone from within—and accelerates to slip past one car and then another edging to the side to grant him room.

At the intersection with Main Street, as the siren howls, he interrupts the traffic; he nurses, pumps, nurses the accelerator as he passes more cars shying away to give him room.

Nor is it easy to talk within the howling sound, and this gives Dulac a chance to let something settle within himself.

The man has said nothing, has acknowledged what is happening, it seems, by remaining silent. On the highway, pressing on, Dulac calls out, "I'll let you off in town. If you don't mind."

"No problem," the man calls back.

Keeping both hands on the steering wheel, Dulac presses on. He has nothing more to say. The news keeps moving through him, and it is new every time, and it is his job to press on and not to give in. He presses on.

NINE

HE WONDERS IF THEY'VE FOUND THE BOY YET. It shouldn't take long. Walking along, approaching a corner where he might turn back in the direction of where he left the boy, he experiences an urge to do so. He could walk by on the other side of the street, he thinks. He could walk by and take a glance to see if anything was happening. The pull to return is appealing and he can't quite resist it. At the corner, he makes the turn as if casually and walks along. It is the best he has felt all morning, or in several mornings, although he doesn't know why. Does he feel safe now? he wonders. Is that what it is? Is it freedom he feels? Or is it because he has finally done the right thing?

Seeing a police car pass up ahead with its blue light flashing, he fears that nothing has changed. A thought comes up in him, too, to turn back. He doesn't. He keeps walking. He wants to see. He isn't sure what it is, but he wants to see, wants to feel something.

TEN

WITHIN THE BARRICADES, in the midst of confused activity and on his way to the heart of things, Dulac feels late, wrinkled with exhaustion, responsible for everything. His car might still be rocking, it seems, its siren still sighing in its illegally parked position back on the street, half over the curb. He stops. All these uniforms. Chaos. Cars. It's his case and he won't have this, he decides. He won't have this.

People are lined up, and lining up, to watch. Citizens. Gawkers. Jokers. Ahead is a concentration of state troopers in leather boots, city policemen, plainclothesmen, Mizener, DeMarcus, sheriff's deputies. He turns back to the entrance. Out in the street an officer is trying to keep traffic moving as people are slowing down in their cars to rubberneck. To the uniformed officer within the barricades, Dulac says, "Step over here," to draw him some steps away from the dozens of people on the other side of the tape.

"Has anyone come or gone other than all these cops?" Dulac asks him.

"One guy went out, sir."

"Who was that?"

"He worked here or something. Was parked here. Said it was important business, so I let him go."

"You got his name?"

"Yessir, and his license plate."

"Okay, good. You get a chance, call it in, have them run it. Don't let anyone else leave. No one. But get the names of anyone belonging to these cars. Have them wait right here. Tell them we'll have to talk to them. And keep those people back."

Dulac glances over the gathering crowd. The person he is drawn to, Eric Wells, is back along the parking lot somewhere. He walks that way. There is the need to establish some control here. And there are all those faces back on the other side of the rope, even across the street; a number of them, many of them, are young men. Checking them out seems nearly impossible, at the same time that he doesn't believe anyway, in his gut, that the suspect would show up here now. Still, driving hard in his car, he had been barking at himself, *he's here, he's been here all along, he's here and all those who were so certain he was on the run were wrong, everyone has been wrong.*

He is moving now, at last, in the direction of the center of attention toward the rear of the parking lot. The boy. All the others are here, standing in groups of three and four, talking, smoking, gesturing; he cannot, does not believe quite yet that in their midst, somewhere, is the body of twelve-year-old Eric Wells. He notices yellow tape then, to the left, reaching around the backs of four cars, containing an area including the cars and the space before the cars, where no one is trespassing. To his surprise, he feels an urge to have them all gone from here, to have their voices silenced, so he might look alone upon the child whose life had been taken, so he might see whatever there was to see, so he might know at last. Where but in his own heart, Your Honor, can a true detective look for evidence?

Mizener is in a near group, and Dulac says to him, to say something, "The lab people aren't here?"

He doesn't note or listen for an answer; perhaps none was given. His attention has already shifted to the area in front of the taped-in cars, although nothing is visible from where he is standing. Somehow, he doesn't want to appear too anxious. Perhaps he fears his own reaction, that he might break something or wail like an elephant gone loco.

To Detective DeMarcus then, turning to duty, he says, "Listen. Line up three more people. Besides yourself. Go in pairs. Cover all directions from here. See if anybody saw anything. I can't understand this car thing. Maybe he's stolen a car. Knock on every door, get into every office, for a block or so. Somebody had to see this."

Once more then, Dulac looks over the taped-in cars, which nose up to a curb. Going on, looking between two cars, he sees the boy's blue-jeaned legs lying on an old crust of winter-dampened weeds, sees that which has occupied most of his thoughts these past several days. Eric Wells. There he is at last. He's here.

The drivers of the two cars before which the body lies have to have seen the body, he thinks. He thinks this as he stands looking. The drivers could not have pulled in and parked and left their cars and not seen the body lying there. So the body wasn't there. It wasn't there until after they were there. That's simple. It means he was dropped this morning, that's what it means. Still, it doesn't say anything about when the boy died. Only the medical examiner will be able to tell them that. Thinking this, Dulac sees, too, again, that the killer, the college boy killer, Vernon Fischer, could be out there in the crowd of bystanders. Now that he had dropped off the secret witness, Dulac thinks, the one person who knew him on sight. Dropped him off, really, because he wanted to be alone, if only for a couple minutes. Stepping back toward Mizener, he says, "Neil, we need the owners of these two cars. Soon as possible. There's no way they could have parked here and not seen the body."

"Someone's inside looking for them," Mizener says.

"Where's the car of the person who discovered the body? Is it here?"

Mizener points to the rear of the lot. "It's that white Olds," he says. "He saw the body *between* these two cars?"

"That's right."

"He stepped between the cars to look?"

"Right, that's what he said."

Dulac steps over, to look again. He still has not seen the boy's face, and even as he knows it is so, knows it is Eric Wells, he is not entirely convinced, not yet. He is, and he isn't.

He returns toward Mizener.

"Any pictures taken yet?" he asks him.

"Just Polaroids," Mizener says.

Dulac steps back. He circles the four cars then, to take a closer look from the other side. He approaches carefully and stops at the yellow tape where it is strung on an angle to the corner of the building.

There is the small boy, lying on the ground, less than a dozen feet away. On his side; the boy could be asleep. A boy would use his arm as a pillow, though, Dulac thinks. And he thinks how simple death is in its way. A mechanism, full of thoughts and feelings, fears and hopes. Walking. Seeing things. Then a mechanism full of nothing. Life gone, carried away on a breeze.

The killer is here, he thinks and feels.

Crouching, he gazes on the body from under the tape. He touches some fingers to the ground, to feel the damp cold there. He's been here all along, he thinks.

Straightening, he calls back to Mizener, "Neil, whose footprint is that?"

Mizener steps closer. "The guy who discovered the body says it's not his," he says. "He's absolutely certain he didn't leave the pavement."

"Listen, remind me to have the state police do a helicopter shot," Dulac says. "We'll see what kind of trails and paths there are around here."

"You think he walked in?" Mizener says.

"Oh, I think he drove in. But the car thing is bothering me. Why in the hell hasn't his car been spotted? Maybe he's driving another car. It's the only thing that makes sense."

"You think he's around?"

"He sure was; all the time everybody said he was in Canada, he was here."

"I guess so," Mizener says.

"It looks like he just placed the body, more or less in the open, so it would be found quickly. We get the owners of these two cars, we should be able to narrow down the time."

Mizener stays in place but doesn't respond.

Dulac is looking once more at the boy. He lights a cigarette. We lost it, he is thinking. There's something in the air for him, as he looks, of a game of childhood. Hiding. Chasing. Raiding a fort and playing dead. He thinks to ask Mizener if anyone has put forth an idea of how long ago the boy died and decides not to.

For the moment, he doesn't want to know.

"Lieutenant, there are a lot of reporters and TV people gathering down there," someone says to him.

Dulac looks over. "Tell them I'll give a statement as soon as I can. No one's coming in here until the body's removed, and that won't happen until the lab people have done what they have to do. Tell them that. That it'll be a while."

"They want to know if we know when the body was dropped, or if we know the time of death," the officer says to him.

"Not yet," Dulac says. "We're working on it. Tell them that. It's exactly what we're working on."

Dulac looks back over the ground and over the young boy lying there. The young boy hasn't moved. It isn't a game of childhood. Dulac looks again. He has to go back around the cars and stand with the others, he realizes, not to appear attached to anything. He has no wish to stand with the others, to hear what they have to say. Yet he does so. He has always done so. As if to show his strength, he returns around the cars, while at his back the child's death keeps talking to him.

ELEVEN

HER TIME TO MEET Betty is here—it's nearly eleven thirty—and the lieutenant still isn't back. Thinking she will return after lunch, Claire approaches a cadet on duty at the front desk, near where she has been waiting almost an hour now. She can be back about one o'clock, she tries to explain. She's supposed to meet a friend for lunch. The cadet says he will pass on the message.

Claire starts away, fixing her coat and scarf. She is just a step from the door when not a cadet but a police officer near the gate calls, "Mrs. Wells."

As she looks back, the man says, "I guess the chief wants to see you."

"I have this friend waiting," Claire says.

"Maybe it'll only take a minute," the officer says, swinging the gate open.

She walks to the opening, where the policeman, who has several powder-blue stripes on the sleeves of his shirt, adds, following her, "It's right along here."

Claire feels self-conscious here again about her clothes, as she has since she cleaned up to come into town. She's forgotten how to dress—if she ever knew—and her clothes, her light beige gloves, the scarf she is wearing, the couple of combs in her hair, seem old-fashioned in comparison with the way other women in town are dressed. She has a fear, in fact, that Betty will laugh at her, and this thought is on her mind as she is directed into the chief's waiting room. The first clue she has of anything—although it hardly registers—occurs when the secretary gets to her feet at once and comes around her desk to meet her, even to touch her. There is the chief in his doorway, saying, "Mrs. Wells, come on in here. There's been a call about something."

Perhaps she knows by now, although following into his office, she says, "A call about what?"

"Here, Claire, why don't you sit down," the man is saying to her.

The secretary has followed at her side. "A call about what?" Claire says.

"Claire, please have a seat," the chief says.

"A call about what?" she says.

"Now, Claire, I don't want you to get upset," the chief is saying. "A little boy has been found. Near Islington Street. He looks about twelve. Well, I have to tell you, he's not alive."

Claire sits there; a flash lifts from her scalp.

"Are you okay?" the chief says.

There is the secretary at her side; Claire feels numb. She says, almost foolishly, "Eric is twelve."

"Claire, it may be Eric," the chief says. "The clothing matches."

Claire doesn't say anything to this. Then she says, "He's not alive?"

"No, he's not," the chief says. "We're not entirely certain it's him, Claire. It doesn't look good. We need positive identification. I'm terribly sorry."

Claire is trying, too, to be uncertain; it isn't working.

"Is there someone we can call? To make identification? Would you want your older son to do it?"

Claire only looks at him; she isn't ready for this conversation.

"Is he home?" the chief says. "We need to notify him, too."

"Matt's at school," she says. And then she says, "You think it's Eric?"

"Well, there aren't any other young boys missing," the man says.

Claire sits there, and over a distance, across the span of her life, a thought comes to her that Betty is waiting and that all things in life are blown around by the wind.

"I wouldn't want Matt to do that," her voice is saying.

"What's that, Claire?"

"To identify his brother," she says.

They are there, about her, waiting.

She is not looking at them. She is looking between them. Eric? she thinks then, as the information seems to come home to her. Is it Eric they're talking about, out there where it's so cold and damp?

TWELVE

VERNON IS ACROSS THE STREET, along the sidewalk. He's fifty yards away. He'd like to be closer, to see better, at the same time that he is reluctant to be too close. He doesn't know what to do or what matters.

As an initial move in the direction of things, he crosses the street between the slow-moving cars and stands on a raised sidewalk surrounding Mister Donut. People are standing and moving everywhere, trying for a better view; the thickness of the crowd, however, close to the roped-off event, holds more or less steady. "They found that little boy," someone says.

Vernon keeps walking, circling, to see if he can get closer. There is a tall woman draped with photography gear, keeping a camera in both hands raised above her head, like someone on television. There, too, are two men, a dozen feet apart, with television cameras mounted on their shoulders. "They found that little boy," someone says. The eggbeater sound of a helicopter is in the air, but the clatter is there for some time before Vernon—like most others, he keeps shifting and tiptoeing and trying to see something of the heart of the matter—realizes what it is or glances to see it.

"These people will sure scatter if that thing lands," someone says.

"You think that's why it's here?" someone says.

"Maybe they want to evacuate him to Boston," someone says.

Vernon keeps shifting and trying to slip between people to move closer. Boston? he thinks. Will they take him to Boston? The idea appeals to him, as if everything would be taken out of town. And taken care of. In Boston, medical things were made okay, as they all knew.

He shifts and moves closer, raises to his toes as do others throughout the crowd. All at once then there is shouting and a surge backward, nearly pushing him from his feet in the crowd. *"Move it back now!"* a voice is shouting. *"Move it back! Move it back!"* There is an ambulance with flashing red lights, Vernon sees; the wooden barricades are being lifted around by policemen—the white vehicle with its orange stripe is more like a large pickup truck carrying a hospital container—as the ambulance backs into the parking lot, into the center of secret knowledge to which they are all being denied access. Maybe now they will just leave him alone, Vernon is thinking. They have the boy; they're all so busy. Duncan didn't really know, did he? Even if he did, would he tell anyone? He wouldn't, would he? Duncan? He cannot imagine Duncan telling anyone.

The barricades are swung nearly closed again, and the crowd surges forward this time. Cigarettes are lighted. Close by, Vernon hears someone say, "What a circus." And he hears, "Who has the snack concession here? I'm missing lunch." A thought is in his mind all along to speak to someone, to talk about what is happening, to ask if it is the little blond-haired boy who was missing? He'd like to talk to anyone, but doesn't. *Is it the little blond-haired boy?* he thinks to say.

The helicopter hovers, centers almost directly above them, and people glance up into the whipped air. Vernon doesn't. He keeps edging between others and in time comes to a place where he is all but in the second row, with a view, over and between shoulders, of the policemen and others on the other side of the barricades and rope. The ambulance lights are in view as he lifts to his toes, and its roof lights continue to flash and circle. Flash bulbs go off in the distance, too, and there are many more policemen and plainclothesmen around the lighted vehicle. There, he sees, yes, there is the same large detective whose picture was in the paper! Seeing the man makes him feel sick in his stomach for an instant, as if he is going to vomit. He doesn't vomit, though. He thinks of going up to ask the man, as he would ask a professor after class, if the boy's being taken away in the ambulance meant he was going to the hospital and was going to be all right. Is that why they have an ambulance? Were they taking him to Boston?

The large man moves, comes several steps his way, then stops. He is lighting a cigarette. He appears to be looking at the mob of people, even at him. The man turns then to speak to two other men, pointing one way and another. He is a flushed and overweight man, Vernon sees. He is jabbing a finger at the pavement then, over and over, as he talks. The man terrifies him, makes him feel another wave of sickness.

Something is happening, out of view, at the rear of the ambulance; all attention, including Vernon's own, shifts there. A rear door, which had been standing open, is closed; a man in a white hospital jacket steps past others to the driver's door of the ambulance. The ambulance is going to leave, as policemen move away from in front of it. Added lights start flashing from the headlight area of the vehicle; the pushing back and shouting comes up again, although less wildly this time. *"Move it back, please, here it comes. Move it back now."*

Vernon sags with the crowd, sees the flashing ambulance slip by, and returns forward with the crowd once more as the barricades are closed. Turning into the street, the ambulance lets out an abbreviated howl as it heads away. In a moment it howls again, again briefly. The sound continues between Vernon's ears, though, and seems to pose a question of the boy's being okay or not, being rushed to the hospital or not. Why else would the siren call out like that?

He lingers still, as do most others. His soul might survive if the boy survives, is what he is thinking, ignoring altogether his lifting of the stiffened body from the trunk and placing it on the ground. His soul might survive. That seems the issue within him now.

He pushes closer through the crowd; still he cannot win a place in front. As if it is important now, sanctified with this attention, he has no wish to leave this place. There is even an urge in him to identify himself to the crowd and to the police, to have credit paid where credit is due, to explain what happened.

Going up on his toes, he looks for the big detective. Has he gone home? he wonders. With the boy recovered and taken to the hospital, is his job over? Has he quit?

THIRTEEN

IN THE CAFETERIA, Matt is sitting at a bench by himself when he realizes someone is speaking to him. Looking up, he sees the three-piece suit first and then Mr. McGowan, the assistant principal. Matt had been thinking and feeling how bummed out he is, and seeing the man's gray suit, he knows, he knows everything, even as he hardly recognizes any of the words being spoken.

He stands, lifting his legs out from under the table, and he leaves his plastic tray, as instructed, an added clue to everything, to anyone watching, and makes his way between the tables to the center aisle. Here he approximately walks with Mr. McGowan, half a step behind him—like any other student, he thinks in this moment, who doesn't own geometry—follows the man through the overall din, on their way to the swinging doors ahead.

Mr. McGowan has said nothing more, nor does he speak again as they walk the endless hallway. It is just as well to Matt that the man doesn't say any more, for the din of the cafeteria continues in his ears and his thoughts keep flashing here and there. He'll be famous now, he thinks. She'll change her tune now. What will Cormac say?

In the main office, he notices the flash of eyes on him from the women behind the counter as he turns, on faint intuition, to the left, into the principal's office, as Mr. McGowan opens the door with its upper pane of clouded, rippled glass. The principal is getting to his feet, coming around his desk. It is Mr. Duchaine, who says, "Matthew, it's about your brother."

Matt looks at him, waits for what he knows is there like a curious present.

"I've had to do this before," the man is saying. "It's not easy, believe me. Your brother's body was found a short time ago."

Matt only looks back at the man. He doesn't know what to say.

"Matthew, I'm so terribly sorry," the man says. "This kind of thing shouldn't happen."

Matt stands there. He is squeezing his eyes, as they smart some. He is against crying, though, as if the tears would seem to be for the benefit of this small audience. "Where did they find him?" he says.

"I'm not really sure," the man says.

They stand there. Matt doesn't know what else to say, as his attention seems focused on keeping his eyes from blinking and releasing tears. His brother, Eric, dead, he thinks. Still it isn't Eric who is dead; it isn't Eric they are talking about.

"A police car is coming to take you home. It should be here any second."

Again they stand there, until Matt says, "What happened to him?"

The one man, and the other, looks blankly at him, at his question, until the principal says, "We don't really know, Matthew. I'm sure they'll tell you everything."

Matt stands there.

The three of them stand there.

"I'll get my coat," Matt says.

"Oh, I'll go with you," the assistant principal says.

"That's okay," Matt says.

The principal nods lightly, to agree that it's okay.

In the hallway, Matt walks on air. He continues to keep his eyes from blinking into tears. When he blinks once, though, against his wishes, a film is drawn over his eyes, which he strains—retrieving his coat, starting back, saying "Hi" to someone in passing—to have evaporate without being sideswiped by another blink.

"They should be here any minute," the principal says, having stepped to the hallway door.

"I'll go wait outside," Matt says.

"Are you sure you want to do that?" the principal says.

"Yes," Matt says, for it is true.

Again, the man nods.

Outside, as everyone knows, it's the winter air that makes a person's eyes water, and this knowledge helps Matt's efforts not to cry. It's an effort which is taking on a certain importance, as if it is he and Eric against all odds.

Nor does he blink in the back seat of a rattling police car as two young uniformed officers in the front return him home. It's only when the car is on his street and approaching his house that something happens. It is the house where they live, have always lived, the three of them. There it is. The police car is pulling up, and from the rear seat, looking through the side window, he sees the house there beside them. There is their third-floor apartment, their black-and-white TV, their bedroom, their life. Matt tries to hold himself against breaking, and he gasps and holds and gasps again, but his face is going to pieces then and all is lost just as he is opening the door.

The young officer in the passenger seat has turned to look at him, is saying, "You gonna be okay now?" and gets out on his side then as Matt has started crying and is unable to speak.

Beside the car, the officer takes Matt's shoulders in his hands, tries to look at Matt as he is bawling and trying not to bawl, gasping and crying as his heart seems to be pulling apart and there is nothing to be done about it. The policeman's arm goes all the way around his shoulders then, and grips him to his side, and he seems about to cry himself, as he says, "Oh, kid, goddamit." And even as he is crying and gasping for air, Matt resists the strong embrace, vaguely aware of the grip and strength of his father holding him, the last man to have held him, a lifetime ago.

FOURTEEN

ONCE, when she was a little girl too small to know much of anything—perhaps five years old and three feet high—there was a moment when a burst of childlike love came up in her and she exclaimed, "Papa, I love you," to her old father, only to have tears come up in his eyes, which started up tears rather of fear in her own, which occasioned his trying to let her know that his eyes had filled in the rush of happiness he felt, all of which kindled in her one of the warmest sensations in her life, a warm sensation within which she peed some in her panties in her father's lap and he held her to him in laughter and tears and told her she was just like a little puppy . . . which old thought she is trying to have within her now, within the hospital smells, following along a corridor, trying to settle herself against an impossible task immediately ahead.

She wishes the lieutenant were here. None of the people leading her along are familiar. Turning to the double-door entrance to an apparently large room, two of them—one a woman in a white jacket who seems to be a doctor—hold the doors open for her to enter.

As she enters, though, the woman reaches to take her arm and whispers, "Right here, Mrs. Wells."

However confused, Claire stops with the woman and the others in the entrance to the room. The woman is turning her around in the direction from which they had just come, still holding her arm in both hands. "Up there," the woman says.

Claire looks up. Mounted above the doorway is a television set, its screen lighted grayish white. At once, as she watches, a black-and-white image appears on the screen, like the odd beginning of a program. There is a young boy lying on a narrow surface, and there is a white sheet up to his shoulders, and it is Eric, and she looks at him and looks at him, and sees how tired and hungry he appears to be, how there are shadows under his eyes from lack of sleep, and she is thinking how he would need to—

"Mrs. Wells?" the woman says. "Is that your son?"

Claire looks to the woman and feels herself nodding as if in the body of another person, and just as gently and urgently as they led her in, they are leading her back out—the doors are held open—and back along the corridor, where she is reluctant to go. Wait, she wants to cry at them. Wait, I have to take care of Eric.

People shift and move before her in a space surrounded by glass and overcast daylight, and to the person squeezing her arm along the way now, another woman, this one in dark clothing, Claire wants to speak, wants to be courteous in response to the attention being shown her, wants to thank people for being helpful, but she wants above all to go back to be with Eric, wants to say something, get out from herself something which is turning just under the surface like a fist, trying to find a way to break through.

She is walked along, though, through the air, across the parking lot. She knows then—it comes up in her—that she must go back to where they have just been, back where she is needed, that *this* is wrong, going away, going the wrong way, being led the wrong way as it seems she has been led the wrong way all her life . . . At the same time Claire knows that Eric is not alive anymore, that she may not go back to him, that there is only this floating along, this being led along, that this is what is left to her, knowing this as they approach a dark car, as she finds some words for the fist turning in her chest, and says, "You're supposed to die first. You're not supposed to live longer than your children."

To which the policewoman, squeezing her forearm, replies, "I guess that's true," as she keeps guiding her into the car's passenger seat, as Claire keeps looking back, keeps feeling the pull to the building they are leaving behind.

Stop! she wants to cry. *Stop! Stop! Don't you understand? I have to go back! I have to be with Eric! I am his mother! I have to be with my son!*

The car doesn't stop, doesn't turn back. The policewoman slows down at an intersection, engaging the turn signal, which keeps poking at Claire as she sits there, as the car enters the street.

FIFTEEN

VERNON IS SITTING in the park by the river, his arms around himself for warmth. Walking here, leaving Islington Street at last when a string of police cars pulled away, he has walked past the police station again, again on the other side of the street. The police station is two blocks from where he sits now, a distance of perhaps a hundred and fifty yards. Sitting on a cement bench, he is staring across the mouth of the river to Maine, where rail cars squeak and squeal and bright flashes of light tell of life and work at the Naval Shipyard.

A man appears, walking a dog along the wharf. Moments later, a woman passes, walking two dogs on leashes, and these dogs, like the other, make added comments on existence to Vernon which he finds troubling to accept.

His mother is on his mind. A thought to telephone her has him staring between his legs at the pavement. The thought becomes a need. He'd like to do it. He'd like to let her know that he loves her. He'd like to hear her voice, no matter what she might say. He wishes to forgive her, for in this moment she seems a child to him and he wishes her peace and freedom, too. He has always disliked her, he sees, and yet, of course, he loves her. He can't help it.

As he walks, his infatuation for the small oceanside town comes up again. Is it possible to feel love for a side street without sidewalks? For parked cars and wooden houses? For gutters and drains? It is love he believes he feels. Now that he can *see*, he thinks, and knows that he could make a contribution—now that he perceives the center of all things—he can see, too, that it is too late. If he has always loved her, he wonders, does it mean that she has always loved him, too? In spite of everything? It's what he'd like to ask her if he called her. Does she love him? If she does, it means something.

There are newspapers before a side street mom-and-pop store. POLICE STYMIED IN SEACOAST KIDNAPPING PROBE, a headline says. Yesterday's news. Walking on, Vernon wishes he had not seen the headline. He will read no more newspapers, he tells himself, nor listen to any more television or radio reports. He will walk and think for a time. He'll look at what there is to see.

No one stops him. Near the river once more, as he looks over an old drawbridge as well as at the soaring new highway bridge, both of them crossing into Maine, a thought runs though his mind of how he might feel there, on the other side, in another state, but the thought expires and he continues walking.

Cars slide by, but he doesn't look at them. Circling through town, he steps around a glossy ten-speed bicycle parked before the city library and looks on the bike's complication of gears and wheels and cables, its seat and handlebars, a magical childflight it suggests. He does have a soul, doesn't he, he tells himself. He can tell now that he does, but he really has no idea if it may live on in any way on its own. These thoughts expire, too, disappear like expressions of breath as he continues walking and looking around.

A car passes—a Camaro—music for all to hear pouring from its opened windows. It is a teenage boy in the car, who should be in school and knows nothing, nothing at all, Vernon thinks. Can no one teach anyone anything at all? he wonders.

He tells the operator he is calling collect, which he is forbidden to do, and waits while the woman puts through his call. There are unusual clicks before the ringing begins. It rings four times and is not answered.

"There's no answer, sir, would you like to try later?"

"Yes," he answers.

He walks again. Having circled away from the police station, he realizes it is acting as a center of his movement. As he moves away, a feeling in him diminishes. As he moves closer, the feeling comes up again. The sensation is unusual but rich and magnetic in its way. He tends toward it again. A warmth spreads through him, too, as he tends toward it.

SIXTEEN

THE MEDICAL EXAMINATION of the child's body is more intriguing to R. Marc Miller, the researcher from the university, than had been the particular intrigue of the sex film. That was speculation. This is quite real. It is not a little amazing to him, spending virtually all his time in laboratories and libraries, that one in fact may lead to another. Here it is. And what a difference it makes, he cannot help thinking. As he thinks, too, notes to himself, how policemen, like the overweight detective who has also accepted reaching into a pea green surgical gown for this witnessing, are in immediate everyday contact with psychology, sociology, and psychiatry and hardly know the names. Amazing.

How *is* the pathology of violence against women and children being verified here? he wonders. Did the film he was shown lead to this death, this loss of life, this theft of life's simple intentions lying there on the chilled stainless steel table—warmed only, it seems, by the repeated flashes from the circling photographer's two or three cameras. Is he here himself, this afternoon, to offer explanation, to pass judgment on these questions?

He would like to leave right now, he thinks, as the overweight detective shifts and he shifts, too, to have a view between the doctors closer to the table. He would like to leave and leave a note indicating that he doesn't do it this way, he doesn't generalize from individual examples of hard evidence, if they seem compelling or not. He just doesn't do it this way. He works in tranquility is what he does. He works in reflection, with words or paper, with concepts, statistics, theories, diagrams. He doesn't do this, doesn't work in the flesh, under pressure of life, under pressure of death.

But he decides to stay. He decides in a blinking against an actual odor, to call up whatever strength it is he needs to stay. It's the real world, made up of real people, he thinks, and maybe it will put hair on his chest. So he decides, shifting his feet, craning his neck for a better view, perking his ears for words spoken, ordering into operation his tried and true personal mechanism of information gathering:

PERSONNEL. *Present at medical examination and autopsy, Portsmouth Hospital, in addition to lifeless body twelve-year-old Eric Wells, two pathologists, senior and apparently junior; two forensic lab people, state police, both male also; two attending nurses, both female; a police photographer, also male; Lieutenant Dulac, Portsmouth detective in charge of investigation of what is now a sex murder; one hospital administrator, who is female; and myself.*

CHARGE. *Per instructions from Lt. Dulac—who, in all due respect, would seem to me to be in over his head on this case—to provide profile of person or persons who would abduct, molest, and kill twelve-year-old boy as indicated by evidence; to provide whatever psychological clues or insights suggested by the evidence of treatment of the child during his captivity, before and after death; to provide professional opinion concerning any possible relationship of previously critiqued porn film.*

In view of the facts reported to me by Lt. Dulac that two separate vehicles are reported to have been observed by witnesses in area where body was dropped, one a silver-gray coupe-type vehicle, the other an off-white or beige-colored, perhaps home-painted, laundry panel truck–type vehicle, more than one person could be involved in abduction and murder, possibly even a female, given the apparent cleanliness of the child's body as noted so far by the two examining pathologists.

EXAMINATION. *Pathologists and lab persons go over every centimeter of the child's body, even before the actual autopsy begins, taking specimens and photographs, measuring exact dimensions of such things as an open wound in his skull. Noted here to me by pathologist that the boy's hair was washed after the wound had been inflicted, whereupon I remark that the cleanliness and care of the body indicate to me the hand either of a true pedophile or of a female, possibly with a mothering instinct, suggesting the possibility of more than one individual involved. To this the taller of the two state police lab technicians remarks it was his opinion, given the advanced condition of the body and its degree of dehydration and the clean smell of the boy's hair and skin, that the boy has been bathed and washed after he died and I am asked if such care of an already dead child might suggest any psychological details of the killer's makeup or state of mind. To this I reply the same as I had already indicated, that a true pedophile with a sexual fixation on children or an individual, female or male, with a particular mothering instinct is indicated by these details of evidence. Also, I point out, the efforts to clean the body after death, to make it presentable, would be part of an attempt on the killer's part to expiate guilt and to minimize in his own mind the amount of damage he would know he has caused. I am asked to step forward also to closely examine tie burns on the boy's wrists and possibly on his ankles, which are not actual rope burns, the taller state police lab technician indicates, but probably caused by neckties used to tie the boy, given the minuscule synthetic fibers, blue-black and blue-green in color, they are able to detect and, however microscopic, to secure as evidence.*
At this point, Lt. Dulac, stepping forward also, instructs all present and has us acknowledge that nothing more than rope burns will be indicated or disclosed outside this room, as the kind and color are evidence only the actual killer would be able to describe or produce; such ploys are common devices to weed out persons making false confessions, a peculiar phenomenon, the Lt. says, of highly publicized crimes. Cannot help wondering here if Lt. Dulac may not be

guilty of playing cops and robbers a bit in a small-town way, but of course criminal detection is his business more than mine.

Further examination and specimen taking of body cavities, including mouth, ears, and nose for possible presence of semen appear inconclusive. All such details of examination and discussion appear disrespectful to the little boy who is lying naked under the eyes of so many persons. A heartbreaking scene, really, if allowed to address one in this way. Amazingly sad to me to think that this very little boy with his very little penis, and without any pubic hair at all, has been the object of a sexual abduction and an assault which have led to his death.

Toe and foot areas found to be remarkably clean, as are finger areas. Toenails and fingernails determined to have been very recently clipped and scraped. Soap smells still present between toes and between fingers. Could be a fetish of some kind, or could be an attempt to remove any traces of evidence from the body, lab technician remarks, adding that in the latter instance—as an attempt to remove evidence—would seem to indicate an individual with some awareness of forensic science.

Examination of anal track areas staggering in its revelation of rupture and dilation from forced penetration. Extensive examination of this area, as initial shock wears off. Neck, back, and side areas examined closely for bruises, which are detected in the left neck area.

Yours truly steps forward at this point to bring out that while underpants were soiled, the buttocks area was clean, except for the presence of stool in the anal track, indicating the apparent dysfunction of the sphincter muscle, and that the child suffered fear or terror sometime before death at the hands of his captor.

Advised those present at this point, too, that bathing of the body after death, as well as manicure and pedicure, could have been in themselves the sexual acts of a pedophile and no less significant sexually to such an individual than the apparent forced anal penetration, at the same time, italics mine, that they could have been attempts to erase evidence. To which, not unexpected, one state police lab technician remarks, he loved him so much he killed him. To which I reply, in his mind he may have felt he had to kill him, but it wouldn't seem likely that the killing in itself would have been pleasurable for him or a sexual act for him. To which lab technician remarks, how do you know that? To which I have to reply, I don't. It's an educated guess.

Lt. Dulac's question at this time: What kind of person would keep this child for several days, care for him, clean him, and place the body in broad daylight, at great risk to himself of being seen, where it might be so quickly discovered?

As to the latter, I reply, that it would appear the person returned the body close to home and cleaned it in an attempt to put things right, in an attempt perhaps to expiate his feelings of guilt. Further, that these acts would indicate that the individual is a caring person, perhaps in a highly desperate state of mind, for he could as easily have dumped it anywhere or buried it, and not bothered to clean it from head to toe.

Examination continues as do photographs. Called upon in pathetic death photos to confirm general deterioration of child's body due to dehydration and lack of nourishment, extended lack of adequate sleep apparent in eyes, which are sunken with dark rings beneath, sallow color, and depth of severe blow to skull with a sharp instrument which remains unclosed. Four to seven centimeters deep, seventeen centimeters long, with nearly all blood washed from wound and hair. At this point, and I feel they are taking out an amount of frustration on me, lab technician asks how the depth and violence of head wound is consistent with a caring person. To which I reply that it isn't consistent and that it could be the result of an emotional explosion or possibly a fight.

AUTOPSY. Senior pathologist notes no apparent genital damage outside the anal rupture. Notes also that exact determination of cause of death extremely difficult to ascertain. Asphyxiation is cause of death, but it may have occurred in one of two possible ways. Death would occur in one instance due to air being cut off to the brain, in the other due to the interruption of the supply of oxygen to the lungs. Strangulation might cause the loss of air to both the brain and the lungs; smothering interrupts the supply of oxygen to the lungs. Forensic lab technician notes there are forensic pathologists who can determine if death was due to lack of oxygen to the trachea, or if it was due to the blood supply to the brain being cut off, and offers to Lt. Dulac that they could seek such determination if need be. Lt. Dulac replies that it is his opinion that such information is not necessary.

Smothering would appear to be the cause, pathologist remarks, due to the absence of bruises on the neck.

How smothered? No microscopic fibers present and therefore no way to determine, pathologist remarks. Could have been anything placed over the boy's face, such as a pillow or even a person's hand.

Time of death also key point. Pathologist sets time at from twelve to twenty-four hours before body was discovered, placing time of death at between eleven a.m. and eleven p.m. the previous day and night, adding that forthcoming lab tests might narrow time more closely, although remaining within the general time frame. Unusual question at this time from Lt. Dulac, as he asks if there is any way to pinpoint time of death more closely, so that it might be determined if it occurred before or after the newspapers were available yesterday between two and three p.m., to which the examining physician only shakes his head no.

Added question to me from Lt. Dulac: Would such a person repeat his actions by abducting another child?

Reply: Highly possible, even possible that he would do so relatively soon given his apparent state of emotional need. Possible, too, that such a person in the process of psychological stress might become a so-called serial killer until caught and stopped, that the recent history of highly publicized serial murders could be suggestive to such an individual. A key element in this case, I point out, is the fact that the child was kept and cared for for an extensive period of time, which would indicate the need or desire on the part of the killer for the ongoing presence of a child, which would support the logic in his mind of attempting to abduct another child. Also, I add, such things are easier the second time. So a definite possibility, even a likelihood, of other attempted abductions.

Added question from Lt. Dulac: Was there torture? Did the killer inflict pain on purpose or for sexual gratification?

Reply: Not per se, apparently. Rape occurred, certainly, for sexual gratification, but otherwise no signs of torture.

How much suffering did the boy experience?

Reply: A great deal. He was bound, he was raped, he was at the mercy of his captor for some seventy to eighty hours, and he was suffocated. His suffering would have been altogether real. Unbearable. At the same time, there is the evidence of his being cared for, so perhaps his suffering was intense at different times.

Given this feeling of caring, Lt. Dulac asks, why would he be raped, an act of sexual violence?

Reply: In his own mind, killer may have believed he was providing sexual pleasure, as the psychodynamics of nurturing and sexuality are confused in the mind of a pedophile. As a child, suspect may have experienced satisfying sexual experiences with other children, boys or girls, or with adults, and he may have been of the belief that sexual pleasure was being given to the victim.

He isn't necessarily homosexual?

Reply: Not neccessarily.

Any possible association or acting out of pornographic film, Children in Bondage, *believed to have been viewed by suspect prior to abduction?*

Reply: Children in both instances bound by the wrists, followed by anal penetration, but nothing conclusive in these details to indicate that one was an acting out of the other, since both might be classified as more or less ordinary activities.

Would suspect have been stimulated to pursue sexual activity?

Reply: Very possibly.

Would he have been stimulated to pursue sexual activity of a particular kind, as with children?

Reply: He did, apparently, pursue sex in a gay bar, with an adult male, which experience was frustrating to him, at the same time that he may have been predisposed, prior to the film, and most of his life, to seeking sexual gratification from children.

Most of his life?

Reply: A pedophile is often a person who failed to receive adequate love and attention in childhood; he both develops a sexual fixation on children, as if to make up for the neglect he experienced himself as a child, and also, possibly in a double-edge of motivation, might express his anger and resentment to parents in general, including certainly his own, by depriving them of their child.

It is known, Lt. Dulac says, that the prime suspect attempted to obtain other, presumably hard-core child porn; if he had been successful, would Eric Wells be alive today?

Reply: Studies were believed to have indicated that yes, pornographic materials might absorb such a person's sexual needs, such studies now in question by some experts. My personal opinion: Like many researchers I believed in liberalization of sexual mores over past twenty to twenty-five years, at the same time that it has become clear that the effects on specific individuals remains unknown and inconclusive. It's a classic dilemma in which what may be good for many may be disastrous for a few.

Has a new pathology come into existence?

Reply: A new pathology? You mean like a new bacteria strain?

Yes, Lt. Dualc says. A new sexual pathology. It's been suggested to me by a caller from a university in Boston.

Reply: This person is suggesting a new sexual pathology is in existence?

Exactly. A new sexual pathology.

Reply: Given to what in particular?

As I understand him, it is given to having its way. Simply that. A belief. An attitude.

Reply: You're asking me if I believe such a pathology has come into existence?

That's what I'm asking.

Reply: I would say definitely not. In fact, I think your caller—I've never heard of the idea—I think your caller may be a fraud or an impostor of some kind. Having one's way isn't a pathology, it's simply a state of mind.

Thanked for my help by Lt. Dulac, I understand I am being granted permission to leave. I do so, to certain relief. Profound relief, I should say. The experience, I know as soon as I am outside, walking to my car, is one from which I will never fully recover. The psychological strain to those persons going on to conclude the task at hand is more, I believe, than I had ever imagined.

SEVENTEEN

MATT IS IN THE MALL, walking, He could not say why he is here, only that he had not wanted to go upstairs to the apartment as the policemen drove away. If his mother was there or not—they had told him she wasn't—the prospect of being in the apartment appeared impossible. What would he do? Sit there? Wait for his mother to call? Sit and think about Eric? In a way he wanted to be alone with his thoughts about his brother, but not alone in their apartment.

Three truant boys from school come along. In no mood to see them, Matt has no escape. At once they are there, gathering around, for they have heard the news, too, and he has to stand with them and hear their words, although they are not quite friends. Nelson Labrecque, a muscular boy who lifts weights and has a reputation for amazing strength and toughness, says to him seriously, "Jesus, man, how are you doing?"

"Okay," Matt says.

"Cops know who did it?"

"I don't know," Matt says. "They have this suspect they're after."

"They'll never get him; they do, he'll just get off."

"Yeah," Matt says.

"I catch him," Labrecque says, "I'd cut off his cock and make him eat it."

There is some laughter; Matt smiles with them, thinking he should not do so, not with his brother dead.

"I'm not joking," Labrecque says. "I'm not joking. You find out who it is, let me know. I don't have no little brother, but I have a little sister. Don't think I'm joking. I'll kill this guy. That cocksucker. I'll tell you, he'd wish he'd never run into my ass."

"The vigilante strikes!" one of the boys says.

"I tell you I'm not joking."

"Yeah yeah."

"Don't fuck with me, man! I tell you I'm not joking."

"*Okay.*"

"Don't think it's a joke. Everybody thinks everything's a joke. You fucking jerks."

"Jesus, take it easy."

"Don't make everything a joke."

"You don't have to go off your rocker."

"Don't make everything a joke, that's all."

"*Okay.*"

"It's not funny. It is not a joke. You fucking cowards. Show me that sonofabitch, I'll show you a joke."

"Jesus, man, sorry for breathing."

"You should be," Nelson Labrecque says. "This guy's brother has been murdered. His life has been *eliminated.* That is not a joke."

"Okay, it's not a joke."

The three go on their way, and Matt walks on again, too. Fear is in him now; there seems something threatening all around, and a thought comes to him that Cormac is who he'd like to see. Of all people. They could laugh or smile over practically nothing, Matt thinks, and there would be a feeling at least of something like everyday life in the air. Or Eric. He'd go for seeing Eric, too. Everything was always so easy with Eric. It was funny, when they were out like this, like looking through the Mall, they always got along easily. They only fought at home. When they were out somewhere they seldom fought. They didn't talk so much, not like when he was with Cormac, but they didn't fight. It was like they were one person. It was like they were the same person, and he wonders if they were in some way.

EIGHTEEN

DULAC IS RUSHED and rattled. Leaving the hospital, he is headed downtown—he *must* go there, he thinks—where a press conference has already gathered, is waiting for him to walk into its center. The news must go out. He has to meet the press, do the job. But other things are in his mind and what he wants to do is to slow down enough to figure out what has happened and what it is he has to do.

The sonofabitch is here! he keeps saying to himself, even as he stops and starts at intersections. He's in Portsmouth! He may be in his classes! He may be going on like nothing has happened! He may return to the cottage! He is here, somewhere! *He's been here all along!*

He has to have another car, Dulac thinks. That white van report. That must be it. But there's the report of a gray coupe, too. Did he switch plates? Did he switch plates and stay low and manage to slip around without being noticed?

Dulac accelerates as a light changes, decides again not to use his siren. Oh, it isn't the killer so much that is in his mind, he suddenly admits to himself. It isn't him. It's the small boy back there on the table. It's the small boy and the awareness within him—it is a kernel, a pebble, in the center of his heart—that he had a hand himself in his death. Had he done one thing or another, or done some one thing differently, it might not have happened. They might have won. No one was likely to blame him. Still, the truth was, he was the loser. It was his game, and he was the loser. Yesterday at this time the boy was probably alive. He was alive all day Sunday, all day Monday. All that time. Then, yesterday sometime, or last night, he was killed. As the cop on duty, he wasn't smart enough, wasn't good enough, and he came in a loser. He had a chance to bring him in and he hadn't been up to it. If they had won, everyone would have shared the credit. But there was only one loser. And it was the person running the show.

Did he hold his hand over the boy's face? Dulac wonders. Is that what he did? Did he watch him die? Feel him die?

Why the pedicure and manicure? Why drop the body off where it would be so quickly found? Was he taunting them? Was he arrogant? What kind of person were they dealing with? Should they get an alert out to keep a close eye on all children? Did they have some oddball child-killer on their hands, some twisted character who was going to imitate the serial killings that had been going on around the country? Here in their small, out-of-the-way town?

Dulac's jaw is tight and he is squinting some as he pulls around the corner before the police station. He waits for a car to pass before turning in—he glimpses a young man standing on the sidewalk across the street; they are everywhere, he thinks—and makes his turn, thinking then of the packet of death photos in his shirt pocket. Polaroid shots, they include pictures of Eric Wells's face, his sunken eyes, the bluish dehydrated pallor over his skin, the wound in his skull, the faint tie marks on his wrists and ankles, his ruptured rectum. He calls into effect his personal mechanism for controlling anger and outrage. For what he'd like to do is show the pictures to the press. Have them played on television. Here you have a dead child. Notice the faint bluish color of his skin. Notice how it blends into that yellowish tint. These are the colors of death. They are the colors we tolerate.

The white laundry truck. Where in the hell can you get to in a white laundry truck? It has to be spotted soon and either cleared or implicated. Could more than one person be involved? Was it *really* this Vernon asshole? Was he working alone? What if the reporters turn on him now? What if they charge him with being ineffective?

There is Shirley, intercepting him on his way to the squad room. She takes him aside. It's the first time he's seen her since he dropped her off early that morning; she is a little worn, not as pretty as she used to be. "Gil, several things are happening," she says. "The father, Warren Wells, called from New Orleans. Someone has been keeping him up on the news. He wants to come up here for the funeral and wants to know if charges will be brought against him."

"Jesus, is it our jurisdiction?" Dulac says. "I don't think it is. He should ask his ex-wife. Or talk to a lawyer. I think it might be up to Claire Wells. Did he give a number?"

"No, he wouldn't do that. He's going to call back. He sounds like a guy with a lot of problems. Money. Booze. Claire Wells called too, by the way, but I did not tell her about her former husband calling. She's got some kind of problem, too. She won't say what it is. The only person she will talk to is you. I don't know for sure, but I have a feeling there was no insurance on the little boy. And of course she doesn't have any money at all. I think the world may be crashing on her."

"Oh, God, okay," Dulac is saying. "Call her back, will you? Tell her I'll call her as soon as I can."

"She's distraught. She's at her friend's; she won't even talk to her friend about whatever it is."

"Well, tell her not to worry. Jesus. Tell her not to worry. Are the pictures here? Did the pictures come in?"

"Oh, yes. The pictures are here. It's a high school graduation picture.

In color. Of course, he doesn't look like a murderer. And," she adds, lowering her voice, "something else is here. The secret witness. He came in. He confirms the picture, by the way, but that's not why he's here. He said, this is what he said: He couldn't stay away. That's what he said. He's a little upset, I think. What happened between you two? He came in, gave me his name, like he's coming out of the closet or something."

"He's where?"

"In your cubicle. But staying secret doesn't seem to be a big thing to him anymore. Or anything at all."

"Okay, I'll talk to him."

Dulac goes along the hall. He doesn't know what he is thinking. Nothing seems willing to hold in place long enough for him to learn from it when, without titles or seams, something else is playing on his mind's screen. Claire Wells. The long-absent father. The white laundry truck. Shirley. Coming around the corner into his cubicle, he sees the secret witness, Martin, sitting in a chair. On a glimpse, Dulac had seen the reporters, photographers, TV camerapeople filling the squad room. "What's the deal?" he says. "Is something wrong?"

"Lieutenant, please, listen—"

"You can't stay away?" Dulac says.

"It's the truth. I—"

"You're going to get identified, you know?"

"I don't care about that. It doesn't matter. My God, I sell real estate. I know who your wife is."

"You might care tomorrow."

"So I'll cry tomorrow. Sometimes you have to do things. I have to do this. I have to be here. I want to help, it's more important to me—"

"Okay," Dulac says, patting his pockets to be sure he has his lighter and cigarettes to take with him into the wolf's den. "Okay. Anyone asks you anything, say you're working for me. Tell them to see me."

"Lieutenant, thank you. You have to know how much respect—"

"Okay, okay," Dulac says, again holding up his stop sign, as Shirley appears in his doorway. "White truck's been found and cleared," she says. "Hampton Beach. It's a delivery van, not a laundry truck; driver had legitimate business there."

"Who checked it?"

"DeMarcus. He's still checking it, but he says it checks out."

"So it was the gray car," Dulac says. "He's driving his own car."

"It looks that way," Shirley says.

"I can't understand why no one is coming in with that car. Could he be cagey enough to be using *another* gray car?"

"I've got the pictures," Shirley says. "You want me to pass them out in there?"

"Yeah, good idea. Let me have one." Dulac is on his way then, taking from Shirley, as she removes it from a manila envelope, one of the five-by-seven color photographs of the face of a graduating high school senior. Turning into the squad room, his presence creating a response followed almost immediately by the beginning of a hush, Dulac keeps looking down at the face in the picture, seeing something there, trying to see something there, trying to understand what it is he is seeing, as he makes his way along the side to the head of the room, still thinking as he looks back at them, as he starts climbing up on a table, what is it? What in the world is it? Is it really some kind of new pathology?

NINETEEN

VERNON IS STANDING on the sidewalk. He walks a few steps, stands awkwardly again in the middle of the sidewalk. A woman pedestrian steps around him, goes on her way. For something to do then, he walks to the corner. He pauses and looks around. He doesn't know what to do. He doesn't know if he wants to go or stay, or if he wishes to sing or cry or step into the street in front of a car. Whatever it is that is within him, he wants it not to go on. If it is a snake family within him in place of his intestines, he wants them to be still. If there is a small monkey there reaching to squeeze his heart, to make it shrill with tidal currents and messages like his testicles being squeezed, he wants it to stop. They refuse to do so. And they sing into his ears. He walks, and stands, and needs or seeks or desires resolution, or confrontation, or conclusion.

Pausing a moment at the corner, looking in all directions, he turns to walk back. It was that big detective he saw driving in, he thinks. He's certain it was, and in another moment, he tells himself—he's building up to it, he knows, and when it takes over in him, he will be doing it—he is going to walk across the street and enter through a door, following the arrow to the side as indicated, and ask if he can speak to the detective in charge of the Eric Wells case—the little boy they found earlier, in that parking lot, he will explain.

And who knows? After a talk with the big detective, after a full explanation and a promise never to do anything like that again, who knows how things might work out? He probably wouldn't make his afternoon class, but he'd sleep tonight, at last, somewhere, and who knew what would happen tomorrow?

Yes, he'd explain everything to the detective, and he imagines the big detective smiling at him, warmly, understanding, as they sit on opposite sides of an official desk and he promises, he assures the man, who watches him closely with his eyes to be sure of his candor and conviction, that he will never, ever, not ever in his life do anything like that again. Never. He will dedicate the rest of his life to making a contribution—

TWENTY

THE TELEPHONE IS RINGING as Matt enters the outside door. It keeps ringing as he goes up the stairs and as he enters. No one is home, he realizes. His mother isn't here—Eric isn't here—as he steps into the kitchen and lifts the receiver from the hook, places it to his ear, and says, "Hullo?"

There is static on the line, and the hollowness of distance, into which a voice says, "Matt?"

He doesn't say anything. He knows who it is and his heart is racing. His thoughts are jumbled at once with confusion.

"Is that you, Matt?" the voice says. "It sounds like you."

"Yes," he says. "Yes. Who's this?" His eyes are filling; he is trying yet again not to cry.

"It's your father, Matt."

Matt has the phone to his ear. He doesn't say anything to this. He looks over the kitchen to the window, sees where they live. Even as he has waited all these years for such a call, a nervous wish is in him to have it over.

"Matt, I heard what happened to little Eric," the voice says.

Matt still doesn't know what to say.

"Matt, are you there?"

"Where are you?" Matt says.

"Well, I'm down here in New Orleans," the man says. "Someone called me."

"Who?" Matt says, becauses he doesn't know what else to say.

"Just someone I know. An old friend. How are you holding up?"

"You're where?" Matt says then. It is his father on the phone; still, he wishes the call would end.

"New Orleans," the man says. "Matt, I'm so sorry about little Eric. I just can't believe it."

Matt holds the phone, having no response to this, as if it is beside the point.

"It just breaks my heart," the man says.

Matt doesn't respond.

"Matt, is your mother there?"

"She's not here," Matt says.

"She's not there?"

"No, she's not here. I guess she's at Betty and John's. I just came in."

"Where were you, Matt?"

"Oh, nowhere. I was just out. They told me in school."

"What's that?"

"Oh, nothing."

"Matt, I remember your voice. It's good—hearing your voice."

"Oh," Matt says.

"Can you—I want you to do something for me, Matt, if you can. I'm in pretty bad shape, Matt. Do you hear me?"

"Yes."

"Do you know what I mean, Matt? I'm not in the best of shape. I'm trying to get things together so I can come up there. Do you know what I'm saying?"

"Yes," Matt says, even as his answer seems more a question.

"Matt, do this. Ask your mother, will you, if she'll have me charged if I come back up there. Arrested. I need to come back up there, Matt. Do you know what I mean? I want to go to the funeral. But I won't be able to if I get arrested. Would you tell your mother that—ask her that for me, Matt?"

"Okay."

"I don't know what else to say, Matt. I feel so bad. What kind of world do we live in?"

Matt holds the phone; he has no reply to this.

"Tell her, Matt, that I'll call again in a while. Will you do that?"

"Yes," Matt says.

"Okay. That's what I'll do. Then you can tell me."

"Okay," Matt says.

"Matt, I'd really like to see you," his father says.

A moment later, the telephone hung up, Matt catches himself standing in the silent mid-afternoon kitchen as if uncertain again of what has happened, of why he is so filled with nervousness.

Should he go over to Betty's or call her? he wonders. All at once, now that the call is over, he wishes they were talking again. He doesn't know what he'd say, but he wishes it were so. His mother will go ape, he thinks, on another rush to his eyes. She will go absolutely ape, and all at once he can't wait to tell her. New Orleans, he thinks. New Orleans, Louisiana.

TWENTY-ONE

STANDING YET ON THE TABLE in the squad room, Dulac is answering questions about the suspect and the photographs of the suspect which Shirley has passed out. In casual groups, people stare at the face in the photograph and look up and listen to Dulac's account of things. They want more photographs; Dulac, promising more for later in the day, has looked to Shirley and received her nod. He hasn't said anything of the death photos in his shirt pocket and wonders again if he should, if he should pass some of them around to validate what he has said about the condition of the body, to let them see as well the innocent size and shape of a twelve-year-old boy lying lifeless on a stainless steel table. He decides no, of course not. They were perceptions for him to absorb, for him to carry; how could he think such a thing?

He says instead, "Are there any questions? I have other things to do."

So many hands and voices come up that he lifts his hand once more and says, "I can take only a few."

"Who are the witnesses? We're told you have eyewitnesses. Who are they? When can we talk to them?"

"Who discovered the body, Lieutenant?"

"One at a time," Dulac says. "As for the witnesses, their identities will not be disclosed at this time, for obvious reasons."

"What obvious reasons?"

"So they won't be harassed by you," Dulac says. "So they won't be compromised if and when we go to trial."

"Do you think their lives would be in danger?"

"No, I don't," Dulac says. "Still, we do have a murderer. An alleged murderer. Who is at large. So we aren't going to identify witnesses at this time. That's not a very smart question. I have—"

"Who discovered the body, Lieutenant?"

"I said, before, it was a man who had business there. He has been cleared."

"Was he a suspect?"

"No, he was not a suspect. We have a suspect. Nonetheless he was checked out."

"What about the time of death, Lieutenant? How was that determined?"

"It was determined by the pathologist, whose name I gave you five minutes ago."

"How was it—"

"You can ask him the question. I'm not a pathologist."

"Twelve to twenty-four hours, Lieutenant—is that as close as it can be called?"

"As far as I know."

"Lieutenant, that means he was harbored from Saturday until yesterday or this morning when his body was dropped. Do you have any idea where he was kept?"

"Not at this time; we're working on that."

"Lieutenant, are you thinking of calling in the big boys on this?"

"Who are the big boys?"

"No offense, Lieutenant. Experts from Boston. Homicide people. Forensic people. The FBI. After all, this is a small town."

"The answer is no. And we do take offense. Lots of people, a whole staff of people, have done and are doing a lot of work, and we feel we're doing the job. As good as anyone else could do it. The state police lab is providing forensic expertise."

"Nonetheless, Lieutenant, there's a killer on the loose. What if he strikes again? Will you ask for help then?"

"We're doing all that we can to bring him in," Dulac says. "We're being assisted all the way around by other law enforcement agencies, local, state, and federal."

"What do you mean, 'all the way around'?"

"In all capacities—what do you think I mean?"

"Is it believed the killer is still in the area?"

"That's what we're working on."

"Do you think this could be related to other groups or other activities coming into the area?"

"Such as?"

"Kinky groups, Lieutenant."

"Kinky groups. Well no, we don't believe at this time that there is any such association. At the same time, we're not closing our eyes to anything."

"Are you going to call in psychics?"

"No comment."

"That mean yes or no?"

"It means no comment."

"Was the boy tied when he was found, Lieutenant?"

"I said he wasn't tied. I said that earlier."

"You said he was tied? He had been tied?"

"That's right. There were marks on his wrists and ankles."

"Any connection with pornography in this area, Lieutenant?"

"Not that we can determine so far. As I said."

"There is a line of investigation?"

"There are some threads or loose ends we're working on."

"Lieutenant, what about free sex or loose sex? Everybody knows what's going on in this town."

"Well, who knows?" Dulac says. "Is that—what you say—what is going on here? Or is it going on everywhere? I don't know who could give the right answer to that."

"Is this the act of a sick person?"

"No comment."

"The boy was definitely sexually molested?"

"We would say definitely, yes."

"How is that known? Was there mutilation?"

"No. There was no mutilation, say, of that kind. He did suffer anal trauma."

"What other signs, sir?"

It is at this point that Shirley appears below him at the table, catches his attention by signaling to him to crouch, and as he does so, hands him a folded slip of paper. Straightening upright, Dulac reads: *Car found in Shaw's parking lot, Islington St.*

"Signs of what?" Dulac says to the reporters, as they wait and watch.

"Molestation."

"We're not certain," Dulac says. "The tests and so on are being done right now. Molestation can take many forms, such as fondling, which do not leave marks. Even language, words, can be a form of molestation."

"When will the body be released for burial?"

"This afternoon, I believe. I don't know the details right now."

"Lieutenant, the state hasn't executed anyone in quite a few years. Would you see this crime as a reason to bring back capital punishment?"

"No comment. Any more questions? I'm afraid I have to go now."

"Who identified the body?"

"Mrs. Wells, his mother."

"What was her reaction?"

"No comment."

"Lieutenant, was he a street kid? Eric Wells? Was he a trouble-maker?"

Dulac looks up at the person asking this question, a young man in a plaid sports coat. "This will be the last reply," he says. "No, Eric Wells wasn't a troublemaker. From all we've been able to tell, he was a good kid. He was a little shy. He was well liked. He was twelve years old is all, and he had a special interest in military things, in building things. He was a general, average boy who caused no problems, for his mother or for the police or at school. That's what he was. Children aren't troublemakers."

Down from the table, ignoring other questions as the reporters move, as some of them push and run, approaching Shirley, feeling angry with the charging mob, Dulac leads her from the room and across the hall to his cubicle, where he closes the door. "Who spotted the car?" he asks.

"Someone called in. Mizener's there. It's just up the street from where the body was found."

"It's positive?"

"Oh, yes, it's positive."

"Jesus, I hope he hasn't touched anything. Did he say if it was locked or if the trunk was open?"

"He didn't say."

"Okay, I'm going there. Will you call the lab people? Tell them we have the car. I'm going there. Anyone wants me, that's where I'll be. Tell Claire Wells, I don't know, the secret witness—just say I'll be back. If you want me, that's where I'll be. I'll be back as soon as I can."

Dulac slips on his jacket then, as Shirley leaves, and checks his hardware, as always, by feel. Something remains on his mind, near three-dimensional images in the front of his mind; still he cannot get them to come into focus. He keeps rushing along, uttering to himself, he's here. He's been here all along!

He slips out and along the hallway, sidestepping people; turning, he slips outside through the side door. He starts along the side of the building to where his car is parked. He is in the chilled winter air. And it is here, in this moment, that he knows and sees what has been picking at his mind. His gait lets up, as if a switch has been thrown; a pins-and-needles chill is passing over him.

He turns to walk the other way. All parts of him but especially his forehead, temples, and ears seem to be buzzing. It isn't the pathology that was nudging his mind. He comes around the end to the red brick building; the disappointment he feels lasts but a second or two.

There he is. There is a young man, near the corner, across the street; he has just turned to walk this way. It is him; it is the person they have been looking for, the young man whose photograph is now in his pocket.

Dulac keeps walking, into the street, crossing the street, headed for the other side. He is going to bring him in, is what is on his mind. He is going to bring him in. He is going to carry him back across the street, carry him over his shoulder as the creature which has befouled the garden, and drop him before all of them to see, hold his foot on his neck, and say, this is him, this is him.

He is spotted. The suspect is alive, in shock, along the sidewalk, is backing away, moving away at once. Dulac lets up a little, but keeps walking. It is only now that he sees what a mistake he has made, what a mistake it could turn out to be if the suspect decides to run.

Oh, it is him. But he is moving away sideways, already at the corner and turning. "Just wait a minute," Dulac hears himself call out. "I'd like to talk to you. Let's talk this over." He hurries, strides hard to the corner, has him in view again.

His words don't seem to work, for the suspect keeps moving, sidestepping, looking at him as he moves. Maybe his face gives him away, Dulac thinks. For he is not calm. He is seized, he is wild to get his hands on the young man. And even as he tries to moderate his hard walking, tries to calm himself and his face, he cannot do it, can think it but cannot do it. "Just wait," he calls. "All I want to do is talk to you."

It doesn't work. It is so false; Dulac is angry with himself, as he strides, that he cannot come up with something, with the right word. Talk will not follow, he knows. He doesn't really wish to talk to the suspect. He will take him in both hands first, and turn him to the gound, handcuff him. That's what he will do. If only he had his beeper, which at that moment is in the door pocket of his car. "You, stop. Right now! I'm a police officer!"

It's the old standby, and it doesn't work. Not this time. It is even less effective, he sees, than his previous approach, for the young man is moving more certainly away, looking over his shoulder as he does so, appearing terrified, increasing the distance between them to forty or fifty or sixty feet.

"Vernon!" Dulac calls. "We know who you are, we know what you've done. Just stop now; we"ll talk about it."

Nor does this work. Looking more charged than ever, more terrified, the suspect keeps moving, is all but running as they are approaching the next corner. Here he angles into the street, as if aiming to cross at the coming corner. He slips around a moving car, as Dulac also angles into the street. "Listen you, stop right there!" Dulac calls after him, not disguising any of his anger this time. "Don't turn that corner. *Halt!*" he bellows.

He is disobeyed; the suspect is out of sight. Half running now, Dulac moves after him, headed for the corner, working to unlatch his pistol.

Coming around the edge of a building, Dulac presses after him, sees him angling across this street as well, receiving a honk from an oncoming Mercedes. On a sinking feeling, Dulac sees that the worst possible small-town thing is happening, that he is caught up in a foot race with a twenty-two-year-old man who is determined to run away from him. Nor can he get off a shot here, and he works to relatch his pistol as he moves. And he bellows as he moves, *"Halt! Police! Stop that man!"*

Few people are there and no one puts anything together anyway. Dulac presses after him, however much his lungs are already begging for air. He cannot see any alternative—if he stopped to call for help he would lose him—and he still has him in sight. He presses on. He thinks how it's like a lousy television show. Only no one knows about the lung capacity of old cops. *Goddamn sonofabitch!* His lungs hurt; they seem able to draw in but slivers of air.

He keeps on, jogging some, gasping. *"Halt!"* he calls again.

Nothing happens. The suspect is a block and a half away; he keeps going, keeps looking over his shoulder, keeps going, keeps going.

So does Dulac keep going, however staggered his pace, as new anger is in him. *You sonofabitch you,* he is saying to himself as he staggers on. *You sonofagoddamnbitch* . . . He slogs on.

TWENTY-TWO

"WELL, I can't believe *you!*" Claire cries at him. "You think I should just let you run to him with open arms? Is that what you think? After all we've been through? Don't worry, I won't have him arrested. I wouldn't do that. But he has no right coming here! He has no right having anything to do with you or with Eric! *He gave up that right—years ago!*"

Matt knew her reaction would be strong, but he did not expect her to go berserk. They are at John and Betty's, where he walked after telephoning and having Betty say that yes, his mother was there. He and his mother are alone in the kitchen and he has only passed on the message, his father's request; still he is feeling hurt and confused himself, as if he is the one who is at fault. Now, even as he knows it will hurt his mother in turn, he says to her, "He's still my father."

She blinks. He expects her to cry out again. She doesn't. She says, "Matt, every time he failed to send any money. Every time he failed to help in any way. He gave up the right of being your father. I'm sorry."

"Okay, forget it," Matt says.

"Every Christmas—every birthday—when he did not send you a gift or even a card, he gave up that right. Now you seem to think it's okay for him to come back here and act like a father."

"Forget it," Matt says, and knows that he is the one who is breaking now, again, and is going to cry. "All I said is that he said he wanted to come. God, I just can't stand this." In tears, Matt is turning to find the door.

"Where are you going?" his mother says.

"I don't know," he cries. "I'm just going. I'm going home. Why should I be here?"

"Matt, Betty and John have gone out of their—"

"*I don't care,*" Matt cries. "*I just don't care. I can't stand all this.*"

His mother stares at him. "Matt, let me tell you what I can't stand," she says. "I'm trying to order a casket and funeral. Without any money. I'm trying to see if the police department will sign for us—if there is some program for people who don't have anything. I can't tell Betty because it's too humiliating for me. Because she's done everything for us. Did you know that? Because your father poured every penny he ever earned down his throat. Did you know that? Because he didn't care if his two sons were fed or clothed, or if they were dead or alive. That's what I can't stand. I'll tell you something else, too. I know you won't want to hear it but it's the truth. So help me God, it's the truth. If it weren't for the man you say is your father—that wonderful little boy, who is your brother, who loved you, would be alive. Right now. That is the God's truth. When he went away, when he did what he did—this is what it came to. *Do you know that?*"

Matt stands there weeping. "I don't know anything," he says then. "I don't know anything. All I know is I can't take this anymore. It's all I've heard all my life. Why is he so bad? He's my father. Why does everything have to be so awful? *Why?*"

Now Claire is the one affected, and she says, "Oh, Matt, please don't say that."

"Okay, I won't. Who cares?"

"Matt, where are you going?"

"I'm going home. He's going to call back and I'm going home. Because I said I would and I'm going to. You're not going to stop me. Because I said I was going to do that; I said I was going to be there and that's what I'm going to do."

He leaves. Going through the door, he hears her say, "Matt, I'm so sorry you feel like that—"

Matt walks away, returns in the direction of home. It's all money, he is thinking. Everything is money. It's all it is. It's money. It's just money. Everything is just money and being poor.

TWENTY-THREE

VERNON IS LUNGING ON. He hardly looks back anymore. Salt and tears and perspiration are in the way, making visibility an on-again, off-again blur. At the same time there seem to be moths in his throat. They are fluttering there, reproducing there, not allowing air or even moisture as he lunges on, as his lungs squeal for air, as he keeps walking-running, running-walking, over sidewalk, past parking meters, down the wrong way on a one-way street, moving, nearly stumbling, into and around an occasional pedestrian, between parked cars, past store windows, thinking oh God, oh God, what to do, what to do . . . ?

He staggers and stumbles on. He crosses an intersection. Now he is going uphill. His legs do not wish to move anymore, but he keeps lifting them one after the other, seeming to think only that he must get away, he must get away, because he doesn't want to die, he doesn't want to be hurt, and he will know what to do, if he gets away he will know what to do . . . He can't even think now, but if he gets away he will know what to do.

As in a dream, as on a treadmill in a dream of running to escape, to escape the Viet Cong with their bamboo knives, he finds himself filled with a sensation of going nowhere, making no progress as they close on him and are going to torture him, are going to slice and shred his skin and penis with razor blades of bamboo. Oh it was so rude not to stop and talk when he was asked to, it was so impolite to run off even if it was his legs, or his stomach, doing the running just because they were so frightened and couldn't do anything else. Why didn't he stop if he only wanted to talk? Why did he keep coming after him if he only wanted to talk? What sense did that make?

His scalp is ringing as he staggers on. He seems to hear nothing anymore. He tries to look again, to see if the man is still coming after him, but turning his head he perceives only salted sweat in his eyes, sees nothing, and tries to rub his eyes free of the stinging, only making it worse, as he drags on, his legs seeming to remain on each step a slight distance behind him while his lungs squeal and squeal and squeal.

Continuing up the hill, climbing up the long gradual hill before him, dragging his feet along, he has to stop, let himself stop as he bends over at the waist, gripping his knees in his hands, nearly toppling, weaving some as he tries, works to draw in oxygen. And is crying to himself. Oh, God, please forgive me, please forgive me, as he gets himself partially straightened upright again, and walking on again, dragging his feet as he continues to gasp for air, telling himself to keep going, to keep going, at all costs to keep going.

A rare car passes, going the other way, as he is staggering out of the downtown area. The river is to his right, the great width of water across to Maine, and he glimpses a freighter, maybe two freighters, tied there along the docks, and a small mountain of white salt, too, a world of salt half a dozen stories high and a block long which it seems to take him a lifetime to pass.

Ahead then, as the uphill grade continues, there are open spaces and no more buildings next to the road. He keeps dragging and stumbling on, telling himself not to look back and not to give up now, to keep going at all costs, to keep going.

He goes on. It is as he pulls up and bends over yet again in an attempt to draw in air, and as he is telling himself not to look back, not to look back, that he swivels some in his pain and lifts his eyes enough to gaze down the hill he has been climbing, that he sees the big detective walking after him, not wearing a coat anymore and not running as he is coming uphill, but walking, still walking after him, oh dear God, still walking after him.

Vernon presses on once more, going uphill one step at a time, and feeling yet again that he is on a treadmill and making no progress. Going on. Going on. Going on. Covering a distance of a yard, and in time a distance of another yard. And crying to himself yet again in confusion and in panic, crying without shedding any tears, crying, dear God, to be left alone, to be given a chance to think, that's all, to be given a chance to think, to be left alone and given a chance to think dear God of what in the world to do.

He gains added yards, in time, but is feeling sickness now in his stomach with the man behind him. *Why doesn't he leave me alone!* If a car appeared, he thinks, he would try to get in front of it, try to be hit by it, to get away from that which is behind him.

Alas then, as he goes, he happens to get his eyes enough above sea level to realize there is something overhead in the air, and so it is that he glimpses the high new bridge, the long green bridge up there reaching and curving through the sky on its way to Maine a mile or so away. The bridge inspires him; he doesn't know why, but the bridge inspires him. He is on a small unused road, he sees, which passes under the great overhead structure. Yet it is something. And as he staggers in the direction of the bridge, he sees that there are fields of brush and weeds spreading away from the roadside here, reaching down over the riverbank, in among sheds and rail sidings there, and spreading in under the bridge itself in its oddly deceptive distance ahead, for even as he moves and moves, gains yard after yard, the bridge seems always to remain in the distance, to lift higher into the sky but to remain evermore ahead, evermore beyond reach. Is he moving? he wonders. Is he moving at all? Why doesn't he come under the bridge? How can he do anything at all if he never comes under the bridge?

He is vomiting then. He hasn't looked back, but something of the man suddenly grabbing him from behind has come into his throat and has him vomiting and heaving to get it out. Nor does he stop or go on either; rather he weaves in a near circle as he vomits and pulls strings of spittle and saliva from his throat, as he crouches and duck-walks and tries to spit free the bile catching in his throat, and tries still to go on.

And does. And doesn't look back. Goes on. Drags his feet. Aims for the weeds and world of brush under the bridge. Goes on, still believing he can make it in under the bridge, if he will only ever get there.

TWENTY-FOUR

LEAVING PAVEMENT, staggering into brush, weeds, and sand under the bridge, Dulac also bends at the waist and retches, tries to spit away his lifelong accumulation of cigarette tar and smoke, a string of slime he has to bite at and pull away. And he comes up looking, gasping as he keeps staggering like a drunk man, looking to see what is before him, to see where the suspect has gone, thinking, too, he may need to reach for his pistol now, may need to go for it, to knock the bastard down.

Dulac has been here before, more or less. It is an underworld under the bridge, within its overhead song, of bridge posts the size the giant sequoia trees reaching a hundred, a hundred and twenty-five feet from their concrete footings the size of garages to the bottom of the massive overhead ceiling. There are footpaths, and dirt roads for city vehicles, small and large piles of sand, pebbles, gravel, cross-stacks of creosoted ties, fences with chained gates, a maze of dozens of obstructions behind which to hide, behind which to attempt to recover some wind, as he is attempting to do himself as he sways and staggers forward and sideways one step at a time, looking, scanning, trying to see anything, to pick up any movement or color.

Thinking, too, uttering to himself, *goddamn him, goddamn him!* And thinking for the first time, even though he withdrew his pistol earlier, of firing a round through the suspect, knocking him down forever, putting a hole through his chest or stomach through which a garden hose might easily slide, leaving a gloss over his eyes—but not removing his pistol this time, not yet at least, as he continues to scan for telltale signs.

He tries to hold still to listen, too, but can draw in nothing above the constant singing-wire sound of so many car tires overhead or between his own massive mouth and nostril intakes of air, his facial openings foaming and flaring like a beast's, then granting the momentary passage of quiet.

In merely a moment, though, as he continues to sidestep in his attempt to regain breath, to recapture equilibrium, he spots something, glimpses a flash of movement, of color, somewhat to the left, back in the direction of the street. Already, automatically, carefully, he has reached to unlatch, to touch his pistol as he is pivoting to scan that angle, to look to identify what he saw, and where, to see more, thinking *he's here! He's here! That wasn't a goddamn bird—he's here!*

He takes a step in that direction. His footsteps cannot be heard. He decides to go ahead and remove his weapon and does so. He is trying to?

think, trying to calculate something. Anything. He can't hear me, he thinks. He will have to look, he will have to look. From that footing? The next footing? The next? They look side by side from here. From that roll of weeds, those piles of washed stones? A foolish move, he tells himself. A foolish move to move at all, because his inclination had been to continue down through the maze to the railroad tracks, to the tidal river flowing by, to look for him there. He wouldn't have guessed that he'd double back.

He takes more steps, watching, looking hard. He kneels, inhaling, exhaling, watching. He is alive, he thinks of himself. His heart has not failed him. He is alive and breathing well enough now, and that sonofabitch is here before him somewhere, here within a thirty- or forty-degree angle. The sound of car tires keeps singing; there is nothing else to hear. He straightens, takes more careful steps.

It's time to be extraordinarily alert, he thinks. Each second. Eyes alive. Stalk that sonofabitch. He is here. He is within a hundred feet. Give all to this. All concentration. Let this speak to Eric Wells, he thinks. Do this well. Let this mean something.

Dulac takes more steps, pauses, takes more steps, slowly and carefully, watching. The wolf is right here, he tells himself. Believe it. Believe in yourself. The fucking wolf has killed and eaten Little Red Riding Hood and you are going to take the wolf. It is here, and you are the hunter in the forest, you are *they* and it is not your option to lose concentration. You will not; you will pause and hold and take steps, and pause and hold and take steps, and you will flush the sonfabitch.

His approach seems not to work, however. No sound may be heard under the singing tires, and his stalking seems not to work. He has to flush him, he thinks. He cannot walk past him, or let him burrow in and not flush him. He cannot do that.

He speaks. On a sudden thought that he can flush him with words, if not with the sound of his footsteps, he hears himself as if another person call out, "Vernon—I know you're here!"

Nothing happens. Scanning, concentrating on the angle, staying in, creating its vortex as he takes more steps, he calls out, "I know you're here. Why don't you come out? I don't know exactly where you are, but I know you're here."

He takes more steps. His pistol, hanging in his right hand, his police .38, feels as heavy as a brick. "I don't want to hurt you," he calls out. "I want to talk to you. I don't want to hurt you."

He pauses, listens and watches. Nothing happens.

"*Stop walking! I can see you!*" a voice suddenly shouts.

Dulac stops. He crouches some, has lifted the pistol some, although it remains in one hand, is looking, studying, trying to trace the sound. "I want to talk," he calls out. "That's all."

It doesn't work; nothing happens.

He takes another step then, and another. *"Stop right there!"* the voice cries out again.

Dulac stops—holds. He has him now, he thinks. Washed pebbles, he thinks. He has him now. He takes another step.

"If you only want to talk, why do you keep walking!" the voice wails at him.

Dulac's focus homes in on the pile of washed pebbles, a pile the size of a car, the right side, he thinks, yes, he thinks; he takes another step.

He breaks! There he goes. From the left. He breaks into a run through other obstructions; as Dulac swings on him, tries as he squeezes off a round to keep him in view, he knows he has missed, doesn't know where the round may have hit, is running at once himself, loping, jumping to the side to see if he can get another angle on him, can spot him in an opening.

He does glimpse him again. Jogging, pistol down, passing through a row of the great reinforced concrete posts, he sees him for just a second, a blink or two, as he is running back across the street. Dulac forces his own legs back into motion, lifts them one after another and curses himself again for not being able to say the right thing. And he remarks to himself as he runs, tells himself not even to think that the suspect is a lifetime younger. Think only that the suspect will quit first, he tells himself. Think only that, that he is frightened and he will quit first and you will overtake him and take him back. Think only that. Think that if he should get away, another child's life will be taken, because you were not good enough, because you did not give all there was to give when it counted. Think that.

He loses sight of him and regains sight. He jogs on, loses sight again, but maintains his line. He chugs and slogs through weeds, and coming to the road again, suddenly—its nearness surprises him—he sees the suspect already across the street and starting up the hill there next to the solid bridge foundation which fills that side of the road. There is no clear shot here, and he begins to attempt to return his weapon to its holster as he is running into the street, but seeing a car coming on holds up both hands, the pistol in his right, skyward—which, he realizes too late, only terrifies the driver, a woman, the only passenger, sending her squealing rubber around him—as he shouts after her, *"Stop, help, police emergency!"*

He goes on, relatching his pistol. Beside the bridge foundation—a massive stone understructure with the bulk of a pyramid—is a path going up the long gradual hill among scrubby stunted trees and brush, and there is the suspect, on the path, almost on all fours, digging and pulling—Dulac is already after him—disappearing from view again within larger trees and brush.

Too soon, going up the hill, Dulac's legs go heavy on him, and he is using his hands, too, to dig and pull as he presses on. Don't give up now, he says to himself. Make him do it. Don't give up.

Face down, he stays after him. Face up, he glimpses him, sees him, and returning face down, for the greater ease of climbing it gives him, he presses on. He digs, claws his hands, his fingers and fingernails, into weeds, shards of dirt and pebbles, scraps of glass, and cries to himself deeply within, *I'm going to get you, you sonofabitch, I'm going to get you*, even as he knows, perhaps more deeply within, that he isn't entirely certain now, which knowledge is already sending through him a new disappointment and a new urgency, as he keeps gasping, keeps clawing and pushing up with the sides of his feet, keeps crying to himself to believe, to persevere.

TWENTY-FIVE

MATT IS IN THE KITCHEN. He has just walked in, is in his jacket still, and is simply standing there. His odd frame of mind is more or less on school, of all places. On Mr. Kazur, who is renowned for always talking politics, current affairs, criticizing the President. Matt doesn't altogether understand the left or right of the man's position, but his notion is that what he is thinking now would anger the teacher. Being poor. He could write a report and present it in Mr. Kazur's face on the consequences of being poor, as he realizes the telephone is ringing.

It isn't his father, though, and his heart sinks. Rather it is a woman calling—from the police department—a woman who seems to know him, to know everything, even to know without asking that his mother is not at home.

"Your father asked me to call," she says. "He wanted you to know that he's spoken to us here, and that he will be flying into Portland this evening, and that he'll be in touch with you tomorrow sometime."

"He's flying to Portland?" Matt says, as if talking long-distance again and missing words and phrases.

"That's right, this evening," the woman says. "Now the problem is, if there is a problem—I'm not sure he quite understands this. It isn't necessarily in our jurisdiction to decide what to do about his being in arrears. Do you understand? If he does call there, could you pass that on to him?"

"He's not going to call?" Matt says. In his disappointment, he is confused by what the woman is saying.

A pause follows. More gently then the woman says, "You don't understand, do you?"

Matt doesn't say; he doesn't know what to say.

"Oh, my," the woman says.

Arrears . . . arrested, Matt is thinking.

"Matt, listen," the woman says. "Let me try again. He asked, your father asked, if we'd have him arrested. I said no, *we* wouldn't. But that doesn't mean someone else might not arrest him. Because the case was never in our jurisdiction. So, if he calls—"

"I understand," Matt says.

"Are you sure?"

"Sure. But if he's not going to call, what difference does it make?"

Now it is the woman who is silent. At last, she says, "Matt, I just wanted you to know."

Off the phone, Matt stands there. Well, his father isn't going to call, he thinks. But he did ask that woman to call and tell him he was coming. That was something, wasn't it? Why waste money on another long-distance call? At least he asked that woman to call and tell him that he was coming.

TWENTY-SIX

VERNON'S MIND WILL not come down to him. He is running; he knows that he is running, that he is digging, pulling, crying to get away from that man, that his hands and feet are grabbing into dirt and weeds, yet his mind is apart, is running a distance above his madly working throat and lungs. Nor does it seem his mind at all, as he climbs and pulls, but his mother's mind. Her mind and eyes are within his own as he climbs, slides and climbs up the ragged path, letting him know that he has really done it this time, that she doesn't know if she can help him this time, and as he struggles on, it seems that neither of them will leave him alone, will let him think for a second.

He slides to his belly, to his chin, and grabs weeds again, gains footholds, to push on. He keeps slipping and falling, bruising his fingers and palms, his knees and shins, his feet sliding, his left ankle paining and throbbing from jamming against something hard. She clings, allowing him no way to duck under her; the big detective stays at his back, too, stays there and stays there so he keeps feeling like he is going to explode, is going to pop like a balloon if they won't leave him alone.

Sliding to his belly, he frantically unhooks his foot from something, shoots a glance back, sees the form of that man, a form like that of a bear, on all fours, climbing after him. He cries within, in his anger and disappointment. Still he pushes on, keeps himself moving through the weeds and brush, at no greater speed than that of a turtle, as it comes to him that he knows more than she does now, that is why she can't help him, because he knows more than she, knows of peace of mind, of salvation, of death, and that no one can help him now.

He continues, as if alone. Losing momentary strength and conviction, he collapses for several seconds, gasping and crying, praying to be left alone by the man, and pushing himself up, returns to crawling and clawing, until he collapses to his face and belly yet again. But he returns to crawling and clawing still again, even as he has little sense of what it is that is making him go on.

Nor, in the next moment, does he seem to know who he is, or where he is, or what he is doing or why. He feels terribly hot, as if he has entered the mouth of a furnace, and he sees that he is opposite the highway railing, is coming opposite the highway surface, where cars are roaring by one after another, two by two, by three, where ground and highway and bridge all merge. On something of a new charge, he gets himself over the ground and over crushed rock and gets a hand on the steel railing, but cannot pull himself higher and clings a moment with knees and one side in the crushed rock. The railing would be less than waist-high if he were standing on the other side, in the breakdown lane, but he has to give up his handgrip on the cold metal and crawl and pull along another six feet, or eight feet, before he can make headway and gain the footing he needs to pull himself up to the lip of the pavement and slide his belly and his legs over the railing, into a collapsed crouch on the pavement, within the immediate *zing-zing* of passing cars, facing uphill yet again, looking up yet another long and gradual hill, but this one altogether over pavement and in the direction of the State of Maine, a mile or so away.

Thus, not even looking to see if the grizzly bear is still after him, Vernon begins moving his feet one after another over the pavement, bending at the waist, looking to the pavement, in the flow of air here, gasping, dragging one foot forward and then the other, upon the skyward angle and curve of the bridge, and feeling some glimmer of hope, a new toss of the dice, until, suddenly, there is a horn blast from one of the passing cars, and all seems dashed, all seems lost yet again as his heart cries out to the unseen driver, *Why did you do that? Oh God, why did you do that?*

He has to look then, has to take a glimpse back to see if he has been seen, and all his worst fears come home to him, for there is the grizzly bear of a man, draped over the railing, lying over the railing and looking after him, sliding over the railing, he sees then, sliding into a pile on the pavement of the breakdown lane and beginning at once to strive to get himself upright again, sending the shock of death directly into his weary heart this time even as he is staggering on, eyes front again more or less, eyes on his knees and on the pavement between them more or less, as the nightmare of his life seems close enough to be flapping its wings not far at all above his back and shoulders and just when he thought he might be getting away.

TWENTY-SEVEN

DULAC STAGGERS, walks on sea legs head-down into the wall of air. There are posts here, square steel columns beside him every twenty-five or thirty feet, aimed upward into the sky. And there is the constant song, the *whoom! whoom!* of cars passing within a dozen feet of him, a sense of being in a massive room, a precarious swaying room in the sky, far above the railroad tracks, above the deep, ocean green river, so high, so precarious that walking here makes it seem foolhardy to proceed with anything as sizeable as an automobile, although a dangerous journey of that kind, at fifty miles an hour, gets over much more quickly than staggering and weaving along one footfall at a time.

Head down into the air, he keeps going. One yard, and another yard. With more strength in his arms than in his legs, he reaches literally, every third or fourth step, to help his thighs along with his hands, to sustain movement, not to give up, not to be beaten, at least not yet. Don't think about it, he tells himself. Move. Don't think. Move.

As he lifts his face once more into the wind, however, he cannot believe what he sees. Nothing. He sees nothing. There is no suspect. The suspect is no longer ahead of him as he has been all along—out there sixty or eighty yards ahead, struggling and staggering at an equal pace. Nor is he, so far as Dulac can tell, in a pile on the pavement, in exhaustion or surrender. And the cars continue to whip past him; there has been no break in their rhythm; there's no way he could have been picked up.

He fears the suspect has jumped; the fear laces through him with the same sensation he felt earlier when he realized, alas, that he was the one on the sidewalk opposite the station. He fears he has stepped from the bridge, has stepped to his death, has slipped over the railing to win a final round, to deny him the satisfaction he has so yearned for of gripping him by the neck, taking him in, leveling charges.

Dulac goes on, keeping his eyes up enough now in the wind, however much it slows his progress, to look around, to look before him and to the side. He goes on. He draws another horn toot from a passing car, thinks to say to them, yes, this is all in fun, an afternoon stroll, thinks, too, to give them the finger, believing he has lost the suspect, pressing on with the wind in his eyes, nose, and mouth, the roar in his ears, the sensation of losing running down through him as he sees he is approaching the summit of the bridge.

Nor does he see the suspect or any sign of him. But then an answer begins to come to him in the face of a child, a passenger in a passing car, a boy of eight or ten. The boy has seen something. His head has jerked to the side to see again whatever it was that startled his attention.

Dulac cannot spot it. He goes on. It is the summit of the bridge, its crest he is on now; looking to the cars zipping by, he sees other faces startled by something, trying for a second look. A look *up*. Their quick looks are shooting *up*.

He sees him then. He sees the suspect. He has climbed one of the vertical steel posts. The posts are hollow, with large chain link–shaped holes on all sides, holes the size of frying pans; the suspect has used the holes as ladder steps to climb overhead. Dulac can see him through a set of holes eight or ten feet overhead; he can see his arm, reaching around the side of the post to grip where there is another opening, and yet again the pins-and-needles sensation is passing over Dulac. He has him.

He steps along. He has him. He decides against unholstering his pistol.

He steps along, watching the shape of a person clinging overhead there. He has him.

To his left, at his hand as he steps along, is the railing, a topping layer of steel over a series of cables as big around as his wrist, the cables swaying in the air. Here at the crest of the bridge the wind is the strongest, and Dulac touches a hand to the railing to keep himself from weaving as he takes the last steps to the post that is attracting the car passengers' eyes.

Expecting to see the suspect clinging overhead like a cat that has exceeded its range, Dulac, keeping a hand yet on the railing for balance, takes the last steps to the other side and turns his neck to look up. There he is, eight to ten feet overhead. His face, however, is turned into his arm in the way that he is gripping the post and is not in view. Only the hair on the back of his head is visible.

Did he think he would walk by? Dulac wonders. Did he think if he climbed up there and buried his face under his arm, he would walk by, would walk down into Maine and leave him alone?

Well, he has him, he thinks. He has him. His neck aching already from looking up, keeping his hand on the railing, Dulac looks out over the countryside, over the tops of trees going upstream, and the tops of houses beneath the trees, and the round tops of oil tanks in the distance. He has him, he thinks, although glancing down to the water, not even directly down but at an angle, glimpsing the faint turning of a whitecap and an outboard the size of his thumb moving away, he experiences a sweep through him of vertigo, a faint awareness that vertigo in itself offers the taste of death.

He looks up again at the form clinging there, and turns his head back down. Inhaling and exhaling, he is trying to settle his disoriented bearings. Don't look straight down, he tells himself. At the same time, looking up is not dissimilar to looking down; doing either he seems to lose balance.

Looking up once more, holding the railing with both hands, he calls out, "Come down. It's over."

Nothing happens; the body clings in the same way; the face does not appear. Beside them, a dozen feet away, cars blast by.

Squinting his eyes to look up again, however painful the ache in his neck, Dulac calls out, "*Goddamit, come down here. It's all over! Now!*"

Against the pain tightening into his neck, he watches, keeps watching. The suspect's face, its eyes, appear then, looking over the top of the arm. There seems to be terror in the eyes; through the air, Dulac believes he detects that the suspect has lost control, has soiled his pants.

The eyes look down. More of the face appears, a face rippled in the wind. *"I want to die,"* the face cries down to him.

Dulac has to turn his neck down again, against the accumulating pain. Looking back up,where the eyes keep staring down, he calls up, "Did you do it?" Guilt seems to Dulac in this moment to be the key question to be ascertained, as if to settle things.

"Did you do it?" he calls again.

"It was an accident," the face calls down to him.

Dulac only looks up at the suspect, in spite of the pain in his neck. The answer is amazingly disappointing to him, although he doesn't know why. He keeps looking at the eyes, at the amount of face visible up there, to see if he can see another answer.

"What kind of accident?" he calls back.

There is no reply.

Dulac stares back. Then he can stand the neck pain no more and looks out over the countryside, to relieve his neck, perhaps to think. Looking up again, he calls out, "That's a lie."

There is no response; the face just looks down at him.

"You're a liar!" Dulac shouts up at him. *"You're a liar!"*

The face only looks down at him now, seems to simply stare at him in unanswered question.

Dulac keeps looking up at him, as the pain points into his neck, then he turns his head down again. Looking back up in a moment, he calls, "Come on down."

The suspect starts down. The holes in the hollow steel posts are three to four feet apart, and stepping, moving from one and reaching to another means he has to extend the full length of his body. In his fear, though, he doesn't quite want to release his hand- or his footholds, and he tries in a way to both cling to the post and to inch or shimmy down, and as he does this, above him, an image comes up in Dulac's mind of seeing him fall to his death.

Dulac doesn't seem to actually think in these moments, as the suspect is trying to make his way down. Dulac's mind seems to be chilled in the grip of the image which has come to him and seems not to reach or to move elsewhere. Yet he will know always that other thoughts and images did pass through his mind, not of the boy or of the suspect there with his apple-colored cheeks, in his terror, but of himself, of his life, of his years growing up in Canada, an image of his father, his time in the U.S. Navy, his years on the police force.

Still holding the railing with one hand, he frees his other hand and extends it overhead to the suspect, where he is clinging to the last hole in the column before coming within reach. Dulac keeps his hand extended. He doesn't know what he is going to do.

Shifting one hand from the post, the suspect reaches with it to grip—both hands are sticky—Dulac's extended hand. Dulac grips the suspect's hand within his own.

Steadying himself, the suspect removes a foot from its perch then, to reach it downward, and as it touches the railing, settles its toe there, on a breath, he removes his other hand to reach it down to Dulac's offered hand, like a child climbing out of a tree.

Dulac may not know that he is going to do anything. Perhaps he doesn't do anything. Before the suspect's second hand arrives to take hold, however, his hand is losing its grip on the sticky hand he has been grasping, and he looks to see the open-eyed expression on the suspect's face as there is nothing holding him but his feet and he knows, they both know, that he is going to fall, that only his toes on the railing and his other toes raised to the edge of one of the holes are holding him, and Dulac is reaching to him as he is sitting backwards, as there is an expression in his eyes—flapping his arms as one does attempting to maintain balance, flapping and lurching to grip air again as Dulac is leaning to reach to him, and cannot reach him, as he folds at the waist in a last attempt to reach his toes, to reach his toe perch, and drops away, on a gasp, into the space behind him.

Dulac doesn't look out or down to see him fall, not yet at least. He is returning his free hand to the railing, to brace himself from toppling sideways, as he hears the merest cry of disappearance, the slightest whimper.

Looking into the wind at last, he sees nothing. There is a distance to the water, the air, the vertigo within him. He sees something then. A small white spash occurs, more to one side than he would have guessed, and he looks up once more, looks upstream against an elevator-dropping sensation rushing through him in this moment, through his brain, down through his life, as he holds tightly, as he braces himself in the ceaseless wind.

HOURS HAVE SLIPPED AWAY; darkness is overall now.

Here is a passenger plane, a Boeing 727, lowering over the dotted lights of coastal highways, offering in its landing pattern out over the dark ocean a night view of Portland, Maine. The plane, a connecting flight from Newark, is all at once, on a line, passing lights, buildings, and trees as high as itself, until its wheels hit and skid, its engines squeal in reverse, and at last, a teetering finned whale with rows of seats in its belly and portholes along its sides, it dips and drifts and rolls uncertainly over the tarmac on its way to the terminal.

At a window seat, in the smoking section in the rear, is a man of forty-nine with a weather-worn face, wearing a western shirt with mother-of-pearl snaps under a mismatching suit coat, open at his dark throat. Not anxious to leave the plane, he watches through the small window at his side, seeing nothing of any greater significance than small ground lights of red and blue, while the other passengers are getting to their feet and unloading belongings from overhead compartments.

It's a new airport, different from anything he ever saw here before. Noticing the highlighted overlapping tails of other planes, and glimpsing a portion of the city skyline in the distance, he wonders, in a way, as he does almost every day of his life still, if things might not have picked up and straightened out for him here if he'd stuck around.

This is Warren Wells. A Maine native, he is coming back tonight for the first time in over seven years. He is the father of two young sons, one of them due to be buried and the other grown up, more or less. Two sons and a previous life. A hometown and a home state. All of which he'd never quite stopped remembering, not for a minute it seemed, although it was true, all these years had slipped by, and it was true, too, that no one would believe him.

In the seat to his right, waiting for him, is his second wife, Vivian—Vi, he calls her—who has never been so far north or seen snow before, and who may be in no more of a hurry than he is to leave the plane and face whatever it is they have to face. "I guess it's Portland," Warren says to her. "Doesn't look like it."

"You don't see your friends?" she says.

"Not from here," he says.

The plane is three-fourths empty by now and she says, "Come on, Warren, let's just go and do what we have to do."

She is up from her seat, giving him room to move into the aisle from his, as he finally presses the release on his seat belt and follows. They retrieve their bags from an overhead compartment, as Vi says, "Come on, your friends will think you didn't make the flight."

As Vi is starting along the aisle and he would follow, he holds his bag on an arm, slides a zipper, and half turning his shoulder, slips out a pint in a paper bag, uncaps it, throws off a sizeable shot, wheezes, blinks his tired, watering eyes, and returns all to its place as he moves on along the aisle to close the gap. Vi seems not to have noticed.

Close to her there is still a short line of people deplaning, and taking in a whiff of the sharply chilled Maine air, Warren seems to know in his heart that the trip is a hopeless mistake. For an instant, he wonders if they might stay on the plane, and fly back south just as they had flown north. Fly anywhere, he thinks, as he follows, as emotions he had forgotten were his seem to be returning to him in the familiar misted air. It's a mistake, he thinks. All his life here, he was pressed and crowded. As if it was any different anywhere else, he thinks. Claire and the two boys. He had loved them, and, it was true, he had run out on them, had worked at not loving them. Nothing in his life had ever really worked out. And it was no one's fault but his own.

Pausing, turning to him then as they are the last passengers making their way into the terminal, Vi whispers, "No more drinking, Warren, the rest of the time we're here, or I'm going right back to Louisiana."

They are on carpeting, as they enter a waiting area and Warren is looking ahead for Bill and Ceil Arthur, his friends from the old days, who had telephoned him about Eric coming up missing and about the discovery of his body. He lets Vi move about half a step ahead of him. He will do, he knows, what she has told him to do. As much as he is able.

He doesn't see Bill and Ceil, but he knows in the instant of seeing two men in topcoats who lift ever so lightly away from a painted wall and start in his direction that something is wrong—even as he doesn't know yet just what it is. He is trembling. Bill and Ceil aren't there. He looks to be sure Vi is close at hand, as he sees the two men coming on. He pauses and wants Vi to pause with him or turn back with him, but she hasn't tuned in to anything and is walking on. "Vi," he says. He is looking at the men, though, and in this instant has the thought that his life is not worth the match it might take to light it and burn it up. Is there any way he can get to the bottle in his bag and have another drink?

Vi has turned. "The police," he says.

The two men close on him, as does Vi, who seems ignorant yet of what is happening. "Warren Wells?" one of the men says in an almost friendly voice.

"Yessir," he says, as if he is a Southerner.

"Sir, would you step over here, please. County Sheriff's Department, Mr. Wells. Mrs. Wells?" the man adds to Vi.

"Some friends were supposed to meet us," Warren says.

"They're just ahead, Mr. Wells. You can speak to them in a minute, as we go through."

"We were told no charges would be pressed," Vi says.

"The sheriff's office has issued a warrant, ma'am, so we will be taking Mr. Wells into custody, where he will have the right—"

"We were told that his wife—his former wife—was not going to press any charges! My God!"

"Mr. Wells's former wife doesn't administer the law, ma'am," the man says. "I'm sorry. Any decision about charges pending against Mr. Wells will be decided by the prosecuting attorney for the county and by a judge. Now, ma'am, you'll be able to join your friends here, if you like. We'll be taking Mr. Wells to the County Building, where you can see him, if you wish to, after he is booked."

"My God," Vi says, with anger, even as her eyes have filled.

"Honey, it's okay," Warren says.

"She said she wasn't going to press any charges," Vi says. "My God, he just came here to go to his son's funeral. To see his other son."

"I'm very sorry, ma'am," the man says. Turning then, as if to draw Warren a step away from her, he says, "Mr. Wells, I'm going to handcuff your right hand to my left. And we're going to have to frisk you, if you'd just step over this way, please."

There are the man's handcuffs, as he removes them from under his suit coat.

"Good God," Vi says. "He's a broken man; give him a chance."

"Oh, Vi," Warren says.

HERE AFTER DARK, leaving the station and driving through the small city, it occurs to Dulac that he loves his wife and that he is no longer in love with Shirley Moss. Yesterday and today he has fallen out of love with Shirley, and in the loss he is experiencing he feels solitary and old.

He desires to be home. He desires to be with Beatrice, and to make up with her, even if she may not know—he gives no thought to actually telling her—what it is he is doing. At most, he knows, he will tell her that he needs her tonight, that he needs badly the abstraction they refer to as home. He will make no attempt to explain any of the complicated matters or degrees of fidelity as he has known them, nor any of the characteristics of reach and responsibility on the bridge, however much the two remain alive and troubling in his very heart.

As he pulls over at the house of Claire Wells's friends, the idea of going out with Beatrice for a drink comes to mind and offers a promise of comfort. Several drinks, he thinks. With Beatrice, whom he does love, loves truly when all is said and done. There is that country music place down on the river and they can go there and have some drinks and hear the jukebox speak of going back to Luckenbach, Texas, with Waylon and Willie and the boys.

He has this last chore. After so much paperwork, this will be his last item of work for the day, and even if he may not be free, he will be off-duty.

Tapping on the door, let into an entryway by the woman, he is told that Claire is upstairs and she will go and call her down. As he asks where Matt is and the woman says he is in the basement—did he want to see him?—Dulac tells her no, no, he just wondered if he was there.

Coming downstairs, Claire Wells appears entirely confused as he greets her, and then she says to him in a low voice. "Can we talk outside?"

He tells her yes, of course, and as they step outside into the chilled night air, he asks her if she'd like to sit in the car. She says yes and they walk to the car, with her friends' lighted house behind them, where he opens the door on the passenger side for her to get in.

Going around, getting into the car himself, he says, "I'm sorry about your former husband's arrest."

She makes no response to this, so he lets it drop. He had been prepared to explain that once her former husband signed an agreement to make up the child support payments—which would mean nothing more than his word, anyway, because they'd have to let him return to Louisiana to his job—he would be released to attend the funeral service. Such at least was his understanding from the authorities in Maine.

They sit in silence. It's her meeting, Dulac is thinking. In this moment, though, he sees again the brief white splash in the swollen green water far below. He experiences, too, the momentary dropping of the elevator. "What's the problem, Claire?" he says to her.

"It's hard for me to say," she says.

"I realize that, Claire. That's okay. What is it?"

"I don't have any money," she says.

A moment passes, and she adds, "I wondered if there might be some city agency I could borrow from to pay for Eric's funeral and burial? I will certainly repay the money."

There is no such agency, and Dulac responds by saying, "What about Eric's father? Apparently he doesn't have any money, but he does have a job. We could have him—"

"No," she says. "No. I couldn't do it. I don't want his money. I want to bury my son myself."

On a pause, Dulac says, "There's no one you can borrow from?"

"I just can't ask Betty and John. I can't do that. They've done so much for me. I don't want to lose them as friends. I just thought, if there was some agency I could borrow from, then I would repay the money as soon as I can. Matt could get a job, too, and we could take care of it."

Dulac pauses again, before he hears himself say, "Well, there is an emergency fund at the police department. I'll tell you what you do. You go ahead and order what you need; charge it to the Portsmouth Police Department. I'll call the funeral home in the morning, so they'll know. Then you just use my name. Okay? So just put it out of your mind for now. Tell them to refer all bills to me, care of the Portsmouth Police Department."

After a moment, seeing her back to the front door and saying good night, Dulac leaves to drive home at last, to see if he may come back down to earth from whatever odd dimension it is he seems to be traversing. He longs all the more to be with Beatrice. She will forgive him. At last, and unlike any other person—it is the product of their years together—she will forgive him. They will go out, go to Jimmy's on the river, and he will tell her how he has committed their savings—they have about three thousand dollars in the credit union—to pay for a funeral, and she will look at him and shake her head at him, but will remain on his side in her way, and they will go ahead and have too many drinks, and probably go out on the small lighted floor and cling to each other in some lumbering forgotten dance of their life together—two oversized creatures seeking equilibrium, matched as a pair, the King and Queen of their bungalow on their small street in their small town—but he will not, not now or ever, reveal to her any more than a little of what he knows.

THIRTY

MATT IS DIALING in a new station. The old radio, repainted avocado by hand and shaped like a toaster, is on a littered workbench in John and Betty's basement. Matt has been reluctant to change the radio's setting, as he had been reluctant to turn the radio on in the first place, for it had been presumed that he came down here to be by himself, to be alone with thoughts of his brother.

In truth, he knows, he is here to be away from all that is going on upstairs. He'd feel okay. Almost okay. Then someone—his mother usually—would start in and her sobbing would have tears coming up in his own throat, headed for his eyes. He didn't want to cry anymore. He didn't want to hurt anymore. Eric himself, he has thought, wouldn't want to be caught in that scene upstairs. It was at times like these, in fact, in odd situations and in strangers' houses, that they did more together, had more fun as brothers, than at any other time. And down here now, it isn't so bad. It's like one of those good times, those fun times. And so he is alone with thoughts of his brother.

It is as Matt is standing with his back to the workbench then that a radio news report comes on, and against an initial urge to search for more music—he's heard and seen enough reports already—he lets the radio have its way. He stands and hears.

The suspected killer of twelve-year-old Eric Wells of Portsmouth has been identified as Vernon R. Fischer of Laconia. The body of the twenty-two-year-old senior honors student, who died late this afternoon in a death leap from the I-95 bridge between New Hampshire and Maine, has been recovered from the Piscataqua River by state police and Coast Guard crewmen. Chased by foot onto the bridge by Portsmouth Police Lieutenant Gilbert Dulac, the ten-year resident of the state is reported to have leaped from the bridge to elude capture.

362

*Although they are continuing their investigation, Portsmouth po-
lice speculate that this is the final chapter in a bizarre abduction-
murder case which has stunned the Seacoast area over the past several days, beginning on Saturday evening when the twelve-year-old
boy disappeared while walking home. His sexually molested body
was discovered before noon today next to the parking lot of an office
supplies store on Islington Street, less than two blocks from where he
disappeared.*

*In a related story, forty-nine-year-old Warren Wells, reportedly of
New Orleans and the father of the victim, was arrested this evening
by York County, Maine, authorities only moments after he stepped
off a plane at Portland National Airport. He is charged with being
over twenty-six thousand dollars in arrears on support payments, a
felony carrying a maximum sentence of three years in prison upon
conviction. A spokesman for the County Sheriff's office reports that
the boy's father will be kept overnight in the county jail but will be
released, on his own recognizance, to attend his son's funeral. Eric
Wells's father is described by authorities as being a man with a lot of
personal problems who is very upset and heartbroken about his son's
death. At the same time, the bereaved father will be asked to agree to
a twenty-five-thousand-dollar personal bond, which requires no posting of money, and to sign a pledge to comply with a court order to
bring overdue support payments up to date. Wells and his former
wife, Claire, were divorced in June 1974.*

Most of his friends, most of the kids in school, Matt knows, would not
have tolerated even that much talking before searching for sounds along
the dial rather than words. Even those words. He knows, too, has a
glimpse in this moment, that by Monday in school the incident, the story
of his brother, will be forgotten and life will be rolling along as it always
has, toward Friday or Saturday, and as it says in all the songs, he will be
the only one who remembers. He and his mother. Maybe his father, too.
And he knows, too, at last, that his mother was right after all, and that he
will not dislike his father for it, but his father could have saved them all,
long ago, could have led them elsewhere than here, and he failed.

Matt knows this as he stands here. A moment standing before a clut-
tered workbench in a basement, while a radio plays and he is alone with
his thoughts and his thoughts of his brother. He has stood here through
the news, and perhaps some of it was news to him, although he has taken
it in rather as he takes in music, as a commodity to feel more than to
weigh and measure, as a shivering over his skin, a stillness in his mind.

He is on his own now, he thinks. More or less. Well, no more or less
about it. It's true. It is what he knows as he stands here. He is on his own
now.

AFTERWORD
Going Home

JULY 1981

TERI FISCHER

Getting rid of his clothes was easy. So was selling his car, for next to nothing. What has her feeling uncertain is what she is doing now, taking this drive this evening, out of town, to dispose of his personal belongings. Letters, photographs, keepsakes, his papers from school. They are in the trunk behind her, in cardboard boxes of odd sizes. The final contents of his wallet are there, too, all but two fives and two singles she removed at last, just an hour ago, separating them from each other and folding them over three times, as she always folded money, and pushing the folds into the rear left pocket of her jeans.

The urn with his ashes is in the trunk, too, lodged between boxes. She is taking it along to throw it away. Screw it, she has said to herself at last, concerning the urn. She has to get rid of it. She cannot stand having it in the house, speaking to her, *telling on her*, it seems, however hidden away it may be in a closet or even in the attic. The little sonofabitch, she thinks. Goddamn him. He messed things up for both of them in life; she'd be goddamned if she'd let him do the same in death. No way.

She has an idea by now for the twelve dollars, too, something she sees as symbolic, a secret gesture of good-bye and farewell. At the end of this drive, this curious mission, she will treat herself to a couple drinks—at work, to be among the only friends she really has anymore. She will have a couple drinks and decide for herself once and for all if she can continue to live in Laconia or if she should sell out and return, say, to San Diego, where she believes she can pick up some of the threads of the life she left behind, even if it was nearly a dozen years ago, when it was excited with the general activity of the war in Southeast Asia.

One way or another, she tells herself, her drinks will mark an end and a beginning. This very summer night. She'll sit at the bar, just like a customer, and take a look around herself. She hopes, she prays, that they kid her for coming in on her night off. They better, she thinks. It's what she needs, she thinks, especially tonight.

People would laugh if they knew of this mission she had undertaken, but it's the only way she has thought of to get rid of his things. She has neither wood stove nor fireplace in her small house, and the town dump, with banker's hours, run like a clinic, was out of the question, even if it did have a central incinerator. For it had sheds and office space, too, and the men who worked there examined everyone's garbage in their bureaucratic authority. She could see them pinning up her son's driver's license, or the newspaper with the headline, TOWN'S FIRST MURDERER IN NINE YEARS, or even some of those pictures of little gay boys which, among other things, had been returned by the police. No, she did not want anyone keeping souvenirs, because if they did, she knew she would have no choice about staying here. She had similar fears about burying his things in the woods. A dog would dig everything up two years down the road, and it would be in the paper all over again, and she'd be paralyzed again in her helpless embarrassment. She has this plan then, heading south on 93, to turn into the elaborate Mall of New Hampshire, near Manchester, find a dumpster in the midst of its loading ramps, dump in everything, knowing it will make its way to a roaring incinerator which will reduce it to nothing, charge a blouse or stockings at Filene's to validate the shopping excursion she has mentioned to friends at work, and return to her meeting with herself at the bar, to two or three or four short screwdrivers, to the first moments of the rest of her life.

She drives on. Right now, to the right, the sun is a dusty orange ball between tree masses and curves in the land, is falling and fading quickly. There are shadows in the highway valleys, where night is coming up from the ground; a car passes across the green, landscaped median with its headlights on—she turns hers on, too—and she begins to have a sense not of driving south but of driving north in her childhood, riding in the back seat of her parents' car in the summertime and heading north for recreation. It's what people are doing here, she decides, what they do all summer. Drive north for recreation. For freedom, really. To be free of heart. Lake water, campsites, high spirits, and cocktails—freedom. So it will be for her, she thinks, in half an hour, when she has completed her task and is heading north again. It will be as it was then. Freedom.

Turning into the mall, which at a distance looks a little like Las Vegas with its lights and neon reaching into the darkening sky, she is having doubts only about the urn. She hopes it will melt. She believes it will. Throwing it into a lake or river has occurred to her, but was rejected on a fear, an image, of some fisherman snagging it with a hook, dragging it in and reading the name, and everyone celebrating all over again the history she had produced. Nor did she care that all that was left of him might be reduced to smoke and disappear completely, for she had yet to burden herself with beliefs of foreverafter. She wants him gone, she tells herself. It's pathetic, she knows, but she wants him to disappear entirely, for it seems her only chance.

The dumpster she finds is in an ideal location. Driving slowly and carefully into an opening in the mall's exterior, she finds herself, under floodlights, at the rear loading area of a supermarket and other rear entrances, next to a blue dumpster nearly as large as a railroad car. Turning off the motor, she slips from her car and goes around to open the trunk lid. Nearby, a generator runs insistently. She pauses, to double-check. An odor of decomposing food is in the air, but no one is around. From ground level, she can see on one end a tumbling stack of folded cardboard boxes and the thin wooden and wire crates used for shipping produce. Maybe the dumpster will be emptied soon. It satisfies her to think that the fire might take place as soon as tomorrow or the next day.

She lifts out the urn first. Now or never, she thinks. Hefting it like a shotput up into the dumpster, she thinks ashes to ashes. It *thunks!* hitting at least close to the steel bottom. It will be covered, she thinks. If not now, with the boxes she has to empty, then with other garbage. She feels some relief. The worst is over. Good luck to you; good riddance, too, she thinks.

Taking one of the cardboard boxes in hand, she carries it to the lip of the long steel tub, which is face high, and spills its contents over the side. Closed boxes would attract attention, she has thought. Loose papers, even that dirty magazine, would go unnoticed. She imagines the urn being covered already. She feels more relief. Okay, she says to herself.

Lifting another box, she dumps it over the side. And another. If there is such a thing as another life, she thinks, I hope you're happier there than you ever were here. Because it just never worked for you here, did it? She empties the contents of another small box, tosses the box in after. Burn, baby, burn, she thinks, as a card or slip of paper falls to the ground.

There is one more box, which is heavy and which she shifts carefully to a resting place on the edge of the dumpster before tipping out its contents. She tips in the box itself. Checking the trunk, satisfied it is empty, she closes the lid. She feels more relief. Only then, stepping back around to the driver's side, does she see again and reach down to pick up the scrap of paper which had fallen to the pavement. It is, of all things, a photograph of her which had appeared several years ago in the local paper when she had won a merchandise certificate for twenty-five dollars.

He saved that, she thinks; she had not noticed it when she packed the cardboard boxes. To think he kept such a thing, she thinks. That he cut it out. Pausing, uncertain, she finally wads the piece of newsprint and tosses it into the dumpster, because she thinks it is going to make her cry.

Starting her car, she backs around and drives out through the opening. In the floodlighted parking lot, deciding after all against shopping, anxious to be on her way, to be where she has thought to be and among others, she crosscuts through the black pasture of glistening cars and returns to the highway.

She drives north. Only moments later, her car's headlights are reaching into the darkness before her. She lights a cigarette. The cooling night air of northern New England flows through her windows as she drives. As on so many summer nights, there is moisture in the air, which is cooling, which makes appealing the dry interiors of cabins and houses and taverns, and as always, there is the darkness ahead.

Something isn't quite working, though, as the feeling of freedom she had anticipated keeps eluding her. She tries to have the feeling come up in her. She tries to recall what it was in childhood, what set of circumstances it was that gave to the rides north on summer nights their special thrill of expectation.

Was it merely childhood? she wonders. Was it just a phase that one might never have back again. Were those small wonders of life spent or traded, never to be known a second time? Why did things so small, so passing, seem at times like this to be everything?

In her wake, meanwhile, in the long steel dumpster, the wadded rectangle of newsprint had settled to a resting place among the other discarded documents and papers, the odd letters and the magazine of photographs, where, under the moving, star-salted sky, all tend slightly toward shifting and reopening under their own power, their own memory. They lie there as a mass of words and pictures, within the deflected light of the mall, within the faintest currents of summer air, as if in waiting, in some secret plan, to be found again.

He is wet-mopping a tile floor. It is the kitchen of a shop called The Bagelry, beyond the reach of the Newington Mall's music but along its main line sixty or eighty yards from where Cormac is working at a midstream island called The Cookie Counter. Outside, outside the Mall's music, it is this weekday in July, and he and Cormac are tending each minute toward a forbidden afternoon excursion, walking some, hitchhiking some, to Hampton Beach, where the midday sun is blazing down on the dark pavement, on green ocean water and blond beach sand, and where, at this time of year, not to be there and to be of an age is not to be at all.

At the same time that Matt's heart is seized with beach fever, he is infatuated with his job. Sixteen now, it's his first job ever, and that he is paid actual money once a week is but frosting on a larger reward. He has taken it on. The kitchen is his when he is there, and it is where he loves to be. Responsibility is something he has never quite known before, in the midst of adults, and when his boss, Mr. Dunn, remarked to him recently that he was a good worker, he couldn't wait to be back at it. He earns minimum.

He and Cormac are friends again, although Cormac may remain unaware that they were ever anything else. They hang out together, walk to and from the Mall when their haphazard work schedules coincide, and rarely telephone each other. It has occurred to Matt that he is pleased to have Cormac as a friend again, although he has never mentioned this to Cormac, no more than he would tell him of the exaggerated satisfaction he finds in his job, or anything of the other concerns which travel as steadily as underground streams through his mind's passageways, such as being on his own, as he knows himself to be.

Cormac is out there now. Hearing his voice from near the counter, Matt concludes his mopping right to the kitchen doorway, hangs up the mop in the storeroom, stuffs his apron into the plastic bucket there as instructed, and checks the clock—12:06—before inserting his time card for his satisfying slam and moving it to the out rack. Starting along the brief walkway, which turns into the customer area, he sees Cormac coming in; catching Matt's arm, Cormac whispers, "Look who's here."

Turning into the shop, Matt is saying, "Who?" but doesn't need an answer as he sees, opposite the glass case by the cash register, Vanessa Dineen and her friend Barbara.

"Matt, hello," she says.

"Hi," Matt says.

"You work here?" she says.

"Yah, in the kitchen," he says.

"Ugh," she says.

"Oh, it's not bad," he says. "In fact, I sort of like it." Caught momentarily between wanting to talk to her and the call of the beach, of Cormac, he adds, "We're in a rush. How are you?"

"I'm just fine. We're going to be ushers, at Prescott Park, for the summer musicals."

Matt nods. He doesn't know what to say. "That sounds great," he says. And he says, "We have to go. Nice to see you. Take care."

"Bye," she says.

Walking away, he feels her at his back. Moments later, walking fiercely away from the Mall, they reach nearby Route 4, where, on the other side of a traffic light, they take up walking forward and backwards, throwing their thumbs out to the train lengths of cars set free periodically by the light. Illegal with Cormac's parents and with Matt's mother, hitchhiking here is illegal with the police, too, and they keep moving along the shoulder, looking to hitchhike *and* to be walking, should they spot a telltale white and blue light rig on top of an oncoming car. Vanessa is with him still, but she is fading now.

"You ever gone to Prescott Park?" Cormac says.

They go along, turn to walk backwards in the rush of another stream of cars.

"I went once," Cormac says. "You know, a musical. What it was like was a cat being squashed by a bulldozer; it kept screaming to this other cat that was being electrocuted. Both at once. Then everybody came out and swirled around for a while. Then the two cats came back to the center of the stage and screeched some more like they were being fed into a meat grinder together."

Matt smiles; he doesn't say anything. After Vanessa—he seems to have let her slip away—other things are on his mind. It isn't "meeting" his father, as he did, during the viewing hours at the funeral home, which moment he has replayed any number of times, perhaps daily. Nor is it seeing him rearrested at the cemetery after the service, and being stricken with an urge to fight for him, to help him escape, and only standing there, which moment he also relives, it seems, at least once a day. What is on his mind is the mailbox at home, which he discovered after his father was released yet again to return to Louisiana and sent a first check along with a note in the envelope asking him to write. After taking part of an afternoon and an evening at the kitchen table, composing the first letter of his life, and waiting a couple of days, he began checking the mail

delivery. Coming home from school, and after school let out for the summer, when he wasn't working, he watched for the mailman's jeep, lis-
tened for his stopping at the three mailboxes on the front of the house,
and zipped down the stairs and around the front of the house to check.

"You don't think that's funny?" Cormac says.

"What's not funny?" Matt says.

They are turning to walk backwards, for another rush of cars. Then
they walk forward again. The mailbox is still on Matt's mind. Old, wrinkled metal, painted white several times over, it is the top mailbox of the
three, and if he walked up to it a hundred times, he came away a hundred
times empty-handed, for there was never a second check or an answer to
the letter he had mailed.

"You're lots of fun, Matt," Cormac says as the string of cars passes.

"I was thinking of something."

"What were you thinking of?"

"I don't know. I couldn't tell you."

"You sure you want to go to the beach?"

"We're going. I'm going. We're gonna have a good time."

"You know something, Matt? You're getting weird."

This time, Matt does laugh. "I know," he says.

"You want to go to Prescott Park?"

"I thought you didn't like it."

"I changed my mind. You want to go?"

"Sure. Let's go."

"When? You want to go tonight?"

"Sure. Let's do it."

They pivot yet again, present their thumbs to another string of cars. As
it is every summer, the Seacoast area traffic is heavy; as they walk along,
as Matt is walking backwards, the excitement of being at the beach is returning to him. Turning, looking ahead once more and walking, he feels
the excitement within him, even as there remains something unexcited
within him, too, a scroll, a stone tablet containing thoughts, it seems,
thoughts instructing him to keep looking ahead, to keep walking along as
he is walking now, to forgo that approaching of the mailbox, which he
knew all along would never present to him what he was looking for, to
forgo looking behind him, to walk on his way as he is doing now.

IN THE MIDWEST, a thousand miles away, driving a rental car he had reserved at Indianapolis International, the heavyweight detective is on a mission he has assigned himself, for its restorative and peaceful possibilities, to pick up and return to his home state a man facing embezzlement charges in the Seacoast area. Cruising along a major truck route into the heart of the country, he is letting his mind wander as it will, where it will, into the future as well as into the past, while he has both windows open in the dryly heated air and is taking in an aroma of the land, of new-mown hay, of timothy and wild basil, a smell he recalls from his childhood in Quebec or perhaps in Alberta where he spent a summer, of wagons rolling along dirt roads filled with rolls of the long green aromatic grasses of summer and home and well-being. On those evenings long ago his appetite was insatiable for all things in life into the night, but as he drives here now, even as he is in the process of kicking his tobacco habit, it is food alone which keeps taking up his attention. He is starved, he tells himself. Roast chicken, his stomach seems to tell him. Mashed potatoes and gravy. Mom's Small-Town Truck Stop Diner in the Heart of the Heart of the Country. Pumpkin Pie. Apple pie a la mode.

Maybe not the a la mode, he thinks. Maybe not the pie either, and maybe not the gravy and the chicken skin, alas. But dinner, even if it is early afternoon. Lots of chicken. At least a memory of better times, he thinks. And having granted himself permission to take in a sizeable chicken dinner, he shifts away from thinking of food itself, cruising along at a comfortable fifty and fifty-five, and lets his mind return to where it seems to have been moments earlier, back in the plains of western Canada, and the general idea of retirement he has been tending toward lately, and the question of whether a new challenge is in order, of whether work is healthy or he should seek out something stress-free and low-key, whether he and Beatrice should ever consider moving away from where they had come to feel so much at home. And back, too, as always, to that other, deeper thought, the necessity within him to tell her. He hasn't; he knows at last—perhaps in this moment—that he must. Every day it has been killing him slightly. He must.

It is in this preoccupied frame of mind and compelled by hunger, picking out the word *Restaurant* among others in a sky-high stack of neon, that Dulac lifts the car's turn signal and glides onto the exit lane as it blends into an uphill ramp leaving the highway. From a stop sign at the top of the hill, he turns right twice, into an expanse of oil-soaked blacktop, perhaps a dozen acres, where as many as fifty or sixty eighteen- and twenty-two-wheelers are parked and an equal number of cars and pickups, all surrounding a complicated central building, rows of gas and diesel pumps, a truck wash and a double row of storage sheds a distance ahead.

Parking, an entire roast chicken on his mind by now, he slips on his sports coat, locks up, and crosses to the building in the heated air, hearing the sparkle and hiss of the great sign above him and the oceanic roar of cars and trucks rolling by on the highway below, and he feels good again as he goes up a flight of wide steps and follows a red neon sign *Restaurant*→ around a partial wrap-around porch where other signs say *Motel*→ and *Arcade*→. Only when he is in a cashier's alcove, though, does he notice something different, even as it doesn't inform him yet in any way. It is a thickness of stale cigarette smoke in the air, and another, fainter smell, ever so slightly sickening, of the deodorant used to sweeten cleaning solvent. Roast chicken remains on his mind, though, and his thought in this moment is that detecting these smells is the price of having kicked the habit, as he sees and continues through a double doorway topped by another red neon *Restaurant* sign.

He has walked to one of the many white tables in the center of a dining room before he realizes how few customers there are, even if it is a couple hours past lunchtime, that the restaurant, except for three or four tables and part of the counter back near the door, is virtually empty. Sitting down, facing the door area, he thinks how much the truck drivers sitting there smoking cigarettes, drinking coffee, resemble the old-timers he saw in the Navy who sat at tables near the door in every galley or mess hall, working, the younger sailors liked to say, on their twenty-year coffee breaks.

Food remains on his mind, nonetheless, even as he detects the lingering odor of stale cigarette smoke here in the dining room as well, and his thoughts are running to the consequences of kicking the habit and to anticipating a less satisfying meal than he had hoped for—never trust a restaurant which smells of stale cigarette smoke and isn't crowded—when he notices a young girl coming his way with a menu.

As the girl approaches to his side and curtsies slightly in handing over the menu, his thoughts of food and his preoccupying thought of the deep secret in his heart get put aside all at once, for the girl looks more prepared for the stage than the dining room.

She wears layers of makeup, and she broadcasts a cloud of perfume, and she is beautiful and provocative in her childlike manner, although she is no more than eleven or twelve years old. False eyelashes, lipstick, rouge, a ribbon in her hair; she appears ready to be laid back on a couch, to be kissed and fondled.

"Good evening," she says, not quite making eye contact. "Topless hours, seven to midnight. Today's special is big tits. After-dinner treats available downstairs."

Dulac is caught off guard, confused; he says, *"What?"* smiling in surprise, struck dumb. "What did you say?"

Her blouse is see-through, he notices; the small nipples on her flat chest are either painted with lipstick or covered with red pasties. She wears black pantyhose, glossy black high-heeled shoes. She looks back at him but does not, as he asked, repeat what she had said.

Smiling, even laughing some, Dulac continues to be nearly speechless. "Look at you," he manages to say. "Do you work here?"

"Yes," she says.

"You're certainly pretty," he tells her.

"Thank you," she says.

"You make good tips?" he says, as if to start a conversation.

"Yes," she says.

"What's your name?"

"Lisa."

"Lisa. That's a nice name. How old are you, Lisa?"

Raising her eyes to him, giving him a coy smile, she says, "I'm old enough."

Dulac laughs some. "Well, who taught you how to be a waitress?" he says, glancing over her makeup and once again into her see-through blouse.

"I learned," she says.

"Come on, how old are you? I bet you're eleven."

"None of your business," she says, almost sweetly.

"Twelve?" he says.

She only looks at him.

"Who told you to say what you said when you came to my table?"

"There's the menu," she says, pointing at it with one finger, glancing over her shoulder, pivoting away a step.

"No, no, just a minute," he says. "Just tell me who told you what to say."

A woman, Dulac sees, is bearing down on them, saying at some twenty feet, "Just go on, Lisa, I'll get this."

The girl slips away. The woman, taking up the view before him, is dressed in a regular lime green kitchen dress, but one unbuttoned a distance down her chest, a shapely woman who is also made up. "Sir?" she says.

"What's going on here?" Dulac says.

"What does that mean?" the woman says.

"What is this? What kind of place is this?"

"You're a cop, right?" she says.

"Right. I'm a cop. That's right."

"This is a topless restaurant. It's legal. Okay?"

"This is a topless restaurant?"

"That's right."

"How old is the little girl?"

"The little girl happens to be my daughter. She's helping me out. There's nothing wrong with that."

"How old is she?"

"She's sixteen, but that's none of your business."

"You tell her to say big tits is the special?"

"I have no idea what you're talking about."

"I'm sure you don't."

"Our special is *beef tips*. You must have misunderstood. Now, do you want to order or not?"

"No, I don't want to order. I want to know—if that little girl is your daughter—what you think you're doing?"

"Listen, I don't have to answer that kind of thing. We're legal, okay? You don't like it, take off. It happens to be a free country."

"You should be ashamed of yourself," he says.

Making an expression of exasperation, turning away, shaking her head, the woman appears about to speak, but there is a man in blue jeans and cowboy boots coming on, saying, "What is it; what's the problem?"

"Asshole cop," she says, walking away.

Coming to Dulac, the man says, "I see some ID, Chief?"

The woman goes on, as Dulac says, "You the girl's father?"

"Nope. You got ID?"

Dulac doesn't bother. He gets to his feet. "City police, Portsmouth, New Hampshire," he says.

"I tell you, Sarge," the man says. "I think you're a little out of your jurisdiction, maybe out of your decade, you know what I mean? We're legal. Sheriff, state troopers come in here all the time time," the man adds, turning to walk away.

Dulac stands there. He watches the man move away and knows he is rattled and knows there is nothing he can do. He leaves. On his way, he looks in the direction of the kitchen, behind the counter, to see if the woman or the girl or the man are there, but doesn't see anyone. He walks past the tables where the truckers sit, quietly now, for they have been watching the scene. They glance, a couple of them, but seem to decide against eye contact with him and look away.

The cashier's alcove, Dulac sees now, is a soft-core porn shop. *Hustler*

377

and *Screw*, *Penthouse* and *Playboy*. The cashier, a geriatric blonde with lips painted beyond their natural lines, works behind bars like those at a bank, and another neon light over another doorway—*Adult Arcade Below*—would lead to the drivers, he realizes, of all those cars and trucks.

The air without is different now, too, although the sky and trees he glances over as he walks to his car would appear to be the same. Craning his neck, he reads the neon sign reaching eighty or a hundred feet into the sky. TRUCKER'S HEAVEN is its headline. Its other lines say, *Open 24 hours, Restaurant, Truck Wash, Adult Entertainment.*

Getting into his car, he backs around to start away and stops to reach and roll down the car's windows. As he does so, something of the past seems to come up in his mind and he decides the least he can do is report them for using a minor to solicit. Driving over near the exit from the lot, he pulls to the side before a row of four open-sided telephone stalls and gets back out of the car.

On a thought to be loose, to somehow fight back, he removes his jacket and tosses it over into the back seat. He can hear the trucks and cars rolling by on the highway below. Deciding a local sheriff might be a mistake, he dials until he gets through to a state police post, in a town called Centerville.

Extending the brief telephone cord, to be out of the booth where the air is a little cooler, he looks over the skyline, to the south and southwest, over trees and lightly rolling hills. Identifying himself, indicating his reason for passing through the area, he says then, "I'm sure you know all about Trucker's Heaven, but have you had complaints of a child, female, age eleven or twelve, waiting on tables and being used to solicit?"

"Lisa, you mean?"

"That's right. Lisa is who I mean."

"You say you're just passing through, Lieutenant?" the dispatcher says.

"Right."

"Well, listen, Lieutenant, we're apprised of what you're talking about. They do have a birth certificate, is what I'm told, which says she's sixteen. That place has been in business there for some time now."

"Have you checked out this girl? She's nowhere near sixteen. The birth certificate has to be false."

"Well, what happened exactly? Was she dressed? If not, it would be a violation. As I understand it, though, they don't do the topless thing there until in the evening."

"She was dressed. She was all made-up though. Wearing a see-through blouse. In her little spiel, they had—"

"Lieutenant, excuse me, I don't mean to question what you're saying, but isn't this pretty mild stuff?"

Dulac pauses, senses disorientation in himself. Then he says, "I don't think it's mild. What I'm talking about, what I'm reporting to you and would be willing to sign a complaint for, is an actual young girl, of eleven or twelve years of age, being used to solicit. That's illegal. The little girl is being used."

There is a pause this time on the officer's end. Then he says, "Lieutenant, listen, hold on a second, let me get the corporal."

Dulac holds, looking over the top of the car into the evening air. For the first time since he started on this trip, early that morning, he misses being home. He had gone looking for something peaceful and nearly philosophical in the middle of the country, and here he is feeling anxious again.

"Corporal Horner," a voice says then. "Lieutenant, where you from?"

"Back east," Dulac says. "That doesn't matter."

"What's the problem, Lieutenant?"

"I thought it was child abuse," Dulac says. "I'm beginning to think it's something else."

"Lieutenant, listen," the corporal says. "I don't know where you been, or where you're coming from, but there's nothing illegal going on at Trucker's Heaven. You can call the local sheriff if you want, and you can lodge a citizen's complaint. I got to tell you, though, what goes on at Trucker's Heaven isn't going to raise a whole lot of eyebrows around here."

"Corporal, you seem not to want to hear what I'm saying. I didn't call about Trucker's Heaven. I called about a young girl they have working there who is underage and is being exploited—is being used to solicit—in violation of laws you are paid to enforce."

"The girl's birth certificate says she's sixteen, Lieutenant. That's old enough to waitress. So far as I know—it's the sheriff's jurisdiction; we're mainly traffic here—so far as I know she doesn't work when they shift over to topless, which would be illegal."

Yet again, Dulac pauses, is aware that he is rattled. "I'd have called the sheriff in the first place," he says, "if I didn't have an idea what he'd say. I thought you guys . . . " Dulac loses voice, loses something which would have had him continue.

"Us guys what, Lieutenant?" the corporal says.

"You're either going to do something about it or you aren't," Dulac says. "If you don't, who is?"

"Who is what, Lieutenant?"

Dulac is looking down, closes his eyes; he is unable for the moment to speak.

At last the corporal says, "Are you there, Lieutenant?"

"Yes," Dulac says.

Then the corporal says, "Lieutenant, are you okay?"

"I'm okay," Dulac says.

"You sound a little tired, you know."

Dulac has lifted his head and eyes and is looking over the countryside and for the moment is lost to himself, as if he doesn't know that he is on the phone or what is going through his mind.

"Lieutenant, listen, you take it easy," the corporal says. "You drive carefully."

There is the click of the receiver being replaced on the other end; Dulac, as he turns and replaces his receiver, is in a struggle, it seems, not to surrender to something he cannot see.

He stands yet in place, in the shade. He has no feeling to drive on, nor any feeling to stay. He stands gazing over the countryside, hearing cars go by on the highway below, trying yet again to see, to believe in whatever it was he had believed in down through the years.

CLAIRE WELLS

As ALWAYS she is the last passenger on what is a school bus painted white and blue and called the Kari-Van. The driver, a university student in khaki slacks and man's shirt, is the same young woman who has been the driver a number of other times Claire has made the trip in the late afternoon after work. They have not had conversation, but each time the driver has pulled the bus into the turnaround patch of gravel and pulled a handle to open the door, she has spoken to Claire as she has not spoken to other passengers, mostly university students, who stepped from the bus along the way. "Be careful now. Have a nice day."

Claire thanks her in turn, gives her a nod and a nice smile, and in imagining things about the young woman, has developed deep admiration for her. She likes to think she'd be more independent like that herself if she had it to do over again, and if she had a daughter, that's how she'd like her to be. In her thoughts, she has said to the young woman, *You just keep it up, you're doing the right thing,* but she has only smiled at her and watched the bus circle around to accelerate onto the highway.

Continuing down the road to the cemetery—the round trip on the University Kari-Van is the only way she has to get there—Claire unsticks her blouse and slacks where they want, from the vinyl seat, to cling to her back and to the backs of her legs. As always, the walk along the two-lane paved road is quiet, and she is pleased again that Eric could return to so peaceful a setting. Occasionally a car or a pickup truck goes by, and people always look to see who is walking along the shoulder of the road, but no one has bothered her. She tries, in her clothes from work, to appear businesslike; she has tried a couple of times to imagine her heart to be as certain as that of the young bus driver, even as she suspects her time for that is past.

Entering the cemetery today, however, and walking along to Eric's plot—he has a brass head marker now, flat to the ground, as are all the other markers in this part of the cemetery—she is frightened suddenly by what she sees coming up before her. Tire marks have ripped through the turf. Fresh tire marks, as fresh as last night or early morning, have ripped through the turf, have passed directly over plots and brass markers, and have all but hit Eric's. Tire-tread mud has dried just on a corner of Eric's pebbled brass marker, a rectangle which says:

ERIC D. WELLS
Adored Son
1969   1981

Claire feels chilled and breathless standing there, but then she closes her eyes and exhales and sees it as less than a serious violation. Vandals, she thinks. Teenagers driving through the cemetery at midnight in their ignorant but possibly innocent cruelty. Although she has begun to weep, she decides to forgive them. Eric wouldn't have minded, she thinks. That's the funny part. He might have enjoyed the visit.

Still, sitting on the grass, she uses her fingers to brush and clear away the touches of dried mud. At last she uses her hanky, and when a shadow of a blur still remains, she leaves it for a rain storm to finish clearing. She feels peaceful then, sitting there with Eric. "Matt's working a lot," she says in the softest of whispers. "But I'm going to have him come with me one of these days."

She looks around. She has tried often to get Matt to come with her, but she isn't unhappy, she realizes, to make the trip and to visit here by herself. The last time he came, back in the spring, he was ready to start back when they'd been here just a few minutes and then he walked around to read other markers. "I guess it's for me to come see you," she says. "It isn't that Matt doesn't love you, too, it's just that—well, that it's for me to come see you." She adds then, "He's doing fine though."

Sitting here for several more minutes, she doesn't speak again to Eric, and she realizes that this, too, is one of the pleasures she derives in coming to visit him by herself. She may speak to him if she wishes, or she may not. She may simply sit here, so they can be together, and however long she stays or what she has to say, she always leaves at peace once more in her heart, a peacefulness which will subsequently elude her, will, on news perhaps of another child falling victim in some similar way, have her in need of coming back, to know again a moment of peace.

It's a hammer she's been hearing whacking in the distance, she realizes, as the sound explodes oddly on the air, and she turns to look in the direction from which it seems to be coming. Gazing beyond the road, using her hand to visor her eyes, she picks out the triangular raw timber framework of a new house, or a barn, reaching into the sky. Eric loved such things, she thinks, and it gives her pleasure to have it nearby. Otherwise, there are no houses in view from here. There are the fields and the line of trees down across the road. It is only a thought of the house Eric always liked to promise he'd buy or build for her that interrupts her scanning the countryside, but only for a moment. "Hear that," she says. "They're building something."

She sits back on the grass, though, and looks away again from the construction over there. What she wants to do is tell Eric of something she saw from the bus window on the way there, but she only calls up the image in her mind, for it wasn't anything very tellable. It was a man with a truck with a flat tire, pulled onto the side of the road. But the man was a father and he had a little boy with him, a seven- or eight-year-old he had propped on the hood of his truck, to keep him out of harm's way, while he fixed the tire there under the child's gaze. The little boy looked so pleased sitting there is what she would tell Eric if she were to try to tell him, which she doesn't. Nor does she tell him how it made her feel awful and wonderful at the same time. Or that what it was that appeared wonderful was the presence in the space between the two of all that mattered in life, of all that time on earth might signify.

She sits. The carpentry continues, the hammer and saw sounds traveling on the slight breezes. A warm summer day is childhood itself, she thinks. Eric will lie here, she thinks, when the building across the road is finished, and when it has housed a family, and when the family has grown, and when they are all gone, he will lie here still. Even as this is what she knows, it is coming to her now, too, that she has to let Eric go, that he dislikes being restrained, especially on a summer day, that she has to stop holding him and let him go. That after the moment in the funeral home of redoing his hair and of standing to hold his hand, and after the moments during the service of the children from his school singing of his keeping his head on high and of not being afraid and of Jesus calling him home, softly and tenderly calling him home; that after giving him one last kiss before the closing of the casket, and bringing him here to the countryside of his birth; that after these moments of holding to him and waiting for him to rise out of his sleep, it is because she loves him that she has to let him go; that in letting him go he may live again. So it is that she releases him, in this moment; so it is that she lets him slip away from her like a child at play, into eternity.

ABOUT THE AUTHOR

A native of Flint, Michigan, Theodore Weesner left school at sixteen, spent three years in the army, and later attended Michigan State University and the University of Iowa. His novels are *Car Thief*, which won the Great Lakes Writers' Prize, and *A German Affair*. His short fiction has appeared in *The New Yorker*, *Esquire*, *Atlantic Monthly* and *Best American Short Stories*. A recipient of NEA and Guggenheim awards, he has taught at the University of New Hampshire and at Carnegie Mellon University in Pittsburgh.